"I think there's been a misunderstanding."

Ryne delivered the understatement in a steady tone. "What our task force needs, what I requested from Commander Dixon, is another investigator. What we definitely do not need is a shrink."

There was a flicker in Abbie's calm gray eyes that might have been temper. "I have a doctorate in forensic psychology—"

"We need a *doctor* even less."

She ignored his interruption. "And since joining Raiker Forensics, I've been involved in nearly three dozen high-profile cases."

At the moment diplomacy eluded him. "Do you realize what kind of case we're working here? I've got a serial rapist on the loose. I need another experienced investigator, not someone who'll shrink the skell's mind once we get him."

She never flinched. "You'll have to catch him first, won't you? And I can help with that. Of the cases I've worked, well over half involved serial rapists. I'm exactly what you need on this case, Detective Robel. You just don't realize it yet."

WAKING NIGHTMARE

THE MINDHUNTERS

KYLIE BRANT

BERKLEY SENSATION, NEW YORK

THE BERKLEY PUBLISHING GROUP
Published by the Penguin Group
Penguin Group (USA) Inc.
375 Hudson Street, New York, New York 10014, USA
Penguin Group (Canada), 90 Eglinton Avenue East, Suite 700, Toronto, Ontario M4P 2Y3, Canada
(a division of Pearson Penguin Canada Inc.)
Penguin Books Ltd., 80 Strand, London WC2R 0RL, England
Penguin Group Ireland, 25 St. Stephen's Green, Dublin 2, Ireland (a division of Penguin Books Ltd.)
Penguin Group (Australia), 250 Camberwell Road, Camberwell, Victoria 3124, Australia
(a division of Pearson Australia Group Pty. Ltd.)
Penguin Books India Pvt. Ltd., 11 Community Centre, Panchsheel Park, New Delhi—110 017, India
Penguin Group (NZ), 67 Apollo Drive, Rosedale, North Shore 0632, New Zealand
(a division of Pearson New Zealand Ltd.)
Penguin Books (South Africa) (Pty.) Ltd., 24 Sturdee Avenue, Rosebank, Johannesburg 2196,
South Africa

Penguin Books Ltd., Registered Offices: 80 Strand, London WC2R 0RL, England

This is a work of fiction. Names, characters, places, and incidents either are the product of the author's imagination or are used fictitiously, and any resemblance to actual persons, living or dead, business establishments, events, or locales is entirely coincidental. The publisher does not have any control over and does not assume any responsibility for author or third-party websites or their content.

WAKING NIGHTMARE

A Berkley Sensation Book / published by arrangement with the author

PRINTING HISTORY
Berkley Sensation mass-market edition / September 2009

Copyright © 2009 by Kim Bahnsen.
Excerpt from *Waking Evil* by Kylie Brant copyright 2009 by Kim Bahnsen.
Cover art by S. Miroque.
Cover design by Rita Frangie.
Interior text design by Laura K. Corless.

ISBN: 978-0-425-23023-7

BERKLEY® SENSATION
Berkley Sensation Books are published by The Berkley Publishing Group,
a division of Penguin Group (USA) Inc.,
375 Hudson Street, New York, New York 10014.
BERKLEY® SENSATION and the "B" design are trademarks of Penguin Group (USA) Inc.

PRINTED IN THE UNITED STATES OF AMERICA

10 9 8 7 6 5 4 3 2 1

To John, who pesters me, challenges me, and never fails to make me laugh. I love you.

Acknowledgments

Special thanks to writing buddies Cindy Gerard and Roxanne Rustand, for having faith even when I didn't, and sharing encouragement and wisdom when I needed it most.

Thanks also to my agent, Danielle Egan-Miller, for your unfailing enthusiasm and support.

Great appreciation and thanks to Wally Campbell, Laboratory Manager, GBI-DOFS, Coastal Regional Crime Lab, for your patience with my unending questions about the workings of the lab and toxicology; to Lieutenant Danny Agan, Atlanta Homicide Detective, Ret., and Sergeant Robert Gavin and Sergeant Mike Wilson, SCMPD, for your assistance with police procedural questions. All of you saved the day! Any errors in accuracy are mine alone, undoubtedly due to my not asking the right questions.

Prologue

It was the cold that roused her. It seeped into her bones, crept along nerve endings already unbearably sensitized. Her eyelids fluttered as she battled unconsciousness, but it was tempting to sink back into that numbed cocoon once again. And perhaps she would have, if her sluggish brain hadn't finally registered what her senses had been screaming at her.

She was in water.

Surrounded by it.

Submerged in it.

Panic shot through her. She tried to lurch to her feet. Her head slammed against the top of her prison with enough force that her body crumpled; stars burst behind her eyelids.

Immediately salt water filled her nostrils, stung her eyes, seared a path to her lungs. She coughed desperately, but found she couldn't open her mouth. Weakly, she fought her way to her knees, the water lapping around her neck and shoulders, and waited for her mind to clear.

When it did, terror rushed in.

She'd been buried alive in water. Cold. Deep. Suffocating. The darkness was absolute. She moved her head experimentally, but couldn't feel a blindfold. Tried to shriek, but could only manage a muffled moan.

She was bound. Gagged. The salt water set her knife wounds on fire. Tiny teeth and pinchers from unseen sea creatures feasted on her shredded flesh.

A scream ricocheted in her mind as she frantically threw herself against the walls of her prison. Metal screeched against metal and her cage pitched, immersing her more deeply into the water. Each ripple and ebb sent waves splashing into her nostrils, taunting her with its reach. A sob trapped in her chest, she rose to an awkward crouch and pressed her face against the top of her prison, hauling in several deep breaths of salt-scented air. Her exhausted muscles started cramping, but she didn't dare move. Her only thought was of survival, and even that seemed more and more unlikely.

For Barbara Billings, the nightmare had just begun.

Chapter 1

Summer gripped Savannah by the throat and strangled it with a slow vicious squeeze. Most faulted the heat and cursed the humidity, but Ryne knew the weather wasn't totally to blame for the suffocating pall. Evil had settled over the city, a cloying, sweaty blanket, insidiously spreading its tentacles of misery like a silent cancer taking hold in an unsuspecting body.

But people weren't going to remain unsuspecting for much longer. This latest victim was likely to change that, and then all hell was going to break loose.

Compared to Savannah, he figured hell had to be a dry heat.

The door to the conference room opened, and the task force members began filing in. Most held cups of steaming coffee that would only make the outdoor temperature seem more brutal. Ryne didn't bother pointing that out. He was hardly in the position to lecture others about their addictions.

Their voices hadn't yet subsided when he reached out to flip on the digital projector. "We've got another vic."

A close-up picture was projected on the screen. There was

a muttered "Jesus," from one of the detectives. After spending the last two hours going through the photos, Ryne could appreciate the sentiment.

"Barbara Billings. Age thirty-four. Divorced. Lives alone. She was raped two days ago in her home when she got off work." He switched to the next set of pictures, those detailing her injuries. "He was inside her house, but we don't know yet if he'd been hiding there or if he gained access after she arrived. She got home at six, and said it was shortly after that he grabbed her. She's hazy on details, but the assault lasted hours."

"Where'd he dump her, the sewer?" Even McElroy sounded a little squeamish. And considering that his muscle-bound body housed an unusually tactless mouth, that was saying something.

Ryne clicked the computer mouse. The screen showed a photo of a pier, partially dismantled, with the glint of metal beneath it. "A cage had been wired to the moorings beneath this dock on St. Andrew's Sound. That's where he transported her to afterwards."

"Looks like the kennel I put my Lab in," observed Wayne Cantrell.

Ryne flicked him a glance. As usual, the detective was sitting slouched in his seat, arms folded across his chest, his features showing only the impassive stoicism of his Choctaw heritage. "It is a dog kennel," Ryne affirmed. The next picture showed a close-up of it. "Sturdy enough to hold a one hundred thirty–pound woman. The medical exam shows she was injected twice. It'll be at least a week before we get the tox report back, but from her description of the tingling in her lips, heightened sensation, and foggy memory, this sounds like our guy."

"Shit."

Ryne heartily concurred with Cantrell's quiet assessment. It also summed up what they had so far on the bastard responsible for the rapes.

The rest of the photos were shown in silence. When he got to the end of them, he crossed to the door and switched on the overhead lights. "Marine Patrol wasn't able to get much information from her when they found her, so they processed the secondary scene. Her preliminary statement was taken at the hospital, before the case got tossed to us."

"Where's she at now?" This was from Isaac Holmes, the most seasoned detective on the case. With his droopy jowls and long narrow face, he bore an uncanny resemblance to the old hound seen on reruns of *The Beverly Hillbillies*. But he had an enviable cleared case percentage, a factor that had weighed heavily when Ryne had requested him for the task force.

"She was treated and released from St. Joseph/Candler. She's staying with her mother. The address is in the file."

"Where the hell is that other investigator Dixon promised?"

McElroy's truculent question struck a chord with Ryne. He made sure it didn't show. "Commander Dixon has assured me that he's carefully looking at possible candidates to assign to the task force." He ignored the muttered responses in the room. If another member weren't assigned to the group by the end of the day, he would have it out with Dixon himself. Again.

"We need to process the primary scene and interview the victim. Cantrell, I want you and . . ." His words stopped as the door opened, and a slight young woman with short dark hair entered. Despite the double whammy of Savannah's heat and humidity, she wore a long-sleeved white shirt over her black pants. He hadn't seen her around before, but given the photo ID badge clipped to the pocket of her shirt and the thick folder she carried, he figured her for a clerical temp. And if that file contained copies of the complete Marine Patrol report, it was about damn time.

"I'm looking for Detective Robel." She scanned the occupants in the room before shifting her focus to him.

"You found him." He gestured to a table near the door. "Just set the folder there and close the door on your way out."

Her attention snapped back to him, a hint of amusement

showing in her expression. "I'm Abbie Phillips, your newest task force member."

"Does the department get a cut rate on pocket-sized police officers?" There was an answering ripple of laughter in the room, quickly muffled. Ryne shot a warning look at McElroy, who shrugged and ran a hand through his already disheveled brown hair. "C'mon, Robel, what is she, all of fourteen?"

"Welcome to the team, Phillips." Ryne kept his voice neutral. "We can use a woman to help us interview the victims. We've been borrowing female officers from other units."

"I hope to give you more assistance than that." She handed him the file folder. "A summary of my background."

The folder was too thick for a rookie, but it also wasn't a SCMPD personnel file. He flicked a gaze over her again. No shield. No weapon. Tension knotted his gut as he took the folder she offered. He gestured to the primaries in the room in turn. "Detectives Cantrell, McElroy, and Holmes. We had another rape reported last night and I was just catching everyone up." To the group he said, "I'll need all detectives and uniforms to the scene. Holmes, until I get there, you oversee the canvass. I'll meet you later."

There was a scraping of chairs as the officers rose and made their way to the door. Abbie turned, as if to follow them. His voice halted her. "Phillips, I'd like to talk to you first."

She looked up at him. At her height, she'd look up to most men. She couldn't be much more than five foot two. And her smoky gray eyes were as guileless as a ten-year-old's.

"We could talk in the car. I'm anxious to get a look at the scene."

"Later." He went to the projector and shut it off. Pulling out two chairs beside it, he gestured toward one.

She came over, sat down. He sank into the other seat, set her file on the table in front of him, and flipped it open. He read only a few moments before disbelief flared, followed closely by anger.

"You're not a cop."

Abbie's gaze was steady. "Independent consultant. Our agency contracts with law enforcement on problematic cases. If you're worried about my qualifications, the file lists my experience. Commander Dixon seemed satisfied."

Dixon. That backstabbing SOB. "I think there's been a misunderstanding." Ryne delivered the understatement in a steady tone. "What our task force needs, what I requested from Commander Dixon, was another investigator. Preferably two. What we definitely do not need is a shrink."

There was a flicker in those calm gray eyes that might have been temper. "I have a doctorate in forensic psychology—"

"We need a *doctor* even less."

She ignored his interruption. "And since joining Raiker Forensics, I've been involved in nearly three dozen high-profile cases."

"Shit." He was capable of more finesse, but at the moment diplomacy eluded him. "Do you realize what kind of case we're working here? I've got a serial rapist on the loose, and with this latest victim, the media is going to be crawling up my ass. I need another experienced investigator, not someone who'll shrink the skell's mind once we get him."

She never flinched. "You'll have to catch him first, won't you? And I can help with that. I consulted on the Romeo rapist case last year in Houston. The perp is currently doing a twenty-five-year stretch at Allred. Of the cases I've worked, well over half involved serial rapists. I'm exactly what you need on this case, Detective Robel. You just don't realize it yet."

The mention of the Houston case rang a bell, but he didn't bother to pursue the memory. "If we have need of a psych consult, we can always get one from a department psychologist."

"And how many of them—how many of your department's *investigators*—have been trained by Adam Raiker?"

Ryne paused, studying her through narrowed eyes. He had no trouble recalling that name; few in law enforcement circles would. The former FBI profiler had achieved near legendary status until he'd disappeared from the radar several years earlier. "Raiker? I thought he was—"

"Dead?"

Maybe. "Retired."

Her smile was enigmatic. "He'd object to either term."

He was wasting his time. The one he needed to be leveling these objections against was upstairs, where the administrative offices were housed, playing political handball. His chair scraped the floor as he rose. "Wait here." He left the room and strode through the squad room. But halfway up the stairs leading to the administrative offices, he met the man he was seeking, followed by his usual entourage.

He shouldered his way through the throng surrounding Dixon. Raising his voice over the din, he said, "Commander, could I have a word with you?"

Dixon held up a hand that could have meant anything. In this case, it apparently meant to wait until he'd finished the joke he was telling to a couple suits that seemed engrossed in his every word.

Derek Dixon had barely changed in the nearly dozen years since Ryne had first met him. The observation wasn't a compliment. He had pretty boy blond looks and the manner of a chameleon. Jovial and charming one moment. Sober and businesslike the next. He was the ultimate public relations tool, because he was damn good at being all things to all people. Ryne happened to know that his habit of trying to be *one* thing to all women had nearly destroyed his marriage.

But being a womanizing narcissistic prick hadn't slowed the rise of his career. In Boston he'd been the department's special attaché to the mayor. He'd come to Savannah three years ago as commander of the Investigative Division. The fact that his wife was the chief's niece might have had something to do with his procuring the job, but Ryne was hardly in a position to judge. When he'd accepted Dixon's surprising offer of a job here a year ago, he'd hitched his career to the other man's.

It was a troubling memory, but not the one that kept him awake nights.

There was a loud burst of laughter as the suits expressed their appreciation of Dixon's humor, which, Ryne had reason to know, could be politically incorrect and crudely clever.

"Excuse me for a moment." Dixon clapped the two closest men on the shoulders. "I need to speak to one of my detectives." The crowd on the stairwell parted for him like a sea before a prophet.

"Detective Robel." He flashed his pearly caps. "Here to thank me?"

"I appreciate the extra person assigned to the task force." Whatever their past, whatever had gone between them, Ryne always maintained a scrupulously professional relationship with the man in public. "But I'm not sure bringing in an outsider is going to be as much use to us as another department investigator would be."

Annoyance flickered in the man's eyes. "Didn't you read her qualifications? Phillips has background unmatched by anyone on the force. You've heard of Raiker Forensics, haven't you? They're better known as The Mindhunters, because of Adam Raiker's years in the fed's behavioral science unit. The training in his agency is top-notch. With the addition of Phillips, we're getting a profiler and an investigator, for the price of one."

"Price." They descended the stairs in tandem. "Resources are limited, the last interdepartment memo said. Seems odd to spend them on an outside 'consultant' when we have cops already on the payroll who could do the same work at no additional cost."

Although he'd tried to maintain a neutral tone, Dixon's expression warned him that he hadn't been entirely successful. The man glanced around as if to see who was within hearing distance and lowered his voice, all the while keeping a genial smile pasted on his face. "You don't have to worry about the finances of this department, Detective, that's my job. Yours is to track down and nail this scumbag raping women in our city. If you'd accomplished that by now, I wouldn't have had to bring someone else in, would I?"

The barb found its mark. "We've made steady progress . . ."

"Don't forget that my ass is on the line right along with yours. Mayor Richards has had me on speed dial since the second rape."

Already knowing it was futile, Ryne said, "Okay, how about adding another person to the task force in addition to Phillips? Marlowe out of the fourth precinct would be a good man, and he's got fifteen years experience."

They came to the base of the steps and stopped. The suits were standing a little ways off and, judging by the looks they kept throwing them, were growing impatient.

Dixon's words reflected the same emotion. "You wanted another person assigned; you got her. Work with the task force you've got, Detective. I need results to report to the chief. Get me something to take to him." His gaze moved to the men waiting for him. "Have you verified the connection between this latest assault and the others?" Ryne had updated Dixon and Captain Brown before the briefing this morning.

"I've got CSU at the scene. My men are on their way over."

"Good." It was clear he'd lost Dixon's attention. "Let me know when you get something solid."

Ryne made sure none of the anger churning in his gut showed on his face as the commander walked away. Keeping the mayor happy would have been the driving motivation behind Dixon's hiring an outside consultant. The second victim had been the mayor's granddaughter, a college student snatched on her way to work and driven to her grandparents' beach home where the attack had taken place. The man had an understandable thirst for results, and Dixon's hiring of Phillips was only the latest offering. Assigning another department investigator to the case wasn't as dazzling as putting a profiler to work on it, especially one affiliated with Adam Raiker, a man practically martyred for the Bureau some years back.

At least he hoped he'd read Dixon's intentions correctly. Ryne turned and headed back to the conference room. He sincerely hoped the man was just playing his usual style of suck-up politics and not engaged in a cover-your-ass strategy, designed to leave his image untarnished if this case went bad.

Because if that were the situation, Ryne knew exactly who'd be left twisting in the wind.

————

When Detective Robel reentered the room, Abbie could tell that his mood had taken a turn for the worse. It wasn't evident from his expression. But temper had his spine straight, his movements taut with tension. "Let's go," he said abruptly.

Without a word, she got up and followed him out the door. He made no effort to check the length of his strides. She almost had to run to keep up with him, a fact that didn't endear him to her. He stopped at one cubicle and dropped the folder containing her personnel information on the desk, then picked up a fat accordion file sitting on its corner.

"Here." He shoved it at Abbie. "You can catch up on the case on the way."

On the way where? To the scene? To the victim? She decided she wasn't going to ask. His disposition had gone from guardedly polite to truculent, and it didn't take much perception to recognize that she was the cause for the change. His attitude wasn't totally unprecedented. He wouldn't be the first detective to resent her presence on his team, at least initially. In her experience, cops were notoriously territorial.

Rather than trotting at his heels like a well-trained dog, Abbie kept the detective in sight as she followed him out of the building and down the wide stone steps. Almost immediately, her temples dampened. Though barely noon and partly overcast, the humidity index had to be hovering close to ninety percent, making her question how the majority of her assignments just happened to be located in walking saunas like Savannah. Houston. Miami.

The answer, of course, was the job. Everything she did

was dictated by it. If there was room in her life for little else, that was a conscious choice. And one she'd yet to regret.

Robel paused at the bottom of the steps as if just remembering she was accompanying him and threw an impatient look over his shoulder. Unhurriedly, she caught up, and they headed toward the police parking lot.

"Do you have any experience with victim interviews?" he asked tersely. "I want to talk to Billings before I stop by the scene."

"Yes."

"Follow my lead when we get there. We've developed a survey of questions I'll lead her through. If you have anything to add afterwards, feel free."

He led her to an unmarked navy Crown Vic, unlocked it. She slid in the passenger side while he continued around the vehicle to the other door. Before following her into the car, he shrugged out of his muted plaid suit coat, revealing a light blue short-sleeved shirt crisscrossed by a shoulder harness. He laid the suit jacket over the seat between them as he got in.

"I'm never going to get used to this weather." He slid her a glance as he backed the car out of the slot. "How do you stand wearing long sleeves like that in the middle of summer?"

"Superior genes." Ignoring his snort, she spilled the contents from the file he'd given her onto her lap. Flipping through the neatly arranged photos and reports, she noted they were sorted chronologically beginning with the first incident reported three months earlier.

She looked at the detective. "So if this latest victim turns out to be related to the others, she'll be the . . . what? Fourth?"

Ryne pulled to a stop at a stoplight. "That's right. And she's almost certainly related. He's injecting them with something prior to the attacks, and they all describe the same effects—initial tingling of the lips and extreme muscle weakness. It turns the victims' memories to mush, which means they haven't been able to give us squat when it comes to details about the attacker. From the descriptions they give, it also does something to intensify sensation."

"Maybe to increase the pain from the torture," she murmured, struck by a thought. If that were the actual intent, rather than just hazing the memory or incapacitating the victim, it would be in keeping with a sadistic rapist.

The hair on the nape of her neck suddenly prickled, and it wasn't due to the tepid air blasting from the air-conditioning vents. The atmosphere in the vehicle had gone charged. She slanted a look at Robel, noted the muscle working in his jaw.

"What do you know about the torture?"

Feeling like she was stepping on quicksand, she said, "Commander Dixon told me a little about the case when we discussed my joining the task force."

"This morning?"

"On the phone yesterday afternoon."

The smile that crossed his lips then was chilly and completely devoid of humor. He reached for a pair of sunglasses secured to the visor, flipped them open, and settled them on his nose.

Irritation coursed through her. "Something about that amuses you?"

"Yeah, it does. Considering the fact that the last time I asked Dixon for another *investigator*"—she didn't miss the inflection he gave the last word—"was yesterday morning, I guess you could say it's funny as hell."

Abbie stifled the retort that rose to her lips. She was more familiar than she'd like with the ego massage necessary in these situations, though she'd never developed a fondness for the need. "Look, let's cut through the unpleasantries. I have no intention of muscling in on your case. Since I was hired by Dixon, I have to provide him with whatever information he requests of me. But my role is first and foremost to assist you."

His silence, she supposed, was a response of sorts. Just not the one she wanted. Her annoyance deepened. According to Commander Dixon, Robel was some sort of hotshot detective, some very big deal from—Philadelphia? New York?

Some place north anyway. But as far as she could tell, he was just another macho jerk, of a type she was all too familiar with. Law enforcement was full of them. Departments could mandate so-called sensitivity training, but it didn't necessarily change chauvinistic attitudes. It just drove them deeper below the surface.

Abbie studied his chiseled profile. No doubt she was supposed to crumple in the face of his displeasure. He'd be the sort of man to appeal to most women, she supposed, if they liked the lean, lethal, surly type. His short-cropped hair was brown, his eyes behind the glasses an Artic shade of blue. His jaw was hard, as if braced for a punch. Given his personality, she'd be willing to bet he'd caught more than his share of them. He wasn't particularly tall, maybe five foot ten, but he radiated authority. He was probably used to turning his commanding presence on women and melting them into subservience.

One corner of her mouth pulled up wryly as she turned back to the file in her lap. There had been a time when it would have produced just that result with her. Fortunately, that time was in the very remote past.

Ignoring him for the moment, she pored over the police reports, skipping over the complainants' names to the blocks of texts that detailed the location, offense, MO, victim, and suspect information. "I assume you're using a state crime lab. What have the tox screens shown?" she asked, without looking up.

At first she thought he wasn't going to answer. Finally he said, "GBI's Coastal Regional Crime Lab is here in Savannah. The toxicologist hasn't found anything definitive, and he's tested for nearly two dozen of the more common substances. Reports on the first three victims showed trace amounts of Ecstasy in their blood. All victims deny being users, and the toxicologist suspects that it was mixed in controlled amounts to make a new compound."

She did look up then, her interest piqued. Use of an unfamiliar narcotic agent in the assaults might be their best lead in the case. Even without a sample, it told them something about the unknown subject. "Have you established any commonalities so far besides the drug?"

"Their hands are always bound with electrical cord, same position. Never their legs. At least not yet. He stalks them first, learns their routine. For most he gets into the house somehow, different entry techniques, so he's adaptable. But one victim he grabbed off the street and drove thirty miles to her grandparents' empty beach house for the attack."

"Same torture methods?"

He shook his head. "The first victim he covered with a plastic bag and repeatedly suffocated and revived. The next he carved up pretty bad. Looked like he was trying to cut her face off. Another he worked over with pliers and a hammer."

"What about trace evidence?"

"Nothing yet." And all the tension she'd sensed from Robel since she'd met him was pent up in the words. "He's smart and he's lucky. A bad combination for us. After the second rape I entered the case into the Violent Criminal Apprehension Program system, mentioning the drug as a common element. Only got a few hits. After the third one I resubmitted, thinking the drug might be a new addition for this perp. I don't have those results back yet, but I'm guessing we're going to get a lot more hits focusing only on the electrical cord as a common element."

"It's unusual to switch routines like that," Abbie mused. "Some rapists might experiment at first, perfect their technique, but if you've got no trace evidence, it doesn't sound like this guy is a novice."

"He's not." Robel turned down a residential street. "He's been doing this a long time. Maybe he's escalating now. Maybe it takes more and more for him to get his jollies."

It was possible. For serial offenders, increasing the challenge also intensified their excitement. The last three victims of the Romeo rapist had been assaulted in their homes when there had been another family member in the house.

With that in mind, she asked, "Are there any uncleared homicides in the vicinity that share similarities to the rapes?"

He looked at her, but she couldn't guess what he was thinking with the glasses shielding his eyes. "Why?"

"He had to start somewhere." Abbie looked out the window at the row of small neat houses dotting the street. "A guy like this doesn't get to be an expert all at once." She turned back to Robel, found him still surveying her. "Maybe he went too far once and accidentally killed his victim. Or something could have gone wrong and he had to kill one who could identify him."

"Good thought." The words might have sounded like a compliment if they hadn't been uttered so grudgingly. "We checked that. Also looked at burglaries. Nothing panned out." But her remark seemed to have splintered the ice between them.

"I'm not surprised the burglary angle didn't turn up anything. This isn't an opportunity rapist. Sounds like he goes in very prepared, very organized. His intent is the rape itself, at least the ritual he's made of the act."

Ryne returned his attention to the street. "I'm still trying to figure out why he *doesn't* kill them. A guy with that much anger toward women, why keep them alive and chance leaving witnesses?" He was slowing, checking the house numbers.

She needed to familiarize herself with the file before she was close to doing a profile on the type of offender they were hunting. But she knew that wasn't what Robel was asking for. "Depends on his motivation. Apparently he doesn't need the victim's death to fulfill whatever twisted perversion he's got driving him."

"Maybe it's the difference in the punishment. Serial rapists don't face the death penalty, even in Georgia."

But Abbie shook her head. "He doesn't ever plan to get caught, so consequences don't mean much to him. He may be aware of them on some level, but not to the extent that they would deter him."

"I worked narcotics, undercover. Did a stint in burglary, a longer one in homicide." He pulled to a stop before a pale blue bungalow with an attached carport. Only one vehicle was in the drive. "I can understand the motivations of those crimes. Greed, jealousy, anger." Switching off the car, he removed the sunglasses and slid them back into their spot on the visor. "But I've never been able to wrap my mind around rapists. I know what it takes to catch them. I just don't pretend to understand why they do it."

Abbie felt herself thawing toward him a little. "Well, if we figure out what's motivating this guy, we'll be well on our way toward nailing him."

"I guess that's your job." Robel opened his door and stepped out into the street, reaching back inside the vehicle to retrieve his jacket. "You get in his head and point us in the right direction. That's what Dixon had in mind, isn't it?" He slammed the door, shrugging into his suit coat as he rounded the hood of the car.

Abbie opened her door, was immediately blasted by the midday heat. The rancor in his words had been barely discernible, but it was there. So she didn't bother telling him that getting inside the rapist's head was exactly what she planned on.

It was, in fact, all too familiar territory. She'd spent more years than she'd like to recall doing precisely that.

Chapter 2

The air conditioner in Nancy Billings's modest ranch-style home kept the place at a comfortable seventy, which didn't account for Barbara Billings's appearance. Huddled on the corner of a multiflowered couch in the living room, she was dressed in sweats and wrapped in a quilt. Her face was still swollen and bruised, her lip split. And she was even less enthusiastic about their arrival than her mother had been.

"I've already spoken to the police." Her tone was flat and her gaze was directed somewhere above Ryne's left shoulder. "Twice. Don't you people talk? I told them everything I know. Instead of making me go over and over it, why don't you get out there and find him?"

The plaintive note in her last few words detracted from her complaint. Ryne didn't blame her for her reaction. Most victims relived the rape during the recounting, and he didn't relish putting her in that position. But neither the officers on the Marine Patrol nor the detectives called to the hospital would have been able to ask the questions pertinent to this case.

"I'm sorry to have to bother you again. I know this is difficult. We've got the other reports, but we just have a few more questions." He purposefully left the chair closest to Billings for Abbie, figuring the woman wouldn't want a man anywhere near her right now. Although when they'd made their introductions, she hadn't paid any more attention to Phillips than she had to him.

"Hi. I'm Abbie Phillips."

Ryne glanced up in the midst of taking out the victim questionnaire they'd prepared for this case to see Abbie leaning forward in her chair, addressing Billings. "If you don't feel up to this now, Barbara, we can come back later. Or if at any time you want to call a stop, we can, and wrap it up another time."

Billings looked at her, really looked at her, and in a flash, Ryne realized Phillips knew what she was doing. Establishing a rapport. Placing empathy above the task at hand. Grudgingly, he acknowledged it was working. For the first time since they'd entered the room, the woman was making eye contact with one of them.

"I'd just as soon get it over with."

Abbie nodded. "Okay. You probably haven't had time to call the rape crisis center, but you were given a card, right?"

The woman's gaze slid away as she gave a jerk of her head.

"Counseling will help. It's hard taking that first step, but after you do, you'll see."

"That's what I tried to tell her." Nancy Billings was fluttering behind the couch, as if to protect her daughter from what was to come. But Ryne knew that no one could protect Barbara from what lay ahead of her. And though he wasn't a fan of shrinks, from the report he'd read, the woman would do well to follow Phillips's advice. She was lucky to be alive. But she was going to need help remembering that.

"The downside is, after you find out for yourself, you'll have to admit your mom was right."

Abbie's words didn't bring a smile to Billings's face, but her expression lightened a little. "She does like to hear that. Maybe I'll make her day tomorrow."

"Sounds like a win-win to me."

Ryne recognized the opening he'd been given. "Ms. Billings, your statement said you were attacked inside your home. When did you first become aware you weren't alone?"

The blood drained from the woman's face. "I went in through the garage entrance and dropped my purse and keys on a small table in the hallway. Then I went to the front door and opened it to get the mail. I don't always lock the garage entrance. I mean, I have an electric door opener with no other way into the garage, and I'd shut that after me. But I know I locked the front door when I came back inside with the mail."

"Your mailbox is next to the front door, right?"

She nodded. "I don't even have to step out of the house. I just reached to get it from the mailbox, then shut the door. I'm sure I locked it." Her fingers plucked at the edge of the quilt and she looked up at her mother, as if for reassurance. "I always lock it."

He was losing her. Ryne recognized the note of panic in her voice, saw her mother respond to it with a hand on her shoulder, a frown directed at him. But before he could say anything else, Abbie put in smoothly, "If your mail is anything like mine, it's mostly junk. Did you look at it right away after you locked the door?"

And that neatly, she snapped Billings out of the self-doubt that had begun gnawing at her. "Mine is mostly bills, actually. There's this place you can write to get your name off the junk mailing list. I did that a couple years ago and it really helped."

Abbie's voice was easy. "Sometimes I just let mine pile up and go through it all after a few days, and others I go through every single piece right then. Depends on my mood, I guess."

There was an imperceptible easing of tension from the other woman's frame. "I like things neat. I always go through it right away. I had a letter from my aunt that day, and I opened it in the hallway and was reading it on my way into the kitchen. She just had a hip replacement, and she was letting me know how she came out. I put the letter by the phone, so I could read it to my mom later. And I put the bills on a little desk I have in the kitchen."

"Did you open them first?" Ryne was running a mental clock in his head, trying to figure the amount of time that must have elapsed since she'd come in the garage door.

She shook her head. "I pay bills every other week. I just put them where I keep the others. Then I went to the refrigerator, to get an idea for dinner. And when I turned around . . ." Her voice faltered. "That's when I saw him."

"Where was he?"

Billings hugged the quilt closer around her. "In the dining room. My house has a galley kitchen with an attached dining area. He was just standing there, all relaxed like, leaning a shoulder against the wall." Her voice had begun to shake.

"What did you do?"

"I screamed. I think more than once. He didn't come at me right away. He waited until I ran for the sliding glass doors before grabbing me from behind and throwing me to the floor. And then he started hitting me." Her fist clenched, and pounded lightly in her lap to punctuate her words. "Over and over and over."

The bruises on her face were neon reminders of her ordeal. From the pictures they'd seen earlier, he knew they were the least of her injuries.

"Why don't you bring Barbara something to drink? A water or iced tea." Ryne directed the words toward Nancy Billings without ever looking away from the younger woman. It was rare for him to conduct an interview with another family member present, but Barbara had flatly refused to meet with them alone. When the older woman moved to obey, he said, "Did you notice anything missing from the kitchen before you tried running? Anything out of place?"

The question seemed to puzzle Barbara. She frowned, shook her head. "I wasn't taking inventory. I was looking around for a way out, a way to . . ." Her words stopped abruptly, as if realization had just slammed into her. "The knives were gone."

He exchanged a glance with Abbie.

"I keep a cutlery set on the counter. When I was screaming, I looked for the knives, for something to defend myself with, and they were gone."

Which meant the attacker had probably been inside before the woman came home, Ryne thought grimly. "Where else did he hit you? How many times?"

"The . . . the face, mostly." Her mother had reentered the room with a glass of iced tea, which she pressed into her daughter's hands. "And the stomach, too, but mostly the face. I lost count of how often."

"Were you resisting?"

Her nod was jerky. "At first. I was struggling like a wild thing, trying to slug him, scratching and kicking."

"Do you think you might have marked him? Scratched him maybe?" In her earlier statement she'd described the man as covered completely in black. Long-sleeved black shirt, gloves, black jeans, and tennis shoes. With no bare skin showing, the chance of him sustaining an injury from a scratch would be slight.

"I don't think so." The glass was clutched tightly in the woman's hands, and she looked down at its contents. "He had a face mask on with slits for the eyes, nose, and mouth. And he wore gloves. I would never be able to identify him."

"No. But maybe you remember other details. His height, his build . . ." Billings was shaking her head before he finished the statement.

"I don't know. I'd just be guessing. I'm not good at that kind of thing anytime, and I wasn't thinking clearly. I just don't know."

"When you were fighting with him in the dining area, how much taller than you did he seem?" Abbie asked.

Billings shrugged, sending her a helpless look. "It was like my mind shut down and all I could do was react. And after he slugged me, I was kind of out of it. I felt a needle jabbing into my arm, and things are hazy after that."

Abbie reached out, covered Barbara's clenched fist with

her hand. "That's understandable. Basic survival instinct kicking in. And whatever he gave you was designed to leave you foggy."

"Try thinking back again to when you first saw him," Ryne suggested. "Do you have anything hanging on the wall he was leaning against?"

Her brow furrowed. "Sure. Some framed antique prints of early 1800 Savannah. And a shelf with some old tins."

"Which was he closest to?"

Barbara sent a puzzled look from Ryne to Abbie. "The shelf of tins."

"Where was his head in comparison with the shelf when he was leaning against that wall? Above the shelf? Below it? Even with it?"

Understanding dawned in the woman's expression. "Below it. The shelf is six feet from the floor?" Her gaze swung to her mother, who nodded. "We hung it when I moved in. Took us forever to get it straight." She swallowed, looked away. "The top of his head was about five inches or so below the shelf."

The rise in inflection at the end of the sentence was more question than statement, but it was something, Ryne supposed. If she was accurate at all in her estimate, the man would have been around five foot nine when he was standing upright.

"What about his build? Was he stocky? Slender?"

"I don't know. He wasn't big. My ex weighed about one ninety and this guy wasn't near as big as him. But he was really, really strong. I couldn't get away no matter how hard I tried." Her voice had dropped to a whisper.

Abbie nudged the hand Barbara held the glass in. "Take some time, Barbara. Drink. Go on." She waited until the woman had obeyed, then sent her an encouraging smile. "You're doing great. And you're still fighting him. With every detail you give us, you're bringing us closer to catching him, so keep fighting, okay? This won't take much longer."

A reluctant respect bloomed in Ryne when he saw the

tremulous smile the woman sent Phillips. She was proving more useful than he would have thought, although given his initial reaction, that wasn't saying much.

"You said things got hazy after he injected you." Ryne watched Barbara's hand creep up to clasp her mother's, where it lay comfortingly on her shoulder. "At any time did you lose consciousness?"

"I think I must have. Because the next thing I remember, we were in my bedroom." She shuddered, squeezed her mother's hand hard. "I was lying on the bed naked, and my hands were tied together, above my head."

"Can you show me the position they were in?" Ryne set down his pen and held his wrists together. "Were the palms facing inward? Or were they side by side like this?"

"They . . . they were . . ." Something seemed to snap inside the woman and her voice rose. "What difference does it make? I mean, really? How my hands were tied or how many times he hit me. How is that going to help? How is any of this going to help?"

"Maybe you both should go," Nancy Billings put in. She rounded the couch and sat down close to her daughter, slipping an arm around her shoulders.

"It's important because you don't know who raped you, Barbara." Abbie waited for the woman to look at her before going on. "Neither do we. But we do know the guy has been doing this for a while, and there's a reason he hasn't been caught. So every minute detail you can provide helps us, because then we put it together with other tiny little details. It's kind of like one of those thousand-piece jigsaw puzzles. You know the ones?"

The woman gave a slow nod, her gaze fixed on Abbie's.

"You dump out the box and you've got like two hundred pieces of sky and you wonder how in the world you're ever going to put them all together. And if even one of those pieces is missing, there's a chance you might not get the others to fit. That's why everything you can tell us is critical. Things that seem inconsequential to you might be important to us because it helps us build a picture of the man who attacked you. A guy like this has a ritual, and the more we know of it, the better we can predict his behavior."

Barbara moistened her lips. "You believe . . . you think he'll do this again."

"He will." Ryne wished he didn't have reason to be so positive about that fact. "You weren't his first and you won't be his last. Unless we can stop him."

"Perhaps we should do this another time," Nancy Billings murmured to her daughter. "After you're stronger."

"No." Barbara let out a long shuddering breath. "The sooner they can get started, the sooner he can be caught." She held her wrists out in front of her, palms pressed together. "I was tied like this. I don't know what he used."

"What about your legs? Were they bound, too?"

Billings shook her head. "No. I kicked at him a few times. At least I tried. But whatever he gave me. . .I was so weak. I don't think I hurt him."

"What was his reaction each time you resisted?" Ryne went back to the questionnaire.

"He'd hit me again. In the face and head. Sometimes on the breasts. He'd just pound on me until I stopped trying to fight at all. I just. . .I just wanted him to stop hitting me."

"Of course you did." Abbie's tone was reassuring. "And the fact that you quit resisting didn't affect the outcome, Barbara. Nothing you did could have changed things. None of this was your fault."

"He never spoke at all." The woman rubbed with her thumb at the condensation that had formed on the glass she still held. "Not once. That made it even more terrifying. It was like he wasn't even human. And nothing I said, not when I cried and pleaded, nothing made any difference."

Although her words weren't quite steady, she seemed to have found a well of inner strength to draw on. And that proved helpful as Ryne led her painstakingly through every detail of the attack. How the victims reacted to the process depended a great deal on the individual. Some dissolved into tears or withdrew completely. Others were reluctant to share the most degrading aspects of the rape, as the horror was revisited in the retelling.

Billings seemed to shift away, as if disassociating herself. She didn't appear aware of her mother's tight grip on her hand. Of Abbie's compassionate expression. Her recital was flat, devoid of expression. And maybe all the more gruesome for it.

Like the other victims, once she'd been injected, her memory got foggy. She did remember that the rapist never undressed, which was in keeping with the statements from the other rape victims. She could recall the types of sexual assault inflicted, but was unable to list them in sequence or recall the exact number. She was able to describe with sickening clarity the nature of the paraphernalia used on her, the excruciating pain, and the torment that had seemed endless.

But despite her cooperation, by the time Ryne had neared the end of the questionnaire, he had little new information to add to their file on the rapist.

"Ms. Billings, do you recall any sudden changes in the rapist's behavior?" When she shook her head, he pressed, "There wasn't any certain moment in which he seemed to escalate to even more violence?"

Her voice was bitter. "He was *violent* from the first minute he touched me. But the only time he seemed out of control was when I resisted. Most of the time I had the impression he didn't have any feelings at all."

That perception could be owed to the mask the man wore, Ryne figured. Without a visual clue of the man's emotions during the assault, he'd seem even more inhuman.

Or it just might be an eerily accurate depiction of a psychopath.

"At any time did he seem to experience sexual dysfunction?"

Ryne looked at Abbie as she asked the question. It was one of the last on his questionnaire, but she hadn't seen the prepared list.

Billings just shrugged helplessly. "Like I told the other

detectives at the hospital, after he shoved that needle in my arm, I wasn't that aware of *him*, you know? It was like all my other senses faded except for feeling. Sensation was heightened unbearably. Like it wasn't enough for him to rape me, nearly kill me," she went on bitterly. "He had to give me something to make it even more painful."

And that, Ryne thought, might be the one most critical detail they had about the scum they were looking for. Certainly it jibed with what the other victims reported.

"Have you received any calls or notes from unidentified persons lately? Either before or after the assault?"

"No." But then the import of his words seemed to strike her and her gaze flew to his, stricken. "Oh God. You think he'll try to contact me?"

"Probably not. But if you get any strange messages, let us know, all right?"

She seemed to shrink back into the quilt, as if trying to make herself disappear. And Ryne knew she wasn't going to hold up much longer. "What's the last thing you remember before he injected you the second time?"

Her chin sank to her chest. "He was packing up. Putting things away and I remember thinking, 'Finally. Maybe he'll kill me or just leave.' And I really didn't care which. I just wanted it to be *over*." She swallowed hard, pulled the quilt more tightly around her. "And then he jabbed me with that needle again, and I . . . I got so mad all of sudden. I couldn't stop thinking, why me? What had I ever done to deserve this? Things started to get fuzzy again, but I was so angry that he was going to get away with this. I wanted to hurt him. I wanted to kill him. And then my hands were free." The quilt was shaking now with the force of her shudders. "I don't know how, he must have freed them, but I tried to sit up and swing at him. I think I hit him. I was aiming for his face." Nancy Billings reached out to hug her, and Barbara seemed to crumple into her mother's embrace. "He went crazy, and this time when he started punching me . . . I must have blacked out. Because I don't remember anything until I woke up in the water."

"Was he gone then?"

She didn't seem to hear his question. "I thought I was going to drown. My mouth was taped and the water kept getting higher until it would get in my nose unless I pressed my face against the top of the cage." Her voice broke then, and she buried her face in her mother's shoulder. "It was just like being locked in a nightmare. Only I couldn't wake up. I couldn't ever wake up."

They wouldn't get more from her today. Ryne flipped his notebook shut, feeling suddenly ancient. The wrecked and weeping woman on the couch was oblivious to them, caught in a vivid wash of memory that might never weaken.

Whoever said time was the great healer was full of shit. He had reason to know that demons could lurk endlessly in the subconscious, just waiting for defenses to be lowered before leaping forth again. Memory could be a ravenous predator, a Technicolor replay of details far better forgotten.

He hoped like hell that Barbara Billings was strong enough to cope with what was to come. The worst wasn't necessarily behind her. Not by a long shot.

Chapter 3

Abbie ducked under the police tape and followed Ryne through the open front door of the Billings house. She was pleasantly surprised—and not a little relieved—to see open boxes of latex gloves and shoe covers sitting right inside the door. She paused to don pairs of both. Surprisingly, even in this day and age, she'd been to scenes where the police had to be reminded to wear gloves.

Raiker, of course, would prefer investigators wear totally sterile Tyvek suits over their clothes. But she was satisfied with the paper shoe covers that prevented them from carrying in particles that could be confused with trace evidence.

She signed in on the security log and, hands behind her back, stepped inside the home. Plastic evidence markers dotted the area. A crime scene tech was standing in the dining room directly ahead of her, operating the electronic crime scene scanner.

Robel was talking to Cantrell, so she moved away from them and continued through the house, stepping carefully around the markers. More CSU techs were in the bedroom in the back, going over grids of the carpet with handheld forensic vacuum units. The bed had already been stripped, the bedding individually bagged and tagged. Black fingerprint dust remained on the white woodwork and glass of the windows. An alternate light source and two sets of goggles sat on the floor next to the bed. From the looks of things, the techs were nearly done with the area. One of the detectives, she thought it was Cantrell, was taking notes of the contents of the closet and drawers.

She halted in the doorway, her gaze traveling around the room slowly. It was unmistakably feminine. Framed matted prints of flowers hung on pale pink walls. The ruffled curtains were neatly folded in bags. The bed was an intricately wrought white metal. And the nude mattress that sat on top of it was patterned with dark brown stains that would turn out to be Barbara Billings's blood.

The evidence of the brutality that had taken place there provided sharp contrast to the delicate décor. A chill worked over Abbie's skin and she moved her shoulders impatiently, shrugging it off. She turned abruptly, nearly running into a large detective she remembered from the conference room that morning. McElroy, the one with the sarcastic tongue.

"What's the matter, squeamish?" He jerked a thumb toward the door. "If you're gonna puke, do it across the street so you don't contaminate the scene."

"If and when I puke, I'll be sure to clear it with you first." Since he didn't appear inclined to move, she brushed past him to get a look at the rest of the house.

Staying clear of the other detectives, she found the side door that would lead to the garage, then traced Barbara's journey to the kitchen. She stopped even with the shelf on the wall, the one the rapist had leaned against, while he'd watched his quarry.

He'd have been filled with adrenaline. The scene he'd planned for, fantasized about, playing out according to his specifications. How long had he watched her? A minute? Two? All the while the anticipation would have built to an unbearable rush.

Abbie wasn't even aware that she'd taken up the rapist's stance, a shoulder against the wall, as she stared blindly toward the kitchen. The instant the victim had seen him would have been delicious. That first expression of shock. That quick transformation to fear. And then amusement would flare when she hunted desperately for the knives that wouldn't be there. Of course they wouldn't. Every precaution had been taken. So there was no harm in playing with her a little. Letting her run for those sliding doors that had been left locked, with the portion of wood she'd jammed in the track to keep out intruders.

He'd allow her to fumble with the lock for a few moments before pouncing. Her struggles would have knocked over that chair that still lay on the carpet. The privacy fence around the small backyard provided assurance that they'd play this scene out without interference from nosy neighbors.

Abbie curled one hand into her palm, as if gripping the syringe. Billings had said she'd been injected shortly after that initial struggle so the rapist had to have had it ready. In a pocket, or up a sleeve, she mused. With a plastic tip covering the needle to avoid pricking himself by mistake.

She felt, rather than saw, Robel's presence beside her. "Which arm was she injected in?" she murmured, her mind still filled with the scene that had played out here two days ago.

"Left."

"Which would almost certainly mean he used his right hand. She said she was on the floor before he injected her." She looked at him then, the movement snapping her out of the surreal mindset of the rapist. "You asked her which fist he hit her with . . ."

"And she said both. I see where you're going with this, but the first two victims were injected initially from behind in their left arms, which would suggest a left-handed attacker. The last two suggest a right-hander. Either he uses both hands equally well, or he's switching things up to throw us off."

"Discovering that he's ambidextrous would be important

information, too," she said mildly. "Have they found the set of knives yet?"

Robel nodded. "Garbage can in the garage. The set's already been dusted." Someone called him and he moved away. Abbie saw a couple men in the backyard checking windows for signs of tampering. If he'd gained access from one of them, there'd be little chance of signs left in the ground below. It hadn't rained in the vicinity for days, according to the online weather source she'd checked on the plane en route to Savannah.

A thought struck her and she retraced her steps to the front door, taking off the shoe covers before slipping outside. The porch was a small slab of cement punctuated with two posts that supported the overhang. Between the porch and the driveway was a small area with carefully tended hydrangeas clustered for maximum effect.

She rounded the area and eyed the shrubs. Nearly five feet high, they'd provide ample cover for someone crouched behind them, ready to roll into the garage as the door opened and its owner was backing her car out. If he timed it right and stayed down, the door would have been lowering before Billings could have caught sight of him over the hood of her vehicle. The car itself could have provided him cover as he tucked himself into the corner of the garage until the door was safely down.

She scanned the area around the bushes, but the crushed rock filler would leave no sign of footprints.

Billings had indicated she'd left the door leading to the house from the garage unlocked. She wouldn't be the only one lulled into a false sense of security with an electric door. Abbie walked into the garage. There were no other outside doors, and only one window too small to allow an adult entry.

Peering into the window of the red Sebring convertible housed there, she saw an opener clipped to the visor. Abbie returned to the front door so she could don shoe covers again before continuing into the house toward the garage entrance. Billings's keys still lay on a table in the hallway there, next to a spare electric opener.

She went in search of Robel, found him in the kitchen on

his cell phone. From the gist of his side of the conversation, she figured he was relaying information to a superior. She waited for him to finish before asking, "Have you determined the point of entry yet?"

The hard line of his jaw was beginning to show five o'clock shadow. With a start, she realized it was nearing suppertime. "No windows broken. All are locked. No doors appear to have been jimmied."

"He could have had a key."

"Billings claimed no one else had a key to the place other than her mother. Never lived here with her ex," he reminded her.

She remembered. She also knew that sometimes victims intentionally withheld information that might cause trouble for people they cared about. "We should follow up on that. An old boyfriend could have had access to the place at one time, could even make a set without her knowing. But it's also possible the perp came in through the garage as she headed out in the morning." Briefly, she filled him in on the scenario she'd checked out, concluding, "Billings said she didn't usually lock the door leading from the house to the garage. But even if she had, the seclusion would have offered him all the time he needed to pick the lock."

There was a half smile on his face as he listened to her. It didn't soften his expression appreciably. "That's how Holmes and McElroy figured it, too. The extra opener would have given the perp access after he went back for his things."

"He probably stashed a vehicle nearby." There would have been a bag or case of some sort to carry the paraphernalia necessary to carry out his ritual. Using Billings's car to transport her wouldn't have given him much maneuvering room, and why risk leaving trace evidence in a car that could be easily identified as missing?

"I've got some uniforms out canvassing the neighbors." Someone called his name and he looked away, nodded, before glancing back at her. "We've got it pretty well covered in here. Why don't you go out and give them a hand so we can wrap things up this evening?"

It was a blatant dismissal. He couldn't have said more plainly that he neither needed nor wanted her help. And if she objected, she'd cement his opinion of her as a trouble-maker on the task force, one who rejected his role as leader. If she agreed, however, she risked looking like a doormat.

She considered her options for a couple seconds before reaching a decision. "Sure." The insincerity in her smile matched his. "You might want to remind your techs to proc-ess the garage as carefully as they did the bedroom. Although it's possible he used the victim's car, most likely he parked his own vehicle right next to hers prior to transporting her. And tell them to take a sample from the crushed rock around the bushes by the porch."

Her pointing out the obvious was enough to wipe that smile off his face, so Abbie strolled away, temper simmering. She had enough experience to know the battle had merely been delayed. Robel was stuck with her, but he wasn't about to welcome her into the inner circle of his task force.

Which meant she'd earn his respect the old-fashioned way. By contributing something no one else could.

Despite the lateness of the hour, Abbie was still wired as she unlocked the door of her temporary home. The familiar rush of adrenaline hadn't yet dissipated. After being dis-missed from the scene by Robel, she'd talked to an elderly woman two blocks south of the crime scene. Even after learning a serious crime had been committed in her neighbor-hood, the woman's outrage had been reserved for the small black SUV that had been parked in front of her house most of the day. Some of the women in her weekly bridge group had had to park down the block as a result.

In her indignation, the woman had jotted down the license number.

After catching a ride back to headquarters, a trace had shown the plates as stolen. And it had been satisfying to al-ready have a DMV list of older-model SUVs fitting the color, make, and model of the woman's description ready for Robel when he'd returned. Almost as satisfying as the flicker of surprise in his eyes when she'd handed it to him.

She walked through the kitchen to the small living room, and set the accordion file she still carried on top of the desk tucked into the corner. It was unusual for the agency to arrange lodging in a house, rather than a motel. But Dixon had demanded immediate assistance, and apparently there was a sellout concert in town, making motel rooms scarce. It didn't surprise her that in twenty-four hours a furnished rental property had been subleased, while she'd flown to Savannah. Where Adam Raiker was involved, achieving the impossible was a daily expectation.

She ought to eat. Although she hadn't done any shopping yet, she could have something delivered. If she got immersed in the details of the case, hours would pass before she thought of anything else again.

But the halfhearted intention wasn't strong enough to keep her from emptying the file on the desk. As she'd noticed earlier, Robel had the contents organized chronologically. She pulled out the chair and sank into it, switching on the lamp. There was a lot of catching up to do. From what Commander Dixon had said, the task force had been formed five weeks ago, shortly after the second rape.

Abbie studied the pictures first. Bundy had favored pretty dark-haired co-eds, but the women in the photos spread before her shared no such physical similarity. All were attractive, and their ages ranged from nineteen to thirty-eight.

It wasn't unusual for some sexual predators to strike indiscriminately, like a kid in a candy store grabbing whatever he could get his hands on. But this guy was patient. A *planner*. He chose his victims carefully and it was evident he spent a great deal of time learning their routines.

So, why these women? Abbie dug through the piles until she found copies of reports detailing the task force's workup until that point. Scanning it rapidly, she found the information she was seeking and slowed to read more carefully.

No solid link had been established between the first three victims. There were no commonalities in their jobs, neighborhoods, or churches. They even shopped at different grocery stores. Two, counting Barbara Billings, were divorced. One had been single, not yet out of her teens, and one a house-wife, assaulted in her home when her husband had been out of town on business.

It looked like this angle had been exhaustively investi-gated, but she was still anxious to see if she could connect Barbara to any of the other victims. These hadn't been ran-dom attacks. Either they'd come into contact with the rapist at some point, or he'd selected them because they somehow fit his own bizarre ritual. And if she could figure out why he chose them, they'd be a long way toward establishing his motivation, and one step closer to nailing him.

Something had been nagging at her since she and Robel had talked about the victims earlier, and she dug through the pile of papers documenting the second assault. Amanda Richards, the mayor's granddaughter, hadn't been assaulted by a man hiding in her home. For her, the rapist had used a blitz-style attack, grabbing her one evening as she crossed the college campus from her job as cashier in the student union. But she'd been transported to the mayor's beach home for the attack, and Abbie thought there was something criti-cal about that.

Attacks them in familiar surroundings, she wrote. After jotting down a few more notes, she laid her pencil down and picked up the first pile, the one concerning the rape and tor-ture of Ashley Hornby. Adjusting the lamp for better lighting, she began to read.

It was well after midnight before she sat back, rubbing her eyes. A glance at the clock on the wall had her groaning. She usually got up at six to work out before getting ready for work. But she knew herself well enough to know she'd be hitting the snooze button several times before being able to rouse herself out of bed the next day. To say she wasn't a morning person was putting it charitably.

She took the time to replace the contents of the file so she could return it the next day. Then she readied for bed, mind still preoccupied with the case. She'd want her own copies of the file contents; she'd talk to Robel about it tomorrow. It would be several more nights like this one before she felt like she had a solid handle on the background. But she was itching to get started on a victim grid, a process she always used for establishing intersections in the victimology. Switching on the lamp on the bedside table, she padded back to turn off the overhead light before getting into bed.

She'd long ago learned the trick of emptying her mind, inviting sleep, and tonight exhaustion hastened the process. In only minutes she'd drifted into a deep dreamless slumber.

––––––––

It was the darkness that wakened her. Complete. Suffocating. Abbie opened her eyes, disoriented. Then she bolted upright in bed, fumbling for the lamp on the table. Two quick clicks confirmed what her sleep-fogged mind should have already figured. It wasn't working. The bulb was probably burned out.

Lungs strangled, she took a deep breath, beating back the old ghosts that threatened to pounce.

Are you alone in the dark, little girl?

The insidious whisper snaked across her mind, leaving a trail of ice. Stumbling from bed, she lurched across the room toward the light switch.

In her haste, her knee banged against the dresser, and she nearly fell. The shadows in the room seemed to rush in, grow more oppressive.

You don't have to be alone. Open the door and let me in.

Her breath sawed in and out. Her pulse pounded like a locomotive. She could feel herself moving, but the distance didn't seem to lessen. She stretched out her hand. Her fingers felt the switch plate, slipped off. Swearing, she lunged to the wall, her palm slapping blindly for the switch. An instant later her fingers found it, and she snapped it on, flooding the room with light.

Her knees went to water then, and she sank in a graceless heap to the floor. She swiped at the chilly sweat on her face with the tail of her nightshirt and waited for her pulse to quiet.

Are you alone in the dark, little girl?

With the strength of long practice, she beat back the echoes of that voice, and the sinister memories it summoned. She wasn't a girl anymore. She wasn't helpless.

And for more years than she could count, she'd made very certain that she'd never be alone in the dark again.

Chapter 4

The woman on the computer screen struggled feebly, her eyes rounded with terror. Blood oozed from the slashes across her breasts and over her stomach. A click of a button had her screams sounding, muted but shrill enough to summon a rush of arousal. An echo of that initial blast of power.

Barbara Billings had been a well-executed catch. With one minor exception, every instant had gone as planned. She may have been the most satisfying yet.

But not the last. The pictures mounted on the bulletin board above the computer displayed a number of equally deserving women. The selection couldn't be rushed. Part of the thrill was the anticipation. The familiar need was—not sated—never that—but only simmering now, not rising and clawing for release. There was plenty of time to consider the next victim.

Even if a tiny slip had been made this time, the police still had shit to go on. Which was probably why they were controlling what was released to the press. If the public knew how little progress had been made in this case, they'd be screaming bloody murder.

Bloody. A quiet laugh escaped at the irony. *No pun intended, Barbara.*

But it was never too soon to prepare. The cell phone lay next to the computer. After a familiar number was dialed and an interminable wait, a sleepy voice finally answered.

"Hey, I was going to call you tomorrow. Where are you?"

"I need more supplies. How soon can you send them?"

"You're really enjoying my little discovery, aren't you?"

Excitement flared hotly as the woman on the computer screen began writhing in agony. Oh, she hadn't liked that speculum shoved up her ass. Not at all. "Very much. But I'll need twice what you gave me last time."

"Hell, you can have three times as much." The pause that followed hummed with expectation. "But you have to do something for me first."

Irritation surged, was ruthlessly tamped down. "Already?"

"She didn't last as long as I'd hoped. I'll be more careful with the next one. Promise."

Fingers drummed the desktop indecisively. It would mean catching a quick flight and back, but it was doable. "All right. Male or female this time?"

"Hmm, how about you surprise me."

Someday, despite their long relationship, a real and very final surprise would await the man. He was getting a bit too demanding. But for now he was needed. "Expect your gift within the week."

"Fast work. I'm impressed." The voice was pleased. "I'll overnight your delivery. Same mail drop?"

"Yes." Business concluded, the call was disconnected. It was tedious to have to deviate from planning to arrange a trip, but well worth the hefty supply of drugs and syringes received in exchange. Totally anonymous. Completely untraceable.

Several clicks of the computer mouse fast-forwarded the movie before halting at the best part. The moment when the woman first realized her suffering wasn't at an end. That there was something more in store for her.

Watching the sheer horror on her face was almost as

thrilling as being there. Almost. Yes, Billings had been nearly perfect.

But the next one would be even better.

———————

Ryne rested his chin on his folded arms upon the kitchen table and stared at the two fingers of Jim Beam in the glass before him. Memory, that sneaky bitch, supplied him with vivid sensory details. He could almost taste the scorching path the liquor would take down his throat. Could feel the burn as it pooled in his belly. Could remember the compulsion to follow the first shot with another. Then another.

Somehow in the grip of that thirst, it was easy to forget the repercussions of too frequent late nights, too many empty bottles. Simple to slip into the rationalizations that could almost convince him the events of a year and a half ago weren't his fault. That Deborah Hanna's blood wasn't on his hands, as surely as if he'd pulled the trigger himself.

But he couldn't dodge the truth when his head was clear, and after eighteen months of sobriety, sometimes in the middle of a puzzling case, or after a particularly exhausting day, the truth pounced with the feral savagery of a wild animal.

Someday that truth would devour him.

But not tonight. The ring of his cell phone shrilled, cutting through his dark thoughts. He pulled it from the pocket of the jacket he'd slipped over the back of the chair, read the number on the screen. Dixon's home number.

Ryne glanced at the clock as he flipped the phone open. Nearly 1 a.m. Surely Dixon didn't have news about the case. Although he'd insisted on being personally involved, his role was merely supervisory.

"This is Robel."

After his answer, there was a minute hesitation before he heard, "Ryne? Did I wake you?"

Wariness rose as he recognized the voice. Not Dixon at all, but the man's wife. "SueAnne. Is something wrong?"

"No. Well, Holly is sick and her fever is really starting to scare me. Derek said y'all had a meeting tonight but I haven't been able to reach him. I was just wondering if you were with him. If I could talk to him."

She finished on a rush, and Ryne could feel lead settling in the bottom of his gut. He'd always liked SueAnne Dixon, with her pretty blond looks and Southern belle manners. He'd wondered what the hell she'd seen in the womanizing prick she'd married. The same prick who'd used him, used this case, as a cover tonight.

"Sorry, I'm at home. But if you need to take her to the hospital, I could come over and stay with Hillary until Derek gets back."

"Oh, I don't want to bother you. I'm probably worrying about nothing. But I'd like to let Derek know. If I just knew when to expect him."

In that moment Ryne realized Holly Dixon wasn't nearly as sick as her mother let on. And while he wasn't going to lie for her worthless husband, neither was he willing to be the one to shatter the precarious trust she still might have in the man. "I expect he'll be along shortly. But I mean it, SueAnne. I can be there in twenty minutes if you need me. Don't know much about babysitting four-year-olds, but I don't figure Hillary can give me much trouble while she's sleeping."

"You'd be surprised." His words had eased something in her voice, and he didn't know whether to be glad or ashamed. "I'll just wait up for him. You're probably right, and Derek is on his way. I'm sorry about bothering you, but now that I've got you on the phone, I'm going to scold you about turning down all our barbecue invitations." Her tone went teasing. "I don't think I've seen you more than twice since you moved down here."

He got up and reached for the glass, carried it to the sink, and dumped it out. "You know how it is. New job. Heavy caseload. I'll make it over again one of these days."

"I'm going to hold you to that. Oh, I think I hear Derek now." She hesitated. "I feel so silly . . . I sure would appreciate it if y'all didn't mention this call to him. He's always accusing me of overreacting."

"Sure thing, SueAnne," he said gently. When she hurriedly said good-bye, he disconnected, then stared for a moment at the phone in his hand. He hadn't lied to her, but he'd misled her all the same. A better man would feel bad about that, but it wouldn't rank too highly on his overburdened conscience.

Ryne plugged the phone into its charger before heading to his bedroom, where he already knew sleep would elude him.

If SueAnne Dixon wanted to believe the lies her husband told her, who was he to knock her faith? They all made choices.

The hell of it was living with them.

———————

Abbie paused to appreciate the historic brick structure that housed police headquarters before heading up the steps. With its tall white-trimmed windows and ornate gingerbread, it looked to be a couple of centuries old. Spanish moss hung like ragged lace from the huge oaks surrounding it, and next door was an old cemetery. Jogging up the steps, she wondered how many of its occupants had been "guests" in this building prior to their demise.

The desk sergeant directed Abbie to the conference room, where she'd found the task force grouped yesterday morning. She slipped in the door, recognizing the detectives she'd met yesterday, as well as several uniformed officers. Only Ryne was absent.

"Good morning."

The others nodded at her greeting, except for McElroy, who looked up from the chair he was lounging in. "Hey, Tinkerbell. Get coffee, would ya?"

Abbie raised a brow and sank into a chair. "I don't want coffee."

"That doesn't mean you can't get it for the rest of us."

She'd met plenty of men like McElroy, those who used charm if they possessed it, intimidation if they didn't to get what they wanted. And he'd intimidate some people. He had a good foot and a hundred pounds on her, an ex–football player's build that had softened but not yet run to fat. His swarthy skin would always make him look like he was suffering from a mild case of sunburn. With his slicked-back hair and cheap sports jacket, he looked more like a used car salesman than a cop.

"Sorry, Nick." The door opened again as she spoke. "I hadn't heard about your accident."

McElroy glanced around at the others in the room, then back at her. "What's that?"

"The one where you broke your leg. Left you unable to wait on yourself."

The other detectives laughed, and McElroy's expression darkened. "You want to see my *leg*, sugar, that can be arranged."

"A tempting prospect, but I'll pass."

"If you want coffee, McElroy, get it when we're done here. I'd like to get started." Abbie looked up to see Ryne standing at the table positioned in front of the room. A fifty-ish man in a rumpled suit took a chair near him. His face was heavily freckled, and his ginger-colored hair stood up in little tufts all over his balding head. This must be Captain Brown, Ryne's immediate superior in the case. Dixon had mentioned him, but had also emphasized that he was personally overseeing the investigation himself.

Ryne's gaze traveled over those assembled in the room, lingering for a moment on her. He didn't look like he'd slept much better than she had, although undoubtedly for different reasons.

"Phillips, you want to update the others on what the canvass turned up last night?"

Abbie rose, faced the rest of the detectives. "The neighbors to the south of Billings, a couple in their sixties, are on vacation in Montana, visiting relatives. There's a divorced guy on the other side of her home, Kevin Williams, a machinist who works second shift. Said he was at work, and he checks out. Officers will be following up today with any neighbors not contacted last night. So far no one saw anything suspicious, with the exception of Ethel Krebbs, who lives two blocks south of Billings's street."

"Don't tell me," McElroy drawled. "Ethel Krebbs saw the whole thing from her picture window."

"No, but she called in to the department with a complaint about an older-model SUV parked in front of her house. She was expecting company and wanted it moved. No one checked it out." Abbie shrugged. "It's not private property, so it was probably considered a low-priority call. When her company left at nine, it was gone. But she was upset enough to jot down the license number of the vehicle." A curious stillness settled over the room. "We ran the plates and they'd been stolen off a '99 Chevy Impala a week ago."

Cantrell spoke up. "She get the make and model of the SUV?"

Abbie nodded and shot Ryne a questioning look. He picked up a sheaf of papers he'd brought in and walked over to Cantrell, handed it to him. "We've run vehicle registrations for older-model Broncos. Also have the stolen vehicle reports for the last two weeks. Wayne, you and McElroy can go through these and see what you come up with. Isaac, I want you to work the dog kennel angle. Check out the manufacturer, who sells that type around here, how many, do they keep records . . . you know the drill."

Holmes's expression managed to look even more hang-dog. "Needle in a haystack," he muttered.

"Yep. But this is the haystack we're shaking today."

"What about Tinkerbell?" McElroy shot Abbie a pointed look. "What's she gonna be doing? She sure as hell doesn't fetch coffee."

Ryne's face went expressionless. "Ms. Phillips will be working on establishing a profile of the rapist."

The air in the room went abruptly charged. Isaac Holmes looked at her. "What precinct you say you're from, Phillips?"

Abbie opened her mouth to answer, but Robel beat her to it.

"She's an independent consultant. Commander Dixon made the decision to contract with an outside agency, Raiker Forensics. Maybe you've heard of it." There wasn't a hint of emotion in Robel's voice. To Abbie's ears, his dispassionate tone was as damning as a shout.

"Un-fucking-believable." McElroy glared at Ryne. "She's not even a cop?"

"You want a profile, you should have just asked." Cantrell's smile was chilly. "White male, between twenty and forty. Marginally employed. History of abuse toward women. Isn't that what you guys always come up with?"

"Depends on the evidence," she answered evenly. "And the pattern. But it's too soon for me to reach any conclusions. At this point, it hasn't even been determined that the rapist is male."

McElroy guffawed and Ryne glared at him. "I think what Ms. Phillips is saying . . ." he started.

"What I'm saying is it's too soon to narrow our focus. It probably is a man. Better than ninety-nine percent of rapists are. But this one incapacitates the victims and never undresses. Given the haziness of the victims' memories, I'm not ready to rule anyone out yet."

"So I guess we know what Robel's doing today," McElroy said in a loud aside to Cantrell. "Tracking down those dangerous female rapists we got running all over Georgia. Lucky bastard."

With effort, Abbie kept a smile on her face as the detectives laughed. "I've worked more than a dozen serial rapist cases in the last five years. Female perpetrators are rare, but I don't rule out anything until the evidence warrants it. Generalizations are dangerous because they blind us to other possibilities."

"Okay, let's get to work." At Ryne's order, everyone rose, including Captain Brown. "If you run across something that sounds promising, I want to hear about it."

The detectives filed out of the room.

"Ms. Phillips." Brown paused before her and extended his hand. "Captain Dennis Brown. I want to welcome you to Savannah and the team." His grip was firm, his faded blue gaze searching. "I'm sure Ryne will get you everything you need, but if there's anything I can do, my office is upstairs."

"Thank you. I look forward to getting started."

He inclined his head and followed the others out the door.

Abbie eyed his retreating figure speculatively. It was always telling to analyze the dynamics of the groups she worked with. And in those brief moments she'd gotten the distinct feeling that Brown was no happier about her being here than Robel was.

"I had another desk moved in, next to mine." The detective gathered up his files quickly then straightened. "That will be your space for the duration."

Next to his. Great. "Thanks."

"You don't believe that, do you?" He fell into step beside her, his voice openly skeptical. "All that you were saying about women raping women. I mean. . . seriously."

She stifled a sigh. Leave it to him to completely miss the message she'd tried to get across. "It's a remote possibility. But it's a possibility until we prove otherwise."

"You really think this guy on the loose in Savannah might be a female?"

"No." She pushed by him and went in search of her desk. "I *think* he's a perverted sadist—a male sadist—who gets off by inflicting horrendous torture on his victims and then fantasizes about it for weeks afterwards. We just don't have enough to prove it yet. But that's what I'm being paid for, so that's exactly what I'm going to do."

———

It was nearly dark before Abbie reached her house again. When she was on the job, there were few other distractions, so she usually kept long hours. If she was going to be here for any length of time, however, she needed to find a gym to work out in. She made a mental note to ask Robel about it tomorrow.

Robel. She parked the rental car in the driveway and then got out, locking it with the remote. His attitude toward her assignment to the task force hadn't softened appreciably. But she'd completed entire cases without having the lead investigators ever make nice. The job was still possible. It just made for a tense way to work.

She started toward the house, still preoccupied with the

case. She wanted to interview all the victims herself. She'd already set up a meeting with Amanda Richards, the mayor's granddaughter, for the next morning, in her hospital room. She was being prepared for her third surgery since the attack. From the photos in the file, it was apparent the damage had been. . .

Abbie stopped. Then in one smooth movement she bent, slipped the weapon from her ankle holster, and trained it on the back door, which was standing ajar.

Glass littered the steps from the shattered window in the door. The method of entry had been crude, but effective. She thumbed off the safety on her Sig, while reaching for the cell phone in her purse. After calling it in, she replaced the phone and circled the house.

The front door was still shut. She climbed the porch and tried the doorknob. Locked. Completing her journey around the house, it was evident that the intruder had entered and left the same way.

If he'd left at all.

Sirens sounded in the distance. Keeping her weapon steady, Abbie climbed the back steps and nudged the door open with the toe of her shoe. She stepped into the kitchen, surveyed the area, and found it empty.

The house was a small L shape. The kitchen opened on to the living room, and the bedroom and bath were on its right. Her gaze flicked to the cellar door. The latch was in place. She continued into the house carefully, the glass crunching underfoot the only sound in the stillness.

The only things out of place were the three framed pictures she'd brought with her and set on the mantle of the small fireplace. These were lying facedown on the floor, as if someone had knocked them off with one swipe of a forearm.

There were few hiding places in the room, but she checked them all. Behind the couch. In back of the recliner. And more cautiously, the front closet. Nothing.

She could hear tires screeching to a halt in front. Giving the bathroom a swift look, she focused on the bedroom. A quick search convinced her the prowler was no longer around. Abbie reholstered her weapon, her gaze trained on the gaping doors to the bedroom closet. Fabric littered its floor. She approached it, stared at the savagery that had been done to her wardrobe, and felt her stomach hollow out. For the first time she considered that the "intruder" was probably all too familiar to her.

She walked back through the house and met the two officers at the back door, hands by her sides. "I live here. I made the call about the break-in."

"Please step to the side, ma'am." One officer passed by her, weapon ready, while the other stopped in front of her. "I'll need to see some ID."

The officer was young, no more than mid-twenties, with the regional drawl rounding the vowels of his words. But his gaze was sharp, shrewd, and he hadn't lowered his weapon.

"Abbie Phillips. This is my SCMPD identification badge." She unclipped it from the pocket of her shirt and handed it to him. He scanned it, looked at her.

"Special consultant? To what?"

"I'm working with the serial rapist task force."

The other officer returned to the room. "Place is empty."

"You shouldn't have entered the place before we got here, ma'am." A hint of censure colored the first cop's tone as he handed the badge back to Abbie. "Whoever broke in here could have still been on the premises."

She didn't want to complicate the matter by explaining that she was armed. That Raiker refused to allow his investigaters to work without weapons. The cop, Dale Mallory, was right, in any case.

"Doesn't look like anything is missing," she said. The only things of value she brought on a case were her Sig and laptop, and she'd had both with her. "Just vandalism. Is this neighborhood prone to that sort of thing?"

Mallory had holstered his gun and pulled a small notebook from his back pocket. "Not really, but there's a high school a block from here. Could've been kids."

An all-too-familiar apprehension knotted her stomach. Now that she'd been over the premises, she was anxious to have the officers gone. Anxious to be alone to consider the complicated ramifications of the situation. But the cops methodically took down her information, asking her questions that she couldn't answer entirely truthfully. No, she hadn't lived here long. She'd only gotten to town a couple days ago. Yes, she was living alone. No, she hadn't met anyone outside of work since arriving. She had no idea who could have done this.

She uttered the last lie without a qualm. She'd long ago mastered the art of delivering one without hesitation. Remarkable how old talents surfaced under times of stress.

"Officers." Abbie's head jerked at the familiar voice. Ryne stepped in the back door and flashed his shield at the two policemen. "What have you got?"

Both men's attention switched to the newcomer, and Abbie attempted to hide her dismay. His presence seemed to shrink the already small area of the kitchen in a way the other officers' hadn't. She didn't miss the deferential tones with which the two men addressed him, nor the fact that after that first lightning glance over her, his attention hadn't strayed in her direction again.

She didn't want him here. She didn't want that shrewd focus narrowed on her, on her personal effects, asking questions she had no intention of answering, and drawing his own conclusions.

His appearance rattled her in a way the break-in hadn't. Abbie got a garbage bag from beneath the sink and left the officers explaining the situation to the detective. Swiftly, she returned to her bedroom and gathered up the fabric littering the closet floor, stuffing it in the bag. Then she removed the ruined shirts from their hangers and discarded them as well. There was no way of salvaging the shirts after the sleeves had been hacked off, in any case.

She suspected the "vandal" had counted on that.

"So, the uniforms said there wasn't much damage."

Abbie rose, the half-filled garbage bag clenched in one fist. The doorway framed him, and she knew, with a sinking certainty, that the image of him standing in it would prove difficult to dismiss from her memory. He was an intriguing man, even when he annoyed her. Which so far was most of the time. "More of a nuisance than anything else."

His gaze went beyond her, lingering on the open closet and empty hangers. "Weird sort of thing for an ordinary vandal to do."

"Breaking and entering falls under the 'weird' category altogether, doesn't it?" She brushed by him, went back to the kitchen, dropping the bag and grabbing a broom tucked into the corner. The policemen were gone, no doubt dismissed by Robel. If she'd had her preference, she'd have taken their presence over his.

If she had her choice, he'd never have come at all.

"I can patch that window for you."

"It's okay." Aware her tone had been short, Abbie softened it. "Thanks, but I can take care of it. Tomorrow I'll call a glass company to come do a permanent fix."

"And a security company. Whoever did this could return. Next time they might damage more than just your shirts."

"And a security company," she repeated, straightening to face him. She'd have agreed to just about anything at that point to get rid of him. To be alone with the worry that had lodged in her chest ever since seeing her closet.

His gaze searched hers, but she kept her expression blank. She knew that fact didn't escape him, but he said only, "I think I've got some things in the trunk to fix the window."

"That really isn't . . ." He was already walking through the door.

Frustrated, she used the handle of the broom to knock out the remaining shards of glass from the pane. His stubbornness wasn't exactly a newsflash, given their association up to this point. But somehow right now she found it even more irritating.

She finished sweeping up the glass and dumped it in the trash bag. Then, when he approached the back porch again, she went back to the living room and picked up the displaced pictures. The glass in each had been cracked by the fall, so she removed each picture from the frame and discarded the ruined glass. Then she replaced the photos on the mantle.

"All done."

She turned when the voice sounded behind her. "That was fast."

Ryne approached. "Just some cardboard and duct tape. It won't hold long. Don't put off calling that glass company."

"I won't."

He passed by her to study the pictures. Nerves skittered along her spine. It was ridiculous to feel exposed as he perused the only faintly personal touch in the entire room. Ridiculous to feel weak, as if his learning anything about her left her vulnerable in a way she was always careful to avoid.

He tapped the unsmiling man next to her in one picture. "Who's this?"

"Adam Raiker."

"I remember reading about his last case for the Bureau. Caught by the serial killer he was pursuing, right?"

Although she doubted she knew much more than he did, she said, "Wilson Corbin. Raiker rescued his hostage, but Corbin got away. Adam pursued him and ended up being captured. He was held for three days before he managed to get free and kill the man, despite his injuries." And the injuries Raiker had sustained had been substantial. That was clear from the picture, even after nearly seven years. A hideous scar bisected his throat. The cane he walked with was clutched in one hand, the eye patch he wore giving him a formidable look. It was an accurate enough depiction of his personality. Adam Raiker was the most formidable person she'd ever met, with a staggering intellect, caustic tongue, and incomparable talent. She considered herself fortunate to be working for him, but that didn't mean she wasn't intimidated by him.

Abbie turned away from the photos, but Robel failed to take the hint and follow suit. Big surprise.

"Looks like you've got hidden talents."

Reluctantly, she turned back, following his gaze to the center picture, taken last summer at the shooting range on the grounds of the agency's headquarters, in Manassas, Virginia. It showed her unsmiling face next to a paper human outline. Six holes were clustered in the vicinity of the heart. "Raiker insists we qualify as marksmen each year." He was also adamant that his operatives be issued weapon permits from any law enforcement agency requesting their services. "I posted a personal best last August."

"Rifle or handgun?"

"This was the handgun qualifier, but we have to qualify with both." She gave a wry smile. "My prowess with a rifle is less impressive, but I passed."

His attention had wandered to the next picture, and she felt the tension settle in her shoulders again. Forestalling the inevitable question, she said, "I want to thank you again for your help."

"No problem." This time when she started toward the back door, he followed. "You might try Stanley Glass when you're calling tomorrow. They're in the book. They're quick and they won't hose you for the work."

"Good to know." He stopped, his hand on the knob of the back door. Silence stretched, long enough to have her nerves jangling. Robel looked at the bag in her hand and his expression grew thoughtful.

Abbie sensed he was about to say something else. And more than anything at that moment, she wanted to avoid further speculation. "I'll see you tomorrow."

"If you need some personal time to come home and deal with the glass or security companies, just let me know." He reached for the bag. "I'll dump this in the garbage on my way out."

"I can . . ." His hand brushed hers, heat transferring at the touch, and she nearly jumped. Her nerves were frayed and at that moment she would have given her very generous monthly paycheck to make him disappear.

"Good. Fine." She relinquished the bag and stepped back, his inscrutable stare making her all too aware that she was flushing. "And I don't need any time off. I'll see you tomorrow."

Without another word, he went out the door, and she closed and locked it after him, feeling a little foolish. It would be easy enough for a prowler to remove the neat cardboard patch job and reach in to unlock the door. She pulled a chair from the kitchen table and wedged it under the knob, although she was fairly certain the trespasser wouldn't be returning. At least not tonight.

Resolutely, Abbie walked back into the other room, intent on losing herself in work when a realization struck her. She was going to have to find a mall to do some shopping. With the exception of the one she was wearing, every dress shirt she'd brought with her had been ruined.

Frustration surged. As if the break-in wasn't irritating enough, now she had to shop. And she'd rather be beaten than to spend hours looking at clothes. But of course, her intruder today had known that.

Inevitably, her gaze was drawn to the photos she'd replaced on the mantle. To the blond woman with the too bright smile standing arm in arm with Abbie.

"Callie?" Realizing she'd called the name aloud, she immediately felt foolish. The small home had been searched several times already. There was no one here.

But there had been earlier, and it had almost certainly been her sister. All the tension of the last hour settled in her temples, and they began to throb painfully. She hadn't spoken to Callie for months, but she'd left messages. Forwarding addresses. She had no idea why Callie would reach out now, in this way, but she was almost certain that she had. The devastation to her wardrobe proved that.

Only Callie knew about her penchant for long-sleeved shirts and the scars they covered.

Only Callie would bare them, literally, for the world to see.

Chapter 5

The woman lying in the hospital bed knew all about scars. If Abbie hadn't seen the photos taken after Amanda Richards's attack, she'd find it hard to believe that the girl had already had two operations. From some newspaper pictures in the file, she knew it had once been an extraordinarily beautiful face.

Now it was a patchwork of seams and puckered, drawn skin, as if there hadn't been enough flesh to reattach and the remaining skin had been pulled too tightly. One eye was noticeably lower than the other, giving her features an off-kilter look. Looking at her, Abbie was certain today's was just one of a long string of surgeries.

She knocked on the open hospital door and the three occupants of the room looked toward her. "Hi, I'm Abbie Phillips, a consultant working with the SCMPD."

"Oh, for heaven's sakes!" snapped the woman sitting next to the bed. Even without an introduction, Abbie knew she was the girl's mother. Her resemblance to Amanda's newspaper pictures in the file was too strong for it to be otherwise. Rising, she turned toward Abbie. "You people have deplorable timing."

"I asked her to come, Mother." Amanda's voice was

pleasant but firm. "The operation isn't scheduled until this afternoon. There's plenty of time."

"There's no reason to upset yourself before surgery." The older woman turned her back on Abbie, and reached over to smooth her daughter's blond hair back from her ruined face. "Whatever this is about, it can wait."

Amanda looked at the middle-aged man on the other side of the bed. "Daddy? You don't mind taking Mother to the cafeteria for a while, do you?"

He hesitated, sending a steely look toward Abbie. But in the end, he managed a smile for his daughter and said, "Sure, honey."

"Phil, really. I don't think . . ."

Ignoring his wife's protests, he rounded the bed, took her elbow, and steered her toward the door. "We'll be back in twenty minutes." Abbie knew it wasn't her imagination that imbued the words with a hint of warning.

When the door had closed behind the couple, Amanda attempted a smile. Only one side of her mouth responded. "Sorry about that. They can be pretty fierce when it comes to me."

"It's parents' jobs to be protective." Even though some parents failed miserably at it. "I can't blame them for objecting to the timing."

"I'll be out of it for days after the surgery." Amanda hit the button to elevate the head of the bed more. "Pain meds have that effect on me. And I didn't want to wait that long. I heard Grandpa Richards tell Daddy they'd brought in an expert, and I wanted to talk to you."

It took Abbie a moment to make the connection. Mayor Richards. Someone, presumably Commander Dixon, was keeping the man informed. "I don't know about the expert part, but I do have experience in these kinds of cases. I want to focus on the victimology pattern, and I have some questions that weren't covered in the earlier interviews."

"You mean figuring out why he chose me. Us."

Abbie gave a slight nod. The girl was quick. "Exactly."

Amanda indicated a chair next to the bed and Abbie sank into it, digging into her purse for her notebook. "I've thought about that. I have a lot of time on my hands these days," she added without rancor. "After it happened, the police asked all these questions about the beauty contests I've participated in. I was crowned Miss Savannah last fall and I'm going to compete—I was supposed to compete—in the Miss Georgia contest later this year. My sponsor thought I had a pretty good chance. . . ." Her voice trailed off for a moment. Then, visibly collecting herself, she continued, "But I don't think it had anything to do with the contest. Any of the contests."

It had been a valid lead to pursue, one Abbie would have focused on herself, though it hadn't yielded anything in the long run. "Why not?"

"Well, it's not like one of the girls I beat out is going to do this to me," she said matter-of-factly. "Though there were a couple vicious enough to arrange an accident for anyone standing in their way of the crown. And don't even get me started on some of the mothers." She shook her head. "But people surrounding beauty pageants are ninety percent female. And no women I know are capable of this. Or even of arranging this for another woman. I just can't believe that."

"But you did come into contact with men at the pageants," Abbie pressed.

Amanda shrugged. "Sure. Sound engineers, emcees, some of the sponsors, agents . . . but what I'm saying is, I come into contact with guys all the time. I attend college here in town, and I see more men on campus every day than I do in the pageants."

As the girl had said, she'd given this a lot of thought. "So let's talk about those guys on campus. The notes say you recently broke up with a long-time boyfriend."

"Chet didn't have anything to do with this." Amanda's voice was sharp. "He's not the kind of person who would deliberately hurt someone. I know the detectives have been all over him about this, and I feel bad about that. This isn't his fault. And neither was the breakup. I just wanted to date other people."

Which was enough incentive for some people to turn to violence. But Chet Montrose was alibied for the night in question. He'd been taking a chemistry final at the time Amanda had been snatched.

"Since this is a multiple offender and the other victims aren't affiliated with the pageant or the college, I don't think either is integral to his pattern."

"Maybe he just saw me in the paper or on TV. There's been a lot of coverage since my win, and as we geared up for the state pageant."

Entirely plausible, Abbie thought, but that possibility led nowhere. "I have copies of your interview with the police. Detective Robel took you over the two weeks prior to the assault, your routine, normal hangouts. I'm going to ask you to think back further than that. Maybe a month or six weeks prior to the attack. Even two months. Can you think of places you might have stopped that you don't normally?"

Amanda's brows were furrowed. "Stopped for what?"

"Anything. Coffee. A different dry cleaners. A place to get pictures developed. A market you usually don't shop at, or a mall you don't often frequent."

"Hard to remember that far back," Amanda murmured, but it was clear from her expression that she was trying. In the end she was able to recall six or seven new places she'd stopped with friends, although she couldn't be certain how long before the rape she'd visited them.

"How many people knew about your grandfather's beach house?" Robel had covered the question in his interview, but something about the location of the rape still nagged at her.

Amanda shrugged. "Of my friends, you mean? All of them. I . . . had a key made a couple years ago. My grandparents don't use it that much. I've had some parties there. You know how it goes. People I know bring people I don't. Seems like my entire dorm has been there at one time or another."

And even if they had only heard mention of a party, it would be easy enough to discover the home's location, given the owner's name.

"It all comes back to this, doesn't it?"

Something in the girl's tone drew Abbie's attention. She looked up from the pad she was writing on. "What's that?"

Amanda's lips trembled before she attempted to firm them. "I just can't stop thinking about it. Like maybe there's some guy I never paid much attention to. Not someone I turned down for a date or anything. I told the detective about them. But I feel like it's someone I've missed somehow. Or discounted. Like maybe I hardly even spoke to him or noticed him at all. And for a long time he harbored this resentment toward me because of that . . ." Her voice hitched.

Abbie could hear Amanda's mother in the hallway. Their time together was almost up. "Well, there, see, that's where you're wrong." She got up and fetched a Kleenex to hand to the girl, who wiped her eyes swiftly before balling the tissue in her palm.

"How do you know that?"

"None of the other victims are associated with beauty pageants or go to the local college. You aren't the same age and you have little in common. But somehow you all came to this guy's attention. Which tells me it probably isn't something you did or didn't do to someone you barely know. This guy is preying on women because they meet some criteria that only makes sense to him. And the sooner we figure out that criteria . . ."

Amanda's eyes were no longer tear drenched. They looked cold and hard as she finished Abbie's sentence. "The sooner you can catch the son of a bitch and put him away."

A faint smile on her lips, Abbie nodded. "Exactly."

Robel wasn't at his desk when Abbie got back to headquarters, and she couldn't help feeling a little relieved. She'd noticed him watching her a couple times earlier that day, a speculative gleam in his eyes, but other than inquiring about her arrangements with a glass company, he hadn't mentioned anything about the break-in.

He hadn't forgotten her request for a complete copy of the investigation, however. There was a fat accordion file setting on her desk, a match to the one on his.

She sat down at her desk and turned on her laptop. It was a half hour after shift change, but she doubted Robel had left for the day. His suit jacket was still hanging over the back of his chair. He kept even later hours than she did. There was nothing to take up her time other than the reason that had brought her to Savannah, but she would assume Robel had a personal life to tend to.

Not even to herself did she want to admit a curiosity about just what his personal life entailed. A wife? A family? It'd be a safe bet to guess he was divorced, since divorce rates among cops were nearly double the national rate.

But guessing was all she could do, because Robel had never so much as hinted about his personal life. And given her reluctance to do the same, her curiosity about his was a bit ironic.

Shoving the man from her mind, she began transcribing the notes she'd taken at the hospital. The selection of the beach house for the location of Amanda's rape still bothered her. Had it been chosen because it belonged to the mayor? For that matter, had Amanda's selection been based on her relationship to her grandfather?

"Are the other guys already gone?"

She started at Ryne's voice behind her, then swiveled her seat to face him. "I've been back about twenty minutes and haven't seen any of them. Why?"

He grabbed his suit jacket. "A black-and-white called in with a vehicle matching the description of that SUV your witness ID'd, right down to the plates. The officers are watching it until I get there." As he spoke, he shrugged into the jacket and headed toward the door.

"I'm coming, too." Abbie pressed Save and sprang out of her chair. Robel didn't slow down and he didn't look back. He couldn't have made it clearer that her presence was neither wanted nor needed. But she'd be damned if she'd let him cut her out of what might turn out to be the first real break they'd caught in the case.

Haskin's 24-Hour Valu-Mart anchored a strip mall on the northern edge of Savannah. Although the rest of the establishments in the mall appeared closed, the parking lot in front of Haskin's was still three-quarters full. The large sign above the storefront proclaimed it the home of discount prices.

Ryne spotted the black-and-white pulled up next to a small compact that had come in bruising contact with a Cadillac Escalade, parked unscathed nearby. He found a parking spot and got out, approaching the officers, Phillips at his heels.

He flashed his shield at one of the uniforms, a craggy-faced man with a buzz haircut. With a quick glance at his nameplate, he said, "Wilhm? You the one who caught the stolen plate number on the Bronco?" At the officer's assent, Ryne led him a few feet away from the other officer, who was moderating the argument between the car owners, a short mustached man and a bejeweled soccer mom.

"We responded to the call about the accident about a half hour ago, and I spotted the Bronco plates a little after that. Next row to the west, almost all the way down." Wilhm gave a slight nod in that direction. "We've got a list of DCBs in the car, that's why it popped for me. Look familiar?"

Ryne had made the decision to release daily confidential bulletins to patrol officers, with relevant case developments. It extended the reach of the task force to every beat officer in the department. Folding his arms across his chest, his gaze lingering on the vehicle the man indicated, he gave thanks now for his foresight.

"It fits," Phillips murmured.

"Have you seen anyone near it?"

Wilhm shook his head. "Not since I've been here."

"All right. Hang around out here and keep an eye on it while we go in to talk to management."

The officer nodded, his gaze drifting back to his partner, who was unsuccessfully trying to calm both drivers. "No problem. We won't be done here for a while anyway."

When Ryne turned around, Phillips was already headed toward the store. He easily caught up with her. Her stride was much shorter than his, and he threw a bemused glance at her legs. They were encased, as always, in black pants. She'd barely meet the old height regulation for police officers, but it wasn't just her height that had warranted McElroy's nickname for her. She was small. Hands, feet, features. Almost . . . he searched for the adjective. Dainty. Yeah, that was the word. Like one of those porcelain statues that cluttered the shelves of his mother's apartment.

The detailed physical description made him edgy. No reason it should, really. It was an effortless, natural observation for a cop.

Noticing that her pants covered a shapely butt and that there were definite curves beneath her fitted shirt, though, was a natural observation for a man.

He scowled, quickened his step. The last thing he needed right now was to be *aware* of Phillips, in any way other than as a colleague. And one that had been forced on him at that. He couldn't afford to wonder about her, about the break-in at her place, at his instinctive recognition that she'd known more about it than she'd let on.

There'd been a time in his life when he'd cut a wide swath through the female population, but the last couple years the number of women had dwindled, and he couldn't much bring himself to care. It was actually pretty damn ironic. He'd started drinking to stop feeling—stress from the pressures of the job, memories of the faces of the innocent—and once he'd stopped drinking, he'd been numb. Now the job was the only thing he cared about, and he couldn't say he much missed the rest. When he needed sex, he found someone who was looking for no more than he. A temporary relationship. With no pretense or promises on either side.

Phillips was here temporarily. But self-preservation was too ingrained for him to start anything personal between them. He'd recognized what had sent him to her house when he'd caught the call on the radio; what had kept him lingering there, when instincts had been screaming at him to keep his distance.

Protectiveness. And a woman capable of making him feel, *anything at all*, was one to stay far, far away from.

"So how are you going to play it? Have management announce the description and plates with a request to move the vehicle?"

"Yeah." He was aware of the curtness of his tone, of her sidelong glance, but ignored both. It was too late to wish that one of the task force detectives, hell, any of them, had still been around to accompany him in place of Phillips. But it wasn't too late to squelch this unfamiliar interest that he had in the woman. One he had no intention of indulging.

The harried-looking plump blonde introduced as the shift manager led them to an office cubicle at the side of store and wrote down the vehicle description and license number Ryne supplied her with. She grabbed an intercom mike, began the announcement, rattling off the information, then paused, released the button, and looked back at them. "Where is the vehicle located?"

"Northwest corner of the lot."

She finished the announcement with that information. Pushing away from the desk, she asked, "Northwest? Under the 'Real Deal' sign?"

Ryne nodded.

"That's where our employees are supposed to park. A black Bronco, you said?" She sucked in her bottom lip, apparently lost in thought. "Seems like Hidalgo Juarez drives a black Bronco. He's on today, too. Showed up ten minutes late for work." She shrugged. "Not my problem, really, since he's not in my department, but he's late more often than not. . . ."

"And where would we find him?" Abbie put in.

"He's a meat cutter, so he'll be in back, behind the meat department. Do you want me to call him up here?"

Ryne shook his head. "Take us to him."

They followed the woman through the long aisles of the store, and into a side door that led to an area with a wall of walk-in freezers. The center of the room was lined with tables, behind which four men were wielding cleavers to chop at large slabs of meat.

It was easy enough to figure out which one was Juarez.

He looked up at their entry, eyes widening when he spotted Ryne and Abbie behind the blonde. Ryne saw the intention in his eyes a split second before he acted.

Instinctively, he stepped in front of the blonde just as Juarez upended his table in their direction and took off toward the exit. The manager shrieked and one of the other men gave a shout, but Ryne ignored them. He leaped over the table and headed after the fleeing man.

"He's still got that cleaver." Abbie's voice sounded right behind him.

Ryne didn't need the reminder. He'd already drawn his gun. "Stop! SCMPD! Put down the weapon!"

Juarez stopped in the act of shoving open the outdoor exit and turned, hurtling the cleaver in their direction. Ryne dodged, knocking Abbie aside. The chopper sailed past them, clattered harmlessly to the concrete floor. She recovered first and gave pursuit, with him a step behind.

When they burst out the door, the man was racing across a short strip of cracked asphalt. Beyond it was a grassy area that was bordered on three sides by highway. If Juarez reached a road and took his chances with the traffic, their chances of apprehending him would diminish appreciably.

He jumped the curb and started across the field. With a sense of amazement, Ryne noted that Abbie had easily pulled away and was gaining on the other man. And although Juarez appeared to be getting winded, she showed no signs of slowing.

Ryne redoubled his efforts. If she caught up with the man, she'd need help subduing him. She wasn't armed, and Juarez easily had six inches and sixty pounds on her.

Abbie had veered right, Ryne noted approvingly. Most suspects in a foot pursuit would make right turns when given the opportunity. In case he didn't, he angled to the left. The odds were in their favor that Juarez would move in either direction. He fervently hoped the man would go left.

The fleeing man went right, heading for the highway with the heaviest traffic. Ryne changed direction. Abbie was now within six yards of the guy. Adrenaline pumping, Ryne figured the distance between the two and the looming highway and realized dismally that they'd never reach him in time.

The land was uneven and he saw Juarez stumble, right himself. To his amazement, Abbie closed the distance between them and then leaped, her body making a graceful arc before straightening into a vertical arrow. She struck Juarez head first, between the shoulder blades, and the guy dropped like a load of concrete. Breathing heavily, Ryne closed the distance between them, his gun trained on the fallen man. But Abbie already had him subdued, one knee holding him pinned to the ground and both arms behind his back.

He stopped a couple feet away. "SCMPD. You're under arrest, dickwad." And when Abbie's gaze met his, there wasn't a thing he could do to prevent an idiotic grin from spreading across his face.

Abbie entered the interview room and handed a folder to Ryne. The fingerprint database had yielded plenty of interesting information on Hidalgo Juan Juarez. She stared at the suspect slumped in his chair, and fought to keep an open mind.

It was dangerous for a profiler to draw impressions from anything other than the evidence at hand. Opinions, unsubstantiated by facts, could blind her to different prospects. Certainly this man's height and weight were general matches to the description Barbara Billings had given. But the sullen answers he'd made to Ryne's questions gave the impression of someone with low-average intelligence. She'd been betting their UNSUB—unknown subject—was batting a heckuva lot higher in the cognitive lineup.

Ryne let out a low whistle. "Appears you've been holding out on us, Hidalgo."

The other man slumped a little farther in his chair. "Told you I did a stint at Dodge."

"For B and E's, you said. Failed to mention you were a weenie wagger."

"I never did time for that."

"Lucky public defender or a lenient judge. Doesn't matter. You like to expose yourself to women. Young, old." Ryne was skimming the record. "Weren't too discriminating, were you?"

Abbie felt her interest sharpen. It was a myth that so-called nuisance crimes never escalated to something far more serious. She'd worked plenty of cases where the perps had started out as Peeping Toms or obscene phone callers.

"That was a long time ago," muttered Juarez. "Not anymore. Besides, what's that got to do with stolen plates on my Bronco?"

Ryne snapped the folder shut. "Unfortunately for you, a lot. Your vehicle was seen in the vicinity of a rape that occurred a couple days ago."

"What?" Juarez rose from his seat, his expression panicked. "I didn't rape no one! I don't have to. I got a girlfriend. You can ask anyone."

"You're going to want to sit down, Hidalgo." Ryne's voice had gone steely. He waited until the man sank into the chair again before continuing. "Your vehicle, bearing stolen plates, was described in a police report a block away from the location of the last rape. If we find any trace evidence inside linking the Bronco to the attack, then we've connected it to the rape, you got that? And given the fact that you ran when we came to question you . . . well, you can see how that looks to us."

Abbie watched the man intently. He was sweating profusely, despite the air-conditioning. "You know why I ran."

"The baggie we found on you?"

Juarez nodded. "I don't wanna get sent back to Dodge. I figured if I took off, dumped the pot before you caught up . . . nothing to tell my parole officer, you know?"

"Let's forget the marijuana for the moment." Ryne braced his hands on the table, leaned closer to the man. "Let's even forget the little matter of assault on a law enforcement officer." When Juarez screwed up his brow, Ryne elaborated, "You threw that meat cleaver, remember? But for now let's focus on the Bronco. If you weren't driving it, you must have loaned it out to someone."

Juarez shook his head doggedly. "No, I never do that. I don't got insurance. If I'm not using it, I have it parked in back of my apartment. I'm the only one with keys."

"So maybe you can tell us where you were three days ago. Between five p.m. and twelve a.m., specifically."

The man swung his gaze to Abbie, as if looking for help. She had none to offer him. Her interest in his answer was as keen as Ryne's.

"I don't know. Sleeping probably. I work two jobs. Usually first shift at Valu-Mart. Six in the morning 'til three."

"You were there tonight," Ryne reminded him.

"Yeah, 'cuz I picked up another guy's shift for him. He needed someone to cover and I could use the money, you know? Usually I get home around four and sleep until midnight, when I go to sweep up at Shorty's Garage, over on First and Levine."

"Do you drive to Shorty's?" Abbie asked.

Juarez shook his head. "Naw, it's only a few blocks. I always walk." A few beats later he straightened, face brightening. "Someone must have taken my Bronco or something. It sits out back from four in the afternoon until I leave for work in the morning. I'd never know the difference."

"Yeah, that's a convenient story, all right." Ryne's sarcasm was all the more cutting for being controlled. He leaned forward, pushed a yellow notepad and pen toward the man. "Write down your whereabouts for last Tuesday night, from five p.m. until twelve a.m. I want every minute accounted for."

The man seized the pen eagerly, then paused to think before he began scribbling. Abbie wished she knew when to expect results from the crime scene techs, who were processing the Bronco at that moment. There would be another round of interviews if the search yielded some evidence, unless Juarez had lawyered up by then.

But most of all she wished she could shake the feeling that Juarez was telling the truth.

Chapter 6

"You can't know that."

Robel's voice was irritated as he slid across the cracked red vinyl of the diner's booth. Abbie followed suit, facing him across the table, already regretting she'd allowed him to bait her into rendering an opinion.

"You didn't ask me what I *know*. You asked what I *thought*. And with what we have right now, I wouldn't have picked Juarez as our guy."

"The techs found blood in the back of the vehicle. If it matches Billings's—and I'll bet you twenty that it will—you might think differently."

Abbie took one of the plastic-coated menus from the rack holding the salt and pepper shakers, opening it without much hope. A quick glance confirmed her worst fears. Leave it to Robel to find the greasiest spoon in the city. But at this hour of the night, there couldn't be many spots to choose from. "I'll be surprised if that Bronco wasn't the vehicle that transported Billings to the sound. But that doesn't mean . . ."

"That Juarez is the rapist. Well, I'm not so sure about that."

She was too used to his annoyance with her to allow it to have much effect. "You're the one who pushed for an opinion. Do you really believe Juarez is smart enough to have committed four rapes, leaving no trace evidence—"

"Yet—"

"Smart enough to steal plates so his vehicle can't be identified, but dumb enough not to get rid of them?"

"Hey, ninety percent of the people I arrest are a couple fries short of a Happy Meal." He held his mug up as a waitress walked by and she came over to fill it with coffee. Abbie shook her head when the woman offered some to her and waited until she'd walked away before continuing. "Guys like that can be cunning about the crimes they commit, even if they aren't exactly rocket scientists."

She knew he was right. One study done on rapists suggested nearly eighty percent of them made little or no effort to disguise themselves to avoid identification. But that was hardly the case with the UNSUB they were tracking.

Their discussion was cut short when the waitress returned with an order pad. "All right, honey, now what can I getcha? You want to hear about our specials?" The words, delivered in an obviously flirtatious tone, were directed at Ryne.

"I'll have the number three on the breakfast menu, eggs over easy, with bacon and toast."

"No hash browns? Cook makes 'em with plenty of butter. Best in the city."

Abbie managed to avoid rolling her eyes. The syrup in the woman's tone was as thick as the spray in her heavily teased hair.

"None for me, thanks." The waitress reluctantly turned her attention to Abbie.

"Do you have any fresh fruit?"

The woman looked blank. "You mean like grapefruit?"

Giving up, Abbie said, "Just get me half a ham and cheese omelet with orange juice, please."

After the woman had moved away, Ryne said, "Sure that will hold you? I thought we decided that neither of us had eaten since breakfast."

Which was the only reason he'd suggested she accompany him to get a bite, Abbie knew. After the interview they'd both been punchy. She'd been on the job since seven that morning, and he'd been there when she'd gotten in. "I'll be fine."

He picked up the coffee mug, drank. "You do much running like you did today, you're going to need more than an omelet to refuel."

He had a slight smile playing around his mouth, but it was a far cry from the sardonic little smile he'd given her a few times her first day on the job. It altered his face, softened the hard angles of his jaw, which was in need of a shave. It made him look all too human. And dangerously attractive.

To distract herself, she took her time putting the menu back in place. "I run. Usually work out in a ring regularly, too. I meant to ask you about a place where I can do both."

Interest sharpened his gaze. "You box?"

"Spar," she corrected. "I train in Muay Thai. But I like to stay in shape on the road."

Ryne sat back in the booth and surveyed her speculatively. "Kickboxing."

"A form of it."

"I don't know of a place like that around here. But the gym I belong to has a ring, a track, and free weights. Nothing fancy, but a lot of cops use it. I think you can buy passes by the week." He took a pen from his pocket and wrote the name of the place and the address on a napkin, then pushed it across the table toward her. "Just don't let McElroy talk you into climbing into the ring with him. He fights dirty."

"Hardly surprising," she said dryly. But she tucked the napkin away in her purse. With no way of knowing how long she'd be here, a gym with weekly passes would be perfect for her. "But if I ever find myself in the ring with McElroy, I think I can handle myself."

His smile reached his eyes. "I'm beginning to believe it. I jog myself, but you weren't jogging out there today. You looked like . . ." He shook his head, as if words failed him. "Never figured someone your size could move that fast. It was like trying to keep my eye on a hummingbird."

She didn't know whether to be offended or pleased. She'd been fighting the battle of bias about her size all her life. In the end, though, it was the warmth in his gaze that decided her. It sent an answering heat sliding along her spine that was both unfamiliar and alarming.

"I'm a sprinter. Did low hurdles in high school, too, but in college my race was the hundred-meter dash." Running had saved her sanity once, a long time ago. Even though she'd given up believing she could outrun her memories. It'd taken her years to accept that her past was wrapped up inside her, no matter how hard she'd tried to shake it loose.

It was time to switch the conversation back to business. Even the scanty amount of personal information she'd shared made her uncomfortable.

Because he saw too much. She'd noted that yesterday, and she wasn't any more willing today to have that shrewd gaze aimed her way. And if he was looking at her as a man instead of as a cop, well, that was unwelcome, too. Nothing shifted her attention from a case she was working. Not even its lead detective.

Especially not its lead detective.

"Any other interesting developments today?"

He shook his head. "Nothing important. No progress made working the list of Bronco owners, although that's no surprise now. Heck of it is, they'd worked through the H's. Probably would have hit on Juarez tomorrow. The kennel lead is a dead end. The manufacturer ships all over the world. That particular brand is sold by a half-dozen pet stores in the area, in addition to being available from department stores, farm supply outlets, vets . . . There are even some breeders who keep a few on hand to sell to customers."

"What about the syringe angle? Some states still require a prescription, don't they?"

"Georgia's not one of them. They can be purchased over the counter and at veterinary supply stores. Hell, they can even be bought on the Internet. If Juarez does turn out to be our guy, he wouldn't have had to work too hard to get his hands on them."

"But from what you've told me about the drug, we're looking for an UNSUB who has the chemical skills to mix his own drug, and access to the ingredients, or—"

"I see where you're going with this." Ryne sat back as the waitress approached and set a steaming plate of food in front of him. "Juarez probably doesn't have the expertise, I'll grant you that. But our perp doesn't have to be scientifically inclined, he just has to know someone who is."

With amusement, Abbie noted that the waitress was spending an inordinate amount of time arranging Ryne's plate in front of him and placing a napkin in his lap. Even more entertaining was his look of discomfit at the attention. Despite his expression, she didn't doubt that he was a man used to a woman's interest.

Abbie's food was delivered with much less care, and they both commenced eating. After the first bite, she discovered that she was ravenous. They were both silent for several minutes as they attacked their meals. She reached for her juice, drank, caught his gaze on her.

He pointed his fork in her direction. "You went shopping."

For a moment her mind went blank. Then she looked down at the blue striped shirt she was wearing and made the connection. Caution slammed firmly into place. "Didn't have a lot of choice. I suppose I should be grateful whoever broke into my place didn't slice up my pants and shoes, too."

"I was thinking about that." He chewed slowly, watching her. "Chopping up your clothes seems personal. A vandal might spray some graffiti, smash up the place, but what was done in your closet . . . sounds like something a woman would do."

For a moment Abbie's heart seemed to stop. It was all she could do to force air into her lungs. With studied nonchalance, she picked up her fork and finished her meal. "Because only women would be interested in clothes? You've never met my hair stylist."

"Okay, maybe a guy. Definitely someone who knows how to get to you." Although she refused to lift her gaze, she could feel his eyes on her. "An ex-boyfriend maybe. Do you have someone who might have followed you here? Someone pissed off at you?"

At first she was so relieved to have him shift his suspicion from a female intruder to a male, that she missed the note in his tone. Surely it was her imagination that there had been a hint of something other than professional interest in the conjecture.

Dodging both, she lifted her glass and drained it. "Hard to imagine anyone being pissed off at me," she said in her sunniest voice as she set the glass back on the table. "I'm absolutely charming."

When she would have reached for her purse, he stilled her action with a hand over hers. "So you're not going to tell me?"

Ignoring the pounding in her veins, she gave him a blank look. "There's nothing to tell." It wasn't necessarily a lie, she thought, nudging aside a sliver of guilt. She'd probably jumped to conclusions last night. There was no good reason for Callie to have followed her here, after months of avoiding all contact.

But good reasons were frequently absent from Callie's behavior, especially if she'd gone off her medication. And any explanation about her sister would lead to revelations that she had no intention of making. Not to this man.

Their gazes did battle for long moments. Long enough for her to see that his eyes weren't always glacial. That they could warm with interest, concern, and maybe something a bit more personal.

He withdrew his hand and she squelched an uncustomary note of regret. She didn't do personal. Hadn't for more years than she could count. And it was better that way. Less complicated.

"When will you know whether you have a match between the blood in the vehicle and Billings?" She took a ten out of her purse and handed it to him for her share of the bill. He waved it away, and handed the check and payment to the waitress, who'd stopped by his side again.

"The sample has already been delivered to the lab. It's not a complicated test. They'll probably run it first thing in the morning." At Abbie's raised brows, he gave a sardonic smile. "I don't know what strings Dixon pulled to get this case stamped high priority, but I'm not complaining. The district attorney's office has already drawn up the paperwork for a warrant on Juarez's apartment, so we're ready if the results come out the way I expect them to."

He stood, and she followed him out of the restaurant. The street beyond the diner's parking lot was nearly deserted. It was after midnight. If Savannah had a bustling nightlife, it was located far from here. "If and when a search is conducted on Juarez's place, I'd like to be there," Abbie said as they stopped next to her car.

"No problem. You've earned that, after today."

She nodded, satisfied. If it had taken the events of the day to gain a measure of the man's respect, the hours had been well spent. Even with the stiffness settling in one knee, warning her that she hadn't escaped the scuffle with the suspect unscathed.

"Why don't you give me your cell number, in case I need to reach you after hours."

As she rattled it off, Ryne punched the number into the directory of his cell. She watched him complete the action, feeling for a moment like a high school girl giving the most popular boy in school her phone number. She shook her head to rid it of the mental flash. She definitely needed some sleep. She hadn't spent her high school years dating, and if a guy anything like Ryne Robel had approached her, she'd have run in the opposite direction.

"Got it." He flipped the phone shut and slipped it in his pocket, extracting his card and handing it to her. "You'll want to program yours with my numbers, too." Seamlessly, he switched subjects. "Did the glass company get to your place today?"

She took the business card and slipped it into her purse. "They're coming tomorrow. Security company will be there at the end of the week." He didn't look pleased by her answer, but she hadn't been able to arrange anything faster. "I doubt the intruder is coming back anyway. They've already seen there's nothing there to steal."

"I could call the security company for you. Sometimes they need a push. . . ." At the look on her face, he held up his hands, as if to stave off an argument. "Okay. End of the week it is."

She started the car door. "Thanks for the meal."

As he opened his mouth to reply, his cell phone rang. Abbie paused, looked back. If this was a new lead reported in the case, she wanted to hear about it. If it was something more personal, well, she could always apologize for eavesdropping.

Ryne turned half away as he answered with a curt "Robel." She noted the sudden stillness that came over him as he listened for a few moments. Then he threw her a glance, his expression a mask of grim satisfaction.

"Good work. This might be the lead we've been waiting for."

Her pulse jumped. The call had to be about the case, but from whom? CSU? One of the other detectives? With mounting impatience, she tried to discern an answer from the one-sided conversation, but he was maddeningly reticent.

"You thought right. I'll be there in fifteen minutes."

As he tucked the phone away, she demanded, "What is it? Did CSU find something else in the vehicle search?"

"You could say that. Balkins said they would have missed it completely if they hadn't pulled out the backseat. It was wedged down pretty tightly. . . ."

He had to be doing this on purpose. "*What* was? What did they find?"

He grinned at the impatience in her tone. "A syringe. And it's full. Looks like we've finally caught a break."

"If the contents can be matched to the tox reports," she cautioned, but the statement was automatic. She could barely restrain the wild leap of anticipation at the news, and impulsively reached out to lay a hand on his arm. "This could be big."

He covered her hand with one of his, squeezed lightly. "Yeah, well, we're due, right? I'll have to be pushier than ever to get the lab to get at this right away, but . . ." He shrugged. "I can do pushy."

"Don't I know it." Belatedly, she became aware that she was still touching him, and withdrew her hand, ignoring the lingering heat on her flesh. A wave of self-consciousness flooded her, and silence stretched, grew awkward.

Ryne relieved it by saying, "I'll let you know if something else comes up. But right now I have to get back to headquarters."

"Sure." A measure of relief surged through her. "I'll see you tomorrow." Abbie watched him as he moved away, considered the fact that maybe she hadn't changed as much as she thought over the years.

She'd been out of high school a dozen years and men like Ryne Robel still had her running in the opposite direction.

———

On the way home she dialed her sister's number again, expecting, and receiving, her voice mail inviting the caller to leave a message. Abbie checked her rearview mirror as she spoke while backing out of the space. "It's Abbie. I'd really like to talk to you, Callie. Can you call me back tomorrow?"

She hung up, strangely relieved not to have reached her. Callie hadn't returned her messages for months, so nothing had changed, really. It was probably a stretch to believe her sister had gone from being incommunicado to following Abbie to Savannah. For the first time since she'd searched her house yesterday, she began to give real credence to the possibility that the break-in was exactly what she'd tried to convince the police of—an act of a vandal.

She turned at the light and headed toward her house on a street almost devoid of traffic. It was sad, but she'd find it infinitely preferable to handle a routine B&E than to deal with the unexpected appearance of her sister.

———

The smoke hung low over the pool tables, and music blasted from the aged jukebox in the corner. Callie Phillips raised her glass and the bartender obediently tipped another two fingers of cheap Tequila into it.

"Hey, baby." The man plastered against her right side leaned down to bite her neck. "Your ass is ringing."

She slapped his hand away when it would have reached for the cell phone clipped to the back waistband of her low-rise jeans. "Doesn't matter. Everyone I want to talk to is right here."

The man on her left slipped his hand into her tight bra top tank and cupped her breast. "And what if we're tired of talking?"

She turned to look at him through alcohol-hazed eyes. She'd long since forgotten his name. Or that of the other man. Names didn't matter anyway. Nothing mattered but the familiar hunger that was rising, that could only be put to rest one way. Well, any number of ways, actually. And she was betting that the two unshaven tattooed men who'd been buying her drinks all night would be only too willing to help in that area.

"We don't have to talk, sugar." He squeezed her breast roughly, and the pain made her catch her breath. Sent excitement humming through her veins. Yeah, these guys would do just fine.

A fight broke out at the pool table in back of them. The bartender leaped over the bar with a club and waded into the fray, swinging indiscriminately.

"Cops'll be here in a few minutes." This from the guy on her right. "Time to choose who you're leaving with, baby. We gotta get out of here."

A smile curved her lips as she dropped her hands to the crotch of each, squeezed suggestively. "No reason to choose, boys. I can handle both of you."

She ignored their quick muttered discussion and slid off the bar stool, stretched, then walked toward the exit, certain they'd follow. When it came to sex, people were predictable. Didn't matter who they were. Where they came from. Women could always be counted on to mix sex with messy other emotions, like fear, guilt, and "love." And men could always, always be led around by their cocks.

She paused at the door and checked over her shoulder, unsurprised to see the two men trailing close behind her. It was good to know that the men in Savannah were no exception.

———

Ryne straightened from his stance against the wall of the crime lab conference room, relishing the look on chemist Mark Han's face when he walked through the door and saw who had "urgent business" with him. The scientist worked in the drug identification section and Ryne had worked with him before. He was good, but famously irritable. At least around Ryne.

The man was dressed, as usual, with a white lab coat covering designer clothes and shoes that probably cost what Ryne paid for a month's rent. Ryne had heard rumors that Han was independently wealthy. It was a sure bet that he didn't afford his wardrobe on a GBI salary. With his slight build, short haircut, and small dark-rimmed glasses, he always reminded Ryne of a Eurasian Buddy Holly.

"Robel." Han glanced around, saw they were alone, and looked wary. "What do you want?"

"Do I have to want something?" Ryne countered. "I brought doughnuts."

He nodded to the box he'd set on the long table.

"Which only makes me more suspicious." Han folded his arms across his chest, looking impatient. "I told you last time you called, it's useless to speculate about the drug your twist is using. I'd need a sample to determine anything. Bad enough that you're burying the rest of the sections with every damn piece of trace evidence you've got on your investigation. This may come as a shock to you and Dixon, but we actually work cases other than yours."

"I'm not feeling the love here, Mark." Ryne was enjoying himself hugely. "You're going to make me think I'm not your favorite cop, and you know how that would hurt me."

"Kiss my ass."

"Maybe you're right." Ryne pretended to consider. "I dropped off a sample of the drug we took from a full syringe we discovered yesterday, but now I feel a little guilty, knowing how busy you are. I had asked the lab manager to assign you to the tests, but I'm sure O'Brien would do just as good a job." He turned, as if headed toward the door, but Han beat him to it, barring his exit.

"You'd better not be kidding."

Ryne arched a brow. "You think I made the trip across town just to yank your chain? I can do that by phone."

Han stared hard at him for a minute, then, as if convinced, demanded, "How big a sample is it? Was the syringe full? God, I've been waiting to get my hands on this. I have a few ideas, but without a sample, it was pointless to waste time on conjecture."

"But now you'll be able to tell what it is, right?" Ryne was hoping if they could get the individual elements identified, they'd at least have another strong lead to pursue. Controlled substances left a nice trail of paperwork, if they were gotten through legal means, or stolen from a place that had acquired them legally. This could open up a whole new avenue of investigation.

The forensic chemist frowned, visibly reining in his excitement. "It depends on whether it's a large enough sample to run all the tests I need to do. This is going to be time-consuming, so don't even think about calling for hourly updates."

The thought hadn't crossed his mind. Hardly. Ryne was well aware that most crime scene evidence languished in labs for months. Although the backlog in some of the lab's divisions had improved drastically in the last few years, it still wasn't unusual for a suspect to be arrested, convicted, and sentenced before the lab work was even done. Given the level of cooperation they'd gotten so far, he'd known Dixon had to have been strong-arming someone to get this case designated as top priority. No doubt Mayor Richards had some pull with the governor, who in turn leaned on GBI. Whatever the process, he was damn glad for it. Especially now.

He also recognized, however, when finesse was called for. "I wouldn't think of it. I know you're busy, but if you can fit it in as soon as possible, I'd appreciate it."

Han studied him carefully, no doubt looking for traces of sarcasm, but as Ryne passed him to head out the door, he said, "Well . . . yeah. I'll see what I can do."

"Thanks." Although impatience was clawing through him, he knew better than to let it show. While he was here, he still planned to swing by the serology section and talk to the biologist examining the blood found in Juarez's vehicle. If the blood type matched that of Billings, they'd have their warrant for Juarez's place.

As for the drug sample they'd transferred from the syringe . . . he knew Han. Knew how fascinated the man had become with the unknown compound and its puzzling effects. He was probably already itching to start running tests, even if it meant staying after hours to get his other obligations fulfilled.

Best-case scenario, they'd get preliminary results in days, not weeks. And with Juarez already in custody, maybe the rapist's next targeted victim would be spared.

Maybe.

———

Hidalgo Juarez's basement apartment was short on natural light, and Abbie figured that just might be a blessing. The man wasn't about to give Martha Stewart competition anytime soon.

"Guy lives like a cockroach," McElroy muttered, kicking through the debris on the floor. As if to punctuate his words, a bug scuttled from beneath a fast-food container across the threadbare carpet.

"I was thinking you two shared the same decorator," cracked Cantrell. The investigators filled the cramped area to overflowing, each carefully covering a predetermined area.

Once Ryne had received word that the blood type found in the Bronco matched that of Billings, the warrant had sped through the sometimes cumbersome legal process. Ryne then had summoned the task force to Juarez's address. Abbie had been across town at Ashley Hornby's house, trying in vain to get the woman to open the door and speak to her. Hornby had been the rapist's third victim, and after her initial statement had become more and more reclusive.

From the looks of things, Abbie was the last on the task force to arrive. She stopped Ryne and asked, "What's the scope of the search?"

He looked tired, and it occurred to her that he must have gotten very little sleep last night, which she could sympathize with. She'd lain awake for hours, thoughts of her sister and the case circling in her mind like frantic ants. Thoughts of the case's lead detective had been just as difficult to banish.

"With the discovery of the syringe, we've got cause to search anyplace we could reasonably find drugs, which gives us a lot of latitude."

Abbie turned to scan the room, her gaze landing on the older-model computer sitting on a stained vinyl-top table in the corner of the living room. "I don't suppose we have access to his computer."

"Nope."

"Why, do you need to check your e-mail, Tinkerbell?" McElroy looked up from his search of the carpet's edge, where a loose area could signify a hiding place. "You into those online singles chatrooms?"

"If Juarez is our guy, I'd expect to find porn. Very specific images." She gave the computer a last regretful glance and headed to the bedroom, which was being tossed by Holmes.

"You want porn? I'm about to make your day." Isaac Holmes got to his feet and handed her a stack of magazines he'd pulled from beneath the bed. Abbie took them gingerly and carried them into the other room. Setting them on the table next to the computer, she sat down to flip through them, suppressing an instinctive surge of distaste.

Ryne had finished with the closet and crossed the room to look through the stack. "An extensive and imaginative collection."

There were magazines featuring adults engaged in a variety of sex acts, including bondage, female on female, group sex, and bestiality. But the presence of the magazines themselves meant nothing. Given the organized precision of the attacks themselves, she'd expect the UNSUB's collection to reflect a similar orderliness. "Any magazines featuring rape and torture?" Fantasy played a major role in a ritualistic offender's crimes, and the perps often developed elaborate porn collections that implied the underlying motivation. The theme of the pornography was reflected in the way the offender interacted with his victims.

Ryne flipped through the pile, checking covers. "None that I can tell."

"See, that's the job I want," McElroy said in a loud aside to Cantrell, as they pulled the cushions from the dilapidated couch and checked inside them. "I'll volunteer to go through the porn. I'll even stay late to do it. After shift. Without overtime pay."

"You're a prince among men," Cantrell agreed laconically.

Abbie straightened, looked around the area once again. There was a TV but she didn't see a VCR or DVD player. Crossing to the bedroom, she peered in, but didn't see any electronics in there. "Doesn't appear that he has a video porn collection, but keep an eye out for any scrapbooks or notebooks."

At Ryne's quizzical expression, she explained, "Some offenders will go so far as to cut and paste images from existing pornography to sketch out their fantasy scenarios, or to have partners act out certain erotic behaviors that are then filmed or photographed."

"She's talking about you, McElroy," Holmes called from the bedroom.

An idea struck her then and she addressed Ryne, who was still flipping through the pages. "Have you interviewed prostitutes in the area regarding this investigation?"

Wayne Cantrell looked up from where he was bent over the couch, his hand shoved into the creases surrounding the seat. "Why would we? We've got low-risk victims in this case. It's not like our guy is out trolling the red light district."

"An offender like this one often evolves, rather than planning and enacting the crimes right away." She went into the kitchen area and checked the freezer compartment and refrigerator. There was nothing to be found but beer and two soggy onions. "Sometimes they'll act out their sexual fantasies with wives or girlfriends to serve as props in their rehearsal of future crimes. If those females aren't available, it's not unusual for them to use prostitutes." She turned her attention to the kitchen cabinets. "We had an offender in St. Paul who nearly killed three call girls prior to his first sexual homicide of a university professor. The complaints filed by the prostitutes weren't investigated fully until after the murder."

"See, we're different here in Savannah," McElroy said. He rose and tipped the couch forward for Cantrell to check beneath. "We take our prostitutes seriously."

"It's a good idea," Ryne interjected. "When we get done here, McElroy, you and Cantrell can follow up on that. We've checked incident reports filed in the last year, but it wouldn't hurt to talk to some prostitutes in the area. They might know about something that never got reported."

"There you go, McElroy," said Cantrell as the two started on the dilapidated recliner. "Your Christmas just came early."

"You're gonna give Tinkerbell the wrong impression of me."

Abbie rose from checking the bottom cupboards, which were empty except for a few pans and what she suspected were rodent droppings. "That wouldn't be possible, Nick."

Holmes came out of the bedroom. "You might want to look at these."

Ryne stood up. "What have you got?"

The detective held up a pair of black tennis shoes, soles out. "Got some crushed rock in the tread. Other than that, they seem fairly new."

Abbie remembered the fill beneath the hydrangeas in front of Barbara Billings's house. It should be fairly simple to compare the samples.

"Anything else?"

In answer to Ryne's question, Holmes held up something he carried between thumb and forefinger on his other gloved hand. "Just this." It was a protective plastic tip. The type that would fit over a hypodermic needle.

Chapter 7

"This really isn't necessary," Abbie muttered, for at least the fourth time. "I'm capable of finding my way to the site on my own."

"It's necessary if you insist on revisiting each of the crime scenes yourself." They'd left the campus of Savannah State fifteen minutes earlier, and were driving toward the ocean. Specifically toward the site where Amanda Richards had been transported for the attack. "I've worked with profilers before. Never had one insist on going to each scene personally. Usually they work from the photos in the case file."

"Then they weren't doing their jobs," she said flatly, gazing out the window.

Ryne could only agree. But then he'd never put any stock in the profiles rendered by the police psychologists used in a few of the cases he'd worked on in Boston. Or in police psychs as a whole. They were worse than Internal Affairs' Rat Squad. IA could fuck up your reputation, but the Psych Service types fucked with your head.

The thought summoned an unwanted memory. *And what*

was going through your mind at the time of Deborah Hanna's shooting, Detective Robel?

As if he'd had the words for all the emotions that had flooded him when they'd burst through that door two years ago and found Glen Powell with his gun against the woman's temple. The exact moment he realized just how badly he'd miscalculated. Adrenaline, fear, anger, determination. Guilt.

The high-rises had given way to housing developments on either side of the interstate. Not scenery that should have kept Abbie's gaze rapt on its passing, but her silence made it all too easy to hear the echo of that long-ago voice in his mind.

Do you think you would have handled the situation differently if you hadn't been drinking the night before, Detective?

Wrong question, Doc. It wasn't the bottle the night before that had been the problem. It was the ones he'd consumed throughout the whole damn case that had blinded him to the perp's identity.

We acted in a manner in keeping with the facts we had at hand. The outcome couldn't have been foreseen.

He'd been too late to save Deborah Hanna, but had managed to save his own ass. The exchange hardly seemed even. His team had been cleared of any mishandling of that final scene. But the stench of failure clung to a reputation, was impossible to dislodge.

"You know, there isn't going to be much for you to see at the beach house," he said abruptly, shaking off the memories. "Mayor Richards barely gave us time to process the scene before he was hiring new decorators to gut the place. Must have decided that wasn't enough, because I hear it's on the market now."

"That's a problem when coming in midway through the investigation," she said. "But I like to see for myself the security that's in place surrounding the scene. The transportation routes and cover provided nearby. I get a clearer picture of the UNSUB when I can look at what environment he chose for his attacks, and what precautions or risks he took.

It would have been even better if I could make these visits at the same time of day the kidnapping occurred."

He knew where she was going with this. "No way to get an accurate picture of the Savannah State campus as it was last spring with no classes in session right now. Besides, Dixon promised Richards that no one would be allowed inside his place without the lead investigator present." The landscape was flattening, the evergreens and towering oaks growing scarcer. "I could have asked for you, but I don't know that he would have changed his mind." He'd have been reluctant to contact the mayor on her behalf, at any case, and be grilled for an hour about their progress. Right now Dixon was handling City Hall, and that's what he was paid to do.

Abbie remained silent, and he glanced her way again. Another woman he might figure was sulking because she hadn't gotten her way, but he was beginning to know her well enough to doubt that. She was working through something in her mind, and he wouldn't hear from her until she did so.

A few minutes later, she proved him right. "So it was dusk when Amanda was snatched on her way across campus after work. The UNSUB used a surprise attack again. He waited until she got on the bike path through a more wooded section and then jumped her from behind. Fewer people than usual were out and about because of finals week."

He took up the verbal reenactment. "Those paths were built wide enough to allow use by small campus vehicles. He probably had a car stowed nearby and dragged her to it."

"She was the only one whose tox screen showed something other than the same elements the others were injected with."

He nodded, checking his mirrors and changing lanes. They were making pretty good time, primarily because there were few people heading to the beach in the middle of the afternoon midweek. The same drive at this time tomorrow would be hellish. "He used chloroform to knock her out immediately. Probably bound and gagged her in the vehicle. Hard to say because she didn't come to until at the beach house."

"And now with Billings's rape, that makes two out of four times that he's transported a victim," she mused.

He didn't follow her thinking. "Billings was a dump site. For Richards, transporting her was necessary to enact the crime."

She was looking at him now, impatience showing in her expression. "Forget Billings for the moment. He took a huge risk with Richards. Even disregarding who her grandfather was. And there was no doubt he knew about the relationship. He's too careful, plans too meticulously for it to be otherwise. And Amanda said the location of the beach house was well known on campus. She'd had parties there frequently."

"That's what she told us."

"Given the kind of assault he plans, he needs time and privacy. Everyone else was attacked in her own home, but a dorm room isn't going to cut it. Why choose a victim you have to go to so much trouble for? Why risk it?"

He opened his mouth to answer, then thought better of it. "You're the profiler. I thought you were supposed to be giving me answers, not more questions."

She made a distracted gesture with her hand. "My preliminary profile is on your desk. I had a copy sent to Captain Brown and Commander Dixon this morning, too."

Neither man had mentioned it when Ryne had checked in briefly to update them on the Juarez search, but maybe they hadn't read it yet. Ryne hadn't been at his desk all day, so he certainly hadn't noticed the file.

Then another thought struck him. "When did you complete it?"

She was looking out the window again. "It's been a work in progress. It was largely done already."

"And you're a terrible liar."

She sent him a cool look. "I happen to be an excellent liar." At his silence, she finally said, "Okay, I finished it last night when I got home. I couldn't sleep. But it only took a couple hours to finish up."

Sleep hadn't been any kinder to him. He'd still been too wired from the events of the day. And the thought hit him that maybe they could have found a more pleasurable way to summon sleep had they been together.

He shook his head to clear it of the totally inappropriate thought. He could work with women, hell, he *had* worked with plenty of women without being tempted to mix his professional and personal lives. So that didn't explain his growing awareness of Abbie in a way that owed nothing to the investigation they were working on.

Getting involved with her, even on a casual level, he decided grimly as he accelerated past a slow-moving RV, was the worst idea he'd entertained since coming to Savannah.

"Why don't you give me the high points?"

"It'd make more sense in written form," she began.

"Which I'm not going to get to read for hours yet, so summarize it for me."

At first he didn't think she'd answer. But finally she said, "I don't claim to have a clear handle on him yet, because I'm still puzzled by his selection of victims. TV depiction aside, serial rapists typically don't engage in specific, symbolic considerations when choosing their targets. He doesn't seem to have a 'type' either, at least aside from low-risk attractive women. But it's clear that we're dealing with a sexual sadist. His attacks will be largely premeditated, never impulsive, and he'll fantasize about them prior to the acts themselves."

He couldn't resist ribbing her. "You keep saying 'he.' You're finally convinced it's a man?"

She shot him a sidelong glance. "As I said before, he almost certainly is, although I won't be *convinced* until we get evidence proving it. But for the record, my pronoun selection is chosen for ease of conversation, not as a reflection of my opinion on that subject, all right?"

He subsided, stifling a grin at the barely discernible edge to her tone. She was normally so composed, getting a rise out of her was an accomplishment.

"The surprise approach is often used by men who are uncertain of their abilities to approach the victim with a con, or to overpower them. But with the care he takes to avoid detection, I don't want to give that fact too much importance. It may be just one more method he employs to ensure he isn't identified. Most of these offenders have above average to high intelligence."

She was warming up to her topic, turning, as much as the seat belt would allow, to face him. "Raiker has largely discounted the disorganized versus organized dichotomy, but I still find it an important descriptor, as long as evidentiary facts and information form the basis of the profile, rather than the descriptors themselves."

He made an agreeing noise, although he had a flashback to a college calc course when the professor embarked upon an "explanation" in which the class got lost completely.

"So given that preface, I'd label this offender as organized, simply by virtue of the extent of preparation he does prior to the act. He takes a great deal of trouble to make sure he can't be identified, which may be because he has no intention of killing the victim or to avoid being ID'd by a bystander. He's been doing this a long time, at least leading up to it, and he won't stop until he's caught."

"And you know that because . . ."

"He can't," she said simply. "We're talking about someone who must intentionally inflict suffering to enhance his own arousal. And once he's experienced that high, that power, nothing else will ever satisfy him."

"So the porn won't hold him any longer."

She gave him an approving look. "Only in the short term, in between attacks. The reports have indicated that none of the victims were missing any personal items. No photo IDs, no lingerie."

"Because this type of offender doesn't take trophies?" Ryne guessed.

"Oh, he does. But he's most likely to photograph or film the victim, either during the assault itself, or afterwards, posed in demeaning ways that will be gratifying for him later when he wants to relive the attack. None of the victims mentioned it, but once injected, they wouldn't necessarily notice."

A grim sense of revulsion filled him. "I hear rapists don't do well in prison. Maybe that is better than a death penalty."

"Sexual sadists, more than other rapists, are highly ritualistic. He's acted these fantasies out long before these offenses. Maybe with a willing partner, perhaps with a paid one."

He glanced at the clock on the dash, wondering if Cantrell and McElroy had discovered anything while questioning prostitutes. "So he's escalating."

She nodded. "And he's bold, but careful. That's why I'm puzzled about his selection of Amanda Richards. He could have chosen any number of other women, heck, any number of other girls on that campus, with far less risk."

Something in him stilled. "You're saying she was chosen because of her relationship to the mayor."

"We have to figure his selection of the victims is done as carefully as is his preparation for the attacks themselves. There's no way he didn't know of the relationship. So why her? It definitely was the most complex attempt made to date, with the greatest risk involved."

"We spent a great deal of time and effort investigating just that angle," he admitted. "Even considered the fact that the first rape was designed to make the second look like the act of a serial offender, when Amanda was the intended victim all along."

Abbie's tone was sharp. "That wasn't in the report."

"No kidding. Was it some sort of payback for someone the mayor pissed off? Believe me, those possibilities are endless. Or could it have been a ploy to distract him from the reelection campaign he's engaged in, which, from all accounts, is brutal."

"So you looked at his rival."

Ryne nodded. "Inside and out. And the fact that he's running against none other than the city's most senior alderman . . . well, you see the need for discretion." His voice was sour. "Can you imagine the press if the media got wind of the fact the mayor was using the SCMPD to investigate his political rival?"

"Politics reek at any time, but especially when they taint an investigation."

"Exactly. Luckily we were able to convince the mayor after doing a bit of checking that Alderman Lewis had little to gain by arranging the rape, since the act casts the mayor in a more sympathetic light."

"God," Abbie muttered.

He wholeheartedly shared the disgust evident in her reply. "And the same thing was true of anyone who had a beef with the mayor. His granddaughter's assault might be arranged, but to perpetuate three other rapes? The odds of that being the case decreased with every assault. And this unknown drug compound being used made it even less likely."

"I agree. I'm not saying Amanda Richards doesn't meet whatever twisted criteria this guy is using to make his selections. But he deliberately included her."

She stopped suddenly, and he looked over at her. "What?"

"I was just wondering what the media coverage has been like surrounding the attacks. There weren't copies of any articles in the case files."

He grimaced, slowing the car as they approached the bridge to Tybee Island. Traffic was thicker here. "Violent crime in Savannah is worse than the national average in nearly every category. So far this year we've had thirty-five rapes reported. So the perp's first assault didn't even merit a blurb on the evening news and was buried on page ten of the newspapers. But with the second victim being the mayor's granddaughter . . . well, you can imagine the frenzy.

"We never released the information about the two rapes being linked, and the media had details of politics and beauty pageants to fill their stories with. It wasn't until the third rape in as many months that some enterprising reporter started asking questions and news of the task force leaked out. I heard Dixon has been up to his ass in media since the latest assault." The man was welcome to the job. As long as the commander kept them away from the task force, Ryne would be happy.

"So maybe that explains his selection of Richards. It might be his way of saying, 'Watch this. Do I have your attention now, Savannah?' Because he couldn't hope to have brought more focus to his acts than to attack that particular girl." She turned her face to the window as they crossed the water.

God, he hoped she was wrong. Alerting the public to a threat was one thing, but whipping up a frenzy in the press created obstacles and headaches for investigations.

"It wouldn't be unusual for this type of offender to hang around a scene, watch the police work."

He nodded. "Can't say any of the scenes drew a large crowd, but we videotaped them. Never saw the same person in more than one tape."

"This UNSUB is motivated by attention. He'll get off at what he perceives as his power over the police, too. He may try to insert himself into the case in some way. I know you've double-checked each of the individuals who found the victims. But it can also be someone who calls in a tip. Wanders into a precinct house for a trivial matter. Frequents a place where cops hang out after hours, hoping to hear some gossip."

He nodded, mulling over her words. "We always check out the identity of people calling in leads, but it could be tougher to check the other areas you mentioned." He made a mental note to have McElroy keep his eye out after hours. He knew the detective often joined other officers after shift at Sherm's, a nearby bar.

"Is that it?" At Abbie's raised brows, he added, "For your profile?"

"A profile is an evolving document. It develops as more evidence comes to light, much as the investigation develops as leads appear. I do suspect he had a poor relationship with his parents growing up. He may have been institutionalized at some point during his adolescence and he may have been sexually abused."

"Cry me a river," Ryne muttered. This was just the sort of psychobabble that solved nothing. And if he was supposed to actually feel sorry for the scumbag, she was wasting her breath. He said as much to Abbie as they began to traverse the Tybee Island streets lined with historic old homes.

"We don't have to sympathize with him to understand him," she said mildly. He had a feeling her mind was only half on him as they drew closer to the site of Richards's assault. "And understanding him is the first step toward an arrest."

"We may be close to an arrest already," he reminded her. They'd caught some breaks with Juarez, but there was a lot of work to be done to tie him with any certainty to the rapes. Even if the rock in the tread of the shoes found in Juarez's apartment matched the fill near Barbara Billings's, it was likely sold by the truckloads for legions of yards and gardens in the vicinity and beyond. But the positive match on the woman's blood found in his vehicle would be damning. Claiming the vehicle must have been stolen wasn't going to hold any weight with the grand jury, if it came to that. Not if they could nail down means and motive.

"Let's talk MO," he said abruptly. "Is the drug part of this guy's MO or his signature?"

"It might serve as both," Abbie responded, "given its properties and effects on the victims. It debilitates them to some extent, which helps him enact the crime. But if it's deliberately designed to enhance sensation, that makes it an important part of his ritual as well. His primary intent is to inflict enormous suffering on his victims for his own sexual satisfaction. Intensifying the pain from the torture would help accomplish that."

He slowed, then swung the car into the long drive of Mayor Richards's sprawling beach home. A two-car garage sat underneath the structure, and he pulled to a stop in front of one closed door. He wondered what kind of sick bastard would think of a drug to increase the agony of his victims. Like torture wasn't enough.

He tried to apply everything she'd just said to Juarez. He had Holmes going through the man's background, and he was anxious to hear what he found. Juarez's sheet had included only misdemeanors before he'd been sent up on a drug charge, but that only meant he hadn't been caught at anything worse. And he wouldn't be the first criminal to evolve while in prison.

Ryne had spent more time than he'd like to calculate hunting down sick fucks like the one preying on women in Savannah. He no longer used alcohol to dull the effects of too much ugliness, and not enough success stories. The life was a part of him, of who he was, and he didn't consider the whys or hows of it.

As he watched Abbie get out of the car to head up to the house, he wondered, not for the first time, what had compelled the woman to devote her life, her career, to tracking down scumbags like the Savannah rapist.

He got out of the car, following her up to the house. That question, and others about her, were beginning to haunt him, during times that would be better spent thinking about the case. Or at least about a much more important question.

Like why he even cared.

Abbie made Ryne show her the exact route into the house he'd figured the rapist had taken. From the file, she knew Amanda hadn't had a garage door opener, only the key she'd had made. Unfortunately, once the UNSUB had her and the key she kept on her key ring, he'd had a way inside the house. The girl had admitted in her interview that she'd written the security code on the key itself with permanent marker.

The home had a huge veranda running around three sides of it, with a breathtaking view of the ocean. Ryne unlocked the side door and she stepped into the house after him.

"I assume the security was changed after the attack took place," she said, looking around the home. Although the outside of the home hearkened back to an earlier century, the kitchen had been completely modernized. It opened onto a family room with vaulted ceilings and a glassed-in wall facing the Atlantic.

"Locks and codes were changed. The company providing

patrol security was fired, although the officer did his job, near as I could tell." Ryne led her down a hallway. "He was the one who called it in when he noticed a window open in the bedroom. Company gave him the go-ahead to check it out."

"And that's how Amanda was discovered," Abbie murmured. "I saw from the report that you thoroughly checked out the officer."

"We looked at him, but his alibi held up, for that night and for the first rape."

When Ryne stopped in the doorway of a bedroom, Abbie stepped around him and took a moment just to *sense*. Raiker was constantly preaching that it wasn't enough to go through photos of a crime scene. You had to *experience* it. Had to see and hear what the victim had seen and heard. And once the scene had been thoroughly processed, you had to touch what the victim had touched. Only then could you be transported back to the events of the assault. To the mind of the offender, who had arranged the events to suit his own needs.

And wasn't she used to that? The sly whisper slid across her mind as Abbie stepped into the room, and stared blindly at the furnishings. Know the victim, know the offender. That's what Raiker would say. And in this case—in most of the cases she worked—knowing the offender meant putting him away. But it wasn't always that easy. It wasn't always that clear.

"This room has been completely redone." Abbie started at Ryne's voice behind her. "Even the floor looks new." The glossy hardwood below their feet gleamed in the light afforded through the blinds. "Furniture is different. So's the paint. The scene was pretty brutal. Blood spatters everywhere."

There was no evidence of the brutality that had taken place here weeks earlier. No lingering sense of evil. The room was fresh, impersonal. It could have been a room in a chain motel. "Is this where Amanda usually stayed when she came?"

"No, that room is next door." She followed him to the next

room and looked inside, at the ruffled spread and matching curtains. There were no personal items sitting about.

The room across the hall was unmistakably the master bedroom. She walked in ahead of Ryne, noting the bank of windows facing the water, the attached bath and walk-in closets. If the offender had wanted to make this a personal strike at the mayor, wouldn't he have chosen this room? Wouldn't it have been one more twist of the knife to not only attack the precious granddaughter, but to do it in the mayor's house, in his room, his bed?

She continued to the next room, mulling those questions over. It was smaller, also with a view. And maybe she was crediting the offender with more preparation than he'd actually taken. Perhaps he'd picked the room he had because it was the first one off the family room. He would have entered the house alone, rather than take a chance being seen carrying a limp Amanda into the house. Then he'd unlocked the garage, driven in. He could have gotten inside and had the vehicle safely out of sight in under two minutes. A small risk, but if he'd familiarized himself with the security company's patrol route, a reasonable one to take.

She went back to the room where the attack had occurred and crossed to the window. Pushing aside the blinds, she looked out over the driveway to the street beyond. "Why would he open this window?" She turned to face Ryne, found him leaning a shoulder against the doorjamb. "Was it unseasonably warm that night? Because even if it was," she continued before he could answer, "why not turn on the air-conditioning?"

"It was normal temperatures for the season, high sixties. The victim couldn't tell us when he opened it."

"The report said the houses on either side were empty," she recalled. "How many permanent residents live around here?"

"None. At least not in this immediate area. These are strictly summer homes and it was the first week in May. A weeknight. The whole area was deserted, for at least three blocks, either direction. Although families occasionally spend weekends here throughout the year, Memorial Day weekend is the kickoff for the summer season."

"The report indicated she'd been gagged, but given the care he takes, I have a hard time believing he would have chanced opening the window during the assault."

"Maybe he heard a noise and checked it out. Or he could have left himself several escape routes as a precautionary measure, and forgot this one before leaving. Whatever his reason, it was one of the few mistakes he made, up until a couple days ago. The window tipped off the security guard when he was doing his rounds about three in the morning. He hadn't seen it open at midnight. He found the victim, got medical help."

Medical help that had kept Amanda Richards alive. Her wounds had been life-threatening, with copious blood loss. A thought crossed her mind, and she started to voice it, only to find Ryne no longer in the room.

She closed her mouth, the words going unuttered as she followed him through the rest of the house. Because the idea was pure conjecture, and she based her profile, her suggestions, on fact. That's what she was staking her professional reputation on.

But if she were going to rely on instinct, she'd wonder if the rapist had had another reason for leaving that window open. Something that had nothing to do with forgetfulness or escape.

Like maybe ensuring that Amanda Richards lived.

"This was a waste of time." Nick McElroy slouched in the front seat of the unmarked car as Wayne Cantrell pulled away from the curb. "How many prosses did Robel expect us to find walking the streets during the daytime?"

"We got some names." Wayne slid him a glance. "It's not like we didn't know the places to hit to talk to some of these girls."

"Yeah, the names of johns who like to slap them around a little. A couple pimps that get overly zealous about their ladies slacking off."

"Maybe we need to concentrate on the prosses that specialize."

McElroy shot him a lazy grin. "You got a habit that needs specializing, Cantrell? 'Cuz if your birthday is coming up, maybe we'll find one who specializes in spanking guys in loincloths. She could play squaw to your noble savage."

"Bite me," suggested Cantrell without heat. There was no use wasting energy on anger toward McElroy. The man's mouth ran on wheels and he had a one-track mind. But he was grateful that they'd work together only for the length of this investigation.

"Bite you? I'm not into that kind of thing, but don't you worry." McElroy leaned over and patted his cheek. "We'll find just the right girl for you." Cantrell jerked away from him and accelerated to turn left on a yellow light.

"Where you going? It's after quitting time already. And we still have to type up our notes from today."

"Figured we could check out Mistress Chan," Wayne said laconically, keeping his gaze fixed on the traffic. "Her name came up a couple times today as one who caters to the S and M crowd. According to Phillips, she might be the type who would role-play with this guy."

"Phillips," scoffed McElroy. He crossed his arms over his chest. "Like she's got anything to add to this investigation. She's just a kid with some fancy letters after her name. She's no cop."

"But we are. So we do our job." Wayne slowed, looking at addresses on the nearby buildings. The street was fairly reputable, lined with storefronts in varying degrees of upkeep. Meat markets were snugged up against boutiques and hair salons in row after row of small businesses. But above the businesses were apartments.

"Let's skip it. Leave Chan to the uniforms. Probably make their night."

"We're here. Might as well check it out." Wayne pulled into a no parking zone and switched off the ignition.

"Jesus, you're like a dog with a bone." McElroy grabbed his suit jacket, which he'd folded and laid in the backseat.

"Tell you what, I'll check up on this Chan pross you're stuck on. You go back and write up the notes for today. Saves us both some time."

Cantrell looked at him with surprise. "How are you getting back to headquarters?"

"Grab a bus, probably. Don't worry about it. If you hurry, you can still swing by the nursing home on your way home. You were going to visit your dad tonight, right?"

"Yeah." Although the man was in the advanced stages of Alzheimer's and wouldn't know him, he'd go, just like he went every week. Then he'd spend the next few days depressed over the shell of a man his father had become, and grappling with the guilt that came from having done too little, too late.

"So go ahead, before I change my mind." McElroy got out and shrugged into his jacket on the sidewalk.

"Yeah. Thanks."

"See you tomorrow."

With a wave, Cantrell pulled away from the curb, leaving the other detective scanning the apartments facing the street.

The woman that leaned provocatively against the opened door was dressed in vintage dominatrix. Black thigh-high fishnets clung to slim legs. The knee-high stiletto leather boots matched the leather thong and bra top she wore. Black elbow-length gloves encased her arms and in one fist she held a short whip. "Detective," she purred. "Always a pleasure."

She snapped the whip alarmingly close to his johnson. "Bitch." Nick reached out and snatched the whip from her. He knew from experience what she could do with it. Stepping quickly inside, he shut the door, looked around. "Did you get rid of him?"

Mistress Chan shook back her waist-length black hair. "You just called," she protested. "And he's a regular. I can't just turn paying clients out on the street every time you get a boner."

Her head swiveled with the force of the slap he dealt her. "You need to learn to do what you're told." But after a quick glance, he was satisfied she had the client safely secreted away somewhere. Probably cuffed naked in a dog kennel, dumb bastard.

She turned back to him, tongue darting out to lick the blood from her mouth. And her eyes, those damn sinful eyes, were alive with desire. "You're in a mood," she murmured. She laid her palms on his chest, stroked them up and down languidly.

He felt his breath quicken. "This is business. Told you that on the phone. I need to talk to you about an investigation I'm working."

Her eyes widened in mock interest. "Do tell." Then she rammed her fist into his solar plexus with enough force to drive the air from his lungs. "I love talking business."

He knocked her to the floor this time, and the sight of her crumpled there had lust abruptly flaring. Reaching down, he hauled her to her feet, shoving her to sprawl over the arm of the couch. With two quick steps he was behind her, pinning her in place and keeping a careful eye on those heels of her. Damned things were needle sharp and hurt like a bitch if she managed to stomp on him.

"Don't forget," she gasped, "I got a client in the next room."

"I'm guessing he'll wait." Shoving her thong aside, Nick unzipped his pants. "And so will business."

Chapter 8

After doing three miles on the track and then hitting the free weights, Ryne took his frustrations out on a punching bag in the corner of the gym. Following the afternoon's task force meeting, he'd met with the DA and the conversation had been depressing. They could only hold Juarez forty-eight hours without charging him, and time was running out. There was no telling when Han would complete the tests on the contents of the syringe, and without something conclusive to tie the man to the rapes, the DA wasn't ready to charge him.

Get me a latent off the license plates or syringe. Or better yet, something that places Juarez in the victim's house.

The echo of the DA's voice in his mind was drowned out by the sound of voices behind him at ringside. Ryne hammered the bag even harder. Like it was that easy. Like anything about this case had been simple. CSU had checked the syringe after he'd transferred the contents to a liquid-tight container, and it had been clean. Nor had they found a print on the tip found in Juarez's apartment. So barring an unforeseen miracle, by tomorrow evening Juarez was going to be released, and they'd have to use a half-dozen officers to watch him around the clock. Which would pay off if he was really the perp they were after, but . . .

The cheer that went up then succeeded in distracting him from the morose direction of his thoughts. He held up a stationary fist to stop the bag's momentum and turned toward the sound of the voices. A crowd had gathered around the ring where two opponents were sparring. A second look had a frown forming. Two seriously mismatched opponents, from what he could see between the wall of bodies surrounding the pair. One of the participants had a foot and a hundred pounds on the other, and Ryne wondered who would be stupid enough to voluntarily climb into the ring for a certain pummeling.

He started to drift in that direction. Some guy with short dick syndrome, probably. A couple likely candidates immediately sprang to mind. He craned his neck, was able to recognize the larger of the two as Jack Barlow out of the second precinct. He was a decent amateur boxer, so Ryne jockeyed for position in the crowd, prepared for a bloodbath.

He blinked when, in the next second, the shorter opponent spun and landed a lightning-speed kick to the side of Barlow's jaw. Another cheer went up from the men around the ring, amid catcalls questioning Barlow's manhood.

Ryne elbowed his way through the front row, earning himself a "Watch it, asshole" along the way. He barely heard the irritated voice. His attention was riveted on the smaller figure moving out of reach of Barlow's gloves. It was obvious from the stance, from the moves, that this participant, though much smaller, didn't lack for experience.

It was also obvious that the second participant was female.

Only the crowd around the ring had disguised that fact from him earlier. She was slight, but there were distinctive, all-too-distracting curves beneath her long-sleeve tee and shorts. And although club rules dictated that sparring participants wear headgear and mouth guards, she was easily recognizable.

Abbie Phillips.

The spandex shorts she wore clung to what, he'd already reluctantly noticed, was an outstanding butt. She pulled her head back a split second before Barlow sent a fast right jab that would have knocked her on that delectable ass had it connected. She landed a punch to the man's stomach that he seemed to barely feel, and from the looks of the shit-eating grin on Barlow's face, he was enjoying himself hugely.

She brought her knee up to deflect a blow that was meant for her midsection and then with a blurring swiftness shifted her weight and used the other knee to strike Barlow in the side, drawing a surprised grunt of pain from the man. Ryne joined in with the laughter of the onlookers.

He must be losing it. Not only was he growing too interested in a woman on his task force, he was getting more than a little turned on watching her beat the hell out of a detective twice her size.

"I'm next, sweetheart," someone shouted. "Be gentle." The crowd laughed again.

He wasn't versed in boxing or martial arts, but he knew enough to be impressed by her footwork. And when she feinted with her left, then quickly shifted position for a kick to Barlow's shoulder, the man staggered back a good three feet.

There was an odd sort of beauty in the way she moved, the fluid strength and jaw-dropping speed. And Ryne found himself intrigued by her in a way he'd been interested in no woman since . . . he failed to remember how long.

"Hey, which one of you guys drives a black Accord? Some punk just shattered its windshield."

Two things happened in quick succession. Abbie stopped, her attention on the speaker, just as Barlow released a punch. She recovered quickly, dodging away, but the blow still clipped her on the jaw, snapping her head back and surprising a sudden oath from Ryne. Jeers rose from the men.

"Cheap shot, Barlow."

"Seeing stars, sugar?"

Abbie shook her head hard, as if to clear it. Barlow came to a stop and pushed up his face mask, regret written on his expression. When he raised his gloves, the gym trainer jumped into the ring and shuffled over to unlace the man, who then spit his mouth guard into his hand.

"I'd already swung, honest. I wasn't cheap-shotting you."

Once the trainer helped Abbie get her gloves off, she dispensed with the face guard and mouthpiece. "Not your fault," she said wryly. "I know better than to lose my concentration. But that Accord." She scanned the crowd in search of the speaker. "Does it have rental plates on it?"

"Yeah, it does. I heard the noise when I was crossing the parking lot and saw someone running. Chased him half a block but he had too much lead."

Ryne didn't recognize the speaker, a stocky balding man in his mid-fifties. Given the size of his girth, though, Ryne doubted the man had chased the guy too far or too hard.

Abbie handed her gear to the trainer, and jumped down from the ring. Ryne rounded the corner to join her as she walked rapidly toward the exit. "How's the jaw?"

She looked at first shocked to see him, then resigned. "Of course you would have to see that," she muttered. "Like my day hadn't already gotten bad enough."

He reached to touch the red mark already blooming on her chin. She jerked away, then wiggled her jaw gingerly. "I've had worse. It was a stupid mistake. I know better than to get distracted like that."

He followed her through the door and across the parking lot silently. He could have told her that "knowing better" wasn't much help when it came to distractions. He should know. He was having a helluva time resisting the one she presented.

Together they surveyed her car, and if anything, her expression grew grimmer. There was a hole roughly eight inches in circumference through the driver side windshield, and the rest of it was a mass of cracks. Ryne went to the driver side door and peered in the window. A brick sat in the seat.

"I'll call it in," he said, already taking his cell phone from his pocket. Abbie just nodded, her gaze never leaving the car. He didn't mention the question uppermost in his mind. Not then. But he couldn't help wondering how someone who'd been in town a matter of days had been targeted not once, but twice.

His call completed, he slipped the phone back in his pocket. Before he was through today, he'd have the answer to that question, and whatever else it was that Abbie was holding back from him.

Abbie slouched in the front seat of Ryne's black vintage Mustang. Ordinarily she would have taken a moment to appreciate the sleekly restored vehicle. She wouldn't have pegged him as a car buff. But she was too busy dealing with the welter of emotion crashing inside her.

She could no longer doubt that her sister was in Savannah. Useless to ask why she'd followed Abbie here, or what had prompted Callie's behavior this time. Figuring out why her sister did the things she did was beyond Abbie, regardless of her degree. Far more practical to focus on the problems her presence presented.

Callie was off her medication; that was clear enough. When she didn't take her pills, she could seem fine for weeks at a time. And then the inevitable crash occurred, and everyone close to her would feel the repercussions. Abbie had lived with those repercussions all her life. Callie was capable of far worse than a vandalized wardrobe and a brick through a car window. And it was that fact that had her worried.

Should she call Dr. Faulkner? She hadn't talked to her sister's psychotherapist for four months, approximately the time Callie had stopped seeing him. He hadn't been able to tell Abbie that, of course. Callie had long since stopped signing agreements to release information to her sister. But Abbie had been able to read between the lines of his guarded responses.

In the next moment she decided against it. If Callie was responsible for the acts against her, it was plain she wasn't under a doctor's care anymore. Abbie had lost count of the number of times this cycle had been repeated. The best thing to do was to meet her face-to-face. Sometimes that had a calming effect on her. At least for a while.

She slid a look at Ryne. He'd slipped on his sunglasses so she couldn't see his eyes, but his expression was neutral. It was hard to believe, however, that he wasn't wondering what the hell was going on, and she braced herself for an onslaught of questions.

"So are you thinking what I'm thinking?"

Mentally preparing herself to do battle, she said, "What?"

He turned to grin at her. "That maybe Barlow paid someone to throw that brick just so you'd stop beating the hell out of him in front of his friends?"

That surprised a laugh from her. "Somehow I doubt it. He's good. I can tell he trains."

"I hear he was on the amateur circuit before joining the academy. From all accounts, he made a name for himself but chose police work instead."

From there, the conversation turned to her training in Muay Thai, the gym facility, and eventually to Ryne's car, which he confessed he'd bought because he'd always coveted one when he was a teenager. And the talk of innocuous subjects had something in Abbie easing. She didn't have to explain her family to Ryne or anyone else. Which left her time to worry about how she was going to get Callie to meet her face-to-face and try to convince her to go back on her medication. To return to therapy.

And for now she wasn't going to consider just how she was going to accomplish either task.

———

"Thanks for the ride."

Ryne got out when Abbie did and reached into the backseat to retrieve her gym bag. She hadn't bothered to change before accepting his offer of a ride home. For that matter, neither had he. After filing the police report and then an incident report for the gym, she'd been ready to call it a day. She still needed to contact the rental agency and order a replace-

ment vehicle. Not to mention dealing with the insurance hassle that was sure to follow.

Her mood darkened again at the thought. It didn't im-
prove any when Ryne ignored her outstretched hand and
instead carried her bag to her back door. He had been suspiciously good-natured about the events of the day. But now
that she was home again, she was anxious to have him gone,
a fact that made her feel churlish.

So she squelched the urge to tell him she could handle
things from here and took the house key from her bag to
unlock the door. He walked through it and she immediately
regretted her action.

The man had a presence that left an indelible impression.
The only other time he'd spent here had been brief, but ever
since, she'd pass through a doorway and have a mental flash
of him framed in it. Each time she looked at the pictures on
the mantel, she'd have an image of him standing in front of
the fireplace, studying each photo in turn.

Those brief flashes were disturbing, made all the more so
by the knowledge that they were powered by her awareness
of him. The awareness was unwelcome. And more than a
little unfamiliar.

She reached to take the bag from him, intent on sending
him on his way. "Thanks again. Hopefully I can get the rental
agency to deliver another car yet tonight."

He gave an absent nod, studying the glass that had been
replaced. "Stanley Glass didn't overcharge you?"

Something about his manner had wariness circling inside
her. "You can't be interested in the details of the replacement
pane."

"No, you're right. He leaned a hip against the kitchen
counter and crossed his arms. "I'm more interested in the
details you've been keeping from me since the break-in. Like
the name of the person who's been targeting you."

In the inner recesses of her mind she could hear the sound
of a trap snapping shut. The easy conversation, the offer of a
ride . . . this had been his intention all along. She'd been a

fool to think that a man like Ryne Robel would let any of this go. He'd only been biding his time.

Manufacturing a tired shrug, she said, "We really aren't going to do this again, are we? I've had some bad luck, but—"

"Bullshit." The steel in his tone had her blinking. "Someone followed you here, or maybe they came with you. But whoever it is has a major hard-on against you, Abbie. And you're going to tell me who and you're going to tell me why."

Abruptly dropping the charade, she folded her arms across her chest, mimicking his stance. "No," she said baldly. "I'm not."

He was upright in an instant, moving toward her. He took her elbow in his hand when she would have walked away from him, and he shoved his face close to hers. "This is my case, and I don't need anything or anyone screwing it up. If you've got some kind of problem that could potentially impact it . . ."

"The case?" For a moment she was nonplussed. "This has nothing to do with the case."

He looked unconvinced. "I'll be the judge of that."

She pulled free of him. "This doesn't concern the investigation, or you. It has to do with my life, and as such, it's my business. Have you seen one example of me being distracted? I spend nearly as long hours as you do at headquarters."

"Maybe it hasn't affected the case yet, but it could. I won't know that until you come clean about what's happening. And if you won't tell me," he added, forestalling her next refusal, "I'm going to Dixon and ask to have you removed."

Shock flared, followed quickly by anger. "He won't remove me. You know why? Because you're overreacting. He'll realize it, even if you don't."

"Maybe not." She didn't like the looks of that satisfied smile on his lips. "But he'll ask you the same questions that I am. Who do you want to explain it to, him or me?"

That stopped her short. She was certain it was meant to.

Of course she didn't want to be having this conversation with Commander Dixon. Only slightly less than she wanted to be having it with Robel.

She sent him a look filled with dislike. "You're pushy."

He inclined his head. "It's been mentioned."

"Not to mention manipulative."

He made a c'mon gesture with his hand. When she remained silent, he said, "It was a guy seen running away from your car today. So who is he? An ex-boyfriend? Husband, maybe?"

"Neither." Still fuming, she picked up her bag and carried it into her bedroom, dropped it on the floor. She turned and found him standing in the doorway. Elbowing past him, she walked back out into the living room. Her gaze went involuntarily to the pictures on the mantel, and a sense of resignation filled her.

"So you're claiming you don't know the guy who shattered your windshield."

She shook her head, her mind filled with too many scenes from the past. All fraught with drama. All that had left her with a lingering sense of despair. "He could have been anyone. She would have paid him or made some other sort of exchange." Promiscuity was just one of the destructive behavior patterns that emerged when Callie was off her meds.

"She . . . who?"

"My sister. She's bipolar, and when she isn't under a doctor's care, her behavior can be . . . erratic."

Although she didn't look at him, she could tell her response had surprised him. And for the moment she was too caught up in the past to resent his prying. Callie was the only real family she had, although they were more like survivors of a natural disaster than *sisters*. The complexity of their relationship would keep a good psychotherapist busy unraveling it for years. She barely understood it herself.

"She lives down here?"

"No." Then she corrected herself. "I don't know. She moves around a lot. And she hasn't been in communication for a few months. I leave her forwarding addresses, so she knew where I'd be." But she hadn't expected Callie to follow her here. She never had before.

"Would she try to hurt you?"

Her gaze snapped to meet Ryne's, surprised at the question. Surprised at the immediate denial that rose to her lips. Few knew the lengths Callie had gone to in order to protect Abbie when they were children. Fewer still understood what it meant to owe such a staggering debt. She'd been paying it, in one manner or another, all her life.

Suddenly chilled, she hugged her arms. "I'm not afraid of her. When she's ready, she'll reach out." At the doubt in his gaze, she added, "I've been handling her all my life, Ryne. Despite the fact that she's older than me, I was named her guardian for a time. This is a complication for me, but it isn't a complication for the investigation."

He was silent for long moments, moments that had tension settling through her shoulders. Then he gave a slow nod. "All right."

Irritation spiked. "Glad the sordid little details of my family drama could put your mind at rest." It was more, far more personal information than she'd shared with anyone in years, with the exception of Adam Raiker, from whom very little could be withheld. And she fiercely resented Robel for forcing her hand.

She walked by him, headed for the door, ready to show him out. As she would have passed by him, he halted her with one hand on her arm. "I'm sorry."

Warily, she stared at him. "For prying into something that was none of your business?"

His mouth quirked. "You'd think so, wouldn't you? But I had to make sure the case wouldn't be impacted. No, I'm sorry about your sister. It must be . . . a worry."

Abbie almost laughed. *Worry* was such a tame description of the inner emotional war that always accompanied thoughts of Callie. But her black humor faded abruptly as his gaze lingered on her, as the concern in his expression changed to something else.

Desire. It lit an answering heat in her veins, one she knew

enough to reject. Although she'd grown to respect the man, she couldn't honestly say she always liked him.

But she was always *aware* of him. There was an attraction that flickered to life at odd moments when they were together. It skipped over nerve endings and ignited long-dormant feelings that had no place in the life she'd made for herself. And it was clear from the heat in Ryne's eyes that he felt it, too. It was, she was discovering, far easier to ignore when he was being deliberately provoking than when he was unexpectedly kind.

Just a few inches separated them. She swallowed, fighting the urge to close the distance and press her lips against that hard mouth and see for herself if it would soften for her. But even as she was struggling to summon the discipline to move past him, away from temptation, he lowered his head and covered her lips with his.

He knew how to kiss a woman. Deep. Demanding. Devastating. There was a sort of resignation in the realization, even as her body responded. It was too much to hope that one taste of him would be enough to quench the attraction for good. And since it was too late to walk away from what was assuredly a mistake, she opened her lips to make the most of the moment. Her pulse chugged and her blood turned molten as his tongue swept into her mouth and his flavor traced through her.

One arm snaked around her waist and brought her closer. His chest was hard; his abbreviated attire showed off the roped muscles in his arms and legs. She clutched his shoulders to explore the bunched strength there and, taking his bottom lip in her teeth, scored it not quite lightly.

Ryne dropped one hand to her butt and squeezed, turning her and walking her backward until she was trapped between the unyielding surface of the wall at her back and the hard hungry man at the front. He braced one arm next to her head while his mouth ate at hers with a leashed urgency that was all the more compelling for being restrained.

Abbie dragged her lips from his and ran the tip of her tongue over the hollow beneath his throat, where bone met sinew. He tasted of salt and sweat and man, and an unfamiliar need clawed through her. Her past relationships had been few, brief, and based on comfort, safety, and most importantly, maintaining control.

There was nothing comfortable about Ryne. He wasn't safe. And she'd battle to remain in control around him. Somehow that made her reaction to him even more shattering.

His lips went to a spot beneath her ear that had her shivering, her knees going to water. Their hands battled with each other's clothing, and her palms skated up his ridged sides at the same moment she felt his fingers at her waist. The feel of him was seductive, lightly padded muscle over bone, and she desperately wanted to test that power with touch and teeth and taste. She reveled in the exquisite pleasure of his hands on her flesh, just shy of rough, and an alarm shrilled in her mind. In a complete detour from her normally innate caution, she muted it. There was an unexpected pleasure to be found in the flavor of him, and a sense of power in realizing that he was just as helpless to control it as she was.

His mouth sealed against hers, he pushed a knee between her legs so he could step between them, to press even more closely against her. A band of heat sizzled everywhere they touched, and a fever streaked through her blood. Ryne's hands went to her breasts, covered in a sports bra that was frustratingly thick and tight. Her nipples tightened in anticipation of firmer contact, and she made a hum of approval when his fingers went to the hem of her shirt, and began to draw it upward.

When cooler air kissed heated flesh, though, reality abruptly intruded. Her hands went to his chest, and it took more effort than it should have to turn away from those wickedly clever lips, to haul in a steadying gulp of air.

He stilled, his breathing labored. They remained like that for long moments, and when he moved away, slowly, reluctantly, something inside her mourned. She busied herself smoothing her shirt down, avoiding his eyes.

"Not a good idea," he rasped, and she jerked her head from side to side.

"Definitely not."

The curse he muttered then had her gaze flying to his. "I'm not apologizing for this."

Her voice was shaky. "I'd have to hurt you if you did."

Hauling in a breath, he took a step back from her, then another. There was an instant, one heated moment, when she glimpsed the hunger on his face, and thought he'd reverse his path and pull her into his arms again. A moment when she was sure she would have gone willingly, and damn the consequences. But then his expression shuttered, and he turned and walked past her. Out of the room. Out of the house.

The snick of the door closing punctured the crazy hope that had flared, albeit briefly. Abbie leaned a shoulder against the wall, not certain her legs would support her. It occurred to her then, as she listened to the sound of the Mustang's powerful engine roaring to life, that Callie's reappearance right now was not the biggest problem she needed to handle.

Not even close.

Chapter 9

Ryne positioned himself behind the one-way glass to watch the scene being conducted in the interview room. Holmes had rounded up Juarez's girlfriend, and he was anxious to hear what, if anything, she could tell them about the man. They had a handful of hours before they had to file charges or spring him. They had the pot and assault charges to level at him, of course, but once they did, he'd be up for bail. And somehow the scumbags always managed to find someone to pony up the dough.

Juarez was still denying any knowledge of the blood or syringe found in his Bronco. And while they were awaiting word from Han on the chemical analysis of the syringe contents, this woman, Geneva Rivera, was their last hope to learn something quickly that would more solidly link the man to the rapes. From the responses she'd given so far, however, that hope was fading fast.

"I told ya, I was only with him a few weeks. Wouldn't call him my *boyfriend*. Can I get a frickin' cigarette? I'm dying here."

"Sorry." Isaac Holmes's expression never changed as he

surveyed the woman from across the table. "There's a no smoking ordinance in the department."

"Figures." She drummed her fingers nervously on the table. "So what'd Hidalgo do, huh? Flash some little ol' lady and give her a heart attack?"

"You knew about his past?"

She lifted a nearly bare shoulder. Narrow straps battled gravity to keep her ample chest from spilling out of her thin pink top. "I didn't know when I met him. Knew he'd been in prison, though. Thought he was kinda *dangerous*. Guys that have been inside, they have a lotta built-up need, you know?" She batted her eyes. "That can be kinda exciting. But Hidalgo, he's about as exciting as a doggy hard-on."

"What does that mean?"

Rivera did a double take. "What does that . . . c'mon, what do you think it means? He's not a top performer. A thirty-second man, if you get my drift."

Ryne watched as Holmes consulted the list of questions he'd given him. "Did he ever threaten you physically? Ever ask you to engage in sexual acts that were abusive?"

Geneva dug in her purse and extracted some gum. Unwrapping it, she popped it in her mouth, chewed. "Naw, nothing like that. He liked to pretend a lot, and wanted me to. It got old fast."

"Pretend what?"

She screwed up her brow, as if the act of remembering was an effort. "Like once he wanted to tie me up, which I thought might be kinda fun. But then he just wanted me to act like he was my master, like a sheik or something. Say weird stuff like I was his slave. Stupid stuff like that."

Interest sharpening, Ryne straightened. He had the stray thought that it was too bad Abbie wasn't here. She'd be better able to tell what, if anything, Juarez's behavior with Rivera might have meant.

In the next moment, realization struck him and his mouth flattened. His first reaction when he'd come in and not seen her had been one of relief. He still hadn't come to terms with the emotion that had slammed into him the first time he'd gotten his hands on her. Or those that had resulted from walking away.

There was no denying it had been for the best. His attention was only half on the conversation taking place in the other room. The last thing he needed right now was to get involved with a woman, especially one working the case.

But it wasn't Abbie's involvement in the case that was his biggest concern, it was the emotions she elicited without even trying. The first time he'd responded after hearing the call about her break-in, he'd backpedaled abruptly once he recognized what he was feeling. *Protectiveness.*

Which would have been funny, if it wasn't so pathetic. The last woman he should have been protecting had wound up dead. The failure still weighted his conscience. If Abbie needed protection, she couldn't have chosen a man less capable of delivering it.

Only half listening to Rivera's litany about Juarez's shortcomings in the bedroom, memories replayed in his mind. Of Abbie sailing through the air to tackle Juarez; of her whaling on Barlow. The mental recollections brought a smile to his lips. Despite her size, Abbie Phillips seemed more than capable of taking care of herself.

Except, of course, with family.

His smile faded as he remembered her reluctant disclosure last night. Even if she was correct, and the vandalism acts were caused by her off-balanced sister, he remained unconvinced that she was in no danger. But he'd recognized the no trespassing signs she'd posted about the subject and had backed away. He valued his own privacy too much to intrude any further on hers.

"Did Hidalgo ever leave anything at your place?" The question had Ryne's attention moving back to the interview room. "Maybe give you something to keep for him?"

"Like what?"

Holmes never seemed to lose patience. "Maybe a sealed box, or a package of some kind. Articles of clothing. Tapes."

Geneva shook her head and said, half-bitterly, "He never spent a dime on me while we was together, other than to pay for drinks when we went out. And he never gave me nothing else either."

"Maybe he left something at your place without asking. Hid it in a closet, under a bed."

The woman gave a short laugh. "I live with two other women, and there's about as much privacy as a shoe box. There's no place you can hide something and not have someone stumble over it. Believe me, I've tried. This one bitch, Greta Marko, she won't stop wearing my clothes, right? So I tried putting my best stuff away, kinda like hiding it, like you said, and she—"

"Can you verify Hidalgo's whereabouts on any of these dates?" Holmes's question interrupted the woman's growing ire, and had Ryne's attention sharpening. But Rivera seemed unsure. A calendar was produced and the woman flipped through it desultorily. Juarez's attendance record at the Valu-Mart had already been pulled. Given his hours, even on days he'd worked, he could have still managed assaults on each of the days in question. Some of the time lines would have been tight, but it was manageable. His second job cleaning up at Shorty's provided no alibi. The owner and other employees had already been questioned, but no one else worked while he was there.

Which meant the man needed to come up with someone else who could alibi him on the days in question. It was clear the woman in the interview room was going to provide him with little help.

"You're sure of that?"

Rivera nodded her head emphatically in response to Holmes's question. "We first started seeing each other the end of April. The last time I was with Hidalgo was middle of June. The eighteenth. I took him to my niece's baptism. Believe me, my family wasn't impressed. It was then I decided to drop him for good."

"How about this date in May." He tapped the calendar page. That would be the date of Amanda Richard's attack.

The woman shrugged. "Can't say for sure. We usually only seen each other on weekends, but sometimes we'd get together on weeknights, too. Not often, though, because he had that job at Shorty's, and he usually had to go there."

Though the detective continued awhile longer, Rivera had nothing else of import to tell them. Ryne headed back to his desk when the interview concluded, his mood dark. He may as well call the DA now and get it over with. Unless something else transpired in the next few hours, Juarez was going to be a free man.

———

As she hurried across Colombia Square, Abbie easily identified Tracy Sommers. The woman was sitting on a park bench waiting for her staring fixedly at the fountain. When Abbie had called to set up this interview, Sommers had insisted on meeting her somewhere outside. When asked for a suggestion, Sommers had come up with this place. From the plaques she'd passed on some of the statues, Abbie knew the area was historic, but wondered what significance it held for Sommers. It was even more humid than usual today, and though the bench the woman had selected was in the shade, Abbie could already feel her shirt dampening.

"Mrs. Sommers?" Abbie smiled reassuringly as the woman jerked at her voice. "I'm Abbie Phillips, working with the SCMPD on your case."

Once she'd sat down next to the woman, Sommers said, "Like I said on the phone, I haven't remembered anything new. I don't know how I can help by talking to you."

"I am sorry to make you go through it again," Abbie said sincerely. "But I have some pictures to show you. Do you think you're up to taking a look at them?"

Sommers visibly recoiled. "You mean . . . you've found him?"

"We have a lead." Despite her own reservations about Juarez as a suspect, she'd agreed to show his photo in an array to the victims. With none of them recalling seeing their attacker's face, it was a shot in the dark, but an avenue they needed to cover.

Tracy moistened her lips, fists clenched in the lap of her

denim skirt. "I don't know how much it will help, but I'll try."

Abbie opened the folder she carried and handed it to the other woman. Each color picture showed a man in a full body shot, with Juarez's picture second in the alignment.

The folder shook in Tracy's trembling hands. "I don't . . . I told the detectives I never saw him."

"I know. But maybe his mask or gloves slipped down, just a fraction, and you saw a strip of skin." The woman was shaking her head before Abbie even finished the suggestion. "In any case, these individuals are different heights, races, and body types. Go ahead and take your time," she urged. "Study them. The purpose here isn't positive identification, of course. But if anything about these men sparks a memory, just by comparison . . ."

Tracy shrugged helplessly, looking up at Abbie. "He grabbed me from behind. And once he jabbed that needle in my arm, I just wasn't that aware of *him*, you know? Only of what he was doing to me."

Her words were eerily similar to what both Billings and Richards had said. "How are *you* doing, Tracy?" Abbie asked, her voice gentle.

"Oh, well . . ." The pretty brunette tried a smile, didn't quite manage it. "I haven't been back to work because I can't bring myself to use the elevators or enter a stairwell."

For this victim, Abbie recalled, the rapist had placed a plastic bag over her head and repeatedly suffocated and revived her. "Have you seen a therapist? They might be able to help you with the claustrophobia, too."

"I'm attending a group. It's not helping much, though." The woman looked away, a bitter expression on her face. "I try to spend as much time as possible outdoors, where the walls can't close in on me. My husband . . . he's been great, but I can't help wondering . . . he's an extreme sports fan. White water rafting, paragliding, rock climbing, you name it. How long is he going to stay interested in a wife who freaks out if a restaurant's bathroom is too small?"

"Couples counseling will help both of you work through this." She knew, better than anyone, that some fears lasted a lifetime. But that didn't mean a person couldn't learn to cope with them.

Tracy appeared not to hear, her gaze on a group of pigeons splashing in the fountain. "I've always had a problem with enclosed places, you know? Todd—my husband—used to tease me about it because I tended to shake and sweat in elevators, but I could still do them if I had to. But now . . . now I can't even get into a *car*. It's too confining."

"Give it time," Abbie advised gently. "And I don't mean to sound like a broken record, but counseling will help." Certainly it had saved her life at one point. It had been less successful with Callie.

She shook the thought away. Callie and Tracy didn't have similar issues. There was no reason to believe that therapy wouldn't help Tracy, especially if her husband remained supportive.

It took another hour to lead the woman through the same list of questions she'd gone through with Amanda Richards. It was a tedious process, but necessary if she was to discover the intersections in these women's lives. Somehow each of them had come to the rapist's attention. If she could just discover that one point, it would be a huge lead in learning his identity.

When they were finished, Tracy looked one last time at the photos, while Abbie began to stow her notebook in her purse. "They're too big," she blurted.

"What?" Abbie's gaze fell to the pictures. "How do you mean?"

"These two are too tall." She pointed at the first and last men. The men depicted were over six foot. "This one is broader through here." She traced the chest and shoulders of another. "The man who raped me was strong. But he wasn't as big as Todd. He's six foot and is in really good shape. The guy was smaller than him."

Feeling a spurt of excitement, Abbie put her bag down

and withdrew the notebook she'd just put away. It didn't escape her notice that Tracy hadn't discounted Juarez. Or that her description of her attacker echoed the one Billings had given.

———————

"I'm sorry, Ms. Phillips, but Barbara didn't sleep well last night. I gave her one of the sedatives her doctor prescribed. You'll have to reschedule your appointment." Nancy Billings spoke from the three-inch opening she allowed in the door, as if ready to slam it at the merest hint of Abbie's noncompliance.

With a sudden shift of plans, Abbie said, "I will reschedule. But as long as I'm here, do you mind if I ask you some questions?"

The woman seemed taken aback. "Me? What could I possibly tell you?"

"In cases like this, we always talk to the victims' families, ma'am, to add background to our case." *Know the victim, know the perp.* Raiker's mantra had been drilled into her. "You could fill in some blanks for me about Barbara's residence history, educational background, employment history, relatives . . . things like that."

The door was closing. "I don't think—"

"Anything I can cover with you is less information I have to go over with Barbara."

The words were an inspired choice. The movement of the door stopped, then the space widened slightly. "You wouldn't need to bother Barbara again?"

It was obvious the woman would do anything to spare her daughter further involvement with the police. Abbie couldn't blame her. "I still need to speak to your daughter, Mrs. Billings. But I think you can give me some of the details I need."

It didn't matter why the woman had decided to cooperate, Abbie figured, as she followed her through the home and was shown to the couch. Only that she had. As she watched Barbara's mother flit around the room, straightening seat cushions and folding newspapers to "tidy up a bit," Abbie noted that the woman really didn't physically resemble her daughter in any way other than hair color. Which made her curious about Barbara's father.

"Is your daughter a native Georgian?"

Nancy never stopped moving. "Oh, my yes. My husband—that's my first husband—and I moved down here while I was pregnant with her. Lived in Mobile awhile, then Atlanta. But we've been in Savannah since Barbara was four."

"I didn't know you were remarried." Abbie jotted a notation down in her notebook. "Do you live here with your second husband?"

"No, thank heavens." At Abbie's raised brows, the woman stopped straightening the curtains and crossed to stand behind a chair opposite Abbie. "I've been divorced for ten years. Purchased this house when the divorce was final. Ron Billings is living in Tallahassee with his new wife, and good riddance to him."

"So he must have adopted Barbara," surmised Abbie.

The older woman nodded. "And she took his name back after *her* divorce, not that she was ever that happy with it to begin with. She idolized her real daddy, God rest his soul. She and Ron never got along that well, especially in her teens."

"Why is that?" Abbie wrote *Ron Billings?* in the notebook and drew a line under it. Although with the evident links in the rapes, it was doubtful that Barbara's poor relationship with her stepfather had any bearing on the case.

"Well, he was a bit of a bully, I guess you could say." Nancy smoothed the sage green fabric on the chair before her, plucking at a loose thread. "Always thought he knew what was best for everybody. Arranged things to suit himself most of the time and expected us to fall in with his decisions. He and Barbara used to have huge battles over that boat of his."

"His boat?" Abbie asked, summoning patience. Oftentimes the most illuminating tidbits of information came when she got the other person talking freely. And Nancy Billings had obviously relaxed since her arrival.

"He bought it—he claimed—so we'd have family time together. Ron had a way of justifying all of his extravagances. Barbara refused to have anything to do with it, and of course I sided with her. Ron could be incredibly insensitive about other people's feelings."

Sifting through the statements, Abbie asked, "Barbara didn't like boats?"

"Barbara didn't like water," Nancy corrected. "She's terrified of it. Has been ever since she witnessed her father's death. She nearly drowned herself."

Abbie's attention bounced from her notepad to the woman across from her. "When was that?"

"When Barbara was seven." Nancy was on the move again, trailing one finger across the glass end table, frowning at a bit of dust she spotted. "I stayed home that day because I hadn't been feeling well. Jack had taken her sailing, just off Hilton Head Island. A storm had come up suddenly and the boat capsized." The woman stopped, took a deep breath. "They were wearing life jackets, and my husband had Barbara and was trying to swim back to shore. They weren't that far out. But the boat must have been lifted by a swell and it came down, striking him on the head . . ."

Leaving his young daughter to watch her unconscious father drown. For a moment she was flooded with empathy. Then an idea reared, one so implausible she nearly dismissed it. But it refused to be rejected. "Mrs. Billings, would you mind sitting down? I want you to tell me everything you remember about Barbara's fear of water since her childhood."

There was a kick in her chest as she caught sight of Ryne bent over some paperwork at his desk. Abbie accepted the sensation with resignation rather than alarm. Last night had proven only too clearly that she wasn't immune to the man. Far from it.

Ryne looked up at the sound of her approach, dropped his pen, and rubbed a hand over his shadowed jaw. "You're keeping long hours."

She didn't bother pointing out the obvious. Sometimes she wondered if he kept a razor and change of clothes there and slept at his desk.

"Heard from your sister?"

The words had Abbie slowing in the process of rounding her desk. "No." She'd barely given Callie a thought for hours, a fact she wasn't proud of. But the kiss she'd shared with him . . . that memory had prowled the edges of her mind throughout the day. On the drives to and from the interviews. During them. Most people would be a lot happier if memory functioned upon command. Since she couldn't order the mental replays to stop, she'd done her best to ignore them.

That attempt wasn't helped by the sight of Ryne, looking lean and dangerous with a black ribbed pullover shirt and a stubbled chin. A wheat-colored collarless jacket hung over the back of his chair.

It wasn't until his gaze met hers that she realized she was staring. Her tongue felt suddenly thick. "Do . . . do you have time to give me a quick rundown of the updates?"

Glancing at his watch, he grimaced. "I'm going to have to leave pretty soon. I'll print out a copy for you, though." He swiveled his chair to the computer on his desk and tapped in a command. A moment later the printer across the room whirred. He got up to retrieve the pages, and stopped at his desk for another sheaf of papers, setting both on her desk. "I wanted your thoughts on the interview with Juarez's ex-girlfriend."

He perched on the corner of her desk, and leaned forward to flip through some pages until he found the one he wanted. "When you talked about this guy practicing or role-playing with wives or girlfriends . . . is this what you were talking about?"

Abbie seized on the subject gratefully. Anything to tear her gaze away from the sight of that black-clad muscled thigh situated too close to her. Scanning the papers rapidly, she said slowly, "It could be. Especially for someone who was just starting to enact his fantasies, before they'd gotten very detailed. How long were they seeing each other?"

"Rivera says just a matter of weeks."

She nodded. "It's possible he would have gotten bolder with her . . . demanded more, if they'd stayed together longer. Of course," she added wryly, "this could just be someone with a master-slave fetish. It's certainly not uncommon."

"So your answer is . . . yes? But maybe no?"

She grinned at his wry tone. "Exactly."

"Very helpful." He straightened, but didn't move away. "And about as definitive as the rest of the leads in this case. Cantrell and McElroy did come up with a few names when they talked to prostitutes about guys who roughed them up. We're following up on those. All we could charge Juarez with at this time was assault and possession, and he made bail this afternoon. I've got guys on him around the clock, though." He stopped, but she didn't respond. "Go ahead and say it."

"I didn't say anything."

"I know. And very loudly, too. You still don't think it's him."

"I think," she said carefully, "that forming opinions before looking at every lead thoroughly can blind us to—"

"Bull. You don't think it's him. But we have every reason to focus on him."

"Yes." Because it put a measure of distance between them, she leaned back in her chair. "Juarez is a valuable lead in this case, whether he's the perpetrator or not." Ryne hadn't said where he was going. Given his dress, she'd guess he had a hot date, and the thought had her stomach clenching.

"Right." He seemed to have forgotten all about having to leave. "Because of the positive blood match in his vehicle."

She nodded. "His SUV was used in the commission of a rape, and regardless of his direct involvement, that makes him one more intersection. We've been concentrating on figuring out how the victims came to the perp's attention. Now we have one more person to consider. If Juarez isn't our UNSUB . . . how did *he* come to the perp's attention?"

"Whether he's the perp or another victim, we'll pull on the threads of his life and see where they lead us." He nodded toward the update he'd printed out. "What the detectives have gotten so far is there. They've talked to his neighbors, his cellmates, and all his relatives around here . . . tomorrow they'll be hitting his workplaces and hangouts."

She considered telling him about the half-formed theory she'd come up with today, decided against it. She wanted to finish researching it, to get all her facts together to support her case. That's what had brought her back to headquarters tonight, to use the databases here.

With another look at his watch, he reluctantly got up. "I have to go. I'm supposed to make an appearance at one of Dixon's BBQs."

The revelation eased something in Abbie. So he wasn't heading off to a date. She had absolutely no reason to feel this lighthearted at the realization. "You sound thrilled."

"Yeah." He crossed to his desk and grabbed his jacket, but didn't put it on. "I hate these kind of things. SueAnne, his wife, is a sweetheart, but Dixon will have the place packed with political types I like to avoid. Only reason I agreed to show up is to get some time alone with him to talk him out of calling a press conference on the case."

The statement had her heart sinking. "A press conference? He shouldn't do that."

"Tell me about it." Ryne's expression was grim. "I know the media coverage has been fierce but the last thing we need is a frenzy. We've got nothing to give them that will be helpful, so we shouldn't give them anything at all."

Abbie wholeheartedly agreed. The media could be invaluable when a description of a suspect or a vehicle was available. Or if a warning needed to be issued to a specific group of people. Neither scenario was the case here. If Dixon was considering using the media just to help bring in tips, a press conference wasn't needed.

Trepidation filled her. Oftentimes the powers that be merely used them as a ploy to calm a panicked public. Or to present a competent face on the investigative effort. Neither would aid the investigation in any measurable way.

"Talk him out of it," she said bluntly.

"Like I said, I'll try. If Brown is there, maybe I can get some help from him." He stopped, looked over at her. "Want to go?"

"Me? Why?" She was surprised at the sudden invitation. Almost as surprised as she was at the pleasure it elicited. After last night, she shouldn't even consider spending more time alone with him. Not that a barbecue presented an opportunity for a reenactment of that kiss, but after it was over . . .

"You could help me talk Dixon out of a press conference." Ryne's smile was lopsided, and all too appealing. "We could double-team him." Her attention was only half on his words. The material of his shirt stretched over the muscled planes of his chest that she had explored last night. Still wanted to touch more intimately. And the strength of that desire was enough to convince her.

She shook her head, with more regret than she'd like to admit. "I'm not dressed for it, and I need to work something out here." The thought of spending time with him, away from the case, away from headquarters was all the more tantalizing for recognizing that it was an incredibly bad idea.

He still hadn't moved, as if reluctant to leave. Because his smoldering gaze was too difficult to return, she picked up a pencil from her desk, worried it with her fingers. "I'd appreciate any insights on getting Ashley Hornby to talk to me," she finally blurted out, compelled to fill the silence that stretched between them. "I haven't been able to get her to answer her phone or her door, although her neighbor assures me she's home."

She'd succeeded in distracting him. His face lost the intent expression he'd been regarding her with, a familiar professional mask shifting back into place. And even as she felt a measure of relief, something deep inside her mourned the change. "I'm not sure if she's even ambulatory yet. The perp did a lot of damage with that hammer. But I never got more than that first interview from her myself."

"Maybe I'll drop by again tonight," she said, cocking her head to look at the watch on Ryne's wrist. An interview with

Hornby could round out the theory she was still formulating, or shatter it completely. One way or another, she felt an increasing urgency to discover which. "I couldn't find any contact information for next of kin in the case file."

"She's got a sister who's traveling in Africa. While Hornby was hospitalized, we sent word through the church that's sponsoring her mission trip, but it's hard to know when the message will catch up with her."

Abbie nodded, already planning to work on any friends the woman had who might help her convince the woman to cooperate. It was unusual for a victim to withdraw completely from the investigation, but not unprecedented. If nothing else, Abbie wanted to make sure the woman's mental health needs were being taken care of. Remaining alone and isolated after such a trauma wasn't in Ashley's best emotional interests, even if it felt like it in the short term.

"So." Ryne took one last look at his watch. "I really have to go." He sounded about as enthusiastic as if he were heading to a funeral. "I'll see you tomorrow."

She nodded. "If you can corner him alone long enough, give Dixon your best shot."

"Oh, I'll corner him." Ryne's smile was grim as he picked up his coat. He gave her one last long look before lifting a hand and moving away. "Don't work too late."

He'd taken only a few steps before he hesitated, then turned back to her. "Listen, about last night . . ."

Panic sprinted up her spine. It took every bit of courage she could muster to meet his gaze and say carelessly, "Forget it. Never happened." An expression flashed across his face, too quick to be identified. Anger? Frustration?

"Oh, it happened," he retorted, his tone silky. "And I'm having a helluva time forgetting about it."

He turned then and wended his way through the sea of desks without looking back. Which was just as well, since Abbie would have hated to be caught with her jaw open, watching those lean hips walk away.

Once he was out of sight, she leaned back in her chair bonelessly, released a shuddering breath. She'd thought he'd be relieved. By treating the matter casually, she'd given him an out. Given both of them one. But he hadn't acted relieved. His admission had blindsided her.

I'm having a helluva time forgetting about it.

Maybe she should be gratified that he'd been as affected by that kiss as she had. Certainly she shouldn't be feeling this blank terror as she contemplated getting involved with a man who didn't meet any of her usual criteria.

Ryne wasn't safe. He wasn't easily controlled. And he wouldn't be effortlessly dismissed. But realizing that didn't lessen his appeal. Just the opposite.

Resolutely, she forced her attention back to the report he'd printed out for her. But after she attempted to read the first page three times, she muttered a curse and stood, stuffing it in her case folder to look it over when she got home.

She walked to the computer in the corner of the office and sat down in front of it, punching in the password Ryne had given her to allow her access to the police databases. There had never been a man alive who could distract her from a case, and Ryne Robel wouldn't be any different, no matter how well the man could kiss.

Within twenty minutes she was so deeply engrossed in her research that thoughts of Ryne were relegated to a distant part of her mind. Not banished. That task seemed beyond her. But once again the case was uppermost. And Abbie knew she was going to have to be satisfied with that.

————

When people made it this easy, they sucked the pleasure right out of it.

The tipsy man stumbled out the side door of the bar into the alley, leaned against the wall of the building. Long seconds passed, but no one came to join him. He fumbled in his pockets, then a lighter flared. He'd come out for a smoke. Unfortunate for him.

"Please. Could you help me?" The voice was just right. Weak. Timid. Not the kind to cause alarm.

The man started, looking around. "Wha—? Oh." Peered through the darkness. "Sorry, dearie. Didn't see you there."

"I had the same idea as you." The rueful tone was masterful. "Came out for a ciggie and tripped over something in the alley. I may have broken my ankle. Do you think you could help me up?"

The man had already tossed his cigarette and was teetering to the rescue in his platform shoes. *Platforms. Where did people find that stuff?*

"Oh, my heavens! Are you in dreadful pain? Do you think you'll be able to walk?"

"Maybe. If you put your arm around me and lift . . ."

"Put your hand on my shoulder." The smoker giggled breathlessly. "We'll be a pair. I can barely walk my—" His words were cut short by the arm around his throat, holding the chloroform-soaked handkerchief to his face.

He put up a struggle. That got the juices flowing. The man spun around, clawing wildly at the handkerchief. But all too soon his struggles faded. His body went limp.

Simple enough to finish it then. To drag the body deeper into the alley. Drop it long enough to open the trunk of the car, then pause, just for a moment. There was something dramatic about the smoker's pose, his arms flung out theatrically.

Impulse had one booted foot lifting, to be brought down sharply on the man's outstretched palm. The resulting snap and crackle sounded like dry leaves crunching underfoot. There were twenty-seven bones in the human hand. Another grind of the heel ensured that every last one was broken.

Snap, crackle pop. Almost like the breakfast cereal.

The thought summoned a smile but too much time had been wasted. A sense of urgency began to grow. The man's body was heaved into the trunk, and the lid shut.

The sound of the car engine sliced through the darkness but there was no one in the vicinity to notice. The man would be delivered alive, although slightly damaged. A small enough favor in exchange for the supply of drugs. Then a four-hour drive to catch the red-eye flight back to Savannah and finalize the next selection.

Although truthfully, the choice had already been made.

Laura Bradford.

So beautiful. And so deserving of something extra special, arranged just for her.

Chapter 10

The task force morning briefing was already in progress when Abbie slipped into the room. Commander Dixon had kept her cooling her heels in his outer office for a half hour prior to their ten-minute meeting. Although he didn't have time to read her updated profile then, he'd promised to do so by the end of the day.

She was much more anxious to get Ryne's take on it. But that would have to wait until this meeting was over.

"So that's it on the newest ViCAP update. I'll narrow down these hits to any that sound remotely like our guy and check them out." Ryne looked at a uniformed officer standing near the back of the room. "Bolen, anything on the surveillance of Juarez?"

"He never left the apartment on my watch, Detective. Nobody in. Nobody out."

Ryne frowned. "So that means no one has seen him since we kicked him loose and he went home?" He glanced at Holmes. "Isaac, did you check with his workplaces?"

The man's nod sent his droopy jowls jiggling. "He hasn't gone to work since. Calls in daily claiming to be sick."

"I'd feel a lot better if we had a visual." Ryne looked at the officer standing next to Bolen. "Sackett, when you relieve Landis this morning, I want you to go to Juarez's door. We need to be positive he's really in there scamming sick leave."

The man nodded and Ryne went on, "Isaac, let's keep working that list of Juarez's relatives and known acquaintances. I want to know this guy inside and out by the end of the day. Who does he come into contact with? Who does he talk to? Wayne and Nick." His attention shifted to the next two men. "What have you got on the prostitute interviews?"

"Well, Wayne here got a bad case of the clap." The only men in the room who didn't show appreciation for McElroy's humor were Ryne and Cantrell. "But it looks like a dead end. Plenty of sickos out there, but no previously unreported assaults or anything like we're looking at." Nick gave Abbie an insincere smile. "Sorry, Tinkerbell. Guess you're batting zero."

"I'd still like to see your notes, particularly for any professionals involved in S and M." When Nick didn't answer, she added, "Something might jump out for me that didn't for you."

McElroy shrugged. "Sure. Whatever. Robel has the copy."

"What about the rock found in Juarez's shoes?"

Cantrell answered Abbie's question. "You mean the shoes that were in his closet, but that he claims aren't his? It matches the rock at Billings's place."

"And so do the particles in the vehicle," Ryne noted.

Cantrell went on, "Lab identified it, and so far we've got it being sold at a dozen places in the vicinity. Discount and home improvement stores, nurseries, landscaping outfits . . . probably find it in half the yards in Savannah."

Ryne said, "Cantrell and McElroy, see if you can get a lead on the shoes themselves. Where are they sold around here, can they ID the customer who bought them . . ."

"That's a long shot," murmured Cantrell.

"Yeah. And so's your next assignment. Research the manufacturer of that syringe we found. Who are their clients, where are those syringes available around here? You know the drill."

"Shit," muttered McElroy.

"That's a succinct and accurate summation of what we've got on this guy so far, Nick." Ryne's voice was sharp. "We have a few prints of Billings's from the vehicle, plenty of Juarez's, and some others from the interior and on the plates. We're still running them all through IAFIS and our state and local databases. Who wants to bet that we're going to get lucky with that?" The room was silent. Ryne gave a grim smile. "Exactly. So we follow every possible lead, long shot or not. I don't know about you, but I don't particularly want to stand around and wait until the next rape, hoping he'll leave us his calling card."

Those words struck a chord with Abbie. She waited until Captain Brown had finished a quiet conversation with Ryne, before he followed the rest of the men out of the room. She strolled to the front table. "You know, maybe he already did. Leave a calling card, that is."

Ryne didn't look up from the papers he was replacing in file folders. "You have a gift for telling me exactly what I don't want to hear, you know that?" He finished putting the papers away and glanced up at her, a wry smile on his face. "You're talking about the use of Juarez's vehicle, right?"

Abbie nodded. "If the evidence doesn't point to Juarez as the rapist . . ."

"We don't have all the evidence yet . . ."

"Then we know why those plates were left on his Bronco, even after the rape was completed," Abbie continued, propping a hip on the corner of the table. "The perp couldn't count on the fact that Ethel Krebbs would identify the vehicle."

"But with stolen plates on it, he upped the likelihood that the police would trace it eventually. And there it'd be, all gift-wrapped for us with blood traces from the victim still inside." He braced both hands on the table to survey her. "You have a devious mind."

"And you've already thought of this yourself." Abbie was half disappointed, half pleased that their thoughts had taken a similar path.

"I have a devious mind, too. So you're the profiler. What kind of guy would go to those lengths?"

The reminder shouldn't have been necessary. She *was* the profiler on the case. A highly skilled investigator. Which didn't explain why Ryne's proximity had her throat drying, her breathing uneven. Irritated with herself, she straightened, putting a bit more distance between them. "He's smart. His goal isn't necessarily to engage the police, but a distraction . . . he's careful enough to plan for that."

"Yeah. We have to consider the possibility anyway. None of the prints on the plates match Juarez. So it was no surprise that we found none at all on the protective needle tip or on the empty syringe barrel." He said nothing more, just looked at her for long enough to make her jumpy. "You should have come with me to Dixon's last night."

The sudden change of topics took her off guard. "You had a good time?"

He grinned. "No, it sucked. Never seen so many bloated egos in one place."

His words surprised a smile from her. "You're right. That does sound like something I'd enjoy." The thought struck her that his charm, when he chose to use it, was even more formidable than the grim sardonic persona he'd worn the first day they'd met. And infinitely more attractive.

Ryne reached back to hook a chair with his foot and dragged it close enough to sink into. "I managed a few minutes alone with Dixon. The captain and I convinced him that a press conference would do more harm than good at this point."

She shared the relief that sounded in his voice. "Good. See? You didn't need me after all."

His gaze went molten. "I wouldn't say that."

His low smoky tone wiped her mind blank. She wasn't good at this. She didn't have experience with the sexual banter that was part of the male-female dating ritual. And the men she'd chosen to get involved with must have been just as inept as she. There was undoubtedly a cause-and-effect relationship there, but she didn't bother to follow it. At the moment, she could focus on nothing but Ryne.

He was wearing a muted striped jacket she'd seen him in before, with a gray shirt, dark trousers. Yet it was too easy to picture him again in his apparel from the gym, with his muscled arms and legs bare. Maybe because that image had taken up permanent residence in the back of her mind, choosing the most inconvenient times to reappear, unsummoned.

"What's that?"

She followed the direction of his gaze and realized with a start that she was mangling the file folder from gripping it so tightly. "Oh. It's yours, actually." Thrusting it at him, she gratefully seized on the reminder of work. "I've updated the profile on the rapist. I think I know how he's been selecting his victims."

The interest in his expression morphed abruptly from personal to professional. The swiftness of the change made her a little envious. And curiously relieved.

"You do? You should have said something. You could have shared it with the team."

"I wanted to talk to you first." Nerves demanded an outlet, so she turned to pace. "I stopped to see Dixon first. Gave him a copy. There's an extra copy there to share with Captain Brown. I worked on this most of the night. At first I thought it was too far-fetched, but there are just too many coincidences."

"And they are?"

She turned to face him again. "I didn't see it at first. He doesn't seem to be choosing them based on a certain type. He isn't finding them in the same sort of occupation or location, aside from the city itself." As she warmed up to the topic, she felt surer. But she knew Ryne was going to be tougher to convince. "We've looked at the victims as a group, trying to find patterns. But it's when I started to really focus on each of them as individuals that it struck me."

"Abbie." She stopped abruptly at his gentle interruption. "What are we talking about here?"

She drew a deep breath, met his gaze steadily. "I think he's choosing women who have some deep-seated fear or phobia. And then I think he's carrying out the rape in a fashion designed to maximize their suffering."

He was silent a moment. Two. "Okay. Most women have a natural fear of being assaulted . . ."

"No, it's more than that." She crossed the room to take the file folder out of his hand. Flipping it open, she extracted the top sheet. "Look at this. He went to a great deal of effort to dump Barbara Billings in the sound. Why? What's the point? It's an unnecessary risk of exposure for him. He had ulterior motives."

Ryne frowned. "Yeah, he did. She had eighty-seven knife wounds on her body. Eighty-seven. Most were shallow enough to make sure she didn't bleed out, but you know what saltwater feels like on an open wound? He's a sadist. You've said it yourself. He just wanted to prolong the torture."

"Exactly." She nodded. "He wants to prolong the torture, but even beyond the time she'd be rescued from the water. He wants her to suffer all her life." At his uncomprehending look, her voice grew urgent. "She's terrified of water, Ryne. She watched her father drown when she was seven. She nearly drowned herself. She hasn't so much as gone swimming in a wading pool ever since."

"An unfortunate coincidence. But what you're suggesting doesn't make sense."

"It makes perfect sense. She's been reduced to sponge baths since the rape, did you know that? Her mother said just the sound of water running in the tub gives Barbara severe panic attacks."

He was wearing that impassive expression that she remembered all too well. But she wasn't going to let him close her out. Riffling through the pages in the folder, she withdrew another. "And Tracy Sommers. She's suffered from claustrophobia all her life. Could barely manage elevators." She shoved the paper at him, but he didn't take it. "The perp placed a plastic bag over her head and repeatedly suffocated, then revived her. Now she can't work. She can't force herself to get in a car, an elevator, a stairwell . . . I'm telling you, Ryne, this is the link."

"It can't be." He shoved back from his chair and rose. "He's picking them because they fit some criteria of his, that's what you said. Some element that intensifies his own sexual arousal. It was in your first profile. At least that made sense."

She ignored the insult. "It still fits. Except the criteria that arouses him is the opportunity to inflict suffering that doesn't stop. It doesn't end when the assault is over." Hearing it out loud, after mulling it over since yesterday, just cemented her certainty. "He thinks he's suffered," she said, half to herself. "He thinks he's been traumatized in a way that can never, ever be healed." Perhaps it took someone with personal experience of that kind of torment, who had been the recipient of that purposeful infliction of emotional pain, to recognize its presence in another.

"And now he's found a way to make other people suffer profoundly. Maybe for the rest of their lives. His satisfaction doesn't end when the assault is over because he ensures his victims long-term agony. And long-term pleasure for himself, because of it."

"Bullshit."

Shocked, she could only stare at him. Ryne had the grace to look embarrassed, but his next words were uttered no less emphatically. "I'm sorry. I don't buy it. You're crediting this guy with way more brains than he possesses. You really think Juarez is capable of this much thinking?"

"I don't think it's Juarez," she shot back, furious. The hell with staying objective. If Ryne wanted to close his mind to options, then so could she. "Look at the profile. That's all I'm asking. Richards fits the theory, too. Her mother started entering her in beauty contests when she was four. She was the favorite for the state title. So what'd our guy arrange for her?"

He looked unconvinced. "And Hornby? Give me one good reason the guy worked her over with crocodile clamps and a ball-peen hammer. Did she have an aversion to construction sites?"

She balled her fists at her side to suppress the temptation to throw a punch at his set jaw. The violent urge shocked her. Abbie Phillips didn't lose control. Not anymore.

She shook with the effort, but somehow managed a dispassionate tone. "I don't have enough information on Ashley Hornby to make a guess. Like I said before, she isn't answering her phone, or her doorbell."

"Look." Ryne's voice had gentled. "I realize you've worked hard on this. You've found some coincidences that we didn't, so congratulations on that."

"Fuck you."

His jaw tightened. "I can't say the thought hasn't crossed my mind, but I'm guessing we aren't talking about the same thing."

Trembling with fury, she tossed the sheets toward him, let them float back to land on the folder. "Don't you dare patronize me. I'm right. Do I have hard evidence? No. There isn't going to be any hard evidence to support a theory like this. But the pattern is there, whether you want to close your eyes to it or not. It might not tell us who, but it tells us *why*. And that's more than we had at this time yesterday."

Their gazes did battle for a long minute, neither willing to give an inch. But then the ring of his cell had him looking away, reaching for it. And Abbie used the interruption as an opportunity to regain her equilibrium.

She was more than a little appalled at her loss of composure. In training, Raiker had challenged her at every turn, forcing her to form ironclad arguments to support her theories. She'd had law enforcement officials scoff at her contributions before; had had her skills belittled. It only made her redouble her efforts because it was infinitely sweeter to later be proven correct.

But none of those experiences had elicited this fiery flood of emotion, and it was all too easy to guess why. None of those men had been Ryne.

Her anger turned inward. She didn't know how the man had been allowed to get this close to her. Close enough that his dismissal of her opinion actually hurt. But recognizing the emotion had all her defenses slamming firmly into place.

The greatest human suffering could only be inflicted by those allowed too close. Emotionally. Psychologically. Intellectually. The rapist they were hunting likely had reason to know that.

And so did she.

"Ah, shit."

Reluctantly, Abbie looked at Ryne. He was rubbing the back of his neck, a bleak expression on his face. "Keep the place secured. Don't let anyone else in but CSU and the EMTs. I'm on my way."

Her stomach knotted with dread. Abbie moistened her lips, which had gone inexplicably dry. "Is it . . . has there been another rape?"

"No." He was shoving the cell in his pocket, gathering up his folders from the table with barely restrained violence. "Ashley Hornby has been found dead in her home. Apparent suicide."

––––––––

Ryne immediately recognized the uniform at the door of Hornby's house. Joe Gomez had been one of the officers used to canvass after the first rape, and the one who'd tipped him off earlier. He motioned the man over. "Who's been inside?"

"The next door neighbor, Iris Knudson, called it in." He indicated the older woman behind him sitting on a corner of the couch, staring blankly down at her tightly folded hands in her lap. Ryne hadn't spoken to her after Hornby's rape, but he recalled her statement in the report. She hadn't been home the night of the attack because she'd been visiting her daughter in Biloxi. "Says the victim gave her a key a month ago and she checks in on her every few days. When I got the 9-1-1 call, I recognized Hornby's name as one of yours, so I contacted you."

Ryne nodded his thanks, and the man went on, "Other

than CSU, no one else has been here except for the EMTs. They pronounced her and now they're waiting for CSU to finish up. ME is on his way."

Two EMTs were leaning against a wall of the living room, talking in low voices. Recognizing the CSU tech in the kitchen bent over the body with a camera, Ryne walked over to him. "Pat. You have some ideas?"

"I'm full of ideas, Robel." The stooped, balding man straightened and set the latest Kodak photo on the counter. "Like my property taxes are too high, and no fault divorce is a femi-Nazi conspiracy to take over the world by putting all males in the poor house. No one ever asks me, though." He shook his head sadly and, picking up a felt tip marker, labeled the picture, then dropped it in an evidence bag and labeled that. Six other photos were similarly arrayed, each a different angle of the very dead woman at the kitchen table.

"Intriguing. But I'm wondering about cause of death."

The man gestured to the evidence bags next to the photos. Five held empty pill bottles and one an empty glass. "Looks like she swallowed the contents of her medicine cabinet, but we'll have to let the ME make the final call on that. If I had to guess, I'd say she's been dead a couple days."

Ashley Hornby's death hadn't been any easier than the last months of her life. A dart of pity stabbed through Ryne. Her hands were still clutching the arms of her wheelchair, her head slumped forward on her chest. Dried vomit was caked to the front of her bathrobe, pooled in her lap, and speckled the table surface and floor. An overdose of medication would have induced first nausea, then possibly convulsions, before she slipped into a coma. The scene looked clear-cut, but only an autopsy would tell them for sure.

Abbie went over to the pill bottles, reading the prescriptions through the clear plastic bags. "Darvocet for pain, Prozac for depression, Naramig for migraines—that prescription was dated almost a year ago—and regular aspirin and Tylenol. All the prescription bottles have her name on them." She looked at the crime tech. "Did you find a note?"

"I didn't. Patterson and Fowler are searching the other rooms, though."

Abbie extracted a pair of gloves from her purse and put them on. Ryne reached into his pocket to get a pair to do the same. The suicide would be treated as a possible homicide, until proved differently. The fact that Hornby had been one of the rapist's victims cast all sorts of doubts about her death.

"Has anyone checked her answering machine? Her phone?"

Pat Rogowski shook his head in response to Ryne's question, sending his wire-framed glasses farther down his nose. "Not yet."

Abbie went over and pressed the button on the machine, and the recorded messages began to play.

"Okay." Ryne pulled a notebook from his pocket and jotted down notes. "I'll get a request in to pull her LUDs. Cell phone records, too, if we find one."

He headed back into the other room. Gomez was speaking to the elderly woman on the couch. She hadn't moved since Ryne got there. With a slight inclination of his head, Ryne motioned for the man to join him near the front door. Lowering his voice, he said, "What's her story?"

The officer consulted the notebook he'd been writing in. "Says she last checked on Hornby three days ago, about noon. Hornby didn't open the door, but Clemons says that wasn't unusual. She just asked if she needed anything and the victim said no."

"I should have checked on her more often," Clemons said, her voice quavering.

Ryne's attention shifted to the woman across the room. There was obviously nothing wrong with her hearing, despite her age. He approached her and asked, "How often did you see or speak with her, ma'am?"

"A couple times a week, since the . . . the incident." The woman obviously couldn't bring herself to say the word *rape*. She was in her early to mid seventies, he estimated. Heavily applied makeup collected in the tiny facial wrinkles of a lifetime smoker. "Ashley was never an outgoing type. Oh, she was pleasant enough," she hastened to say, as if not wanting to speak ill of the dead. "But she wasn't one to neighbor. After she returned from the hospital, she wouldn't see anyone. But every once in a while she'd let me come in to do something for her. I'd tidy up, dust, or fetch things."

"How often did she leave the apartment?"

"Oh, she hadn't left for . . ." Clemons pursed her lips. "At least three weeks. Said she wasn't going to physical therapy anymore. That it was a waste of time. I know because someone from the hospital came to talk to her about it and Ashley wouldn't let her in either. Not that I was listening, you understand. But I was watering my tomatoes and I couldn't help overhearing."

Ryne was willing to bet she "overheard" quite a bit that went on with her neighbors.

"She was just so alone." Her voice broke on the last word, and she dabbed at her tears with a wadded-up Kleenex in her hand, leaving a dark smear of mascara under one eye. "She'd moved here this year after a nasty divorce. I'm not sure she even had any friends to speak of."

"I'm sure she appreciated everything you did for her, ma'am."

She nodded miserably. Ryne spied Abbie talking to another tech, so he left the woman to Gomez and headed over there.

"Look for any written correspondence she may have received," Abbie was telling him. "Let's check her trash cans. Find out when they were last emptied."

When the other man moved away, Ryne murmured, "Are you thinking the perp reached out somehow? Would he do that?"

"He hasn't contacted any of the other victims." She'd been as angry as he'd ever seen her less than an hour ago, but there was no trace of that emotion in her tone, or in her expression. She was totally dispassionate. And he found he much preferred her fury to the remote air she now wore. "It's always possible, but I'd be surprised if he contacted Ashley."

"Not even to make sure she was suffering?" It was a cheap shot. But even realizing it didn't prevent him from trying to provoke some reaction from her. He'd rather see her gray eyes go stormy again than have them regard him with that flinty stare.

"I think he pretty well assured that already, don't you?" Not waiting for an answer, she went on, "She doesn't have caller ID, but redial shows the last call made from her phone was to a nearby grocery store last week. I called and they confirmed she'd placed an order on Thursday, which was delivered at three p.m. that same afternoon."

"And the messages on the machine?"

She consulted the notebook in her hand. "Aside from the ones I made to her, there were six others. One was a telemarketer. Four were from various hospital personnel—her physical therapist, her doctor, a nurse—all recommending that she continue her therapy. The most recent call was yesterday, from her sister. She'd just finally gotten the message about Ashley's attack and was arranging a flight here. She'll be in by the end of the week."

Yesterday. And there had been no one to hear the message. From the pictures he'd seen, he'd concur with the tech's assessment. Ashley Hornby had already been dead by then.

"I'll get a warrant to follow up on the medical end. I want to talk to everyone from the hospital who had contact with her to see what we can learn about her mental state."

Abbie nodded. "Her sister might get here soon enough to help out with that. As next of kin, she could grant us permission."

She turned away to head back to the kitchen before he could say anything else. Which was just as well, because at the rate he was going today, he'd soon need to have his foot surgically removed from his mouth.

After taking a couple of steps, she halted. "Do we have any idea what used to be on those shelves? Or on the walls?" She pointed to the bookcase in the living room.

The shelves were jammed with books and CDs. In front of them were set the sort of knickknacks women seemed compelled to buy. Gaze narrowing, he noted the empty spaces she was indicating between the statues and vases, before his gaze traveled to the wall next to the bookcase. There were several framed posters of what might be Broadway plays. He'd be no expert on that. But there were several empty nails on the wall as well.

"I did that. The last time she let me inside."

Ryne looked at Clemons. "What did you do exactly?"

"Ashley had me get a box from the bedroom and put a bunch of things away for her. Said she couldn't bear to look at them anymore. I put the box in the spare bedroom closet."

Turning on his heel, Ryne followed Abbie into the smaller of the two bedrooms. She already had the closet open and was on all fours, pulling out a good-sized box that had been shoved to the back of it. He squatted down next to her. "What do we have?"

Silently, Abbie drew one object after another out of the carton and handed them to him. Plaques. Medals. He read the engraving on one and frowned. "Princess Grace Award. What's that?"

She put a framed photo in his hands in answer. He recognized a younger Ashley Hornby in the image, dressed in one of those frilly things dancers wore. The photographer had caught her in a gravity-defying leap.

"She was a ballerina." Abbie spread the rest of the photos out on the floor next to them. "Or at least she had been. And judging from the awards, she was good." She looked up at him now, and this time her face wasn't expressionless. Bleakness had settled in her eyes. "An award-winning dancer reduced to a wheelchair. I think the UNSUB picked a great way to make her suffer, don't you?"

Chapter 11

"How did Dixon learn of Hornby's suicide so fast?"

Abbie and Ryne were heading up the stairs to Dixon's office. They'd been ordered—there was no other word for it—to appear in the man's office by two. And given Ryne's expression during the course of the terse cell phone conversation with his superior, it hadn't been a pleasant exchange.

"Who knows? But when he called, he'd already been contacted by the *Savannah Morning News* and WTOC."

Given the press this case had gotten, Abbie shouldn't have been surprised the news had broken so quickly. Some enterprising reporter had been monitoring the scanner, probably, and followed the emergency personnel to the home. Once its occupant had been identified, it was only a matter of time before the media would be alerted.

She slid Ryne a sidelong glance. "I take it Dixon is . . . agitated."

He gave her a grim smile, leaned to open the door to the man's outer office. "I'll let you judge that for yourself. Don't know why he felt the need to have you here, though. I'm the one he wants a piece of."

"Detective." The attractive middle-aged woman behind the desk looked relieved at their appearance. "Commander Dixon has checked twice to see if you've arrived. You're to go right in."

Abbie raised a brow. She'd never been in the office when she hadn't been kept waiting. Her stomach muscles tightened as she followed Ryne through the next door, into the inner office.

Dixon was standing before the bank of windows, arms clasped behind his back. Fingers of sunlight stretched through the blinds to gild his hair an even brighter shade of gold. Abbie had the cynical thought that the pose was a photo-op in waiting. Although their meetings had all been cordial, she was more familiar than she'd like with his type. He was an inch or so shorter than Ryne, a bit slighter in build, but any physical similarities stopped there. He lacked the detective's outer toughness; he was more bureaucratic spin machine than cop.

Which only meant he presented a very different kind of danger.

The commander turned at their entrance, a somber expression on his face. "Ms. Phillips. Detective Robel. Thank you for coming so promptly. I know you both can appreciate how this suicide complicates an already complex investigation."

"Right. It was pretty inconsiderate of Hornby," Ryne replied laconically. Abbie wondered if she was the only one aware of his veiled sarcasm. Dixon seemed oblivious.

"Exactly. But as I mentioned on the phone, if you had kept up regular personal contact with her, perhaps this could have been prevented."

The unwarranted accusation had Abbie springing to his defense. "Ashley Hornby's despondence is most likely related to the assault and the lack of a support system around her."

Dixon nodded. "Just as I—"

Abbie went on, "I'd tried to contact her numerous times in the last few days myself with no success. It appears that she'd cut off contact with her neighbor, with her doctor and physical therapist . . . short of breaking into her house and forcing a conversation, I'm not sure what else you could expect of Detective Robel."

With a wave of his hand, Dixon dismissed her words. "We'll never know, will we? Now we're left with a situation, one that has to be handled in a proactive manner. I've contained the media up to now with press releases, but the mayor and the chief feel—and I agree—that today's discovery calls for a different approach."

A curious stillness came over Ryne. "You can't believe that's a good idea."

Lost, Abbie looked from one man to another. There was an unspoken message passing between the two. The air in the room grew charged.

"You just assured the captain and me last night that you could put them off." Ryne fairly bit off the words, his fingers curling into fists. "Hornby's suicide is tragic, but we have no reason to believe it will change the scope of the investigation. Involving the media at this point will serve no useful purpose, and might even hinder us."

Dixon took two steps to his desk, and braced his hands on it. His voice hardened. "Everything has changed, don't you get that? I know you like to sneer at the public relations responsibilities of my job, but I have enough experience to know we're about to reach a critical juncture here. If we don't give the media something substantive, they're going to start crucifying us in the press. And then, in short order, the public is going to be in a panic."

He was actually considering a press conference. Abbie's frustration matched Ryne's. "I suspect this perp gets gratification from media attention. Why give him what he wants when there's no benefit to us?"

The commander pinned her with a hard look. "Can you say with any certainty that the attention will cause him to escalate?"

She hesitated, shot a look at Ryne. He was regarding his superior with a carefully blank expression. "No," she admitted with reluctance. "He doesn't have a set pattern, but he acts fairly quickly. I think he gathers several prospective targets that meet his criteria, then singles one out and begins stalking her to learn her habits."

With a humorless smile, Dixon said, "Well, then we have nothing to lose on that end. According to the profile you gave me this morning, you believe he's already on the hunt for his next victim."

That drew Ryne's attention. His gaze nearly blistered her, but she answered honestly, "I think he's selected her, yes."

Slapping his hands on the desktop, Dixon straightened. "Even more reason to alert the public then. As a safety precaution. God knows we've got nothing of substance to give them. No description of the perp or vehicle . . ." He stopped, directed a look at Ryne. "Unless Juarez is looking good for the rapes."

"We have no reason to eliminate him as a suspect."

He couldn't have said any more clearly that he still put no stock in the theory she'd run past him this morning. His skepticism still stung, but it wouldn't be allowed to affect the way she did her job. It couldn't be.

"We'll have to tread carefully there," mused Dixon, rubbing his chin. He was the picture of a man grappling with a weighty decision. Abbie wondered cynically if he was already practicing for the press conference. Every move he made seemed rehearsed, like an actor remaining in character. "If we say we have a suspect and then there's another rape, we risk looking incompetent. But we have to provide assurance that the investigation is making progress."

"The investigation *is* making progress." The snap in Ryne's voice was barely discernible. "But giving away too much will impede it. Nothing can be said about the rapist's signature—the drug, the torture. Leave us something to use in any suspect interviews."

Dixon's expression had gone deadly. The palpable antagonism between the two momentarily distracted Abbie from her concern over the publicity. There was history here, something that went beyond the professional to personal. She was finding it difficult to reconcile the man who had spoken so glowingly of Ryne's abilities when she first arrived to the one who was skewering him now.

"Don't forget, I'm still a cop, Robel."

"Sometimes I need to be reminded."

For an instant Abbie thought the commander would lose his careful poise. His nostrils flared, and patches of scarlet painted his cheekbones. But with a quick glance toward her, he visibly reined in his temper. Drawing his chair out from his desk, he sank into it.

"We're done here. Press conference is in fifteen minutes. See Jean in the outer office for details. You have time to get your jacket, Robel." The smile he directed at Abbie didn't reach his eyes. "There's time for you to freshen up, although I can't say I can find room for improvement."

Ryne's expression mirrored her own wariness. "Us? Why do we need to be there?"

"Didn't I mention that?" Dixon picked up a slim gold pen and threaded it through his fingers. "You two are the face of the investigation. You'll be on camera, by my side."

———

". . . and although we are deeply saddened by the death of Ms. Hornby, we cannot allow ourselves to be distracted from the hunt for the serial offender who assaulted her. This department is sparing no expense toward that end. We have nearly forty officers devoted to the case and they are pursuing each and every lead with all due diligence."

Just stick to the sound bite, Abbie thought. If Dixon didn't stray from generalities, he at least would do no damage to the case. She suppressed the urge to steal a look at Ryne, standing between her and Dixon. Captain Brown flanked the commander's other side. The simmering fury that had been seething in Ryne when they'd left Dixon's office probably looked good on camera. It could be mistaken for steely determination. She had less confidence in her own demeanor, which she was fighting to keep carefully expressionless.

"Is it true you have a suspect?" a reporter from the crowd called out.

"I'll let Detective Robel respond to that one."

Abbie hoped her shock didn't show. Dixon had never indicated that either of them would be speaking. Ryne's face when he took over at the microphone was grim.

"We have an individual of interest," he said. Ignoring the excited buzz created by his words, he went on, "But everyone is a suspect until they're eliminated. There is no call for public alarm, but basic safety precautions are always a good idea. Keep the entrances of the home well lit. Landscaping around the house should be low enough that it doesn't offer concealment to an intruder. Dead bolts should be installed on all doors, and lower-level windows outfitted with tamper-proof locks or grills. Look out for your neighbors' homes. Report any suspicious people or vehicles in the neighborhood. In short, be alert."

He stepped away from the mike as another journalist shouted, "Commander, how do you answer the criticism that your department hasn't made an arrest yet?"

Abbie held her breath. Even on their short acquaintance, she knew that type of question was sure to provoke a reaction from Dixon. While the conference had maintained an informational style, it was controlled. But there was usually nothing to be gained in taking questions.

"I can assure you that no one familiar with the case would level such a criticism." For all his faults, Dixon's composure was flawless when dealing with the press. "I happen to know the man-hours going into this investigation, and the overtime being put in by my lead detective to bring this offender to justice. We've put unprecedented resources toward that end, including hiring a private expert."

Abbie's bones turned to ice as the man raised a hand to indicate her before continuing, "Abbie Phillips is an expert in criminal profiling, and with her help we have a detailed picture of the sort of individual who would perpetuate such crimes. We will, of course, release the profile she's prepared to the media."

The clamor of voices intensified, but Abbie was oblivious to it. The blood was pounding in her ears, and nausea churned in her stomach.

And the hell of it was, she couldn't be sure whether the sensations were due to Dixon's unexpected ambush, or the cold hard condemnation she read in Ryne's eyes.

———————

It was the sort of place Dixon would pick, Ryne thought, as he wended his way through the restaurant bar to the table in the back where the commander sat. Lots of gleaming oak and brass, live plants, and polished mirrors. Nothing like the dives he'd frequented when drinking had been his number one pastime.

It'd been eighteen months since he'd taken a drink or stepped foot in a bar. But he'd choose the smoky haze, scratched counters, and cracked leather stools anytime over a yuppie spot like this. At least those places had been free of pretense. They hadn't pretended to attract anything but serious drinkers and quiet desperation. No wonder he'd felt so at home there.

He drew up to the table, pulled out a chair. "Derek," he said, by way of greeting. Outside the job they were still on a first-name basis, but they were no longer friends, if they'd ever been.

Which was why he was sure there was a helluva lot more to Dixon's suggestion for this meeting, regardless of the man's excuse to get him here.

Dixon raised a finger to summon the waitress, who responded quickly. Ryne's mouth twisted. Women had always responded to Derek. And his response to them was just as predictable. "Bring me a draft of Premium Light," he told her, flashing his toothpaste ad smile. "And two fingers of Jim Beam for my friend, straight up."

"I don't want that."

"Bring it." Dixon shooed the woman away and Ryne knew she'd do the man's bidding. Just like he knew the order was a way to slice at him.

"Come here often?" Ryne let his gaze drift around the large area. "I'll bet SueAnne likes it." With its thick oak columns and tall-backed booths, the place was meant for privacy. He'd wager his monthly paycheck that SueAnne Dixon didn't even know it existed.

"Try not to be a prick, Ryne." There was no heat in Derek's words. "You and I have both made choices others might not agree with."

Ryne gave a cynical smile. "As long as we're on that topic, I've got something for you to add to the list. Releasing that profile was a publicity stunt, nothing more. It'll end up obstructing our investigation rather than helping it."

"You can't be certain of that." Dixon fell silent as the waitress returned with their order. He gave her a large bill and a phony smile to send her on her way before returning his attention to Ryne. "At any rate, it was a calculated risk. What better way to counter criticism of the department than to exhibit proof of our expertise? The profile doesn't compromise any leads you're pursuing, but it puts a modern forensic face on the investigation. The public will eat it up."

Ryne shook his head. It was useless to argue with a man who thought in terms of sound bites and public image. And too late, in any case. The damage was already done. "If the purpose of this meeting is just to convince me of the purity of your motives, it's duly noted. We'll have to agree to disagree."

For the first time Derek looked slightly uncomfortable. He picked up the glass of beer and took a long drink before answering. "No, I have something else to discuss with you. Something that will require your utmost discretion."

Ryne leaned back in his chair, instantly wary. If the man intended to use him, or this case, to mislead his wife again, it was time to tell him to go to hell. "And that is?"

Dixon took another swallow of beer, as if for fortification. "It came to my attention that there might be another victim out there. One who hasn't come forward. One who has never been questioned by your task force."

Stunned, Ryne could only stare at the man. An unreported rape victim? Was it possible? He knew the statistics, of course. It was estimated that less than forty percent of all rapes and sexual assaults were ever reported to law enforcement. But given the media coverage surrounding this investigation, it was hard to imagine a victim remaining silent.

Shoving his glass aside, he folded his arms on the table and leaned forward. "Who? When?"

"Her name is Karen Larsen." Derek reached into his trouser pocket and withdrew a small piece of paper, which he handed to Ryne. On it was written the name and two addresses. "The first address is where she lived up until six weeks ago, when it burned down. The second is her current place."

Ryne tried to wrap his mind around the enormity of this development, and failed. "What makes you think she was a victim?"

"I can't be sure. It's your job to check her out." Dixon drained the rest of his beer and held it aloft to capture the waitress's attention. He paused while the waitress delivered his beer, this time not wasting any charm as he handed her a bill.

Ryne was still grappling with the possibilities. "Did she claim to be raped? 'Cuz I checked out all the reports made in the last year, and I didn't find anything else that sounded like our guy."

Dixon looked away. "No. She hasn't mentioned an assault at all. But I happen to know she went to the hospital the next day and had a friend run a discreet tox screen. Turns out it matches the initial hospital tox screen results showing up in all the victims in this case."

"What?" Aware that his voice had raised, Ryne consciously lowered it. "I talked to docs all over this city months ago. None of them had ever seen anything like this compound the perp is using, which is one of the things that convinced me it wasn't just some new mutant party drug. If it were, it would have surfaced in the bar scene, and given its properties, there's no way people wouldn't have ended up in the ER with . . ."

He stopped then, comprehension slamming into him belatedly. "How would you know what her tox screen shows? Do you know her? Did she tell you?" HIPPA laws precluded them getting access to anyone's medical information without consent or a warrant.

Dixon rubbed at the condensation on the glass with his thumb. "Listen, Ryne, this is where your discretion becomes imperative. I have a copy of the tox screen. And my . . . informant tells me that Larsen is starting to experience some posttraumatic stuff. She asked . . . my friend for recommendations for therapists. Counselors who deal with victims of sexual assault."

A dull ache rapped at the base of his skull. Ryne stared at the man, sorting out the spoken from the unspoken message here. Because it was damn certain that what Dixon *wasn't* saying was far more important than what he was.

"And who is this informant?"

Dixon raised his glass for a sip. "That really isn't the issue."

"Of course it is. If I can't verify the character of the informant, the legitimacy of the information is in question, you know that."

"I can vouch for the character of the informant," the other man snapped. "And you'll have the damn copy of the tox screen on your desk in the morning."

Cynicism traced through him as all the pieces clicked into place. "And I'm supposed to trust you to be completely objective about this . . . person's trustworthiness, right?"

Dixon bared his teeth. "You're enjoying this, aren't you? Okay, my informant is the woman I've been banging for the last few months, happy? She knows this Larsen, actually ran the test for her, which could get her in trouble, since it wasn't on the books. She made a copy of the tox screen and gave it to me."

"You're fucking unbelievable." A man at a nearby table turned to look at them, but Ryne ignored him. It was a new low for Dixon, but he shouldn't be surprised. He was, however, entitled to be royally pissed. "You told your girlfriend about the drug used in the course of the rapes? The most important piece of this asshole's MO—the information we're keeping out of the press—that qualifies as pillow talk for you?"

Dixon had the grace to look discomfited. "It's not like

that. Paula . . . the woman I'm . . . seeing is the lab supervisor at St. Joseph/Candler. She documented the results from two of the other victims treated there. Of course when she saw another similar screen, she told me."

It was Ryne's nature to be suspicious. Came in handy on the job and it sure as hell helped when dealing with Dixon. "Exactly when did you find out about the tox screen?"

Leaning back in his chair, Dixon checked his watch. "That really isn't pertinent."

"Humor me."

"Three weeks ago. And don't start unloading on me. It was just a few days ago that she let me know about Larsen's PTSD. I decided the similarities bore checking out, so I'm turning it over to you. End of story."

Incredulity fought with anger. Ryne shook his head in disbelief. "And so you decided to play God with this information and keep it to yourself until now. To hell with the fact that another woman got raped in the meantime, right? What was important was keeping your screwing around quiet."

"I still expect that to be kept quiet," the man snapped back. He leaned across the table, his expression grim. "My possession of that tox screen is illegal, but it might be a link to the rapist. That's why I'm turning it over to you." His mouth twisted. "And spare me the holier-than-thou shit. We all have our addictions, don't we? It's hell when they interfere with our work."

The remark hit Ryne in the gut like a well-aimed jab. He sat back, an eerie sense of calm coming over him. He had a feeling that the words were the most sincere ones Dixon had spoken to him since he'd come to Savannah. "Why don't you say what's really on your mind, Derek. You want to talk about Boston? Let's talk."

Dixon dug in his pocket for a bill, and tossed it on the table. Rising, he shrugged into his tailor-made suit jacket. "You know the problem with being the brightest star in the sky, Ryne? All eyes are on you when you burn out and fall to the earth. I saved your career from the trash heap, buddy. How about showing a little gratitude?"

He walked away then, his acid-edged words etching a path through Ryne's tattered conscience. His gaze dropped to the untouched glass before him, but it was the past he was really seeing. Deborah Hanna's vacant eyes. The censure on his captain's face. The too-impassive mask of the department shrink. No one to blame but himself. Nothing to do but find a way to live with it.

Without conscious decision, he reached for the glass. The liquor seared a path down his throat as he downed it in one gulp. Slamming the glass down, he shoved away from the table and strode out of the bar.

Senseless tragedies occurred every day, a sad fact of nature. But those that resulted from a personal failure were the bitterest of all.

———————

A couple hours at the gym hadn't done much to take the edge off Abbie's mood, so she'd given up, showered, and gotten dressed. If five laps and a punishing hour in the ring weren't enough to get her mind off the case, nothing would.

The thought of her empty house was unappealing. Although she wouldn't trade her job, the constant travel and equally impersonal temporary living quarters were its biggest drawbacks. She'd saved a long time to buy a small wooded acreage in Virginia that she'd then spent years stamping with her own personality. She'd slowly begun to fill it with antiques and primitives she'd discovered when she had time to browse the back road shops in a three-state area. The result was a serene, comfortable residence, and the only place she'd ever really felt at home.

She'd long since discovered that one way to make the constant travel easier was to always pack a few favorite special items to give her a sense of home. But those items weren't enough to lure her back to the rented house either, because it would be the charts she'd made that would engross her upon returning. The grids and logs detailing every fact of the case that led to knowing the UNSUB better.

And thoughts of the case would invariably lead back to Ryne.

In an effort to prevent that, she headed for the historic district. An hour spent driving along the streets lined with moss-draped oaks, admiring the intricate ironwork and varied architectural styles, went a long way toward doing what the workout had failed to accomplish. It was difficult to remain self-absorbed in the face of over two centuries of history. A city that had withstood wars, fires, epidemics, and hurricanes with such elegant grace had a way of putting personal turmoil in perspective.

And there was little reason for her turmoil, in any case. Abbie turned on Oglethorpe, the street police headquarters and the Colonial Park Cemetery were located on. She was here for one reason only, and it was time to refocus on that reason, and stop considering the reactions of Ryne Robel. Whether he agreed with her assessment of the rapist or not, she'd done her job on the profile. She was on to something; she could feel it. And she'd follow up tomorrow with renewed questions for the surviving victims and see if she could paint an even clearer picture of the offender they were hunting.

Mind more at ease, she headed for her rental. It had been well over two decades since a man's moods had been allowed to affect her in any appreciable way, and that wasn't going to change now. She wouldn't let it. Ryne had a right to his opinion, but opinion wouldn't decide the course of this case. Evidence would. They were united in their search for the facts in this investigation.

Checking her side mirror, she accelerated and changed lanes. But still the memory of the look in his cold blue eyes had a shiver snaking over her skin. Because in some ways they were farther apart than ever. And the desolation that filled her at the realization was as unfamiliar as it was frightening.

Chapter 12

Dusk had painted long shadows across the small yard by the time Abbie pulled up to her rental. The property wasn't equipped with either garage or carport, so she always parked at the end of the drive close to the back of the lot.

She'd just gotten out of the car when she saw the figure on her back porch. Her reaction was instinctive. In one smooth move she ducked, grabbed the weapon from her ankle holster, then rose, with her Sig in her hand, using the car for cover. The entire sequence took just a few seconds.

But in the next moment recognition slammed into her. Apprehension quickly followed.

"Abbie, love, I know I haven't been good at returning phone calls lately, but don't you think you're overreacting?" Callie Phillips rose from her perch, a careless smile on her face. "What? No hug for the prodigal sister?"

In a distant part of her mind, Abbie was aware of long-held defenses clanging into place. She replaced her weapon and rounded the car, into her sister's outstretched arms.

"Oh my gosh, it's been too long." Callie gave her a

squeeze before holding her away, a critical eye sweeping her. "Ab, you're positively wasting away. Do you eat?"

Sidestepping the question, Abbie countered, "Why didn't you let me know you were in Savannah?"

"I wanted to surprise you." A laugh gurgled out of her as she mimicked Abbie's earlier police stance. "And I did, didn't I? I'm lucky I didn't get a bullet for my efforts."

Forcing a smile, Abbie led the way up the back steps to unlock the door. "I've been targeted by some vandals lately. I guess I reacted before thinking."

But she was thinking now, furiously. Without seeming to, she watched Callie carefully as she regaled Abbie with her latest exploits, a recent trip on a friend's yacht to the Grecian isles that had ended with motor problems, a police raid, and a marriage proposal. Her first impression was that the last four months had been rough ones for her sister.

Callie's blonde bombshell looks were just as striking as ever, but there was a brittle air about her that had been absent the last time they'd seen each other. Was it Abbie's imagination that her sister's voice was just a little manic as she prattled on about boyfriends, breakups, and job prospects? Although she hated herself for it, habit had her forming a mental checklist to tally warning signs that would indicate whether her sister was off her medication.

Was the constant stream of chatter a bit too frenetic? Were her actions overly dramatic, her choice of topics too random? Abbie sent a circumspect glance at her sister's arms, bared by the form-fitting tank top she wore. There were no visible tracks, but when Callie was abusing drugs, she was more apt to take something she could inhale or swallow.

She smiled and nodded in conjunction with Callie's infrequent pauses, while all the time weighing every nuance in her sister's voice, each expression on her face. The silent evaluation was second nature to her.

Probably not on anything chemical, including, unfortunately, her prescription drugs. Her movements were quick, energetic, and the monologue hadn't stopped, but segued into a humorous recounting of Callie's attempt to bring some French brandy through airport security. She was possibly already in a hypomanic state.

But it was possible she was just excited to see her sister, wasn't it? That her long absence had her missing Abbie and wanting to reconnect?

Even while reason overrode emotion, Abbie was surprised at how much she wanted to believe that. To believe for at least a time that they were normal sisters, with a relationship forged in love, rather than trauma.

Following her sister into the house, she continued to study Callie, noting her lack of color, despite the tale of the long cruise, and she knew the truth. But it didn't change her feelings. Not then. Despite the worry that always accompanied thoughts of her sister, she was the only family Abbie had. And for the next few hours she was going to concentrate on that fact and that alone.

The other woman unerringly stepped over the too-high lip where living room carpet met kitchen linoleum. Abbie had tripped over it more than once her first few days living there.

"Callie?" She waited for her to turn, her perfect profile in sharp relief as she looked over her shoulder.

Abbie shut the door behind her. "It really is good to see you again."

———

Ryne knew he ought to feel worse about ending eighteen months of sobriety. But it wasn't the two fingers of Jim Beam he'd been regretting for the last couple hours. Once he'd gotten past wanting to follow Dixon out that door and kick the shit out of him, he'd been unable to get the man's disclosure out of his mind. He'd come back to headquarters and checked the databases for everything he could find on Karen Larsen, and the fire that had destroyed her home. The information he'd uncovered had only led to more questions.

Was it really possible that there was another victim out there? One who had failed to come forward, despite the media coverage of the rapes? Or perhaps because of it? And if so, could she have information that might, finally, give them a valuable lead in this case?

Questions without answers, at least until tomorrow. Larsen wasn't picking up her phone, and that was probably just as well. If she'd been willing to speak to the police about the incident, she'd have done so. He had to get a handle on her mind-set to figure the best way to approach her.

And unfortunately, the person best able to predict that for him was going to be in no mood to talk to him right now, about the case or much else.

Thoughts of Abbie had his jaw tightening. Whatever his opinion of her latest theory, he'd have preferred to keep her profile within the department. Dixon had blown that possibility by releasing it to the press, who, from all accounts, were having a field day with it.

That wasn't her fault, but he couldn't deny blaming her earlier today when Dixon had announced his intent. He shoved back from the computer. The only thing he hated worse than apologizing was recognizing how badly he needed to.

Scowling, he rose and grabbed the jacket he had hanging on the back of the chair, before heading out of the building. Abbie might be tempted to throw the apology back in his face, but she was too professional to allow her temper to impact the case.

He lifted a hand in an absent farewell to the desk sergeant and pushed open the double doors to the outside, jogged down the steps. Even while he remained adamantly unconvinced of the validity of Abbie's theory, he wanted—needed—her opinion on another aspect of the case. The irony wasn't lost on him. He had a feeling it wouldn't be lost on Abbie either.

———

But the woman who answered the door was definitely not Abbie. Blonde and stacked, her skimpy clothing showed off a figure that was centerfold material, minus the staples.

"Well, hello there," she purred, leaning one hand against the doorjamb as she opened the door wider. "If you're part of

Savannah's welcome wagon, I just might make my stay here permanent."

Over the woman's shoulder Ryne saw Abbie approaching quickly. He noted the exact moment she saw him. Observed the falter in her step. The way her expression closed. There was a kick in the gut at her reaction, but he pushed aside the response.

"Detective Robel." Abbie's formal tone was surely for the other woman's benefit. "Callie, I need a few minutes with the detective. We won't be long."

Callie. Ryne's attention bounced back to the blonde. Whatever he'd pictured from Abbie's brief description of her troubled sister, this woman didn't come close to matching it. There was no family resemblance to speak of. She was several inches taller than Abbie, light to her dark. Everything about her, from her casually tousled long hair, to her careful makeup, to the clothes that could have been spray painted on, was designed to draw attention. Next to the flash of her sister, Abbie should have faded into the woodwork.

But she didn't. He wondered now if she'd spent her childhood trying to, starting with the clothing she chose, which covered up as much as her sister bared. Callie would draw a man's attention, but Abbie would keep it. Her smoke gray eyes whispered of secrets that were a hundred times more seductive than the blatant promise in her sister's gaze.

"Don't be rude, Ab. Let the man in." Callie moistened her lips with the tip of her tongue and stepped aside. Abbie was about to move past her sister, clearly set on a brief conversation with him on the porch. He forestalled her action by stepping inside.

In a movement meant to seem accidental, Callie shifted as well, so that he had to brush up against her to get into the house. She gave a husky laugh, laying one hand lightly on his chest. "My sister isn't used to having men show up on her doorstep unannounced. Unless . . ." She threw a speculative glance at her sister. "Were you expecting company, Ab?"

"Detective Robel and I are working together on a case." Abbie's tone was flat.

"And here all this time I thought your work was boring."

When Callie's fingers started to trace lightly down his shirtfront, Ryne caught her wrist and removed her hand. "You're Abbie's sister, right? How long have you been in Savannah?"

She pouted a moment, then backed up to rest a hip against the cupboard. "Not long."

He considered her for a moment. If she was responsible for the break-in and the brick through Abbie's car window, she'd been here since the beginning of the week, at least. "Savannah's a beautiful city. I'll make you a list of 'don't miss' sights if you want."

Callie's smile was enigmatic. "I'm not much for sightseeing."

He folded his arms across his chest, ignoring the simmering impatience emanating from Abbie. "If you're into the night scene, I understand that Houlihan's or Starz are pretty popular. Steer clear of Joe's on Forty-Ninth. And there are some dives over on Locust that get pretty rough. Someone got stabbed at Topsiders earlier this week. I think it was the bartender."

"It was a customer. But don't worry." She fingered her necklace, an action meant to draw attention to her cleavage. "I can take care of myself."

"Good to know."

"Was there something pressing that brought you here?" Abbie's tone was pointed.

Ryne allowed his gaze to drift back in her direction. There were storms brewing in her eyes. He seemed to have a knack for putting them there.

"Is that pizza?" He walked by them to the box sitting on the stove. "Any left?"

"Help yourself." Callie sauntered over to open the box for him, revealing four slices of pepperoni. He would have preferred sausage, but beggars couldn't be choosers.

"You can take it with you," Abbie said from behind him. She wasn't attempting a dispassionate tone anymore. He took a bite of pizza and looked at her. She was well and truly pissed, and something inside him lightened. He didn't know what it said about him that he'd rather see her irate than to look at him with that blank expression she had down pat, but there it was.

"Abbie, stop. The man's hungry." Callie gave him a slow wink. "I enjoy healthy . . . appetites . . . myself."

Because he suddenly had trouble swallowing, Ryne continued chewing. Subtlety obviously wasn't a trait Callie cultivated. "Did you fly into Savannah from Atlanta? Any problems with that?"

As Callie launched into an animated tale of her travels, he listened silently while he demolished the rest of the leftover pizza. And it occurred to him somewhere between the second and third slice that there was yet another difference between the two women.

Abbie had secrets. No trespassing signs were firmly planted. But she was otherwise straightforward.

Callie Phillips was a liar.

He dangled the occasional carefully worded question in front of her and she fashioned her own noose with her answers. He wondered if Abbie was catching all the discrepancies in her conversation, or if she was too irritated with him to notice.

When Callie had run down, he said, "You staying here with your sister?"

Somehow the other woman seemed closer, although he didn't recall her moving. "Here? No, too small." She reached up and wiped at the corner of his mouth with the tip of her index finger. "I like my privacy. And I insist on my own bedroom." She slid a sly glance toward Abbie. "We've never shared a bedroom, have we, Abbie?"

"No."

The word seemed strained. Ryne stilled, aware of the undercurrents, but unable to interpret the source.

"Maybe if we had, you wouldn't have so many fears." Callie's too-innocent gaze moved back to Ryne. "My little sister is afraid of the dark. Among other things."

He felt Abbie stiffen beside him, and abruptly tired of the game being played. "All of us are afraid of something."

"Not me, Detective." Callie trailed the nail of her index finger along the buttons on his shirt suggestively. "I'm not afraid of anything. You can't imagine how . . . liberating that is."

"If there's nothing else, Detective Robel . . ." Abbie walked to the door, opened it. "It's been a long day."

But it was Callie who walked through it, after a quick glance at the clock on the wall. "I've got to run. I'll call you tomorrow, Abbie."

"Wait. Do you need a ride?" Abbie followed her sister out to the back porch. "Where are you staying?"

"I've got someone picking me up. Don't fuss. I'll be in touch."

Ryne watched the two exchange an embrace, then Callie disappeared from his view. It was another long moment before Abbie turned back to him. When she did, she didn't bother to hide her annoyance.

"There's an interesting new piece of technology you might have heard of. It's called a telephone." She held up her cell for emphasis. "Try using it the next time you're tempted to show up unannounced."

He folded the box and stuck it in the garbage can. "If I had called, would you have told me to come over?"

"What do you think?"

"I think that's why I didn't call." He nodded in the direction of the door. "I didn't mean to run your sister off, though."

"Callie usually does exactly what she wants. She must have had plans."

He regarded her steadily, but when she added nothing more, he said, "She's lying to you, you know. She's been in town at least all week, maybe much longer. That stabbing occurred on Monday. And she claimed there was no hassle at the Savannah Airport. There have been renovations going on there for months. You flew in there, right? It's a major clusterfuck. I haven't heard one person who has flown in there who can talk about it without cussing."

She smiled without humor. "So she's lying. You think

that's big news? It's what she does. It doesn't mean anything."

He wasn't so sure. "Did she have an opportunity to look around here? Because she knew that it was a one-bedroom."

Her expression was impassive. "And?"

"And? And she might have known that because she has already been here. Because she's the one who broke in."

She let the door close behind her and leaned against it. "It doesn't take a hotshot detective to figure that one out. So what?"

Narrowing his eyes, he wondered if she was being deliberately dense. "Did you ask her about the break-in? And the brick?"

"No. Confronting Callie is the worst way to get information. I was more concerned with assessing her . . . mood."

The finality of her tone indicated better than words that she would say no more on the subject. Ryne felt a surge of frustration, but it was tempered by concern. "Just be careful, okay?"

Abbie just stared at him. "Why are you here, Ryne?"

It was a question he should be asking himself. He could have waited until morning to share Dixon's revelation. Barring that, he could have called to discuss the news.

Which meant that taking a drink might not be his only lapse of judgment tonight.

"Something came up after you went home that I wanted to run by you." In succinct terms he relayed his conversation with Dixon, at least the part pertaining to Karen Larsen and her tox screen. Abbie's eyes widened, before her expression grew pensive.

"You mentioned that you'd looked at all the other rape reports for the last year."

He nodded grimly. "Nothing came close to matching the elements of this case. And I would have expected the publicity of this investigation to flush out any victims we didn't know about."

"So she didn't report it. Why?" She turned and hurried into the other room, leaving him to trail behind her. He stopped short in the middle of the room, recognizing the chart she had on the wall, above the desk.

It was similar to the case chart he kept at headquarters, to keep track of evidence, leads, offense dates, and locations. But other than a time line across the top, Abbie's was covered by a large grid, with victim names on the left side and details of their lives in successive boxes. Neighborhoods, church and store preferences, occupation, acquaintances . . . she'd painstakingly lifted every detail gleaned from the victim interviews and transferred them to the paper.

He moved closer to get a better look. Instead of using the colored pins he favored, she'd used different-colored string to link victims to their information in each column. He saw instantly what she'd been depicting. Each place the lines crossed indicated a commonality between victims. There were depressingly few intersections.

Except, of course, for the last column. Every one of the victims had a notation under "Personal Trauma."

He jammed his hands into his pants pockets. "They're already calling him the Nightmare Rapist, you know. The press."

She made a face. "They were bound to sensationalize it."

"I don't want you to be right. About how he selects them."

"You made that abundantly clear." Ice frosted her words, straightened her spine. It was tempting, more tempting than it should have been, to see what it would take to melt it.

Because the urge annoyed him, he let the emotion sound in his voice. "Not because my ego can't take it, or because it's your idea or whatever the hell you're thinking." He rocked back on his heels and stared at the damn chart. And its limited intersections. "Because if you're right, where the hell are we? We can't exactly start Googling every female in the city of a certain age and see if there's some trauma in their past. Unless . . ." He threw her a look. "Did any of the victims get phobia counseling or therapy . . . ?" If they had, then maybe that could be where the UNSUB had come into contact with them.

She shook her head. "It's really only two who had actual

phobias anyway, Billings to water and Sommers to enclosed places. But for all of them . . . it was like he learned enough about each of them to discover a fear, and then specifically created a torture designed to personalize it. And believe me, that scares me as much as it does you, if for different reasons."

At his raised brows, she went on, "This is a departure for a 'normal' sexual offender, even given that they're abnormal to begin with. But always, always, the rapes are ultimately about the perpetrator, not the victim. His wants. His needs. Everything else—who he chooses, how he chooses them, what he does to them—all of it stems from his own desires. Sure, he'll stalk them to learn their routine, to make the attack easier. But it's highly unusual for an offender to make his selections so deliberately."

He tried to recall her words of—was it just this morning? "You said he thinks he's suffered."

Abbie was frowning, her attention on the chart. "Past abuse of some type, most likely. Emotional, physical, or sexual. Something messed this guy up, big-time. And now he's returning the favor. In spades."

"Amanda Richards and Ashley Hornby didn't have a trauma in their pasts until they crossed his path," he pointed out.

"Right. But Richards was all over the TV and newspapers because of the pageant wins. It wouldn't be much of a leap to figure how a beauty queen would react to the deliberate destruction of her looks. Or how an award-winning dancer would respond to being made a cripple. As to how he finds them, there's a bunch of archives online these days that will search hundreds of newspapers. I typed in 'Savannah drowning' in one and know how many hits I got?"

Unfortunately, he could imagine. "And you found the Billings story?"

"Bingo. One of your detectives had done an online search of each of the victims, but Billings was Barbara's stepfather's name."

"What about Hornby?"

Her gaze strayed to the bright yellow string connecting the woman's name to sections on the grid and shook her head. "Those awards were under Hornby, her maiden name. But I couldn't find any mention of her in the local papers. Her neighbor said she'd been trying to get on with a Savannah dance troupe. Ashley wasn't the type to go to bars, or have any sort of social life, according to Knudson."

"I have a feeling she'd know." He'd bet a twenty the older woman kept an eye on the comings and goings of everyone on her street.

"I plan to ask the other victims about personal information they might have posted online." She went to the desk and opened the center drawer. "Chatrooms, blogs, online messaging, My Space, Facebook . . . I'm constantly amazed by the stuff people are willing to post for complete strangers to read."

"We checked that avenue for Richards thoroughly, but we can follow up with the other victims." He shook his head. "I can't even believe the personal stuff women tell strange women in public restrooms."

Withdrawing a paper clip, she closed the drawer again. "Oh, you mean when we all excuse ourselves from dinner and go in to play Rate a Date?"

He eyed her carefully, but her expression remained bland.

"Yeah, there's this hidden signal, see, and then we all get up and meet in the restaurant restroom to assign scores to each other's dinner companions. It's a one-to-ten scale for several categories, based solely on our observations of the other diners. Good conversationalist. Spending habits. Stamina in bed."

Damned if she'd hadn't almost had him. "Very funny," he said mildly. "But it does make me reevaluate the only meal we've had together."

She toyed with the paper clip, smiling at him. "Bet you're wondering now about all those times second dates failed to transpire, huh?"

He didn't bother to tell her that it rarely took a second date for him to get a woman into bed. Or how long it had been since he'd met one who'd interested him enough to want to see her again.

"So where's Larsen fit in?"

It took him a moment to follow her non sequitur, "Larsen?"

She gestured to the chart. "In the order. If she does turn out to be a victim, where does that place her in the sequence?"

He directed his attention to the time line. "I pulled up the incident report after talking to Dixon. The date of the fire was June seventh." He watched as she placed the clip on the time line, between the dates of the Richards and Hornby rapes. Together they studied the sequence silently.

"So if Larsen does turn out to be a victim, he only waited four and a half weeks after Richards. And the next two assaults were three weeks apart," she said slowly.

"Which means he's escalating."

Backing up a few steps, she perched her hip on the corner of the desk, her face sober. "We really need to talk to her."

He crossed to the couch and dropped heavily onto it. Exhaustion was seeping in, sapping his energy. "I thought you might have some ideas on how to approach her. Supposing for a minute she was a victim, why wouldn't she have come forward?"

"Denial. Fear. Too traumatized."

"Or covering for someone."

She considered it, nodded. "Until we talk to her, it's just speculation. But if she isn't another victim, that leads to even more questions."

He'd been partnered with guys for years before getting this in sync with them. If he weren't so damn tired, the realization would have alarmed him. "Like why her tox screen indicates the same mutant drug compound in her bloodstream."

"She's connected to this case." Abbie stretched her legs out in front of her, crossed them at the ankles. The action shouldn't have been sexy. Wouldn't have been for any other woman. His gaze crawled up the length of her legs, clad in black pants, lingered on her slim thighs, before moving to the black long-sleeved shirt she wore. The buttons marching down its front made a man fantasize about undoing them, one by one. Baring an inch of flesh at a time, driving both of them a little crazy by going real slow. Drawing it out.

He rubbed his eyes with the heels of his palms. Jesus, he was losing it, sitting here entertaining R-rated fantasies of a member of his task force. But his concentration was shot to hell. He'd completely missed what she was saying.

". . . have come in contact with the UNSUB at some point. Or maybe with the offender's drug supplier. Do you have a copy of her fire investigation report?"

It took him a moment to switch mental gears, a fact that annoyed him. "I have the incident report, but I've got a request in to get the complete fire and police investigative reports by tomorrow morning. Left messages for the officer and fire investigator to call me."

"It'd be best to be fully apprised of all the details of the incident before talking to her. We can go over the facts of the reports tomorrow and plan a way to approach her, hopefully later in the day." She waited, but when he didn't say anything, she continued, "I want to go with you."

Her tone said she was expecting an argument. He didn't give her one. "Okay."

At her surprised expression he continued, "That's why I came. You're the best qualified to figure out what she's thinking, what approach will work with her."

Yeah, Robel that's why you came. Remember that the next time you start thinking about taking off her shirt, for chrissakes.

"It occurs to me that you've left out a few details."

The wariness that flickered to life was instinctive. "Such as?"

"Such as how Dixon happened to get this information."

She was no fool. He knew she'd read between the lines of whatever he chose to tell her. Which would be as little as possible, for many reasons. "Larsen apparently confided something to a friend. That friend told Dixon."

Her smile was knowing. And cynical. "A female friend." She lifted a hand to wave away any reply he would have made. "Don't bother to respond. It's pretty easy to see Dixon's the type to have any number of . . . *friends*. Men like him are looking for something. When they can't find it in themselves, they try to find it in every woman they meet."

Stunned, he could only stare at her. He'd known Dixon for years. She'd known him for—what? Less than a week? And had probably talked to him three or four times, max. In his experience, women didn't see through Derek Dixon. Just the opposite. "Has anyone ever told you that you're spooky?"

Her smile disappeared. "You'd be surprised. That doesn't explain how he got a copy of Larsen's tox screen." She gazed at him expectantly but he kept his mouth shut. "Or maybe it does." Lifting a shoulder, she went on, "However it came about, the information is compelling. Who knows? It might turn out to be a break in the case."

"He'd never let me hear the end of that."

With both hands braced on the desk, she boosted herself up to perch on the edge. The act pulled her pant leg up several inches and exposed the edge of leather above her ankle.

An ankle holster. He had no idea why he'd always assumed she was unarmed. A dangerous assumption to make in his line of work. She'd never said anything to change his opinion. But then, that was probably the least of what Abbie Phillips hadn't shared.

"How long have you worked for the SCMPD?"

He lifted a shoulder. "About a year."

Her eyebrows skimmed upward. "Really? From the undercurrents I sensed between you two this afternoon, I'd have guessed you'd known each other much longer than that."

"We were rookies together in Boston. I gravitated to undercover work; he did more public relations stuff."

Her expression grew thoughtful. "Maybe that explains it, then."

"Explains what . . . exactly?"

"He's jealous of you, at least on some level."

He barked out a laugh. *Dixon jealous of him? God, that*

was rich. "Better hang on to your day job. Character analysis isn't your strong suit."

She looked at him coolly. "Character analysis *is* my day job, remember? In a manner of speaking."

Shit, now he'd offended her. He was getting too good at that. "I just mean . . . Dixon's got a pretty healthy ego. Hell, so do I. I think he gets off on being my boss."

I pulled your career out of the trash heap, buddy. How about a little gratitude?

Dixon's words from earlier that evening echoed mockingly. It was pretty safe to say that the man enjoyed being his superior. Hell, maybe that's why he'd offered him a job. He'd wondered at the offer, but he hadn't exactly been swimming in options at the time. His career in Boston hadn't been over, but it had been dead-ended by his screwup. He knew it. His captain had known it. Dixon's invitation had surprised him, but he hadn't examined it too closely. Whatever the man's reasons, Ryne had figured he could live with them.

"He admires you. That first day I spoke to him, he went on and on about your narcotics undercover work, and then your stint in homicide. He must have your jacket memorized. He recited a list of commendations and awards you received."

Something in him stilled. "He told you all that?"

She nodded. "Some of it might have been to impress me with the team he's put together for this investigation, but there was something in his voice. Sort of like the high school football team's manager talking about the star quarterback, you know?"

He looked away, embarrassed by the analogy. "Listen to you. Next you'll have us as prom dates. You misread him, that's all."

"I don't think so. And you won't have to worry about the 'date.' He dislikes you, too, in spite of your success. More likely because of it. And since you don't seem too overly enamored of him, I just wondered . . ."

Her voice trailed off, inviting him to pick up the thread. He didn't.

"Why did you come here to work for him?"

Deborah Hanna's face flashed into his mind again. His gut clenched, and he shoved the mental image aside. "I had my reasons."

She waited, a silent invitation for him to say more. When he didn't, she said, "You must have felt the need to punish yourself."

He stared hard at her, logic receding behind a red wall of emotion that surged too suddenly, too abruptly to be contained. The humor in her voice went unnoticed as haunting memories swarmed to the surface. He was on his feet and closed the distance between them with two quick strides.

Grasping her arms with ungentle hands, he shoved his face close to hers and ground out, "Do us both a favor and stay out of my head, Abbie. Believe me, you wouldn't like what you find there."

Chapter 13

Abbie drew in a breath, and belatedly Ryne became aware of how tightly he was gripping her. He consciously loosened his fingers, appalled by his loss of control.

"I was joking. I meant the weather." His confusion must have shown on his face, because she went on, "The heat and humidity? I don't remember all the times you've complained about it." She looked wary, but unafraid. She should have been afraid. He sure as hell was. Afraid of the tidal wave of emotion that had crashed through him when he'd thought she'd angled a little too close to the truth.

For an instant he'd assumed that Dixon had opened up to her a bit more about his career than just to sing his praises. He was usually better at keeping the ghosts of his past locked away. And the last thing he wanted was to discuss them with her.

"Sorry," he muttered, dropping his hands. And he was. Sorry and ashamed. There had been too many hits today, one right after another, touching on nerves he'd thought better protected. It was best to leave now before he did any more damage. She must already think he was crazy. Based on his performance today, he wasn't so sure he didn't agree.

"I won't ask what you thought I was talking about."

Slowly his gaze met hers, held.

"Like you said earlier, everyone is afraid of something. Some are just better at hiding it than others."

He crooked a finger, tapped the knuckle lightly against her chin. "Scariest thing about you? You see too damn much."

"And that frightens you?"

"To death." He became aware then that he hadn't moved away since releasing her. His legs were crowding hers. Without conscious thought, he spread his feet to straddle her legs with both of his. And watched her eyes go to smoke.

"You should be afraid now, Abbie." He sure as hell was. "You would be, if you knew what I'd been thinking most of the time I've been here." He toyed with the top button on her blouse with thumb and forefinger. Her breath drew in, and her lips parted.

"I haven't been at my most rational the last few hours. So I'm going to leave reason to you." He dipped his head, inhaled her scent. "Tell me to leave."

"So the decision is all on me?" There was a catch in her voice when he pressed his mouth to the pulse, where it beat wildly at the base of her throat. "Doesn't seem exactly fair."

"I'm not feeling 'fair.'" What he *was* feeling would be unmistakable, given the way he was pressed up against her. He had no doubt she'd call an end to this, bring him to his senses and send him home, where he ought to be.

But until she did, he was going to indulge himself. He cupped her head in his hands, threading his fingers through the baby soft hair at her nape. With his thumbs, he traced the line of her jaw. It felt too delicate to be capable of setting so firmly.

It wasn't set now, though. There was a tremble to her lips when he covered them with his, a shudder to her limbs when he moved closer. Her hands came up to clasp his wrists, but she didn't push him away. And because he still expected she would—that she *should*—he took the kiss deeper.

Her flavor was tantalizingly familiar, calling up the memory of the last time he'd touched her. Tasted her. The recollection only whetted his appetite for more. He drank deeply from her, hormones kicking to life. Despite his warning, he had no doubt he could stop this before he crossed the line of good sense. But before that happened, he'd take his fill.

Her tongue met his, a long velvet glide. The muscles in his gut clenched. Angling his mouth over hers, his kiss turned demanding. There was heat here, so at odds with her usual impassive manner. It tempted a man to see if he could fan that heat further, stir it into something hotter, wilder, that sent both of them up in flames.

And if it meant both of them forgot, for just a little while, well, that couldn't hurt either.

Her hands released his wrists and slid up his arms to twine around his neck, urging him nearer. He snaked an arm around her waist, hauling her close, mouth still slanted over hers. Tongues battled. Teeth clashed. He should be worried about the greed that sprang to life so easily. But it was more pleasurable to focus on the desire that flared inside him. And he was nowhere close to getting his fill.

He ran his palm over her ass, squeezed. She was slightly built but she didn't lack curves, and her backside had been fashioned by a very benevolent god. He wanted to strip her down and explore with hands and lips and tongue every inch of the silky flesh she kept hidden. Maybe then he'd quench the thirst for her that had been slowly building since he'd first laid eyes on her.

She tore her mouth from his, and his arms tightened instinctively. But instead of moving away, she brushed her lips along his stubbled jaw, back and forth, before testing it lightly with her teeth. Her hands went to tug his shirt loose from his pants. Then her palms were skating up his sides, across his chest, and the feel of flesh on flesh caused his pulse to riot.

Her neck was a long sleek line that begged to be explored. His mouth sped down it, then up again. He lingered at the hollow of her throat, bathing it with his tongue. She was a study of contrasts, delicacy on the outside hiding a will of steel. A professional exterior that almost successfully concealed the exquisite femininity beneath.

Her lips returned to his at the same time her fingers went in search of the buttons of his shirt, and he stilled, trying to recall his earlier reservations. But it was difficult to think while he found himself holding his breath, body shuddering at each brush of her knuckles against his skin. He swallowed a groan. Need was rising, too fast, too urgent. And his earlier certainty that he could walk away if she called an end to this was fading fast.

She was still working on the third button and her unhurried movements were their own kind of torment. He released her long enough to yank the shirt over his head and toss it aside before hauling her against him again.

Abbie gave a slight sound of satisfaction as she ran her hands over him, and he paused a moment to look at her. There was a flush on her cheeks, her lips were swollen from his, and her eyes were slumberous. He reached out a finger and laid it against the pulse at the base of her throat, felt it skipping wildly. And he knew in that moment there would be no turning back this time. For good or bad, the hunger would be satisfied at last.

The realization helped him regain a measure of restraint. His fingers went to the top button of her shirt, the one that had drawn his attention over and over that evening. He watched her eyes as he deliberately unfastened it, noted the way her lids drooped. Heard her indrawn breath when he bent to press a stinging kiss to the skin he'd bared.

The small sound kindled something primitive inside him, something better kept tamped down. He knew how dangerous it could be when he didn't keep all his appetites tightly leashed. But touching her was enough to have those tethers fraying, and at the moment he just didn't give a damn.

Another button undone. The expanse of flesh widened to hint at the shadow of cleavage. He took his time, torturing them both, delving his tongue into the vee he'd bared. Her nails bit into his shoulders, but the slight sting barely registered. All his attention was focused on the intimate task at hand.

The next unfastened button revealed the top of her breast swelling above a black lacy scrap of bra. He stopped long enough to trail his tongue along the border made where skin met fabric, but his lungs grew strangled. Finesse was forgotten as his fingers grew clumsier, hurriedly undoing the rest to finally push the shirt open.

It framed her slender figure, the dark fabric of shirt and bra contrasting against her creamy skin. His hands splayed on her hips as he brought her closer, bending to catch one lace-encased nipple in his teeth. Her low throaty cry had all his senses roaring.

He knew how to satisfy a woman. Knew when and where to linger and how to draw the act out until both of them were steeped and satiated. But he wasn't familiar with this whipping in his pulse, with this hunger that had the blood hammering through his system. Control had never seemed so difficult to summon.

He lifted his head, pausing to enjoy the sight of her nipple, rosy and peaked against the wet fabric. Demand was raging inside him. He wanted her naked, against him, under him. He wanted to possess her fast and hard and deep in a way that finally quenched the hunger that was slashing at him with jagged teeth.

Abbie trailed a teasing finger along the top of his waistband, and his stomach muscles jumped in response. He reached up to shove her shirt over her shoulders, intending to rid her of it completely. But she evaded the action by leaning back, increasing the distance between them. With her gaze fixed on his, she leisurely unfastened her pants, moving the zipper down with excruciating slowness.

Hooking her thumbs in the waistband, she worked them languorously over her hips, revealing first a whisper of black silk panties, then slender thighs. After she kicked the pants off, she bent to her holster, but he was already reaching for her, guiding her leg up to rest the small foot against his knee as he unbuckled the strap and removed the weapon snugged inside the sheath.

She took it from him and set it on the desk behind her and

he stepped closer, urging her leg around his waist. Her body would tempt a saint. He'd never even made it to altar boy.

Releasing the front clasp of her bra, he peeled the lace aside to reveal small perfect breasts. He covered one with his hand and rolled the taut nipple between his fingers, learning the shape, the weight, and the texture of her. She was rose petal soft, silky and fragrant, but touch alone couldn't satisfy the dark and desperate need crashing through him. He bent his head to take her other nipple into his mouth and sucked strongly.

Her back arched as he feasted on her, driving them both mad with teeth and tongue and lips. She was twisting beneath him, her heels digging into his back, her nails biting into his skin, and the evidence of her desire only fanned his hotter. He was dimly aware that the urgency riding him had been set loose. He wanted her now, right now. Wanted everything she would offer freely, and anything she'd seek to hold back. He wanted to stamp her with his possession so fiercely that neither of them would know where the other left off.

His hand went between her open thighs, rubbed lightly at the damp silk covering her mound. Her body jerked against his and a fierce male satisfaction filled him at her involuntary response. Pushing the fabric aside, he entered her with one finger, stroking deeply.

The broken cry she gave had him leaving her breast to cover her mouth again with his, his tongue mimicking the action of his finger. She was liquid fire against his hand, her slick moist heat issuing promises that his body was desperate to collect. He pressed open her soft folds and tapped his thumb against her clit rhythmically, and she bucked and twisted against him in response.

Razor-edged desire sawed through him as he worked her with his fingers, releasing her lips to go on a frantic search for flesh. And when the first climax ripped through her, when he felt her body clench around his finger, he felt his vision haze.

His own need was pumping through him, a brutal demand

for satisfaction. He released her to grasp her hips and lift her, turning to lean her against the wall and sweep off her panties with one continuous motion. He withdrew a condom from his pants pocket, his heart jackhammering in his chest. It stuttered to a halt when he felt her hands unfastening his pants, reaching inside to grasp his cock firmly.

Thought all but shattered. He was capable only of sensation, as every movement of her body summoned an answering response from his. She stroked him in a rhythm designed to drive him to madness. He was going to disgrace himself if he didn't end this soon. Pushing aside her hands, he managed to don the condom and then lifted her again, urged her legs around his hips, then drove into her with barely restrained hunger.

Their moans mingled. He paused, trying desperately to summon a flagging bit of control.

"The bed," she gasped.

"Next time."

He dragged his eyelids open, looked at her, felt his entire body quiver at the sight. Her eyes were closed, her face and chest flushed with desire. She was wrapped around him, arms clutching his shoulders for support, breasts flattened against his chest. Her heels were digging into his lower back, and he could still feel the subtle clench and release of her inner muscles against him. Conscious thought faded, elbowed aside by sensation and a fierce primitive hunger that demanded release. He thrust, with all the brutal greed pent up inside him, and the world receded. There was only the woman in his arms, the lust crashing through him and spiraling desperation.

He hammered into her, incapable of finesse, of anything but the savage search for oblivion. He wanted, needed, to see her eyes as they mated, but the violent desire that had risen blinded him to everything else. He heard his name on her lips, a ragged cry that seemed torn from her, felt the delicate inner convulsions as she climaxed, and need turned to madness. Burying his face in her throat, he plunged harder, deeper inside her until his passion erupted, ripping through him and shooting him headlong into pleasure.

———————

They made it to the bed. Eventually. And then spent the next few hours exploring and exploiting each other's bodies until they fell asleep from sheer exhaustion, limbs still entwined. When Abbie opened her eyes, early morning light was seeping in the room from beneath the shade. And she had the thought that little could be as anticlimatic after a night of mind-blowing sex than to wake up alone.

But she was wrong.

As she sat up in bed, she realized two things simultaneously: She wasn't alone. But it would have been infinitely easier if she were.

Ryne stood in the doorway, clad only in his pants, a towel clutched in one hand, his shirt in another. His chest was still damp. His wet hair looked like he'd only finger-combed it. The shadow on his jaw had deepened; he hadn't availed himself of the disposable razors in the bathroom. He looked rumpled, sexy, and dangerous.

And extremely ill at ease.

Her earlier disappointment was swallowed by dismay. The expression on his face had her scrambling for defenses. There could be little as demeaning as being someone else's regret.

Deliberately, she looked at the alarm on the bedside table, while tugging the covers to a discreet level. "It's late. You'll have to hurry to make it back to your place to change and get to the daily briefing."

"It's Saturday."

Her eyes closed briefly. Of course. Which meant she couldn't depend on the pressing need for work to defuse the tension. It was a struggle, but she managed a level tone. "I forgot. I'll be at the station within the hour. I know you're as anxious as I am to see Larsen's reports as soon as they come in."

He hadn't moved, so she pulled the sheet loose to wrap

around her shoulders as she slipped from the bed. She knew it was ridiculous, but she wasn't up to parading by him buck-naked. She felt exposed enough as it was.

"Abbie."

His voice was low, the awkwardness in his stance evident in the tone. Because there was no way to avoid it, she forced herself to meet his gaze.

"Last night was . . ." He hesitated, as if searching for words. She wanted, desperately, to hear him finish that sentence, even while she feared what he might say. Last night was what? Wonderful? A mistake? But the adjective he chose really didn't matter. Her eyes had been wide open last night, figuratively, at least. She knew exactly what they could have between them. And what they couldn't have.

"Last night doesn't change anything," she said clearly. "We work together. Nothing can cloud that."

He couldn't quite mask the flicker of relief that crossed his features, and she felt a sardonic sort of amusement. Nature should have equipped men with built-in parachutes to assist them in dealing with sticky morning-afters. They could just go out the window and avoid having these conversations altogether.

She moved toward him and he stepped aside to allow her through the doorway. "Give me an hour and I'll meet you downtown, okay?" If he made a response, she didn't hear it. She shut the bathroom door behind her and leaned against it, the blood pounding in her ears. She'd played this scene in one variation or another before in the past, so there was no reason for it to be having such an effect on her now.

But it *was* affecting her. There was no denying it. Limbs wooden, she let the sheet drop, crossing to the tub and turning on the shower. Not for the first time in her life, she wished she could be "normal." She wished she could learn to trust a man enough to allow him close to her.

And she wished, quite desperately, that *this* man wasn't the first one to elicit this sharp-edged longing in her.

There wasn't enough hot water to erase the darkness of Abbie's mood, but it helped, as it always did, to concentrate on the case. She was anxious to learn what she could about Karen Larsen. She wasn't particularly eager to spend the day with Ryne, but the sooner they got their relationship back to a professional footing, the better.

Shutting off the water, she grabbed a towel and briskly dried her hair before wrapping it around herself. Immersing themselves in a new aspect of the case would ease the awkwardness between them. Logically, she knew that. Now if she could just put logic ahead of emotion, she'd be ready to face him again.

She finished her morning rituals with lightning speed, then headed to the bedroom, mind still lingering on the morning ahead of her. She reached for the light switch and flipped it on, then froze.

Ryne should have been gone. Certainly she'd given him every opportunity to take the easy way out. Every man she knew would have accepted the chance to make his escape.

But then, she'd never met a man like Ryne Robel.

He was fully dressed, sitting on the corner of the bed, hands clasped between his open legs, his gaze on her. And his voice, when he spoke, was husky, but determined. "You and I have a few things to get straight before we . . ."

He stopped, and she realized in an instant what had distracted him. She snatched her hand away from the light switch but he was already on his feet, striding toward her. He caught her by the shoulders when she would have turned away, took one of her arms in his hand and turned it upward. Her gaze followed the direction of his, toward the crisscrossing of old scars lining her inner arm from above the elbow to the wrist. Scars that had been hidden from him last night by her shirt. By the dark.

Most of them were white now. Those that still remained pink and puckered had been deeper than the rest, and would never truly fade. The observation was detached, as though it had originated from someone else.

Ryne let her arm drop, repeated his examination of the other. And when he looked at her again, it was with that same impassive mask she remembered from the first time they'd met. The same little smile that had nothing to do with humor. "You a cutter, Abbie?"

She flinched, pulled away from him, and this time he let her go. Feeling strangely ancient, she moved toward her closet, although she wasn't about to dress in front of him. Regardless, it was imperative that she establish distance, physically at least. "What are you still doing here?"

"You're changing the subject."

"It's the only subject I'm interested in discussing."

"Those scars are too straight, too even, not to have come from razor blades. Either you did it yourself, or . . ." His voice broke off, and then he was by her side in two long strides. "Did someone abuse you? Was it your sister?"

Callie. Her stomach turned over. Oh, God, she did not want to get into this. Not now. Not with him. "Callie never hurt me." Not really. Just the opposite. And that was the source of all her sister's problems, wasn't it? Prolonging her own pain to save Abbie. She released a long shuddering breath. "It was a long time ago, Ryne. And it's absolutely none of your business."

He cupped her shoulders with his hands, gave her a little shake. "That's bullshit. Last night made it my business."

"Last night?" She tried for an incredulous laugh, failed miserably. "So we bare our souls because of one night of sex, is that it? In that case, you go first. Why don't you tell me the whole story about what happened in Boston? The real reason behind your move to Savannah?"

She saw his expression go blank, and allowed herself a bitter little smile. "So last night gave you rights to pry into my life, but none for me, is that it? Are personal disclosures linked to number of orgasms? Because if so, I'm pretty sure we're close to even on that score."

His eyes burned into hers, angry in a way she couldn't quite fathom. "You're right, it isn't fair. You don't owe me any explanations, but you're going to give them to me anyway. You know why? Because seeing those scars planted an image in my head. Of you, in the past, hurt and bleeding. And I don't want that picture there. You have no idea how much I don't want it. So either you tell me or I'll get the answers another way." At her silence, he gave her a nod, released her to step away. "All right then. I'll have Callie picked up and ask her. Somehow I think she'll be more forthcoming."

Panic sprinted up her spine. Callie had seemed close to the edge last night already. The last thing she needed was to be pressed about their past. It was, after all, the cause of all her sister's problems. She grabbed Ryne's sleeve as he would have turned away. "Leave my sister out of this. You're not going to manipulate me again into revealing something that's none of your business. I'm not a suspect you're interrogating. Stop treating me like one."

Temper ignited, he gritted out, "No, you're not a suspect, you're a woman I . . ." He stopped, as if shocked by the incomplete thought. Voice raw, he continued, "You matter, okay? To me. You probably shouldn't, but there it is. And whatever happened to you . . . it matters, too. And believe me, that scares me more than it does you."

His words acted as a fast right jab to the solar plexus. Inwardly reeling, she stared at him, grappling with his revelation. She'd have suspected him of using words to get his way if he didn't look so miserable at having uttered them.

Shaken, she turned away. She couldn't think, couldn't reason, while looking at the concern etched on his face.

But her thought processes scattered even further when he crowded close to her, drawing her back to lean against him, skating his hands down her arms and up again. "I'm the last person to judge, you need to know that. And if you really can't tell me . . ." He hesitated, long enough for her to realize how hard the words were for him to say. "I'll try to leave it alone."

His last statement abruptly deflated her, had all the fight streaming away on a shuddering sigh. His thumbs brushed against the skin on her inner arms. She wondered what he'd say if she told him that sometimes the scars still throbbed with a phantom pain that owed nothing to the physical. Or how long it had taken her to break herself of the habit of rubbing those scars whenever she felt threatened.

Such futile battles, really, in the scheme of things. Just as holding out against his concern was. After all these years, no one could be hurt by the truth anymore. The damage had been done long ago.

"Callie is four years older than me. She was ten when my father started raping her." She felt him jerk against her, was glad she couldn't see his face. It was easier, far easier, to pretend she was talking to herself.

"I don't know how old I was when I realized what was going on. Not completely, of course." Children couldn't really fathom that kind of horror until they were thrust in the midst of it. "But I knew he was hurting her. Going to her room in the middle of the night and doing 'bad things.' Things that made her cry and bleed. Things little girls don't know how to describe to someone else."

His voice was raw in her ear. "Your mother?"

"Died of pneumonia when I was only a couple years old. We moved around a lot. He worked for a big construction company. We went where their projects were." The years were a blur of new neighborhoods, new schools. She could see now how their lifestyle worked to keep them isolated. Kept them from establishing any relationships that could lead to them entrusting someone with their secret. She'd always wonder if that had been part of her father's plan.

"I was eight the first time he came to my room." She was barely aware of Ryne behind her. Unaware of his stillness. His held breath. The past had sucked her in, sucked her down. And the memories still burned. "He didn't get in. As soon as we'd moved to that house, Callie put a lock on the inside of my room. I have no idea where she got it. How she knew to install it. But she did and made me swear I'd use it every night." So he'd stay outside the door and whisper to her, his voice coaxing and threatening by turns. While she shook and prayed in the darkness to be delivered from something she couldn't even fully understand.

"And how long did the lock keep him away?"

She knew what he was asking, but she shook her head. "Callie made sure he never came in. She would . . . distract him." Offer herself as sacrifice to keep him from brutalizing Abbie. How did someone repay a debt so steep? Especially knowing it had most likely cost her sister her mental health?

Ryne's body was strong and steady behind hers. It was tempting, so tempting, to lean against his strength for just a moment. She refused to allow herself even that small indulgence. If there was one thing her past had taught her, it was the danger of relying on anyone but herself.

"One night I was so scared he was going to get inside that I tried to get out the window. Ended up breaking it and cutting my arm on the broken glass." She stopped, her throat closing at the memory. There was no way to describe that slash of pain, starkly pure and somehow beautiful. No way to explain what had made her reach for a shard again once she heard the footsteps, still clad in work boots, move heavily past her room and down the hall in response to her sister's call. And every time she'd hear Callie cry out, she'd bring that shard of glass across her arm again. As if the infliction of pain could absolve her of responsibility for the agony her sister was experiencing, on her behalf.

"I graduated to blades later." Her voice was flat. She knew better than to tell him that Callie had bought them for her. He would never understand how the two of them had bonded over shared suffering. Only through her training, and the distance of adulthood, did she understand how dark and twisted that reasoning had been. But at the time it had made perfect sense.

His voice was tight. "Is he alive?"

She warmed at the grim intent in his voice. She could have told him that no one could right old wrongs. There was nothing to do but find a way to live with them. But it touched something inside her that he felt the need to do so.

"He died when I was ten. We were in foster homes after that." And once the truth had been shared with a caseworker, there had been long-term therapy, for both her and Callie. It had probably saved her life. It had been less effective for her sister.

He didn't utter any meaningless platitudes, for which she was grateful. There was nothing to say, and they both knew it. Abbie dreaded turning around, seeing for the first time the difference in his expression. If he looked at her with unease or—worse yet—pity, their working relationship would be strained unbearably. Their personal relationship would be irreparable.

But there was no opportunity to turn around, not then. Instead, his arms tightened around her, and his chin rested lightly against her hair. And as he held her, the silent understanding he offered was in many ways more healing than time, more therapeutic than all the years spent in a therapist's office.

Slowly, as if operating absent of conscious thought, her hands came up to cover his. And for an instant, she allowed herself to let go and enjoy his warmth. His embrace. And the steady solid feel of his strength as she leaned her weight against him.

Just for a moment.

The beer can hurtled through the air, crashing into the television set controls, abruptly silencing the pious news anchor. The fucking talking heads on the local news kept going on about Ashley Hornby's suicide. And every time the news story ran, that familiar rage boiled up all over again, spilled over.

The cowardly cunt had ruined everything. *Everything.* All the thought and planning that had gone into arranging her experience, and she hadn't even had the courage to accept her destiny. Instead she'd taken the easy way out and ruined the whole thing.

With the sweep of an arm, the contents of the table were sent flying to the floor. She'd been flawed. Weak. And—the fact couldn't be escaped—she'd been a mistake. The whore hadn't had the strength to face her fate.

Fists clenched. Temper hazed vision. It was getting harder

and harder to keep that old rage leashed, channeled into the one thing that gave it purpose. Errors couldn't be tolerated. There was too much at stake to waste it all on an undeserving bitch like Hornby.

A deep breath. Then another. Slowly, tension eased out of a body stiff as a board. The next one would be better. *Perfect.* Laura Bradford would be a masterpiece. And nothing would be allowed to go wrong. The rest of her life would be a horror, and she'd live through every second of it, as she was meant to.

And that horror was going to begin even sooner than originally planned.

Chapter 14

"You're sure she's home?"

Abbie shrugged at Ryne's question and rang the doorbell again. "She said she'd be here until she leaves for her eleven o'clock shift. It's only ten." Her phone conversation with Karen Larsen had been brief, but the woman had sounded open to speaking with them. Of course, when she'd immediately assumed Abbie was calling about the investigation into her house fire, Abbie had done little to make her think otherwise. They knew the woman was skittish about the details of the case. She and Ryne had formed a game plan for this interview prior to making the contact.

A voice sounded from inside the house. "Just a minute."

Abbie glanced at Ryne. His burgundy shirt was the only splash of color against his black suit and tie. Dark sunglasses hid his eyes.

Despite her trepidation after their conversation this morning, it had been amazingly easy to face him again at headquarters, and she knew she had Ryne to thank for that. When she'd entered, she'd found him at his desk, poring over Larsen's arson investigation report. Other than an initial searching glance, he'd been all business as he'd given her a run-down of what he'd learned so far. It had been simple to follow his lead.

She could almost forget that the revelation she'd shared with him hadn't been entrusted to anyone else in years. Not since her third interview with Raiker, prior to being hired. And that had been unavoidable. Adam Raiker didn't tolerate secrets.

And now, apparently, she'd met another man who demanded the same level of candor. She was less sure how she felt about that.

The door opened as far as the security chain would allow. "Yes?"

"Ms. Larsen?" Abbie recognized the woman from a photo that had been included in the arson case file. She shifted to position herself in the woman's view. "I'm Abbie Phillips. We spoke on the phone earlier. With me is Detective Robel."

"I'm going to need to see some ID."

Ryne held his shield up where she could see it, and the door closed. The rattle of a chain sounded and then the door opened to reveal a woman wearing what Abbie thought of as the new medical uniform: patterned smock, white pants, and pink rubber crocs.

"Sorry. I'm still a little nervous after all that's happened." Larsen stepped back and waved them inside.

"Perfectly understandable." Abbie gave her an encouraging smile and glanced quickly around the small living area. The house was slightly bigger than the one she was staying in, and sparsely furnished. But there were fresh flowers in a vase on the TV. Some framed prints on the wall. Brightly colored throw pillows were placed on the couch. The room was as tidy in appearance as was the woman herself.

Larsen's dark blond curls fell to her shoulders, framing a narrow face, carefully made up. Her lipstick was the exact shade of the polish on her neatly manicured nails, and the small hoop earrings she wore. "This is about the fire, right? Because I'd really like to get things settled with my insurance company. I lost all my things and I can't afford to buy much until I know what the settlement is going to be."

"We'd like to talk to you about the fire, if you have a few moments." Ryne took his glasses off and indicated for the woman to sit. She looked from him to Abbie and back again before sinking slowly onto the couch.

"Where's Officer O'Hare? He's the one I've always dealt with before."

"He's still active on your investigation," Ryne replied. "We're here because there's a possibility that your case is related to one we're working on."

The woman looked puzzled. "I don't understand. The fire was started by a candle I left burning that caught my bedroom drapes on fire. Stupidly careless on my part, I admitted that. But how could my case be connected to any others?"

Ryne sat on the opposite end of the couch, facing her. "Some details in the fire investigator's report caught my attention. For instance, there was some burned cable near your bed that has been identified as electrical cord." He waited a beat. "Since most people don't keep it lying around, it raises some questions."

Larsen sent a quick glance toward Abbie, as if looking for help, found none forthcoming. "Exactly what kind of case are you two working on?"

"The cord?" Abbie pressed.

Larsen lifted a shoulder jerkily. "I had some leftover TV cable in a closet from when I had cable installed. But it wasn't connected to anything. I'm not sure what that could have to do with the fire."

Cable wiring and electrical cord were two very different things, but Ryne let it pass. His interest in the woman, however, deepened. He pretended to consult his notebook . "You told the investigator that you'd been out earlier that evening at some nightclubs."

Larsen flushed, and her gaze dropped to her hands, linked in her lap. "I'd had a bad day. I decided to go out for a few drinks, something I *never* do. I mean, hardly ever. And yeah,

I was pretty wasted when I got home, which is the only reason I would have been so careless with the candle."

"And the locks on your doors."

She looked up sharply at Abbie's words. "What do you mean?"

"Woman living alone, coming home late . . . it was after the bars closed, right?" She didn't wait for Larsen's nod before continuing. "The report says you managed to escape before the fire truck came by smashing the bedroom window with a chair and climbing out. But the lock on your front door wasn't secured when the firemen got there."

Karen checked her watch. "I have to get going soon. I've got to be at work."

"By eleven, you said." Abbie smiled easily. "We have a bit more time. Do you remember locking the front door?"

"If you say it was unlocked, I believe you." The woman shrugged, looked embarrassed. "You have to understand, I don't normally hang out in bars. I'm not much of a drinker."

"How much did you have to drink that night?"

"A half-dozen margaritas. And my usual limit is two, so I topped the stupidity factor in all areas that night. Now I'm living with the consequences, right?"

Because she detected the self-recrimination in the woman's tone, Abbie sent her a commiserating smile. "Must have been a *really* bad day. I've had them myself. Something happen at work?"

"No." Karen twisted a silver ring on her finger. "I was just feeling kind of blue. Lonely, I guess. I've only lived in Savannah since March and I haven't met that many people."

"So you just wanted to get out for a while to a place where crowds gather and interact with people," Abbie said encouragingly. She didn't look at Ryne but was aware of the way he was sitting back, letting her assume the lead in the interview. "Sounds perfectly normal. Did you meet anyone special to pass the time with?"

"Ran into some women I know from Memorial."

"Is that the hospital you work at?" asked Ryne.

"One of them. I'm a temp nurse. I go wherever there's a

shortage. So I've worked at all the hospitals and some of the private practice clinics in the area, filling in as needed. You can actually make better money doing that than you can in a full-time nursing position," she explained. "If you don't mind the uncertain hours and last-minute calls."

"So you hung out with these women most of the night."

Larsen shook her head slowly, her gaze sliding away from Abbie's. "Just chatted for a few minutes."

"Meet any interesting guys while you were out?"

The woman's expression closed. "I wasn't out looking for men. I'm not a slut. I don't do that. I'm not like that."

The vehemence in her voice made it obvious that Abbie had struck a nerve. Striving for a note of humor, she said, "Sometimes we don't have to be looking, we just have to be there. Men are like flies. They don't wait for an invitation to land."

An unwilling smile tugged at Larsen's lips. "Yeah. Well, I encountered a few bar *flies*, but no one special. And I really have to go, or I'm going to be late for work."

She rose, and Ryne and Abbie followed suit. "One more thing, Ms. Larsen," Ryne said. "Could you verify the places you went that night prior to returning home?"

Larsen looked wary. "Why?"

"Just part of our investigation." He checked a page in his notebook, reading off the list she'd given to the officer on her case. Looking up, he said, "Are there any others that you forgot to mention earlier? Maybe one you didn't stay long at?"

She swallowed hard, shook her head. "I don't understand. Why are you here? What difference does it make where I was? What case are you working on?"

"We'll be in touch," Abbie said. She already had more questions than when they'd come here, but she knew they'd get no more from the woman right now.

They walked themselves to the door, as Larsen seemed to be rooted in place, next to the couch. Ryne opened the door and Abbie turned, as if just remembering something. "Oh, Karen. The fire investigator's report mentioned as many as a dozen partially consumed containers, of the type used to hold candles. Did you light them all that night?"

"I must have." Her voice was flat. "I probably did. Candles are romantic, right? Until one burns down your house."

———

"Men are like flies?"

Still in the process of buckling her seat belt, Abbie smiled at the wry note in Ryne's voice. "Just establishing a rapport. I didn't mean it. Much."

He flipped his glasses open and settled them on his nose before turning the key in the ignition. "I can imagine you've had your share of men circling around you. And we didn't cover this earlier, but just so you know . . . I'll be the only one 'landing' on you for the near future." The look he sent her was unmistakable, even with the shades shielding his eyes.

"What a lovely sentiment," she said tartly, smarting at the crude innuendo. "Maybe you can have it inscribed on a greeting card."

He turned his attention back to the street as he pulled away from the curb. "It was your analogy. And it's been a long time since I've done exclusive. But this . . . with us . . ." He halted, then muttered what sounded like an obscenity. "As long as this lasts, I won't share," he said flatly. "If that's a problem for you, better tell me now."

Her throat clogged, her ire of a moment ago fading as abruptly as it had formed. She believed his assertion that he hadn't had a long-term relationship for a while. If anyone had "lone wolf" written all over him, it was this man.

Which made her reaction to his demand all the more powerful. The fact that he wanted an exclusive relationship now, with her, had tiny bursts of pleasure pulsing through her system. And alarm. That, too, of course. His notion that she had scores of men waiting in the wings was as ridiculous as it was flattering.

As was his assumption that she would know how to handle an "exclusive" temporary sexual relationship with him.

She busied herself tightening the seat belt that didn't need adjusting. "I can live with that."

"Good. So what's your take on Larsen?"

Not for the first time, she was grateful at the way he could skate from personal to professional in an instant. "She's hiding something, that's a given. How far did the officer go to check out her story about the bars?"

"Not very." Ryne took a left to head back to headquarters. "There was nothing suspicious about it. The fire investigator determined early on the source of the fire, and the insurance company is claiming negligence and balking at paying. It looked pretty cut and dried, although Shepard, the investigator, says she was damn lucky to escape through a window. The flames had already spread to block Larsen's exit from the bedroom door. She got out a few minutes before the first fire truck rolled up."

"She'd have to be sleeping pretty soundly for the fire to have gotten that far without her waking up."

"Maybe she was passed out."

"And maybe she was tied up, and couldn't get free before then."

They shared a glance. "A definite possibility. A good length of cord was found on the floor next to the bed."

They mulled that over for a moment. "All those candles," Abbie mused. "A dozen, you said."

"That's right. Nearly three o'clock in the morning, she comes home from a night of drinking, 'wasted' by her own account, and lights what would be, by anyone's estimate, a large assortment."

"Not that it happens frequently, but when I've had too much to drink, all I want to do is go home and go to sleep. What about you?"

His hesitation was barely noticeable. "I don't drink anymore."

Anymore. She hadn't missed the inflection he'd given the word. Nor had she missed the no trespassing signs in his voice. She filed the statement away to be explored later. "But she doesn't go to sleep; she lights candles. Leaves the front door unlocked." She shot him a glance. "What's that sound like?"

"Like she was expecting someone."

Abbie nodded. "The way she nearly lost it when I asked about meeting a man downtown . . ."

"Guilty conscience, maybe. Like someone who invited a guy she met downtown to meet her at her place. But why try to hide that? Why not give the guy's name up?"

"Could be like she said," Abbie picked up the thread effortlessly. "Inviting a strange man home might be totally out of character for her. Maybe she's embarrassed about it."

"A different MO, if it's our guy, though." Ryne braked suddenly when another car switched lanes without signaling. "He doesn't pick up women in bars, risk being ID'd later."

She gave it some more thought. "Does this drug have to be injected? Can it be ingested instead?"

"No idea. Hopefully that's something the GBI chemist will able to answer for us. You're thinking something could have been put in one of her drinks?"

She nodded. "One way or another, the drug is the link. She came into contact with it during the night or once she got home. We just need to have a few more answers before approaching her again." And she needed time to research Larsen's background. She didn't want to mention that to Ryne right now, unwilling to disturb the easy camaraderie they'd fallen into.

"I want to get a look at the scene of the fire. Want to come along?"

Although she was tempted, Abbie shook her head. She could always check out the site later. "Take me back to headquarters to get my car. I'd like to start checking out those bars she listed. I want to learn everything I can about Karen Larsen by the time she gets off work this afternoon."

He was silent for a moment. Then he said, "Might as well show Juarez's picture around those places, too. We'll kill two birds with one stone."

"Any sign of him since you assigned a door knock?"

"He was holed up inside the apartment, just like we

thought. After our guy talked to him, he started back to work the next day. We've still got someone on him. Maybe he'll venture out to resume his crappy social life this weekend. No one can stay locked up in a dive like his forever."

Remembering the state of Juarez's apartment from their search of it, Abbie was inclined to agree. "It will probably take me a while to find out who was working at each of the bars on the night in question and get those people in to talk to them."

"I'll send a couple officers with you."

She'd need the show of SCMPD muscle, she realized. She had no visible means of authority to convince the management to talk to her otherwise. He pulled into the parking lot of police headquarters and cruised to a stop beside her rental. She released her seat belt and opened the door. His voice stopped her exit.

"Abbie?"

Turning, she found him looking at her, expression impassive, his hands clenching and unclenching on the steering wheel. But he said only, "Keep me posted."

———

Five hours and a gallon of water later, Abbie had little to report but rapidly eroding patience and limited progress. She'd underestimated the amount of time it would take to gather time sheets and work schedules in each of the drinking establishments from that far back. After the first stop, she'd wised up and dispatched two of the three officers Ryne had assigned to the next two bars on the list, to get the process started there. And even after all that effort, she got the same story from every waitress and bartender she spoke to.

No one could say with any certainty that they recognized Larsen, although waitresses in two establishments had hesitated over her picture. She'd scored no better showing Juarez's likeness. The only thing lifting her spirits as she walked into The Loose Goose was that it was their final stop of the day.

A blast of cold air hit her as Abbie pushed open the door, and squinted in the dim light to find Officers O'Malley and

Dugan. O'Malley spotted her and crossed the room. "Got someone who recognized her, Ms. Phillips." He jerked his head toward the man behind the bar, slowly wiping its surface. "Jim Cordray. He was working that night till closing time."

"Thanks, Tom." Moving past the man, she approached the bar, aware of the bartender's searching gaze all the while.

"Mr. Cordray, I'm Abbie Phillips, with the SCMPD. I'm told you recognized a photo Officers O'Malley and Dugan showed you."

The bartender's shaved head gleamed under the light overhead. From the breadth of his chest and biceps, he looked like he bench-pressed Volkswagens in his off-hours. She wondered if he doubled as a bouncer when he wasn't mixing drinks. He was a walking poster boy for steroid use.

"Recognized the broad, not the guy."

"Okay. So you were bartending that night?"

"That's right." He made no effort to hide the interest in his gaze as it raked over her form. "She was downing birdbath margaritas like they was water."

"Birdbath margaritas?"

He turned and got an oversized goblet and sat it on the bar in front of her. Abbie's brows rose. Given her height and weight, she was a real lightweight in the alcohol department. Two drinks of that size would have had her incoherent.

Karen Larsen was half a foot taller than she was, but if she'd had a few of these, it was little wonder that she'd been wasted. "How long was she here that night?"

He shrugged. At least she thought that's what it meant when those massive shoulders rippled toward his neck. "Don't know when she came in. But she was sitting up here at the bar for a couple hours and she was still here at closing time. Already pretty loose by the time I noticed her. And it was hard not to notice her."

"Because?"

"'Cuz she was showing off the goods, ya know what I mean? Tight top, short skirt . . . got a nice rack on her, but her ass is a little flat for my taste." He gave up the pretense of mopping the bar and leaned his elbows on it, giving Abbie another once-over. "I ain't got nothing against smaller packages, though." When he smiled, a gold front tooth glinted.

"I'm sure you're intimately acquainted with small packages," she replied blandly. Officer O'Malley turned his chortle into a cough as Cordray's brows furrowed. "Did she leave alone? Did you notice anyone in particular spending time with her?"

"She left alone. And she was chatty. Talked to lots of people while she was here. No one special."

Abbie studied the man then took a guess. "Did you go home with her?"

Sending a glance at the man, presumably his boss, at the end of the bar still talking to Dugan, he replied, "Nope." He resumed wiping the bar in a desultory fashion.

"But she invited you, right?" When he didn't issue a denial, Abbie went on, "See the way I figure it is, I've been to five other places and no one can recall her being in there for sure. The places were packed, hard to remember someone weeks later. But you not only remember her, you recall what she was drinking and wearing. That tells me there was more than simple observation going on. You and she were flirting, right? And when closing time came, the two of you were planning to see a little more of each other. Nothing wrong with that. Two consenting adults, right?"

"Right." Cordray gave her a slow wink. "And you know what they say about ladies all being 'tens' at closing time."

"So how'd it go? She gave you her address? You followed her home, or did she wait for you?"

He shook his head. "Neither. I was gonna head over to her place after we closed, but then my prick of a boss"—he jerked his head in the direction of the middle-aged man at the end of the bar talking to Dugan—"he counts the take and says the register is off a couple hundred bucks and he about goes ape shit. None of us can leave until the dough is found, and that means we're all standing around here for three more hours, unpaid, 'cause he's threatening to call the cops and turn us all in." He gave his employer a hostile glare. "Asshole."

Three hours. If his story checked out, that would mean it was at least five before he left here, and the emergency call from Larsen's was placed at four-fifteen.

"Were you the only one mixing drinks while this woman was in here?"

Cordray ignored the question, clearly filled with self-righteous anger. "'Course after all that time he finally figures out that he counted wrong—twice—but does he apologize? Hell, no. We're all out several hours' sleep because the asshole never passed fourth grade math."

Summoning patience, Abbie repeated the question.

"Naw. There were a couple of us. Benny was working the bar that night, too. I know he fetched at least one drink for her because it was him who pointed her out to me."

"What about when she left? What kind of condition was she in then?" Given the drug's disabling properties, Abbie doubted whether Larsen could have come in contact with the drug prior to her arrival here and still be functioning. But then, she'd managed to break a window and escape her bedroom, ostensibly with the drug in her system.

"Same condition as most who left here. Drunk. But not so drunk that she wasn't thinking straight. She called her own cab on her cell. Made it outside without help."

Almost certainly the woman wouldn't have managed that if the drug was already in her system. Abbie made a mental note that they were going to have to get Larsen to voluntarily offer them a copy of her tox screen to justify their possession of the copy Dixon had given them.

The possibility seemed no more improbable than retrieving any more useful information here today. Even realizing that, Abbie settled more comfortably on the barstool and asked resignedly, "The other guy bartending that night. Is he here?"

———

Laura Bradford smiled as her date excused himself from the table. Having to take a cell phone call on a Saturday night might have raised warning flags had it been anyone else, but Warren Denton was a high-powered local criminal attorney. Given his job, she could believe he was never really off duty.

Nerves jittered pleasantly in her stomach as she took a sip of what tasted like a very expensive wine. As a court stenographer, she was used to being invisible. It had taken Denton well over a year to even speak to her when they'd run into each other outside the courtroom; another year before he'd asked her out. And she definitely wanted this to go well. Although twice divorced, Warren was articulate, charming, well dressed, and handsome. It didn't hurt that he was also wealthy and obviously didn't mind spending his money. The Balustrade Revolving Restaurant, perched atop a downtown highrise, was one of the city's most exclusive.

She reached into her purse to withdraw a compact, checked her makeup in the mirror. The pains she'd taken with her appearance showed. She hadn't missed the subtle appreciation in Warren's expression whenever he looked at her.

Laura allowed herself a little smile as she slipped the compact back into her purse. After the string of dead-end dates she'd experienced in the past several months—the last of which had been an unemployed thirty-five-year-old Trekkie enthusiast still living in his parents' basement—she was entitled to feel a little excitement at the prospect of a date with a *real* man.

And maybe not just one date. At least she hoped not. Maybe this would develop into a real relationship. She wasn't necessarily in the market for white lace and organdy, but if a prize like Warren Denton came along, she wasn't going to close the door to options either.

"Beautiful view, isn't it?"

Laura started at the sound of a voice. A stranger had approached to face the glass wall behind her, which looked out over downtown Savannah.

Deliberately keeping her eyes from straying toward the view, she said deprecatingly, "I wouldn't know. I haven't looked at it."

"You haven't . . . well, turn around and see for yourself. A little later, with the lights from the city below, it will be truly spectacular."

Just the thought had Laura's stomach hollowing out. "No, thanks. Heights scare me stiff."

Chuckling, the stranger said, "Odd place to pick to come and eat then."

"It was my date's idea. I'm trying to impress him." Laura chanced a quick glance at the newcomer, keeping her eyes deliberately diverted from the window. "I didn't want to tell him that I'm terrified of heights. At least not yet."

The stranger gave her an intimate wink. "Well, don't worry, my lips are sealed. Your fear . . . will be our little secret."

Chapter 15

Abbie halted her approach and just took a moment to look at the man seated at the desk next to hers. Ryne's jacket was off, hung carelessly on the back of his chair, and he was reading something on the computer and scribbling notes in a notebook next to the keyboard.

His hard jaw was shadowed—it was past eight already—and his short brown hair showed signs of careless fingers being jammed through it more than once that day.

She had an urge to lift a hand to smooth it, a gesture that was distinctly feminine and totally unfamiliar. She didn't recognize where the wave of tenderness stemmed from; couldn't remember experiencing it for a man before. She was certain that if he knew of it, it would frighten Ryne as much as it did her.

She curled her fingers into her palms to keep them from reaching for him and continued her approach.

"You didn't call."

His back was still turned when he spoke. How long had he been aware of her standing there? Before her surprise could turn to embarrassment, he swiveled his chair to face her. "I expected you to check in before now. Did you hit a snag with the employees at the bar?"

Shaking her head, she set her purse on her desk and propped her hips against its corner. "You know how it goes. By the time you get someone down there with access to the time sheets and then call the employees in, it's hours."

"Tedious work. You should have left it to the uniforms to finish."

She stifled a yawn with the back of her hand and shrugged. "We didn't talk to every person who worked in all the bars that night, but we got most of them. I think the bartender at The Loose Goose is our guy, though." She gave him a run-down of that conversation she'd had with him and Ryne gave a bemused nod.

"So it's like we figured. She arranged to have him follow her home afterwards, and that accounts for the front door being left unlocked, and all the candles. He doesn't show, she falls asleep—or passes out—and the candle catches the drape on fire. Which would be the end of the story if she didn't appear to have the same chemical in her bloodstream as the rape victims. His alibi check out?"

"His boss backed up his story about keeping them all there an extra three hours or so, and can say with certainty the bartender remained with everyone else." And after fifteen minutes of conversation with the man, she'd been inclined to agree with the bartender's assessment of him.

Ryne worked his shoulders tiredly. "She could have issued the same invitation at a bar she hit earlier and the employee lied about recognizing her picture. Or maybe she came on to one of the patrons, too. One might have even known the bartender was going to be held up and decided to take his place."

"I thought of that. But according to both guys behind the bar, she spoke exclusively to the one bartender for the last hour before closing time. I've got O'Malley and Dugan following up on the patrons the employees recognized in the bar that night. But if there was an attack," and it was beginning to seem probable, "it's just as likely the rapist was hidden in her home, the same way he was in most of the other victims'. Larsen said it was unusual for her to go out at night. With her temporary nursing status, her schedule was likely erratic. He would have to be watching her closely to know when he could slip into the house."

"Next time we approach her, we'll bring up the arrangement with the bartender and see if we can get her to admit to inviting him. Maybe she'll be ready to talk once she sees what we know. What's his name?"

Abbie gave him the bartender's personal information. "I came back to run a background check on him myself."

"It'll keep." Ryne stood, picked up his coat. "I'll follow up on it when I come back in tomorrow morning."

"Might be simpler to pitch a tent at your desk," she noted, trying without success to keep concern from tingeing her tone. He kept long hours. Well, when she was on a job, so did she, but she'd be the first to admit there wasn't much else in her life to concentrate on. A pathetic admission, if there was ever one.

"I'm not much of a camper." He studied her, the corner of his mouth kicking up. "Although I could be talked into it if you're offering to share my sleeping bag. Protect me from these wild animals." He jerked his head in the direction of the nearest detectives.

Abbie's cheeks heated, and she threw a quick glance around them. The crew at this time of night was thin, and none of them appeared within hearing distance. And in spite of his light tone, the mental picture of the two of them wrapped around each other in a sleeping bag took on sudden vivid imagery. It was a moment before she could respond, and when she did, it took real effort to match his easy tone. "Somehow I think you'd be fine on your own. But if one of these guys makes a move for your s'mores, I've got your back."

"S'mores. Geez, I haven't had them since I was a kid." He was silent for a moment, and the heat in his eyes had her flesh tingling. "Have you eaten?"

"Are you kidding? After talking to those employees today, I may never eat again. At least not in a bar."

"Another guy would take you out. Decent restaurant. Wine."

"But you're not that guy?"

His voice lowered, and the intensity in his gaze had her pulse stuttering. "I'm the guy who's had his concentration shot to hell and back today, thinking of last night. The kind of guy who'd just as soon grab a bucket of chicken and get you in bed again as quickly as possible." He paused a beat. "But we can go out. If you'd rather."

She knew that she had only to say the word and he'd do exactly that, despite his weariness. Go home. Shave. Get changed and go out for a late dinner in an expensive restaurant. She could appreciate the offer, even while she wasn't tempted by it in the least. Not when she wanted exactly the same thing he did. To get him in bed, hot and naked, with the long hours of the night stretching invitingly before them.

She cocked her head, smiled slowly. "Extra crispy?"

———

In the end the chicken waited until an appetite of another type had been sated. It was only after, once his mind had cleared and his breathing returned to normal, that Ryne had done the honorable thing and fed her. Because all of a sudden they were ravenous.

They ended up picnicking in her bed, still naked, propped with pillows against the headboard and a towel across their laps to catch the crumbs. And as picnics went, this one kicked ass. There were no ants to worry about, and the view, he thought, eyeing Abbie's bare breasts, couldn't be beat.

Scooping up a dab of mashed potatoes with one finger, he dropped it on one of her nipples, then leaned over to lick it off.

"Interesting table manners."

"I don't see a table." He reached over and turned the bucket around to read. "But now I understand how mashed potatoes can turn this into a 'Valu-pak.'"

Abbie snickered, gave him a light push. "You're depraved.

I'm not sure when I started liking that in a man." She waggled her oily fingers at him. "Hand me a napkin, will you?"

Instead he reached for her hand and brought her fingers to his mouth, sucking the pad of each. And watched her eyes go to smoke. Satisfaction curled in his stomach. She was usually so guarded, it was all the more gratifying to observe her expression when he surprised her. Pleasured her. Evidence of her desire was heady, especially given the strength of his attraction to her.

The power of her appeal should have alarmed him. It had been a long time since he'd let himself get this close to a woman. Longer still since he'd done exclusive. But since he'd stopped drinking, he'd spent a year and a half denying himself one kind of craving. He had no intention of denying this one.

Tugging the towel from their laps, he wiped his hands on it before dropping it to the floor. He rolled to his side and the roundness of her shoulder caught his attention. Brushing his lips over it, he explored the shape and softness with his mouth. Abbie would be here for the length of the investigation, and then she'd be gone. A pang of regret accompanied the thought. But he'd regret it more if he didn't use this time to steep himself in her, to get his fill before their time was over.

He covered her hand, linking their fingers to stretch out their arms, his lips skimming over her bicep. There was toned muscle beneath the silkiness there, reminding him of the toned perfection of her body elsewhere, too. Softness belying strength. Much like her personality. Upon first meeting, he doubted most would see beyond the quiet composed exterior to the sharp mind beneath, or to her steely determination.

And no one would suspect the secrets she harbored, or the cause for them.

He lifted his head slightly to study the fine white lines crisscrossing the inside of her arm. A testament to past suffering. His gut clenched, as it always did when the mental image of her flashed into his mind, of a young girl, alone and terrified, mutilating herself out of misguided guilt and fear. All of them carried scars of some sort. Some just kept them buried.

Ryne bent her arm to skim his mouth over a scar that had remained pink and puckered, and Abbie shifted to press one leg the length of his. Her hand brushed his thigh, teasingly skirting the area showing remarkable signs of interest.

"You went to the scene of Larsen's fire today?"

His mouth was busy at the inside of her elbow. "Mm-hmm."

"Describe it for me." She crossed her leg over his, skating her foot up to his knee, and then down again.

By lifting her arm, he had access to the soft outer curve of her breast. He traced the shape of it with the tip of his tongue, smiled when she shuddered in response. "Small two-bedroom with two exterior entries. Northern-facing front door, the back is accessed by a set of three concrete steps. No garage or carport. Parking on the street in front. No security system, but there were deadbolts on both doors."

"Signs of entry?"

Her fingers were kneading his thigh, ignoring the heated length of him only inches away in what had to be by design. His voice was more strained than he would have liked when he answered, "Front door was unlocked, which we already knew. The other was locked, but the deadbolt wasn't engaged. The heat from the fire blew most of the windows out and the fire investigators didn't notice any signs they might have been tampered with. Of course, in light of Larsen's statement, they didn't really have reason to look."

He relinquished her hand to smooth his palm over the curve of her hip, and at his urging, she rolled to face him. A measure of satisfaction filled him at the access provided him by her position. He stroked the warm slope of her narrow waist, his fingers inching upward to brush a velvety nipple.

"Front door opens directly into the living room," he continued. "Across the room and down a six-foot hallway is the bathroom and spare bedroom on the right with Larsen's bedroom opposite. Her room had two windows, one facing the street and the other facing the east, toward the neighbor's house, which is about ten feet away. It was the east window drapes that caught fire first. The flames followed the southern wall, blocking off escape from the bedroom door. Larsen went out the north window. That portion of the home was consumed by the fire. Most of the living room and the kitchen are also damaged. Benson, the fire investigator, said it's a total loss."

"Our UNSUB wouldn't follow her home from the bar and into the house." Her hands skimmed up his chest, and down again. "He'd have been waiting inside for her. We know he has a talent for locks, with finessing alarm systems. And if the deadbolt wasn't secured on the back door, he could have exited through either door. I don't suppose they canvassed the neighbors?"

He still wasn't willing to say with any certainty that Larsen had been a target. But he was getting there. "They talked to a few of them, but I'd like to do it again, more thoroughly."

"How many windows in the spare bedroom?"

He swept his hand up one silky thigh, over her hip to squeeze her butt lightly. She had the sweetest ass. Toned and curved like it had been fashioned to haunt a man's dreams and scramble his thoughts. It took effort to shift his focus to answer her question. "One, facing the back of the property. Fairly secluded backyard, with a hedge around the east and south sides. A small storage shed sits on the southwest corner."

"So if this was our guy, why didn't he use the back bedroom?"

He frowned, not following her line of thought. "Why?"

"With only one window, which faces to the back of the property, he'd be assured of more privacy. He must have realized that the flames would be visible from the street. Unless . . ."

Somehow it didn't seem strange to be lying in bed with a woman he wanted, discussing a case with her. It should have been. It certainly shouldn't have felt so natural, so right, to discover that their minds were as much in sync as their bodies were. "Unless what?"

She tipped her head up to look at him. "He doesn't want his victims to die, does he? Not if their long-term suffering is his end goal. It occurred to me when we went to the Richardses' beach house and saw that opened window, the one that alerted the security guard to check the house and subsequently discover Amanda Richards."

"I'm not following you." And he didn't think it was the distraction of her naked curvy little body pressed up against him that had him so dense. At least not totally.

"I did a little checking on the tides for St. Andrew's Sound. The UNSUB put Barbara Billings in the water at high tide, or close to it. Even then, she was able to avoid drowning by pressing her face to the top of the kennel. The water was only going to get lower for the next several hours. If she hadn't been discovered by Marine Patrol, she almost certainly would have been by local fishermen early the next morning."

Ryne was silent for a moment. Since the UNSUB hadn't killed any of the victims, it was obvious their death wasn't the guy's intent. "Yeah, okay."

"He wants them found. After he rapes and tortures them, the ultimate payoff is the psychological suffering that will ensue. He has to make sure they don't die before they're discovered or he doesn't achieve the purpose of his ritual. Sommers was found by her husband. Knudson investigated Hornby's house after the alarm clock radio didn't turn off. It was on maximum volume, right?"

"So, if Larsen is another victim, you think the UNSUB purposefully chose the bedroom with a window in view of the neighbors so they'd call the fire in. Pretty risky. What if they had been sound sleepers?"

She scraped her nail lightly across his nipple and he flinched a little. When he saw a smile cross her lips, he could be fairly certain it hadn't been accidental. "I think sometimes he might hang around in the vicinity to make sure discovery takes place. If it hadn't, he would have brought attention to it some way himself. He doesn't want them dead. He isn't going to go to all that trouble and have them die on him."

Ryne smiled grimly. "So he must have been pretty pissed when he found out about Hornby's suicide."

She nodded. "It would have incensed him. He would have felt . . . cheated in some way. And as I said before, it would accelerate his cycle of choosing a new victim."

He didn't need the reminder that they were running out of time. The twist had likely chosen his next victim already. He agreed with Abbie on that. It was probably only a matter of days before he struck again. The news accounts recently would mean the women of Savannah were more aware of the dangers, but they couldn't count on that to stop the guy. He was too smart. Had been too damn lucky so far. And the leads they had so far weren't going anywhere fast enough to make him certain they would catch him in time. The certainty lay like lead ballast on his shoulders.

He could be sucked under by that knowledge, let it weigh him down and eventually destroy every shred of judgment, until he second-guessed every decision and allocation of manpower. Or he could use it to hone his determination. To focus his attention and do his damnedest to stop the perp in time.

He stroked a finger over the pulse that beat slow and steady at the base of Abbie's throat. The only absolute in police work was the folly of allowing a case to consume you. A cop had to take a step back once in a while to keep his instincts alert. Casual sex could be an easy way to accomplish that, but there was nothing casual about the way he felt about the woman beside him. And worrying about that just might distract him from the inner darkness that sometimes threatened to swallow him.

Abbie tilted her head and kissed him, slow and languid. As if they had all the time in the world to explore what was between them. And for a moment, he could almost believe they did. He took the kiss deeper and felt the kick to his system as desire arrowed through him. They were pressed together, lips, chests, hips, legs, and her soft warmth beckoned like a promise.

He could think of no better way to forget the pressures of the case than to steep himself in her. Ryne closed his teeth lightly on the delicate cord of her throat, and she shuddered against him. He wanted to spend the night exploring her, finding every sensitive spot on her body where lingering would have her moaning and quivering beneath him. But his intent was thwarted a moment later when she pushed him to his back and slid down to take him in her mouth.

His vision abruptly grayed. The soft moist suction was enough to smash his intent to go slow. It was enough to smash *all* conscious thought to hell and back.

His fingers threaded through her hair as he endured the sweetest kind of torture imaginable. The rest of the world faded to include only the two of them.

He endured the torment for long moments, until he doubted his ability to last any longer. With his hands on her shoulders, he urged her up, snaked an arm around her waist, and hauled her closer, sealing his mouth against hers. There was a careening in his blood, a primal beat that throbbed for this woman. Now. Right now. Without releasing her, he reached out his free hand and felt for the foil packets he'd left on the night table. And cursed when he instead knocked the empty food container to the floor.

The sound of Abbie's husky laugh was like a match striking flint, and his passion flared hotter. Wilder. He didn't recall a woman who could get to him faster, make him forget the best intentions in his hunger to have her. Now. Fast and hard and the hell with the precautions.

It was finally Abbie who got the condom out of the packet, rolled it with excruciating slowness over the thickness of his cock. And then, when he didn't trust himself not to pull her beneath him and take her with a senseless savage urgency, she lowered herself on him, one hand on his shoulder and the other wrapped around him to guide him into her hot depths.

Ryne could feel the sweat beading on his forehead, the

blood pounding in his veins. Senses were unbearably sensitized as Abbie took both his hands in hers, linked their fingers, and pressed them against the pillows on either side of his head.

It was heaven and hell. The slide of her skin against his, her taut nipples grazing his chest as she rode him, slowly at first, and then faster as her own desire took over.

Sensation slapped against sensation, too fast and wild to be identified. There was the slippery hot feel of flesh on flesh, the sound of her gasps, of the groan ripped from him. Because he had to see her, he dragged his eyes open to look into hers, to watch as passion turned them the shade of fog.

Her hips pumped a quicker rhythm, and a steel bar of desire tightened in his gut. His muscles went taut. He surged upward, driving himself deeper inside her, trying to get closer. She filled his vision, his world, as the ferocious battle raged over them, between them. And then she leaned forward to press her mouth to his, and passion snapped abruptly, wiping his mind, his senses, clean.

And when he exploded, he thought of nothing but her.

————

"You need to lighten up," Callie advised, inhaling deeply from a cigarette. "All work and no play makes Abbie dull, dull, dull."

With effort, Abbie maintained the smile on her face, while repeating to the waitress, "You can take my plate. And I don't want another beer, thanks." She looked at her sister after the woman shrugged and cleared the table. "I've never developed much tolerance for alcohol. If I had more than one, I wouldn't be able to drive home."

"Did I tell you about the Maserati I drove in Paris last month?" Callie picked up her beer and tipped it to her lips without putting the cigarette down. "I've never been much for cars, but Jesus, that one was fast. Took a half a minute to get it up to a hundred." She laughed, loudly enough to have several people looking their way. "What a blast."

"I thought it was Greece."

"What?"

"I thought you said before you were in Greece."

The other woman shook her hair back impatiently. "This was before Greece. Pay attention."

Abbie *was* paying attention. Had been since Callie had surprised her with a call about the time she and Ryne had been leaving work. He'd actually suggested leaving early—it was Sunday after all—to show her a few of the Savannah sights. She'd anticipated talking him into one of the haunted history tours that explore the city's eerie past.

Most of all, she'd looked forward to just being with him, without work or sex—however incredible it may be—shading their interactions. But the phone call from her sister had effectively put their plans on hold.

She hadn't heard from Callie since she'd shown up unannounced at her house, and she'd been in a constant state of unease worrying about what she was up to. Callie's sudden invitation to dinner was all the more surprising for its apparent normalcy.

But the more time she spent with her sister, the less likely it appeared there was anything normal about Callie's behavior.

"Abs, look at that guy over there. No, over there. He's totally checking you out."

Abbie flicked a glance in the direction of the loner nursing a beer at the corner of the bar. "He looks like someone minding his own business to me."

"No, you know who he looks like?" Callie snapped her fingers. "Like that older brother of the Fentons'. The second, no, the third foster family. Remember them?"

Abbie did. The couple and their family had been simple people, and particularly ill equipped to deal with a rebellious teen and her traumatized sister. After Callie had run from that home, they'd been removed again, but she and Abbie had never been placed in the same family again.

But it wasn't the Fentons occupying Abbie's attention at the moment. It was her sister's frenetic state. "Do you have a supply of meds with you, Callie?" She watched her sister's expression close down, but continued doggedly, "Because if you don't, we should call Dr. Faulkner. You're cycling again. You have to recognize it."

"I don't need to be doped up or to have my mind shrunk." Callie ground her cigarette out in the ashtray with short vicious stabs. It was already filled with half-smoked stubs. "Can't I even be happy to be with my sister without you wanting to call in the white coats?" She lit another cigarette, puffed, and then blew out a thin stream of smoke. "And the reason I quit going to Dr. Faulkner was because he wouldn't stop hitting on me. Got to be a drag." She narrowed her gaze at Abbie. "Wanted me to do him on the desk and reenact playtime with dear old dad. Said it would cure me. So I walked out and saved five hundred dollars an hour. Cured myself."

Abbie kept her gaze steady even as her throat dried. Leveling accusations of sexual abuse at people in authority, or those who tried to help her, was yet another of Callie's self-destructive behaviors. She'd accused two foster fathers, a social worker, and a teacher. Now Dr. Faulkner. "If that's true, it should be dealt with by reporting him to the police. To his licensing board. It's not a reason to forgo therapy and meds altogether."

For a moment she thought her words would bring on one of Callie's explosive tantrums. Her sister drew in an outraged breath, fingers clenched on her glass. It could, at a moment's notice, go hurtling through space. Then a moment later she burst out laughing.

"If you could hear yourself," she said ruefully. "If that's true . . ." she mimicked. She drew on her cigarette, blowing one perfect smoke ring. "Okay, so I made it up. But sitting in some drone's office twice a week for fifty minutes isn't doing me any good. I know what I need, and it isn't dropping a grand a week looking at ink blots. I'm thinking of going back to school, did I tell you that?" Callie scanned the room before crossing one leg over the other, the act causing her skirt to ride up even higher. "Everyone needs a purpose, right? You have one, even though I've never pretended to understand it. I could, too. I was pretty good at nursing before I quit the program, remember?"

Abbie did. If she recalled correctly, nursing had been one
of Callie's longer stints in school and had come directly after
her brief time as an airline stewardess and right before she'd
been convinced she could make it on the drag race circuit. "I
know you can do anything you put your mind to," she said
quietly. "But you'll be more successful if you give yourself a
real shot at it this time. Get focused first."

Her sister had a gift for ignoring anything she didn't want
to hear, so Abbie wasn't surprised when she switched topics.
But the subject she brought up then shook Abbie to the core.

"Did you ever wonder what would have happened to us if
our old man hadn't taken that header down the steps?"

It wasn't a subject she wanted to discuss. Or to think
about. Especially now, under Callie's all too avid gaze. But
she answered honestly, "Sometimes. Sometimes I do." When
she found herself alone and shaking in the dark, with the
echoes of that voice all too real in her mind, she wondered
that exact thing. And worse.

"Best thing that ever happened to us. Sometimes the end
really does justify the means, don't you think?"

Abbie stared at her sister, uncomprehendingly. Then as
logic filtered through, a horrible thought occurred. "What do
you mean? *What* end justifies *what* means?"

Callie ground out the cigarette she'd taken only a few
puffs of. "Filthy habit. I don't even know why I started again.
I only smoke when I'm drinking."

But Abbie found it impossible to leave the subject alone.
"Callie, what do you know about . . ." She'd never been able
to bring herself to call him her father. "About his death?"

But her sister's eyes were on the screen above the bar.
"Hey, you're on TV again."

Abbie stared at Callie, wanting to press her, knowing the
futility of it. Everything her sister said in her current state
had to be taken with a grain of salt anyway. She knew that.

"You shouldn't wear so much black," Callie said criti-
cally, her eyes still glued to the screen. "It makes you look
washed out."

Abbie sent a quick glance to the TV, which was muted,

but the newscast had already gone on to something else. They'd taken to showing just the clip of Dixon, Brown, Ryne, and her on the police headquarters steps, while the anchors rehashed what was known about the investigation. Dixon's hope that the press conference would keep the media happy was unfounded, so far as she could see. It seemed to Abbie that it only provided fodder for a sensationalized daily summary, which provided no useful assistance at all.

"You're famous," Callie said, turning back to her with an odd little smile on her lips. "And so's your cop. The cameras love him. Takes that edge of mean he has and makes him look dangerous."

She could only shake her head, unable to keep up with the jumps in her sister's concentration. But Callie had called it right enough; Ryne had an edge, and he was dangerous. On levels she had no intention of sharing with her sister.

"You know I've never cared for what you do," Callie said suddenly. "All those cops and bodies." She wrinkled her nose. "But you must be good at it. And that makes me proud. Sometimes I think you're the only good thing I've ever done, Ab."

Abbie's eyes burned with tears that refused to form. She reached out to cover her sister's hands with one of hers. And the sense of futility that filled her was as familiar as it was heartbreaking. "I know what I owe you. I've always known. I can be grateful for your bravery while still being miserable at what it cost you."

Callie squeezed Abbie's hand and for a moment there was a rare clarity in her eyes. A moment when Abbie felt a genuine closeness to her sister that had always been lacking.

Then Callie pulled away and reached for her beer, taking a long swallow. "I've always told you, worrying about me is a waste of your time. Didn't you know? I'm indestructible."

———

Callie widened one bleary eye to focus on the grimy clock face on the tavern wall. Abbie had run off hours ago. But that was when they were at the restaurant, she recalled. A couple hours and a few bars ago.

But no, Abbie was back. She swayed, clutched the edge of the bar, and peered at the flickering TV screen mounted next to the clock. That familiar footage was being played, of her sister and the cops, talking about the handful of nothing they had on the Nightmare Rapist.

"There she is, everyone, my little sister." Callie held up her shot glass, toasted Abbie's image. "Special consultant to Savannah's finest. Guess that makes me a celebrity, too. She'd be nothing without me, know that?"

She downed the tequila, barely noticed the path it scorched down her throat, and rolled the shot glass down the bar to the bartender. "Next one should be free, Ty. Got a famous sister, you know."

A male voice called from the pool table, "Hey, Callie, that really your sister? She don't look like you."

"She don't got your tits," another put in, and laughter sounded.

A bearded man pressed up against her. Slowly she swung her head to look at him. She didn't remember his name, but she recalled being on top of him a few nights ago, in the front seat of his pickup, with his jeans pushed down around his boots. What he lacked in grooming he made up for with stamina. "I like sisters." He grinned, showing a missing left bicuspid. "I mean, I like *doing* sisters. She into three-ways?"

"Fuck off." Suddenly furious, she grabbed an empty pitcher off the bar, and swung at his head. He ducked, barely managing to avoid being clobbered with it.

He backed away. "What the hell's wrong with you tonight? Crazy bitch."

She smiled nastily, and watched anger seep from his expression, to be replaced with caution. "Think I'm crazy? You have no idea. The only three-way action you'll be getting is you using both hands on your scrawny dick in the john."

"Here's your shot." The bartender set the glass down in front of her. "Chandler," he addressed the man behind her. "Shove off. I don't want no trouble."

Reaching for her purse, Callie withdrew her billfold.

Strange, how that impulse to protect her baby sister was still sharp. Still instinctive.

Or maybe not so strange. She'd protected Abbie most of her life, hadn't she? Sacrificed more, God, more than anyone could imagine, just to keep her safe.

"Put your money away. I got it."

She threw a flirtatious look at the newcomer beside her, but her mind was still on her sister. She *was* proud of Abbie. She'd told her as much, hadn't she? But it got hard sometimes to see her going about her life, like the past was some untidy mess she'd mopped up and forgotten. Like it didn't still live inside her, a living breathing darkness that touched everything she did. Everything she was.

"Forget your sister." The stranger leaned both forearms on the bar, looked over at her. "Bet you're more interesting than her anyway."

Callie looked at him more carefully then, smiled slowly. She wasn't a fan of long hair, but at least his was pulled back away from a face that would almost be considered pretty if it wasn't for his eyes.

They were hard. A little cruel. And she knew she'd take him home tonight and try him on. She was having one of those nights where she felt a bit cruel herself.

Because Callie had sacrificed herself to the monster that had been their father, Abbie had escaped their childhood unscathed by the nightmares that haunted Callie's every waking moment. If she didn't love her so much, it would almost be enough to hate her sister for that fact alone.

It would almost be enough to wish for such a nightmare to befall Abbie.

Chapter 16

"What've you got, Tinkerbell, one of those fancy coffee drinks?" McElroy dropped heavily into a chair beside Abbie in the interview room, the steaming liquid in his Styrofoam cup splashing precariously. He eyed her disposable cup with lid.

"It's a cappuccino." She waited for the expected jibe, but it didn't come. The man nodded, sipped from his coffee.

"Those aren't bad. I used to have a machine. One of the things my wife took with her when she left."

Ryne looked up and over the room, and it gradually quieted. Which was fine with Abbie, because she found herself more than a little creeped out by McElroy in an affable mood. Captain Brown opened the door just as he began speaking and slipped into a chair in the corner.

"Isaac came up with a possible lead on the syringe found in Juarez's vehicle." Ryne nodded at Holmes, who rose, straightening his dark ill-fitting suit. "The syringe is brand name *Reston*, which is one of the best-selling in the country. Client base is around five hundred thousand, including an expanding Internet market. But there are lot numbers, which will narrow the search. We finally got their client list this morning, after haggling forever over the court order."

"We'll be using a dozen uniforms to help with the grunt work on this," Ryne said, "concentrating on clients in an area within a hundred-mile radius of Savannah, especially the mail drops. This could turn out to be a strong lead, and we're going to wring it dry." He turned his attention to the detective who had just sat down again. "Isaac, you and Wayne will concentrate on the mail drop clients. McElroy, you'll coordinate the uniforms talking to the rest of the clients. Did any of the businesses experience a theft of syringes? Are they disappearing faster than usual? If anything sounds promising, follow up the phone calls with a visit."

"Anything from the lab on the syringe contents yet?" Captain Brown asked.

Ryne shook his head. "But I hope to have at least a preliminary report soon." His gaze shifted to Cantrell. "Why don't you update everyone on the shoes found in Juarez's apartment."

"We reached a dead end." The detective delivered the news with his usual impassive manner. Abbie couldn't recall a time when she'd heard expression of any sort creep into his voice. Or for that matter, seen a change in his demeanor. That kind of control must come in handy when working with McElroy.

"The sneakers are mass produced and available in discount stores across the country. Local outlets have had them available for over a year. The only peculiar thing we found is that they're a size larger than Juarez's foot measures. Bigger than the shoes he was wearing when we picked him up."

That news brought silence to the room for a moment. Then Holmes said, "He might have thought that would throw us off if he left prints with a larger shoe than he normally wears."

Abbie remained quiet. It was entirely possible that the detective was right. It would take an informed offender to be aware that there were ways to measure depth and width of a footprint left at a crime scene that could determine such a thing.

It was equally possible that the shoes didn't belong to Juarez at all.

Ryne was speaking. "We've got a solid handle on Juarez's hangouts, so I'm putting on-duty officers in street clothes in each of his favorite bars between eight and two a.m. They'll take some pictures of the patrons with camera phones and we'll see whom he's been associating with. Someone may pop for us."

"Who do we have to know to pull that duty?" McElroy called out from his slouched position. "Because I'm willing to sacrifice my liver and my sleep. You can even skip the overtime pay."

The others chuckled, and even Ryne smiled. "Sorry, Nick. The last thing I want to do is short you on beauty sleep. The officers need to fit in, so they'll be drinking nonalcoholic beers. But I promise to give you first shot at the photos they take."

He consulted his notebook before continuing. "I've got the LUDs back on Hornby's phone. All the calls for the last two months have been accounted for. Preliminary results are in from the ME and they support suicide as cause of death. Her prints are the only ones on the drinking glass found next to the body."

"You didn't think this guy would come back and finish the job, did you?" Isaac Holmes directed the question to Abbie.

She shook her head. "If the UNSUB had wanted her dead—if he'd wanted any of them dead—he'd have killed them during the course of the assaults."

"Looks to me like he made a pretty good attempt each time," Cantrell drawled, and there was a murmur of agreement in the room.

"If they hadn't been discovered, any one of the victims could have died from her wounds. But each of them *was* discovered. And that's too coincidental not to have been planned. Once, maybe, okay. But every time?" She shook her head. "Whether you agree with the profile theory or not, you have to look at the odds. The more victims he doesn't kill, the more it looks deliberate. They live because he wants them to. Above everything else, these attacks are all about his power. What's more absolute than the power over life or death? It's the ultimate in control. For whatever reason, he's chosen to let them live. For now."

Ryne looked up sharply, and Abbie saw that the other detectives were just as focused on her words, so she chose them carefully. "I still think he leaves them alive to carry out some twisted long-term suffering he's arranged for them. But he isn't always going to be lucky. Things are going to go wrong at some point. He's going to be surprised by a victim who takes longer to subdue, one who maybe gets a glimpse of him while she struggles. He's too careful to leave a victim who can identify him." She paused for a moment, then added, "Or he'll lose control at some point. Either situation means a woman dies."

The mood in the room turned even grimmer. Ryne didn't mention the possible Karen Larsen connection and Abbie knew that he wouldn't. Given the way Dixon had come up with that information, they'd have to tread very lightly until they got more to go on from the woman herself.

Instead Ryne focused on the exhaustive background that had been compiled on Juarez's family and acquaintances. Of special note was the fact that Juarez had leveled complaints with the warden of the prison where he'd served time. According to his claim, his former cell mate had raped him continuously during his first few months behind bars, until he'd been moved.

McElroy shot her a sideways glance. "What about it, Tink? A guy who's been turned into some hillbilly's butt buddy might have a little pent-up anger, don't ya think?"

She didn't respond, but there was no ignoring the truth in his words. Abbie was aware of the sort of rage that built up from years of that sort of abuse.

And rage could motivate people to do horrific things.

———

She went back to her desk, keeping an eye out for Ryne. He hadn't assigned her a task during the meeting, but they'd discussed the case again this morning over coffee. And even earlier, she recalled with a flush of heat, as they dried each other off from the shower, where they'd stayed, limp and sated, until the hot water had finally run out.

It was a curious sort of intimacy to find herself just as fascinated with a man's mind as she was with the chemistry that sparked to life so easily between them. Well, almost as fascinated.

Although she was fastidious, she didn't lack experience. But she'd selected other men in her life because she could so easily keep them at a distance. That distance meant that they'd also lacked the combustible sexual connection she'd found with Ryne. And since she'd deliberately kept the parts of her life compartmentalized, she'd never had a lover she could discuss her job with.

But those discussions were a natural part of her relationship with Ryne, and she found it a novel pleasure. Even if they hadn't been working on the same case, it would take someone affiliated with law enforcement to understand the frustration and demands of their investigations. That understanding gilded an explosive desire that seemed only to burn hotter the more time they spent together. She was hardly in a position to judge, but it seemed to her that a relationship like that was about as close to perfect as she could ask for, even if it was only temporary.

She gave herself a mental shake. *Especially* because it was temporary. Just the thought of embarking on a long-term relationship with a man could still turn her veins to ice, and she knew Ryne well enough to realize he felt the same. In that way, if in no other, he was safe. He'd expect no more from her than she was willing to give.

But that thought was immediately elbowed aside by the memory of two instances when he'd demanded more, much more, than she'd wanted to share. When he'd insisted on answers she hadn't intended to provide, with a dogged persistence that had been impossible to evade. He'd already elicited much more personal information about her than she'd shared with anyone in over a decade, with the exception of Raiker.

And it hadn't escaped her that he hadn't reciprocated in kind.

With a pang, she watched him head toward the desks, deep in conversation with Dennis Brown. Ryne Robel had his own secrets, and he was as guarded with them as she was with her own. She wouldn't pry, because she knew what it was to value privacy.

But that didn't mean she didn't want him to trust her enough to tell her what haunted him. She smiled mirthlessly. And that must mean she topped the charts for inconsistency. For the first time in her life she wanted the very intimacy that was sure to send her running if it were offered.

Abbie waited until the captain headed toward his office to approach her desk. Seeing Ryne's expression, she raised her brows. "You don't look happy."

He scowled. "Dixon contacted the captain before the briefing. Apparently he had a meeting with the chief and got a real ass chewing, because he saw fit to pass it on. I've got a meeting with the commander this afternoon for probably more of the same."

Abbie spun her chair around to face him more fully. "It sure would be nice to get a preliminary report from Han on the contents of the syringe. That should divert Dixon's attention."

Nodding, he replied, "Exactly what I was thinking. I'm heading over to the lab right now to talk to him. I hope to God he's got something for me." He went to the bottom drawer of his desk and withdrew a thick binder, handing it to her. "This is the newest information I've gotten from ViCAP."

She took the binder, eyeing it dubiously. "I thought you said you hadn't found any close matches." The database compared signature aspects and similar patterns in MO for violent crimes. The most notable aspect of their UNSUB's signature was the use of the drug, which had failed to match any cases in the database. Resubmitting the information minus the drug, using only the electrical cord as a commonality, they'd gotten substantially more hits, but these would be long shots.

"Don't look like that. You're the one who said something about this guy evolving." He propped his hips on the corner of his desk, folded his arms. "If the drug is a new part of his MO, maybe we should be looking harder at the cases involving bondage with electrical cord. It's possible that perp evolved from less violent rapes to the ones we're seeing now, right?"

"It's probable." Abbie leaned back a bit in her chair to look at him. "It's also possible that he evolved from sexual homicides to the ones we're seeing in Savannah."

Ryne looked skeptical. "A serial rapist who's deescalating? Is that likely?"

"He wouldn't be deescalating," she corrected him. She'd tossed the idea out without thinking it through, but the more she considered it, the more credible it seemed. "Again, it would depend on his motivation. If he's allowing the victims to live because he's arranged long-term psychological torment for them, then it's likely he's killed victims in the past, and no longer finds it satisfying. Remember, this guy thinks he's suffered. It would follow that he's still dealing with issues caused by abuse. So why should his victims get the easy way out? The toughest part of life isn't death, after all. It's living, and dealing with our pasts."

He went still, and she stopped, recalling in a flash what she'd been thinking about before he joined her. His ghosts were just as persistent as hers. She wondered how well he dealt with them. He'd mentioned once that he didn't drink anymore. Had drinking caused the ghosts or been used to keep them at bay?

But a moment later he'd recovered, shooting her a wry grin. "Like I said. You're a scary lady."

To defuse the awkwardness, she strove for humor. "You should know. You saw me in the ring."

"That I did. Although honesty forces me to admit I found the sight more arousing than frightening."

That surprised a laugh from her. "It would appear then that you're easily aroused."

"By you?" He pretended to give it some thought, then gave her a slow wink. "Yeah, I guess you could say that."

She could feel heat crawling up the back of her neck and had the urge to look around to be sure no one else was within hearing distance. But her gaze was trapped by his, and the wicked glint in his eyes made it impossible to look away. His eyes weren't arctic now. They were deep blue pools of wicked promise. And Abbie knew from delicious past experience that if they had a modicum of privacy, she'd be in his arms, naked, under him, in a heartbeat.

Because the man moved fast. She was growing increasingly familiar with his moves, and wholeheartedly approved of them.

Clearing her throat, she tore her gaze away to stare blindly at the binder in her hand. "I'll take a look at it today," she promised, attempting to gather her scattered thoughts. "Oh, and I had an idea about the shoes."

He cocked his head, seemed amused. "Okay, you had me right up to that last statement. What shoes?"

"The ones found in Juarez's apartment. Have you considered what it means if they were planted there?"

A flicker of annoyance passed over his expression. "After what we found out about his life in prison, I'm more interested in him as a suspect, not less."

She lifted a hand to stave off the argument. "I'm not discounting that. Just trying to look at all sides. Because if they really don't belong to him, we've got an UNSUB who did more than scope out a random available vehicle to transport a victim. He's deliberately drawing attention to Juarez as a suspect, which means he's engaging the police, at least on some level."

Ryne stretched out his legs, appeared to give it some thought. "*If* Juarez doesn't turn out to be the twist we're looking for . . . sure. I've run into that before, where the perp tried to point us toward someone else to make us expend time and resources looking in the wrong direction. Doesn't usually go that far, because we eventually see through it."

"Eventually," she reminded him. "After wasting valuable man-hours."

He conceded her point with a nod of his head and pushed

away from the desk. "I've got to get moving if I want to corner Han before my meeting with Dixon. The colored highlighters are in my desk drawer. Help yourself."

She started to thank him, then snapped her mouth shut and slanted him a glance. "What makes you think I'll need them?"

A half smile played across his lips as he surveyed her. "What's it going to be? Pink for cases with electrical cord and blue for sexual homicides that share some commonalities with our case? Yellow for assaults where the assailant hid in the home?"

Because she had every intention of color-coding the documentation, the accuracy of his guess was more than a little annoying. "Think you know me pretty well, do you?"

The look of male satisfaction on his face was impossible to miss. "I think I'm beginning to."

"Then you won't be surprised to learn I have every intention of working the Larsen and Cordray angle today, too. If I spent all day on the binder, my eyeballs will be bleeding in hours."

"Suit yourself." His smile was suspiciously close to a smirk. "And keep me posted."

"No problem. Enjoy your meeting with Dixon."

Her gibe succeeded in wiping the humor from his expression and he winced. "You've got a cruel streak, Abbie. I don't know when I started finding that so damn attractive in a woman."

———

Ryne leaned against the wall of the crime lab's conference room and mentally rehearsed his spiel for Han. The chemist wouldn't be pleased to see him, but Ryne thought he'd shown great forbearance in not contacting the man earlier. And let's face it, he needed to arm himself with good news before the meeting with Dixon.

It would have been far easier if he had only Dennis Brown to answer to. The captain had been in the trenches, had worked difficult investigations before and realized the excruciating process of fitting hundreds of seemingly disconnected pieces of information together to make a case. Back in Boston, Dixon had always been more political tool than cop. Nothing in the last year had convinced Ryne he'd changed.

Mark Han entered the room, a familiar expression of impatience on his face, and Ryne straightened, reached for diplomacy. But the need didn't arise. The man saw him and grunted. "Good. I was hoping it was you. I was about to call."

For Han, those words were tantamount to a pleasantry, and Ryne was momentarily taken aback. Then comprehension filtered through him and excitement flared. "You've identified the drug?"

"It's a beauty." Han crossed quickly to a conference table and set down the notebook he carried. "From a purely scientific standpoint, of course. Someone spent a lot of time designing this compound."

He flipped the book open and pointed to a page. Ryne glanced down at the scribbled formulas and notes. They may as well have been written in Greek. "Why don't you tell me what you discovered."

"I'm not done with all the tests. I have to be careful with such a limited amount of the sample. I don't suppose you've found any more?"

Ryne hated to dash the hope in the other man's expression, but he shook his head.

Han gave a philosophical shrug. "In any case, I think I've identified the two main components of the compound. One is MDMA, methylenedioxymethamphetamine."

"Ecstasy," Ryne murmured. The tox screens had shown traces of it in each victim.

"Right. Often people will report enhanced tactile sensations with use. But you'll never guess the second element I identified."

"You're not going to make me, are you?"

Han reached up to push his glasses more firmly on his nose and flipped a page in his notebook. "Tetrodotoxin, or TTX." He paused expectantly for a moment, awaiting a response, but when Ryne merely raised his brows, the chemist blew out a breath. "It's a highly poisonous neurotoxin that is fatal well over half the time it's ingested. Ten thousand times deadlier than cyanide. A single milligram is enough to kill."

"Wait a minute." Ryne jammed a hand through his hair, as a new thought hit him. "He was trying to poison them?"

Han shook his head impatiently. "This drug is a derivative of TTX, which tells me the guy was going for some of its effects, but not death. If he wanted to kill them, he'd have mixed in a larger amount. No, from what you told me about the victims' reactions, he probably wanted to immobilize them. With large dosages, the first symptom would have been numbness or tingling in the lips, followed by complete paralysis, cardiac and respiratory distress, and then death."

Ryne pulled out a chair and reached for the chemist's notebook, flipping through pages, although none of the chemical formulas or writing made much more sense than the pages he'd already seen. "All the victims reported the tingling in their lips," he affirmed. "But although they were weak after he injected them, most of them still spoke of struggling, so they weren't completely paralyzed. They were all injected twice during the course of the assault."

Shrugging, Han said "Like I said, trace amounts. If he was going to mix his own drug cocktail, so to speak, I can't figure why he didn't use a form of scopolamine, which also could have been tweaked to produce the paralysis and hazed memory. It would have been a lot easier to access than TTX."

Ryne recalled scopolamine from his early days working narcotics undercover. He'd once infiltrated a gang-related drug ring selling it, along with roofies and GHB, as date rape drugs.

"What would be the major outlets for TTX?"

The chemist smirked at him. "The Indo-Pacific Ocean."

Looking past the man to the clock on the wall, Ryne was reminded that he didn't have much more time before his meeting with Dixon. "Can you be a little more specific?"

"Sure." Han grabbed the notebook from him and looked through its pages, until he found the one he was seeking, tore it out, and handed it to Ryne. "Tetrodotoxin is found in several forms of marine life, but the most common is the puffer fish, otherwise known as fugu or blowfish. They're considered a delicacy in Japan, which not coincidentally leads the world in TTX-related deaths. It's even used in voodoo to create zombie poisons."

Ryne eyed him askance. "Get out."

The chemist slapped a hand over his heart. "Swear on my mother's grave. That's mostly in Haiti, I think."

"So I just need to start tracking down voodoo queens, sushi chefs, and geeks raising puffer fish in their home aquariums." Ryne's tone was sardonic. "Thanks, Mark. This is really helpful."

"You can skip the home aquarium enthusiasts. The fish don't produce the TTX on their own, a bacteria does it for them. And the bacteria is only present in the marine world. Puffer fish cultured by humans don't carry it."

"That really narrows it down."

"Probably not, but this should. There has been some recent interest by the pharmaceutical community regarding the use of TTX for medicinal purposes."

That buzz of adrenaline was back. Ryne stared at the other man, his mind racing. "How much interest?"

Han shrugged. "Couldn't say. But I know I've seen periodic studies in journals for the last few years on the possible medicinal benefits, primarily for pain suppression or anesthesia."

"That doesn't make sense," Ryne interjected. "This perp isn't giving something to the victims to lessen the pain. Just the opposite."

That familiar impatience was back in Han's expression. "TTX has a relative molecular mass, right?" Han flipped through the notebook to find a formulaic drawing and stabbed a finger at it. "Pharmaceutical scientists regularly make derivatives of drugs that produce desirable effects while minimizing or eliminating the unwanted effects. They change the structure of a drug slightly to see if this makes it more effective or reduces side effects. They'll add or remove a methyl, a hydroxy group, or some other functional group here or there on the original drug molecule and then see how it changes its effectiveness."

"Then how could you identify it as TTX anymore?" Ryne asked. "It's properties or whatever would be altered, right?"

Han looked smug. "You can still determine the drug it was synthesized from, but that wasn't the tricky part. Another chemist would have used a scheme of acid and base extractions. But TTX breaks down in strong acid or strong base. A neutral extraction was needed, and that isn't common."

It took Ryne a moment to realize that he was supposed to be impressed. "So you must have had an idea of what you were going to find."

"There are no screening tests for TTX or its derivatives. But I thought of it when you first described the effects to me. The structure of this drug is very close to the original compound, with slight changes that must have been deliberate. Someone spent a lot of time experimenting with minute alterations until the desired effect was achieved." There was a shade of admiration in his tone. "Like I said, scientifically speaking, it's genius."

"And designed with one specific purpose in mind," Ryne said grimly.

———

Abbie rubbed her eyes with the heels of her palms and turned away from the ViCAP notebook. She'd take a break from the tedium to focus on Larsen for a while. She'd want to talk to her again, but not before she was armed with as much background as she could compile on her.

She put the cap back on the highlighter she was using— she still owed Ryne for that dig—and got up to sit behind his desk to run a check on the woman.

Her cell phone rang, and checking the number, she saw it was Ryne. Answering it, she said, "You lied. You don't have any blue highlighters. That's going to throw my whole system off."

There was a pause, then a low chuckle. "Sorry about that. I'll have to make it up to you. Does that mean this isn't a good time to ask for a favor?"

Abbie leaned back in his desk chair, enjoying herself. "I've learned a little about you, too. Enough to avoid making any promises without knowing up front what the favor is."

"Usually a wise choice, but this is related to the case. I just left Mark Han and he's got a lead on the drug." Humor fled, and Abbie straightened as he went on, "He thinks it's a derivative of tetrodotoxin"—he spelled it for her and she jotted it down on a paper on his desk—"which has drawn the attention of the pharmaceutical community, and I was wondering if you could do a quick Internet search, see if you come up with anything."

She moved to her own computer again and opened the search engine, tapped in the subject, scrolled the page rapidly. "Lots of articles on its origin . . . it comes from puffer fish?"

"Among other things. Try medicinal effects or something."

She obeyed and a moment later let out a whistle. "Bingo. Looks like a press release from Ketrum Pharmaceuticals." She scanned the page. "They're currently in stage three of clinical trials—whatever that is. Looks like they're having some success using it for a heavy-duty pain blocker." She frowned. "That's not how it works on the victims."

"I'll explain later. I'm just pulling in to meet Dixon now. See what you can find out about the parent company and where their labs are located. And if you could discover the location of the specific lab involved in this testing, that'd be great."

"No problem," she said wryly, eyeing the ViCAP binder. On top of everything else she'd been involved in today, what were a few more hours of research?

They disconnected and Abbie got up to position her laptop on the edge of her desk. She could use the two computers simultaneously, running checks on Larsen and Cordray while searching the web for more facts on Ketrum. Maybe she'd discover the answer to the most urgent of the questions she hadn't had time to put to Ryne.

Like how a poison from a marine animal could be found in the veins of each of their rape victims.

———————

"Abbie. Check this out."

She looked up to observe Officer Joe Reed walking by, jerking a thumb behind him. Craning her head, she tried, and failed to see what he was indicating. But now that her concentration had been interrupted, she could certainly hear the commotion that she had previously tuned out.

"I'm not leaving until I see him, so the sooner you get him back here, the sooner you'll be rid of me." As the woman's voice filtered back to her, Abbie pushed away from the desk and headed up front.

"Ma'am, I already told you. Detective McElroy is out and could be all day. If you'll just leave a message . . ."

Abbie walked up to where the weary-sounding desk sergeant was addressing a dark-haired woman dressed completely in black.

Which was a little like describing the Sphinx as piles of interesting rocks.

She was clad in a skintight cat suit and thigh-high black boots with pencil-thin heels that added a good five inches to her height. She wore studded leather fingerless gloves, a matching choker, and a palpable fury that threatened to erupt at any moment.

"Is there a problem, Sergeant Foster?" Abbie asked pleasantly.

"Not at all." The officer replied with remarkable composure. "I was just trying to explain to this . . . lady . . ."

"*Mistress* Chan, you miserable worm," the woman snarled.

". . . that Detective McElroy isn't here and may not be back for hours. She was about to leave a message."

"I was about to do no such thing. Get him on the phone."

She slammed a hand on the policeman's desk and leaned forward threateningly.

Foster's tone was still even, but his face had reddened. "You'll want to step back, ma'am, before I have you cuffed and put behind bars again."

Mistress Chan. Abbie flipped through her mental Rolodex until she recalled where she'd heard the name before. The dominatrix that Cantrell and McElroy had interviewed. She observed the woman with renewed interest. Nothing in the detectives' notes had jumped out at her when she'd reviewed them, which in itself had seemed curious. It was hard to believe that a woman who made her living as this one did had never run across an S&M client who had come to her with bizarre demands.

She raked the woman's form with her gaze and smiled inwardly. *Bizarre*, of course, was in the eye of the beholder.

"Perhaps I can help you, Mistress Chan," she put in smoothly, edging her body between the woman and the desk sergeant. "If you want to step over here with me, we can talk about it."

Chan straightened, stared at her suspiciously. "The only way you can help is to get that bastard McElroy here so I can take him apart."

"A tempting prospect," Abbie muttered under her breath. From the corner of her eye she saw the sergeant smother a smile. She took the woman's elbow gingerly in her hand and steered her toward her desk, saying in a louder voice, "I think I can give you an idea of when to expect Detective McElroy."

On the way to the desk, however, Abbie noted the avid interest in the detectives and officers around her, and abruptly veered off course, showing Chan to the conference room where Ryne conducted the task force meetings.

"Have a seat."

"I prefer to stand." Chan clutched the back of a chair and shot Abbie a narrowed glare. "Are you a detective, too?"

She dodged an explanation by saying merely, "I'm with the task force Detective McElroy is working on. That's how I can be fairly certain that Sergeant Foster was correct. The detective isn't expected back here for hours." She prepared herself for another outburst from the woman but Chan had an arrested expression on her face.

"You're looking for that guy, too. Whattaya call him. The Nightmare Rapist."

Abbie inclined her head. "I believe you answered some questions from Detectives McElroy and Cantrell a couple days ago, but I wonder if you'd mind if I asked you a few."

"Not Cantrell." Visibly calmed, Chan released the back of the chair to prowl the room. "I don't know him. Only Nick."

"Detective McElroy"—Abbie gave the words faint emphasis—"asked you about any clients of yours that might have had unusual tastes."

The woman turned and smiled over her shoulder, real amusement on her face. For a moment Abbie felt like she was glimpsing the real person behind the S&M persona she cultivated. "Honey, in my line of work, they all have unusual tastes, y'know?"

"Can you think of anyone in the last several months who seemed to take it a bit more seriously than others? Maybe got too rough, or wanted you to do things even you weren't comfortable with?"

"Most of my visitors want the fantasy." Chan had lost interest and was on the move again. She rounded the corner of the table, picked up the carafe of day-old coffee, and sniffed it, before grimacing and putting it down again. "And I'm usually the dominant. That's the way I like it."

"You said you're *usually* the dominant." Abbie kept her voice steady even as she seized on the woman's words. "What about your visitors who have other demands?"

"There is one I can think of. Likes to inflict pain, sometimes with what he penetrates me with." She sent a sidelong look at Abbie, as if to assess whether she'd shocked her. "It excites him that I fight. That I give as good as I get. Occasionally he gets carried away." She lifted a shoulder, continued around the table, trailing her fingers sporting long scarlet nails over the tops of the chairs. "I never really thought about it until I started hearing all the news about that guy you're

looking for. What he does to those women. Got me to thinking . . ."

"Thinking what?"

"About this client of mine. And that's when I started to get
a little afraid of him. I've seen him lose his temper, and it
isn't pretty."

Abbie threw a longing glance at the door, wishing she had
her tape recorder. Or her notebook. "You'd better tell me the
name of this client, ma'am. We're going to want to talk to
him."

When she glanced back at Chan, the woman's sly smile
had caution rearing. "You already know him. It's Nick. I'm
really afraid that Detective McElroy might be the Nightmare
Rapist."

Chapter 17

"You stupid son of a bitch." Ryne tried to control the fury seething through him, but it was a losing battle. Every time he looked at Nick McElroy's face, he wanted to plant his fist in it.

"Robel, you've got to talk to Dixon, get me reinstated. Tell him I'm necessary to the progress of the case." The big detective swallowed, his usually ruddy complexion pale. "I need this job. It's the only thing that gets me out of bed in the morning."

"Necessary?" Ryne barked out a humorless laugh. "You've compromised the entire investigation. Every lead you followed is tainted, don't you get that? It's all suspect." His gaze narrowed as a thought struck him. "Did Cantrell know about you and the prostitute?"

Miserably, McElroy shook his head. "The bitch is just trying to stick it to me because I didn't bail her out when she got picked up in a vice sweep last night. She wanted me to get the charges dropped and I blew her off. That should show I haven't let my relationship with her affect my job. I didn't use my position to get special favors for her."

Incredulous, Ryne stared at the man. "Yeah, that proves you're a prince, all right. You really don't see the jam you put us in here?" Driven to move, he rose to pace. "You let your dick do your thinking, screwing a prostitute for months. Chan suggested you were the rapist, you know that?"

McElroy glowered. "She's just trying to get back at me. Anyone can see that."

Ryne strove for a modicum of patience. It was a reach, when he wanted nothing more than to swing at the man. "That may be, but we have to waste valuable time disproving it, the same way we follow every tip that comes in. Besides which, we're shorthanded. It'll take at least a week to bring the new guy up to speed on the case."

"I've been replaced already?" McElroy surged to his feet, his expression ugly. "That didn't take you long, did it? Must have had someone all picked out. You never wanted me on this investigation anyway. That's been clear all along."

The other man took a step forward, and Ryne braced himself. With the fury churning inside him, he'd almost welcomed the opportunity for a brawl.

The strength of that urge had him drawing in a breath, releasing it slowly. "We shouldn't be talking," he said, somehow managing an even tone. "Anything you have to say should go through Captain Brown."

McElroy deflated, the anger streaming out of him as quickly as it had come. "I figured you'd understand better. I need to keep busy. My wife . . . she left six months ago and took my little girl with her. She hasn't let me see the kid in twelve weeks. Sometimes the job is the only thing I got, you know? I'll go crazy sitting at home."

Ryne remained silent, but a stab of pity pierced him. He hadn't realized McElroy had a child. Before he'd been placed on the task force, Ryne had only known him from seeing him around the gym.

"For what it's worth, I agree that it sounds like Chan is just jerking us around by fingering you. You'll be off the hook for that as soon as we check out your alibis for the nights of the assaults. The rest of it . . ." He shook his head.

"You're going to have to wade through the disciplinary process." And no matter how much he disliked McElroy right now, he could sympathize with what the man had ahead of him. "You have a meeting with your rep lined up?"

"Four o'clock."

"Listen to what he has to say. Find something to fill your days so you're not sitting around brooding over this." He'd become something of an expert on brooding himself, not that long ago. It solved nothing, merely paving the way to a deeper, darker, emotional hole.

He went to the conference room door, pulled it open. "Once we double-check your schedule with the nights in question, you'll be alibied. At least that will be one less thing for you to worry about."

The other man nodded morosely, headed through the door without saying another word. Ryne watched him go for a moment, noted the studied busyness of the others at their desks, and swung the door shut. Sinking into a chair, he rubbed the back of his neck wearily.

News of Han's findings and the possible pharmaceutical lead had defused a great deal of Dixon's ire—at least until he'd learned of the development with McElroy. The man had gone ballistic, and Captain Brown hadn't been any too happy either. What had started out as a promising day in the investigation had abruptly turned to shit.

Bleakly, Ryne wondered if he was inviting trouble by figuring the day couldn't possibly get any worse.

———

Abbie gave another insistent ring of the bell. Karen Larsen's car was still parked in the drive, so she was guessing the woman was in there. The results from the database inquiries she'd made on Cordray and Larsen had been waiting when she returned from talking to Mistress Chan.

The memory had her grimacing. Talk about a dropping a bombshell. The woman had known it, too, and Abbie would bet a week's salary that she had leveled the accusation at McElroy to get just this sort of reaction. Unfortunately, they had to treat it as a legitimate accusation until it was proven otherwise.

It was almost enough to make her feel sorry for the detective. Almost.

After another ring of the doorbell, the door finally cracked open a few inches and Larsen stared out unenthusiastically. "This really isn't a good time."

Abbie pinned on her cheeriest smile. "I'm sorry to bother you again, Ms. Larsen. But we had some follow-up questions for you. When you didn't answer the phone, I decided to take a chance and drive over."

"Anything you need to know should be in the report I filed with the fire investigator," she said firmly, inching the door shut again. "I have to work third shift tonight and I need to get some sleep before then."

"Actually, Jim Cordray isn't mentioned in the fire report, although he probably should be." A sliver of satisfaction traced through her as the name of the Loose Goose bartender had Larsen freezing in the act of closing the door. "We wondered why you didn't mention to the investigator, or to Officer O'Hare, that you were expecting company on the night of the fire."

There was a tremble to Larsen's mouth, before she firmed it. Stepping back, she opened the door wordlessly, and Abbie stepped through it.

The place was as neat as the last time she and Ryne had been there, but dark, with the shades drawn. A pillow and a comforter were lying on the couch, and there were creases in the oversized T-shirt and yoga pants the woman wore. It was obvious Abbie had wakened her.

"So." Larsen swept the blanket aside and sat cross-legged on the couch. "Sounds like you've been busy."

"We followed up on the places you said you'd been that night. Cordray was the only one who recognized you."

Larsen's mouth twisted, her gaze cast downward. "Always nice to be remembered, I guess." She swallowed hard, then lifted her chin and looked squarely at Abbie. "You may as well tell me what else he said."

"I think you can guess." Their gazes met, held, until Larsen's dropped away. She clasped her hands in her lap tightly.

"I don't do this. That. I mean, whatever he told you . . ." She pursed her lips tightly and looked away. "That's just not me. I'm not a slut."

"No one's judging you, Karen," Abbie said gently. "We just need the whole story so we can figure out what really happened the night of the fire."

The other woman lifted a shoulder jerkily. "I wasn't withholding information. It just doesn't have anything to do with the fire. Really. The investigator agreed it was the candles that caught the drapes on fire."

"He also said there were more than a dozen candles lit in your bedroom. A woman doesn't light that many candles if she's planning on crawling into bed alone."

Larsen dropped her face into her hands. "I'm so stupid!" Her voice was muffled. When she lifted her head again, her eyeliner was smudged slightly under one eye. "It's not like it was going to be romantic anyway, with that big creep. Obviously I wasn't thinking clearly." She shook her head. "I must have picked up the rest of the candles on the way home somewhere. I only had the one in my house before then." Her voice trailed off, and she looked like she was about to cry. "You must think I'm horrible."

Abbie gave her a sympathetic smile. As confessions went, Larsen's was more pathetic than shocking. "What I think is that you're being too hard on yourself. All of us have done things that we're ashamed of. Things we wish we could undo. The first step in moving on is forgiving yourself for your mistakes."

The other woman scrubbed at her eyes, smearing her makeup even more. "Yeah, well, when I screw up, I do it major, don't I?" She let out a shaky breath. "I'm hazy on the details. I'd had a couple good-sized margaritas at The Loose Goose before coming home."

More than a couple, according to Cordray's statement, but the detail wasn't important so Abbie remained silent and let the woman go on.

"He'd said it'd be an hour or so before he could meet me, but he was there ten minutes or so after I got home." Her voice broke. "It was horrible. *He* was horrible. Sick and violent. I think he must have put something in my drinks, because once it started I lost consciousness several times."

Everything in Abbie stilled. "Who, Karen? Who was there?"

The woman frowned at her. "Cordray, of course. He . . . he grabbed me from behind, and at first I . . . at first I *laughed*. I thought . . ." Her throat worked and she unfolded her hands to wrap her arms around her middle. "I actually thought, 'Well, he's certainly eager.' " Her voice was filled with self-loathing. "That's the worst. I invited him. I brought all that horror upon myself."

Abbie leaned forward and said urgently, "Karen, are you sure it was him? Did you see Cordray's face? At any time during the night?"

Larsen seemed to fold in upon herself. "I . . . I don't know. I must have. I was just so out of it. I really think he slipped me something because all I can really recall is fading in and out of consciousness. Which was probably a blessing," she said bitterly. "He hurt me so bad. But I was drunk, and I invited him. Believe me, I know what the police would say if I filed charges. And I . . . didn't want anyone to know what I'd done." Her voice broke on the last word, and she bent at the waist, a loud sob escaping her.

Abbie rose and crossed to the couch, sinking down beside the woman to put an arm around her shoulders, her mind racing. She didn't know how much more Larsen could take right now, but there were more blows to come, and she didn't know any way to soften them.

"Karen, listen to me." The woman drew in a hiccupping breath, but lifted her head, although her gaze skirted Abbie's. "The man that night . . . wasn't Cordray. We've already checked his alibi thoroughly. He was held up in the bar that night with his manager and all the other employees until after five a.m."

Karen did look at her then, confusion and misery warring on her face. "That's impossible. He was there. I admit I was in and out of it, but I know he was there."

"*Someone* was there, Karen," Abbie said as gently as she could. "But it wasn't Cordray. I know this is hard for you. But I need you to answer another question for me." She gave the woman a few moments before leveling the question that had been on her mind for the last few minutes.

"Had you ever been in a fire before?"

"Is it safe to come in yet?"

Ryne looked over his shoulder to see Abbie approaching with exaggerated caution, and for the first time in hours, something lightened inside him. "Hey." He let his pencil drop to the desktop and spun his chair to face her. "Have you been with Larsen all this time?" He glanced at his watch. "It's nearly seven."

"Yeah, well, after our discussion she was having a very bad day." She leaned against the corner of his desk. "I finally called her neighbor to come over to stay with her. She was pretty upset."

He was listening, but wasn't as focused on what she was saying as he should have been. The headache that had been threatening all day was a dull rapping at the base of his skull, despite the pain relievers he'd swallowed an hour earlier. He was used to putting in long hours, but there came a time when he wasn't even effective anymore. He was perilously close to that point right now.

He'd like nothing better than to head out with Abbie to her place. Or his for that matter. Close the door and forget this case, forget this day, forget everything for the next several hours but the two of them.

The thought had interest, and more, stirring in the pit of his belly. She wore a gray shirt today, one of those fitted ones with the buttons hidden beneath a . . . what'd they call those things? A placket? Whatever. The shirt matched her eyes, the color of dense fog.

Her eyes darkened with emotion, he recalled. With temper. With desire. Pleasure. His stomach muscles clenched at the memory. The sight of Abbie when passion took her was a gut-wrenchingly sexy image that had burned itself onto his mind. It recurred at the most inappropriate of times, disturbing his focus. Disrupting his concentration.

That should alarm him. *Did* alarm him on some level. But damned if he could get his fill of her.

She batted him lightly on the side of the head. "And you're not listening to a thing I say."

"On the contrary," he lied, forcing his gaze away from the fabric hiding the fastenings on her shirt. "You had Larsen's neighbor come over to stay with her."

"I should have hit you harder," she observed. "I told you that a couple minutes ago. You're in another world."

"Would it make you feel better to know you were there with me?" God, he loved that expression on her face, that mixture of shock and pleased embarrassment. It made him think that, regardless of her experience, she hadn't experienced *this* before. Whatever this was between them.

He gave himself a mental shake. Apparently lack of sleep and Tylenol were enough to turn his brain to mush. He leaned back in his chair, stretched. "Let's start again. What had Larsen so upset?"

Abbie folded her arms across her chest. "She was convinced Cordray was there. That he drugged her, raped her, although she didn't report it as such because she'd invited him back to her place, just like we'd figured."

The news succeeded in snaring his attention. "Except it wasn't Cordray."

"And that's what sent her into near hysterics." He didn't miss the flicker of sympathy on Abbie's face. "And there's more. Her home started on fire when she was seventeen. A neighbor pulled her from the flames before she suffered major injuries, but . . ."

He could almost guess what she wasn't saying. "The rest of the family?"

"Her brother was away at school, but her parents died."

A fire survivor, who had been assaulted and had her bedroom aflame later that night. He'd always hated coincidence.

"Did she mention the tox screen?"

"Eventually." Abbie tapped the fingers of one hand against her shapely thigh. "She had the neighbor take her to the hospital instead of waiting for the ambulance because she doesn't have insurance."

"A ride in an ambulance is eight hundred bucks a pop," he noted.

"But while she accepted treatment for smoke inhalation, she didn't breathe a word about her other injuries. Thinking it was Cordray, she blamed herself for the attack. But she did have her friend, Dixon's girlfriend, run a tox screen. She was afraid Cordray—at least who she thought was Cordray—had drugged her. I got her to agree to give us a copy of the tox screen so now our possession of it will be legal."

Ryne frowned at her reference to Dixon but didn't correct her. "So she arrived home from the bar at two-thirty, according to her statement. And there's no way Cordray could have been there before five."

"Another interesting thing—she claims she had only one candle in the house, and thought she might have stopped to buy more on the way home. But where would she buy candles at that time in the morning?"

"If this is our guy, he probably brought them with him," Ryne guessed.

"That's what I thought. He grabbed her about ten minutes after she'd been home and the fire was called in at four-fifteen."

"Leaving only about an hour and a half for the attack," Ryne said slowly. "That would rush this UNSUB. He likes to take his time. Inflict a lot of damage."

"Maybe things didn't go as expected," Abbie suggested. "If he watched Larsen as closely as he did the other victims, he'd have expected her to be home. According to her, she didn't have much of a social life."

"All he'd have to do is watch to see if she leaves the house dressed for work and from there guess the time she'd be home, if she usually works eight-hour shifts."

"Only this time she leaves again, and by her account, it's

still early. Five-thirty or so. And she doesn't return for hours. That must have really thrown a wrench into his plans."

"But if he followed his usual MO, he'd have been inside the house by the time she got home from work. He could have grabbed her while she was changing then. He got Billings around six thirty, so he isn't worried about starting the attack in the daylight. Why didn't he just take her when he had a chance?"

She shook her head slowly. "Hard to say. Unless her leaving caught him by surprise, since she so rarely went out." She thought for a moment. "Did Han say anything about the effects if this drug was mixed with alcohol?"

Ryne shook his head. "I doubt he'd be able to take more than an educated guess about that. Why?"

"Because I wonder if all the booze she consumed interfered with the effects. She's hazy about the attack. More so than the other victims. It sounds like she was unconscious a lot of the time."

He leaned back to study her carefully. "I'm thinking the perp would be pretty pissed off by that. He'd want her subdued but awake to suffer through the whole experience. The whole time line hurries him. Maybe that's why she was able to get loose from her bonds—he had to act more quickly than usual."

"There's still a lot of details to her story that need to be filled in," Abbie admitted. "Tomorrow I want to visit the scene of the fire, talk to her neighbors."

"Were you able to access that information about her family's fire on the Web?" he asked, without much hope.

"It wasn't available to the general public. I had to pay a fee for the newspaper archive, and of course, I already knew what to look for. I followed up with the same question I asked the other victims, about any personals postings she might have made to an online bulletin board, blog, or chat site. She claims she isn't into that sort of thing."

It had been a good line to follow, but hadn't panned out. Out of all the victims, only Richards regularly used the new

Web gadgetry that allowed people to share what was, from a police perspective, an unwise amount of personal information.

He rubbed at the base of his skull, where the pounding had taken on jackhammer status. "You filled out the interview questionnaire? Victim checklist?" He didn't need her nod to have his answer. Abbie was as thorough as he was himself. When it came to victimology, probably more so.

"Nothing in her daily routine or habits jumped out for me, but I'll be certain once I add the information to the victim grid."

"So tell me where you think this leaves us."

"He's not relying on a single method for selection," she said regretfully.

He shared her disappointment. It would have been a helluva lot easier all around if he were. They'd have nailed it by now. The victim grid Abbie had put together was comprehensive, with only the most superfluous intersections.

"Some of the information he could have gathered through the media or Internet, and I think it's probable that he did so, at least in the case of Richards and Hornby. But for the others . . . somehow, some way, they gave up the information about their fears freely, in a completely nonthreatening environment."

Abbie's face went pensive as she continued, "He's in a position to win women's trust, or in a crowd, like a party where you mingle and have innocuous conversations with lots of people over the course of the evening. Maybe he even overhears the information, and then follows up on it."

"Someone who wins their trust." Ryne mulled the statement over. "Who is a woman going to talk to so freely?"

"Girlfriends. Their mothers. Pastors. Therapists. Gynecologists."

He was following Abbie's rapid litany until the last. He raised his brows. "Gynecologist?"

"Or doctor." Abbie shrugged. "Think about it. You already have very few secrets from the person doing your annual Pap smear."

Ryne felt what he considered a very natural squeamishness at examining the idea too closely. Some of women's mysteries should remain just that. Mysteries.

"And so far we've gotten nowhere looking for connections in where they doctor or worship. Maybe we should look harder at the friends and acquaintances angle."

She nodded unenthusiastically and he suspected Abbie understood what he did himself. They'd covered that angle pretty thoroughly already. It was going to be nearly impossible to predict the actions of an offender who was using random methods of selection.

"I didn't get through all the ViCAP hits, but I did highlight the cases in which electrical cord was used to bind victims, regardless of whether it was arms, legs, or both." She half turned to reach for the binder, which she'd placed on his desk, and opened it to indicate pages bearing yellow highlighter. The sight brought a smile to his lips, in light of their earlier conversation that day, but he knew better than to let her see it.

"I had a forensic knot analyst look at what pictures we could get of the cord," he reminded her. In most cases, whoever had found the victim had released her before the police were there to salvage the knots. But the security guard who had rescued Amanda Richards had had the foresight to cut the bonds carefully enough so that they could be reconstructed, as had Marine Patrol when they'd pulled Billings out of the sound. The analyst could only tell them the knots hadn't been military, nautical, or connected with any occupation requirement.

"Yeah, and I'm still not sure whether the use of the electrical cord means only that the wire is accessible to him or part of his ritual. But if it is part of his signature, it might pay off to look further at the cases I highlighted. There was a string of sexual homicides in New Jersey three years ago that were particularly violent, in which electrical cord was used."

Ryne frowned. "I think I remember those. I was still in Boston at the time. Followed the case in the newspapers."

"It rang a bell with me, too, because Callie was going to

nursing school in Connecticut at the time. At any rate, there are several others, most sexual homicides, involving some sort of cable or wire. I'll continue looking at them tomorrow."

Pushing away from the desk, she rounded his chair to pluck a file folder out of the drawer of her desk, and handed it to him. "Maybe this will cheer you up. I contacted Ketrum's PR department under the pretext of being an enterprising young reporter, and got you a list of their labs and locations, including the lab that's working on the trials with TTX."

Pleased, Ryne opened the folder, scanned the sheet inside. "Good work."

"The PR rep I was talking to got real guarded when I wanted to discuss their trial tests, but after some more digging online, I discovered that the clinical tests they're doing involving TTX are being done at Ketrum's newest lab facility, in Shelton, Montana. And . . ." She paused dramatically. "You're going to love this—I cross-checked Ketrum with Reston's client list."

"They're on it?"

Abbie nodded. "Double-checked with their headquarters and was told they've used Reston syringes exclusively for the last five years."

There was a racing in his chest that he recognized as adrenaline. They were on to something here, finally. He could feel it. "You had a lot more productive day than I did." He needed the identities of the team members working on that clinical trial for Ketrum and to check each of them out. But how . . .

"A-a-a-and . . . I've lost you again." Abbie's smile was indulgent. "There's a lot of new developments. Want to discuss the next course of action over dinner?"

He was tempted. The strength of that temptation was nearly overwhelming. He'd like nothing more than to go home with Abbie, bouncing ideas off her while they ate, before eventually giving in to another sort of appetite that was never far away when they were together.

Regretfully, he shook his head. "I'm up to my ass in paperwork, and I have to think this through, be ready with new assignments for tomorrow morning's meeting. I'll probably be late."

"Sure." She agreed a little too readily, turning away to reach for the ViCAP binder. "I'll take this with me and continue working on it after I add Larsen's information to the victimology grid. We can compare notes tomorrow."

He watched her closely, but she avoided his gaze. He wasn't willing to admit that he didn't think he'd get a damn thing accomplished with her seated at the desk next to him. His concentration was already too fractured by the events of the day as it was.

"Abbie." He waited until she finally looked at him, her smile a little too fixed. "I'll be late. But I'd like to come over after. If that's okay."

Her smile amped up, infused with genuine pleasure. She said only, "That'd be fine." But that, coupled with her expression, was more than enough.

Abbie's cell rang as she was crossing the police parking lot to her car, and one glance at the caller ID had her stomach sinking. Because the disloyalty made her feel guilty, she answered with more cheer than she was feeling. "Callie. I'm glad you called. You're hard to get a hold of."

She hadn't spoken to her sister since the night they'd had dinner together, but she'd called her several times, to no avail.

"I'm bored," Callie announced. "How about I pick up Chinese and head over to your place."

Reaching her car, Abbie unlocked the driver's door and slid inside, setting the files she'd hoped to work on beside her on the passenger seat. "Sounds good," she said with false enthusiasm. "Or I could pick you up if you like." More than simple curiosity was behind the offer. Seeing where Callie was currently staying might help her glean valuable insight into her sister's emotional state. Callie's manic cycles were marked with expensive extravagances and buying sprees, while her depressive states would have her staying in a fleabag hotel with questionable occupants.

But the opportunity didn't present itself. Callie said merely, "See you in twenty minutes."

As she drove off the lot, Abbie was grateful for the work that would keep Ryne at his desk for hours yet. She wasn't especially anxious to have him and Callie in one place again.

———————

The table was littered with half-empty cartons when Callie pushed her chair back and rose to prowl the small home. "How can you stand being cooped up in here?" She went through the doorway into the small living room, and rounded the couch. "I'd go crazy in such a small space."

Abbie left the mess to trail after her sister as far as the living room doorway. Callie seemed especially brittle this evening. On edge. "I don't mind. I'm not here that much. Mostly just to sleep."

"And are you sleeping alone these days, or have you had that hot detective keeping you company in bed?" Callie sent her an arch look as she continued pacing the room, trailing a hand over the mantel, skirting the pictures there.

That was a question she had no intention of answering. Her sister had been just as unforthcoming about some questions Abbie had put to her earlier, uppermost being where she was staying.

That in itself wasn't cause for alarm. Callie had always been secretive about things that barely mattered, and overly open about things Abbie would rather not hear about.

But pressing her on the subject would divert Callie from the topic of Ryne, one Abbie was eager to steer clear of. "I'd really like to know where you're staying while in Savannah. In case I have to get in touch with you and can't reach you by phone."

"I move around," Callie said vaguely. "Oh, I have a brilliant idea! We should go out." She whirled to face her sister, her face bright. "When's the last time we did the town together?" She gave an impatient wave of her hand as Abbie opened her mouth. "No, I don't mean for dinner, like the other night. I mean get dressed up and rock this town back on its heels." Her tone turned wheedling. "C'mon, it'd be fun. I have some people I want you to meet."

She felt guilty about dampening her sister's enthusiasm by demurring, even though Abbie would rather chew glass than spend the next several hours in smoky bars watching her sister spin further out of control. "I have to work tomorrow." She injected a note of regret into the words, could see that her sister didn't buy it. "I'm well past the age when I can carouse all night and not suffer the effects the next day."

"That's because you never got enough practice." Petulantly, Callie slapped her hand on the mantel, knocking the picture of the two of them to the floor. "Always sensible, capable Abbie. Doing the right thing. Making the right choices. Perfect, perfect Abbie."

Her chest went tight. "I'm far from perfect."

"Why, because you're still afraid of the dark? You can just turn on a light and the darkness is gone, isn't it? I'll bet you wish it was as easy to be rid of me."

"You know better than that," Abbie said quietly.

"Do I?" There was something wistful about the smile Callie gave her. "I don't know you at all anymore. Not really. When's the last time we were close, Abbie? I mean really really close?"

Now wasn't the time for honesty, that true closeness was never something they'd shared. So Abbie gave her as much sincerity as she could muster, and hoped it'd be enough. "You know I love you. I always will. We're sisters."

"We could be close again." Callie's eyes were bright, her expression avid. "You know when we were always the closest?" She whirled away from the mantel and approached Abbie rapidly. "When I gave you this. Remember?"

Abbie's gaze dropped to the object Callie had taken out of her pocket, and felt the breath rush out of her. A razor blade. Still inside its protective paper shield. And the past flooded in with a frigid force that was impossible to avoid.

Here, Abbie. You can throw that piece of glass away. Use this tonight. I'll know you're there for me. I'll know.

"Put that away." Her throat had closed. The words sounded strangled. And she couldn't look away from the blade. Couldn't push aside the memories it elicited.

"I never felt closer to you than when I knew you were bleeding down the hall from me. You felt it, too, didn't you?" Callie took the blade from its wrapper, held it out. "I know you felt it, too. Don't you ever miss that pain, Abbie? Aren't you ever tempted to pick up a blade again, just to see the blood?"

"No." Abbie tore her gaze away from the razor blade and stared steadily at her sister. Callie needed calm right now, she needed someone to be rational.

She didn't need to know that just the sight of the blade had those old scars itching again. Brought the memories hurtling back of that first slice, the burn, followed by a curious numbness. And then the scalding pain that had followed. Pain like her sister had been experiencing just yards away.

"Take it."

When Callie tried to push the blade into her hand, she stepped away. "We need to get you lined up with a therapist down here, Callie. Someone who can see to your medication. I'll come with you. I'll stay with you the whole time."

But her sister was insistent. "I don't need therapy, I need *this*. *You* need this. *Take* it. Just one cut. Feel it again, Abbie. Can you feel it?"

"Callie, you and I can—"

"I said feel it!" Callie shrieked, bringing her hand swiftly across his sister's arm, above the elbow. And then stared, eyes round and horrified, as the slice in the sleeve rapidly soaked with blood.

There was a familiar buzzing in Abbie's ears, that light-headed feeling of being disconnected from it all. From the pain. The fear. And then air hit the open wound and the numbness was replaced by burning. A burning that would turn to agony with one more slice. And then another.

"Abbie, I'm sorry. I'm so so sorry." Callie's face crumpled

and she dropped the blade, flinging her arms around her sister. "I didn't mean it. I never want to see you hurt. You know that, don't you?"

"It's all right," Abbie whispered, staring blindly over her sister's shoulder. "It's going to be all right." Awkwardly, she disengaged herself, spread the rip in her shirt apart to assess the damage.

With a sinking stomach, she realized that the wound wasn't going to be taken care of with a couple butterfly bandages. "C'mon, Callie, I need to go get this stitched." She reached out to lift her sister's chin with one hand, gazed into her stricken face. "And you need to get a new prescription."

"I'll drive you." Callie seemed to pull herself together then, looking frantically around for her purse. "Let me just get you a clean towel to put over your arm."

Abbie watched her sister bustle around, taking charge, bringing out a dampened washcloth, finding her keys. But when it was time to leave, Abbie remained in place. "I'm not going unless you agree to place a call to Dr. Faulkner. Now. Tonight."

Something flickered in Callie's expression and she crossed the room to tug on Abbie's uninjured arm. "We can discuss it later. C'mon now. Before you bleed all over."

The blood was seeping between Abbie's fingers. She could feel it trickling down her arm, dripping to the floor. But she didn't take her eyes off her sister. "Not until you promise. You call him tonight. I pick up the medication. I watch you take it. Promise, Callie."

Callie moistened her lips, looking everywhere but at her sister. Then she stared at the hand Abbie had clamped over her wound, where the blood was seeping through her fingers, and her throat worked convulsively.

"I promise."

Chapter 18

"What can I do you for, Savannah?"

The gravelly voice on the other end of the phone matched the image posted on the department website for Montana's Elk Run County's sheriff. Mick Jepperson was a balding, red-faced, burly man, a twenty-two-year veteran of the department. Ryne was hoping the man's experience matched his capable demeanor.

"I'm working a serial rapist investigation here, and—"

"That so-called Nightmare Rapist? Saw something about that on the news."

Great. So the media attention had gone national. Ryne pushed the realization aside to be worried over later. "We've gotten a recent break on the drug the UNSUB uses to subdue his victims. Something that points to a possible connection with Ketrum Pharmaceuticals."

"Ketrum?" The sheriff's voice went guarded. "They're big business in our parts. Biggest employer in the area. We're pretty isolated out this way. You can imagine what it means to our tax base to have a fancy new company start up with almost two hundred new jobs."

"Yeah, I get that." He gave the man a brief rundown on Han's findings, finishing with, "I'm checking the pharmaceutical end first. I have a list of other companies working with it, of course, but Ketrum is using it in clinical trials, putting them well ahead of the pack. Not surprisingly, they aren't releasing the names of the team members working on the trials."

"Interesting, but I'm still not sure how I can help."

Ryne could hear the dwindling patience in the man's tone and abruptly switched gears. "I was wondering if you've had any incident reports that stand out. Rapes or assaults where the victim claims to have been drugged."

"Nope. We have our share of violent crime, but nothing like urban areas. Had us an attempted murder case last night, but I'm thinking we'll be solving that as soon as we track down the estranged husband."

His shot in the dark appeared to be going nowhere. "So no sexual assaults?"

He could hear the shrug in the sheriff's voice. "Sure. But not like what you're dealing with." He was silent for a moment. "Had a case eight, ten months ago where a girl was attacked. A runaway, who'd been doing some underage drinking in the bars. Rape kit showed violent intercourse, and she was roughed up pretty good, but she wasn't much help identifying her attacker, or giving us anything to go on. Kept saying she'd been really out of it during much of the assault."

Interest sharpening, Ryne asked, "Do you have an address? I'd like to talk to her."

"An address wouldn't do you much good. A few weeks after she was delivered back home, she took off again. Far as I know, she hasn't returned."

Shoving aside a stab of frustration, Ryne said, "What about her tox screen? Do you still have a copy of it?"

"Sure. It ought to be in the case file. You want a copy? Near as I can remember, it didn't come up with anything definite."

"But it can be compared to the victims in my case." Ryne gave him his fax number. "We've got lab priority on this. I'll be able to get back to you within a few days." Now that he had the man's interest, he shifted tactics. "What would be really helpful is the names of the individuals working directly on the TTX trials for Ketrum."

The man was silent for a moment. Slowly he admitted, "Well, I do have a deputy whose wife works in human resources out there. It's no secret in these parts that she can talk the ear off a jack mule. If anyone knows what goes on at that facility, it'd be her."

Squelching a surge of excitement, Ryne elicited the man's promise to follow up with the deputy's wife and get back to him tomorrow. Only minutes after ending the call, the fax in the corner of the room began to whir. Giving another look at the empty desk beside him, Ryne got up to collect the tox screen Jepperson had sent.

He hadn't heard from Abbie since she'd left work last night, and he was starting to worry. Her car had been in the drive but she hadn't answered the door or her phone when he'd gotten to her place close to midnight last night. He'd figured she'd changed her mind and gone to bed rather than wait up for him and he couldn't say that he blamed her.

But it had been impossible not to be disappointed.

He scooped up the tox results and started back to his desk. That disappointment should be a wake-up call. He was beginning to rely too much on seeing her at the end of the day; discussing the case with her, or not talking at all, which was even better. There was nothing like mind-blowing sex to ease the normal stress and pressure of the job.

But he'd be lying to himself if he claimed it was just the sex that kept him going back, like a damn homing pigeon to the roost. He liked being near her, liked the feel of her in his arms all night. Liked the look of her, tousled and drowsy in the morning. And he was very much aware of what kind of trouble that meant.

Hell of it was, he'd never been one to walk away from trouble.

He went to the receptionist's desk. "Marcy, has Phillips called in?"

The blond woman never looked up from her keyboard. "Not since this morning."

Which had been a short terse message informing him only that she'd be late today. With a shrug, he headed back to his desk, prepared to go through the cases she'd highlighted in the ViCAP file. His cell phone rang before he'd gotten through half a dozen cases.

"It's Abbie." Her voice sounded weary. "Something came up with Callie last night. That's where I've been today, too. I'm on my way across town now, though. Thought I'd swing by and start interviewing the neighbors at Larsen's first address, unless you have something else for me."

"That sounds fine." And it was a relief, more than it should have been, just to hear her voice, even if she sounded distracted and impersonal. "Ashley Hornby's sister is in town. I told her you'd be contacting her." He gave her the number. "If I'm not here when you get in, give me a call. I want to hear what you come up with."

After she'd promised to do so, he disconnected, and stared blindly at the binder. She hadn't gone into details about the events of last night, but that didn't stop him from wondering. Didn't stop him from worrying about the effect the antics of her unstable sister might have on her, and what the hell was he supposed to do with that?

Shove it aside, he decided grimly, and forget about it. Abbie didn't need protecting, and he sure as hell didn't have the time to spend worrying about something that was none of his business. Four, quite possibly five, rape victims and an offender they still couldn't ID were more than enough to occupy his mind.

Letting a woman take up residence there was downright dangerous.

Wearily, Abbie nosed her car into the driveway and pulled around to the back. She'd always hated coming home in the dark, but had a small keychain flashlight for nights such as these. Right now she thought she might be just tired enough not to mind the shadows. All she wanted was to fall into bed and sleep for eight straight hours.

The ER visit had turned into an all-night affair, first to get the twelve stitches in her arm, and then waiting for the psych consult for Callie. The psychiatrist, Dr. Solem, at St. Joseph/ Candler had consulted over the phone with Dr. Faulkner, and Abbie had watched Callie take the resulting medication herself. Her sister had an appointment for later that week to see Solem, and if the time lapse had Abbie nervous, she had no one to blame but herself.

She turned off the engine and took her keys from the ignition, finding the keychain penlight and thumbing on the switch. What was she supposed to have said when asked if Callie was a danger to herself or to anyone else? The act of bringing the blade to Abbie's place showed just how far Callie had cycled. But she hadn't meant to injure her. Abbie honestly believed the vows her sister had made over and over during the course of the night. Hurting her little sister had been the last thing Callie had ever wanted.

Swinging the driver door open, she reached for her computer case and got out of the car, pushing the door shut with her hip. She'd put her sister to bed in the hotel where she'd been staying, a fairly respectable if low-budget place, and sat with her while she'd finally slept, tears of regret still damp on her face over the harm she'd caused Abbie.

And then Abbie had sat for hours beside the bed, staring blindly out the window as early dawn had turned into daylight, caught up in the past and reflecting on the hold it still had on them both.

She pointed the beam of the small flashlight toward her back porch and rounded the car. It had been nearly six before she'd returned to headquarters after interviewing several of Larsen's former neighbors and consoling Hornby's grieving sister. Ryne had been nowhere in sight, nor had he answered his cell. She'd worked a few more hours but he'd never returned, and she'd been more than ready to call it a day.

She'd made two phone calls to Callie throughout the day, both of which her sister had dutifully answered. Tomorrow, though, she needed to see her, to determine for herself that Callie was taking the meds the way she . . .

She saw the flicker of movement from the corner of her eye. Instinct had her dropping the computer case. Reaching for her weapon. But a weight caught her and slammed her against the trunk of her car forcefully, catching her injured arm between her body and the metal.

She cursed, both from surprise and pain, and struggled for a moment as fear, old and new, collided.

The shadows pressed in, dark and oppressive. The heavy breathing sounding close. She was alone. Vulnerable in the darkness.

Shaking free of the past, she swung back with the keys, hoping to catch her assailant in the face. The blow was deflected and her keys went flying. In the next movement she struck back with one of her feet, connecting with a hard knee.

"Shit!"

She was crowded closer to the car, her face forced down to the trunk lid as a big body pressed against her. "Smart little bitch, aren't you?"

She stilled, straining to recognize the venom-filled voice in her ear. "Knew you were trouble the first time I saw you. Had to go running to Robel, didn't you? Couldn't come to me first. Let me explain."

Comprehension filtered in and Abbie drew a breath, her mind racing. "I had to tell Robel, Nick. You know that."

"Bullshit." He stepped back and roughly turned her over to face him, one hand braced on her chest. "You had it in for me from the first. You bitches are all alike. You're the one who never belonged on that task force. I should still be there, doing the job. What the hell have you contributed, huh?"

Abbie stared up at Nick McElroy assessingly. He was drunk, but not incapacitated by any means. Was he drunk enough not to weigh the cost to his career if he hurt her? She didn't think so. But she also didn't know the man well enough to predict what he was capable of.

In the last twenty-four hours or so, she hadn't done especially well assessing potential harm to herself.

"What do you want, Nick? What is this going to solve?" If she could distract him, she'd have a chance to pull her gun. And regardless of Nick McElroy's intentions, she'd feel a lot safer with her Sig in her hand.

"I want you to undo the damage you did by repeating Chan's garbage to Robel. You're going to go to Dixon himself. Tell him I don't fit the profile and that it's your opinion I'm needed on the case."

Abbie felt the urge to laugh, knew it was ill advised. "Dixon isn't going to believe that. You're better off—"

With one hand around her throat, he pressed her head back, rapping it smartly against the car. "I belong on this task force. I belong on the job. You're going to help me get my suspension retracted."

Swiftly, Abbie recalculated her earlier assessment. McElroy wasn't rational. And she wasn't about to wait and take her chances with the man. "Maybe you're right, Nick. There is one thing I could do."

His grip on her throat eased. "Damn right there is."

Abbie rammed her knee with all the force she could muster into the man's groin, rolling away when he folded in on himself and fell heavily against the car. Pulling free of his weight, she spun and aimed a kick at the side of his head and then bent to pull her weapon from her ankle holster.

Hearing footsteps crunch on the gravel behind her, she sidled away to keep both McElroy and the newcomer in her sight. "Stop right there. Both of you."

But as soon as she uttered the words, she knew they'd be ignored. Because McElroy was already straightening, his face a mask of rage illuminated by the beam of the other man's Maglite. A familiar figure was stepping between him and Abbie, pushing Nick away when he would have taken a step in her direction.

Ryne. Abbie didn't know whether to be thankful or dismayed to see him. His presence here was sure to inflame an already volatile situation.

"Step back, Ryne. I've got it under control."

But her words were lost on him. She could see the fury on

his face, could guess his intentions even before he dropped the light and sent his fist into McElroy's face.

The other detective swung back, a heavy haymaker that would have rendered Ryne unconscious if it had connected. But Ryne ducked and sent a swift jab into McElroy's solar plexus, before clipping him again in the jaw.

Nick lunged, head-butting Ryne, and they both tumbled to the ground in a flurry of blows.

It was sorely tempting to just fire a shot in the air to get their attention, since it was clear that neither of them was in any position to listen to reason. The resulting paperwork, however, wasn't worth it.

Abbie strode up to where the two men were grappling. Ryne was throwing punch after steady punch at McElroy's head, while the other detective had both hands wrapped around Ryne's neck.

She placed the muzzle of her gun against McElroy's temple and said, "Stop now."

If the warning in her voice didn't get through the alcohol haze, the pressure of her weapon against his skin did. His hands loosened from Ryne's neck, fell away.

"Get up, Ryne."

"Abbie, let me—"

"Back off!" Right now it'd be a tough call to say which of them she was more pissed at.

With a seething look at her, he obeyed, shoving away from the other man and getting to his feet. McElroy sat up, wiped the blood from his mouth sullenly. "What the hell are you doing here, Robel?" Then in the next instant his mouth twisted. "Don't tell me you're putting it to Tinkerbell." He gave an ugly laugh. "Now that's something Dixon should find interesting."

"Shut up, Nick." Abbie wouldn't have been capable of diplomacy even if it had occurred to her. "If you were sober, you'd realize that you have no one to blame but yourself for your current situation. You're in this mess because of your involvement with Chan, and that doesn't have a damn thing to do with me, or with Ryne. Now go home and sober up.

You come near me again and you'll be pulling your balls out of your throat."

"Already am," the man muttered, struggling to his feet. "You never would have landed a kick if I hadn't had a couple beers."

"A couple?" Ryne's tone was derisive as he stooped to recover the flashlight. "I told you to stay out of trouble, not to spend your days boozing. This isn't going to help your situation. You're just making things worse."

McElroy made a show of brushing off his jeans and T-shirt. "I just wanted to talk to her. This had nothing to do with you."

"Yeah?" The low lethal tone of Ryne's voice had all of Abbie's senses on alert. "Well, the next time you want to *talk*, pick up a telephone. You go near her again and you won't be walking away, McElroy. I'll see to that."

Nick glared at him. "Fuck you, Robel. You're just Dixon's bitch, think we don't all know that? How else would a homicide cop end up lead detective in this task force? Hell, how else would a Boston cop wind up in SCMPD?"

Ryne took a step toward McElroy, then halted, a physical threat radiating from him. "This is the only warning you'll get. Steer clear of the case and stay away from Abbie. Or I will hurt you. And I'll damn well enjoy it."

Abbie watched as McElroy wheeled around, stalked down the drive. It hadn't occurred to her until then to wonder where he'd parked before he'd been skulking outside her place. His vehicle must be on the street, but she hadn't noticed. There were always cars parked out there. Many of the houses in the neighborhood lacked garages.

She holstered her weapon, then retrieved her laptop. Finding her keys and the attached flashlight proved more of a challenge. Peering at the ground, she retraced her steps around her car.

Ryne found them before she did, sweeping the area with the beam of the Maglite and scooping them up, before playing the beam over the path to her back door. "Why the hell didn't you get a light installed out here when the security company came?"

The anger in his voice took her aback. Grabbing the keys from him, she made her way to the house, uncaring whether or not he followed. "I have a penlight for the rare nights I come home in the dark. It's not worth the expense to put a bunch of money into a short-term rental."

"It's worth it when your safety is an issue. It's worth it when you're afraid of the dark."

That stopped her cold. Setting her jaw, she turned to face him. She didn't like to recall that instant of mind-numbing fear when McElroy had knocked the light from her hand, his body keeping her captive against the car.

"I handled myself, darkness or not," she reminded him, his words still smarting. They all had their vulnerabilities. She'd worked hard to overcome hers. Reminding her of a weakness didn't endear him to her. "Things were under control. You just made it worse with your caveman theatrics." She turned and stalked up to the house, reaching for the key to unlock the back door.

"Well, excuse me all to hell for thinking that a woman struggling with a drunken idiot who outweighs her by eighty pounds just might need a little help." He followed her into the house, his voice truculent.

"Your *help* made matters worse. I'd already gotten away from him when you arrived. If I'd had a chance to defuse the situation, I might have been able to—"

"You might have been able to what? Talk him to sleep? Invite him inside for a couch session and shrink his head?" Ryne stopped short in her kitchen, and eyed the cartons stuffed high in the trash can, before continuing, "Even you have to admit he was beyond talking sense to. There was only one thing that was going to get through to him and that was a good ass kicking."

She stood in the doorway to the living room to block him from coming any farther into the house. Because she was abruptly anxious to see him go.

After the sleepless night she'd spent with Callie, followed by eight hours of work and then the run-in with McElroy, she found herself completely devoid of the patience to deal with Ryne, who was inexplicably in the grips of testosterone overload.

"Perhaps it escaped your notice that I'd already pulled my weapon when you arrived." It was hard to say what infuriated her more—his disparaging remarks about her profession, or his disregard for her capability to take care of herself. "No one asked you to ride to the rescue." Her voice had risen to a near shout, which was yet another reason to get Ryne out of there. She didn't want to lose control in front of him. That would top off the last twenty-four hours. "I'm not one of those women who needs a man in my life directing every damn move I make."

His voice was sharp as a blade. "All evidence to the contrary."

She was shaking now, with combined fury and fatigue. "Get out. I don't want to be around you right now."

A shadow passed over Ryne's expression and he took a step toward her. "Abbie . . ."

"Get . . . out." She didn't stay to watch him comply. Instead she turned and walked through the small living room, flipping on a lamp and setting her laptop on the desk. She stood there, fists clenched, muscles bunched, until she heard a small noise. The unmistakable sound of the back door closing quietly had the tension seeping from her, a little at a time.

She scrubbed both hands over her face, wincing when she came into contact with a knot forming over one eye. As a matter of fact, a chorus of aches and pains were making themselves known. She had a matching lump on the back of her head, both of them courtesy of close contact with the trunk of the car.

Grimacing, she considered that maybe she should have kicked McElroy harder. She crossed to the bathroom, rubbing a tender spot on her hip, and assessed the damage in the mirror.

Gingerly, she probed at the lump above her eye. If she

iced it, she might be able to keep it from swelling any more. The last thing she wanted was to have to answer questions about her appearance tomorrow at . . .

Catching a glimpse of her shirt in her reflection, she lowered her arm to examine it. It was spotted with blood. Uttering an oath, Abbie quickly unbuttoned it and shrugged it off to examine the injury beneath.

The wound between the neat stitches was oozing in a couple places, but it didn't look like she'd pulled a stitch loose. Which was lucky, since the ER doc last night hadn't looked too convinced by the story she'd come up with to explain the injury.

She cleansed it with a dampened cloth, then applied some first aid ointment to it. Ordinarily she'd spend hours working late into the evening on the case, going over the results of the day's investigation, and putting them in some sort of order. But exhaustion was bearing down on her like an out-of-control truck. She doubted her ability to remain upright much longer.

It was when she headed to her bedroom that she heard it. A scrape of a shoe on worn linoleum. Her blood chilled and she froze, straining to listen for another noise. But one didn't come.

She hadn't locked the back door.

Her eyes slid closed in self-reproach. It was an unforgivable oversight, especially after the events of the evening. But if this was McElroy coming back for another round, she wasn't going to be nearly as gentle this time.

Swiftly she bent and drew her weapon, training it steadily on the doorway separating the two rooms as she inched closer. Could it be Callie? She didn't think so—both times Abbie had spoken to her that day she'd mentioned staying in for the evening.

There was another noise. Closer now. Abbie deliberately controlled her breathing as she ducked behind the overstuffed chair, using it for cover. The angle would allow her sight of the kitchen. And the intruder standing in it.

"Hands up, then don't move," she commanded.

"Abbie?"

Their voices sounded almost simultaneously. She stepped away from the chair, her gun trained on the person in her kitchen. The one person she hadn't expected to see.

The one she least wanted to talk to right now.

"What are you doing here?" Her voice was unwelcoming.

Ryne gestured toward her back entrance. "You didn't lock your back door."

She relaxed her stance, lowering her weapon. "So this is just a security check? You wanted to add to your list of my perceived ineptitudes? Congratulations. Make a note of my carelessness and then leave. Again."

His gaze flicked over her figure, and she was suddenly aware that she was facing him down in black pants and a black on black striped bra. Not exactly an appearance guaranteed to boost her avowal of competence. But right now, she was long past caring what Ryne Robel thought.

"I wanted to say . . . I know I was a dick a while ago."

"You *were* a dick," she agreed. The apology was unexpected. There was no reason to let him know how it disarmed her. She could feel some of the ire that had seemed so all-encompassing only minutes ago fade away. "It's been a long day and I'm ready to turn in. If I promise to lock the door behind you, will you stay gone this time?"

His expression altered, alerting her that he was no longer listening. He approached her with a few long strides, taking her injured arm in one hand and turning it upward to examine the wound there. His gaze when it met hers was grim. "What the hell, Abbie?"

She hesitated, reluctant to share the whole experience with him, especially in light of his earlier behavior. "I don't want to get into it."

"Can't blame it on McElroy, he just left." Comprehension flickered across his expression. "This is why you were late this morning? The deal with your sister last night? Did she do this to you?"

She had the dim thought that maybe she should be grateful he didn't leap to the conclusion she'd taken up self-destructive habits again. It was small consolation, to be sure.

Another wave of weariness hit her and she felt herself sway a little. Pulling her arm from his grasp, she half turned away. "It was an accident. For once, just let it go."

"Don't you think I wish I could?"

The bitterness in his tone surprised her into glancing back toward him. She was startled by the bleak expression on his face.

"Believe me, it'd be a helluva lot easier if I didn't give a damn. If the thought of you hurt, bleeding, didn't tear something up inside me that I don't want to feel." A muscle in his jaw jumped. "I don't want this. I never asked for this."

The meaning of his words rocked her back, threatening her last vestige of composure. She couldn't—wouldn't—let him see how they wounded. "I've never made any demands on you." She could hold on to that, at least, even while an inner voice jeered. No, Abbie Phillips would be the last to expect something from a man. Expectations meant trust, something she'd never learned to give.

Ryne seemed not to have heard her. "It wasn't as hard for me to stop drinking as you might think. Because even without the alcohol, I was numb, and that wasn't so bad. I could do my job. Could think a damn sight clearer, but didn't feel a thing. And you know what? That was fine with me. Best thing in the world."

"No, Ryne," she said quietly. "It wasn't. Every mind has its own way of dealing with trauma. But the absence of emotion isn't a sign of healing. Just the opposite."

He jammed a hand through his hair. "I wasn't *traumatized*, I was blind. I was on the fast track in Boston. Dixon might have been the political golden boy, but I was the cowboy. I didn't mind taking the dangerous jobs early on, going undercover, infiltrating gangbangers. And even later, when I made detective, I had the instincts for the work. I knew I was drinking too much, but it wasn't going to affect the job. I told myself that." His tone was filled with derision. "Biggest mistake I ever made was believing it."

"What happened?"

He didn't seem to hear her question. He was talking more to

himself than to her. "Homicide investigation looked pretty straightforward. Marriage on the rocks. Wife arranges to have her husband whacked and stands to inherit a hefty chunk of change. Had a witness willing to testify he overheard the wife making the arrangements for a hit. Everything pointed to Deborah Hanna, the wife. I never looked elsewhere. Not seriously. Not until it was too late."

"It wasn't her."

He gave a short mirthless laugh. "It wasn't her. But she was the next victim. My 'witness' turned out to be her ex-lover. He'd had plans for the two of them, but she broke it off. He waited a year for his revenge. Arranged the whole thing to point to her. When she still refused him, he put a bullet in her brain. So, yeah. That eats at me."

She knew intuitively his words were an understatement. She'd long suspected something haunted Ryne Robel. Now his ghost had a name.

He shoved his hands in his pocket, leveled a gaze at her. "But I can handle that. *Was* handling it. Until you. This. I can't help worrying when I think of you being hurt. Can't seem to stop myself from stepping in to protect you. And I don't want to feel like this."

Panic sprinted up her spine. The emotional punch of his words was more powerful than the blows she'd sustained earlier. "Then don't," she urged almost pleadingly. She didn't want the kind of attachment he was talking about any more than he did. Less.

And she especially didn't want to examine her own feelings too closely. Didn't want to think about what it was going to be like when the case was solved and she left.

His smile was twisted. "That's the best advice you can come up with? Because it's . . ." His words broke off as he looked more closely at her. Afraid of what he'd see in her expression, she turned away. But it was too late.

"I've seen you run down and tackle a suspect. Saw you pound on a sparring partner twice your size. Watched you humiliate McElroy with a few well-placed kicks." With a gentle tug on her elbow, he turned her to face him again. "But this is the first time I've seen you look scared, Abbie."

His tone was wondering as he stared hard at her. "Hell, you're more terrified than I am."

"I'm not 'terrified,'" she corrected him. Her words might have sounded more convincing if they hadn't held a slight tremble. "We just need to be . . . sensible."

"Okay." He sounded a little too agreeable. With his index finger, he began tracing the slight swell of flesh above her bra. "I can do sensible. How's sensible work?"

"Well, we . . ."

Her voice broke off as he took the weapon from her hand. "You've decided not to shoot me, right? So we can get rid of this?" He set it down on the couch and pulled her closer, one hand sliding down to cup her butt.

He was, she decided, a bit too easily distracted. "The case comes first. We see it through."

"Of course."

Her senses scattered as his mouth skimmed over her throat and settled at the hollow of her shoulder. He had the most amazing tongue. "And after that . . ." She could sense the stillness in him. Could barely draw the breath to finish the sentence. Because once the case was solved, she'd be gone. What was between them would have to be finished. Surely he didn't need her to say it.

"After that . . ." He pressed a stinging kiss to her throat and she shuddered.

"Then . . . we'll see."

She heard the smile in his voice. "We'll see? Good plan. Definite. Precise. I like that."

Abbie slipped both hands into his hair and tugged ungently. "Shut up, Robel." She smothered his laugh by pressing her lips to his and immediately got lost in the taste of him.

He knew exactly how to kiss a woman. Hot, and wet, and deep, as if staking a claim. She may be blind when she tried to envision what lay ahead of them, but now, in his arms, it was the immediate future she cared about. She wanted to bask in the smoldering sensuality he exuded merely by breathing. She wanted, most of all, to forget the events of the last twenty-four hours and to fill up greedy pockets of memories of the two of them together.

And she didn't want to consider the time when memories were all they'd have left.

He hooked his finger in one of her bra straps, drew it slowly off her shoulder. When his mouth touched the skin he'd bared, it felt hot as a brand, and all of a sudden it was she who was too easily diverted. She knew him well enough to realize he'd take control if she let him, setting a fevered pace to the climax they both sought. And with the passion he so easily incited, whipping her blood to churning whitecaps, she'd be in no position to argue.

But she wanted to take her time. Wanted to savor every taste, each touch. And wanted, quite desperately, to see him sweating and shaking before it was through.

She tugged his shirt free of his pants, leisurely undoing the buttons, one at a time. It was hard to concentrate on each inch of hard masculine flesh she bared while his mouth was busy, skimming over her shoulders—both bared now—and up the side of her throat. But there was a reward to be had in maintaining focus. As the widening vee of his loosened shirt framed his muscled torso, she gave a pleased hum.

He could be a model for that gym he used, though he'd scoff at the idea. Wide shoulders, roped with enough muscle to leave intriguing hollows where flesh met bone and sinew. Well-defined pecs, sprinkled with hair a shade darker than that on his head. Flat belly, the muscles jumping when she stroked a finger above the waistband of his trousers.

She felt her bra fall away under his hands and moved closer to press against him. Her nipples drew tauter when she went on tiptoe to drag them over his hair-roughened chest. Drawing his bottom lip into her mouth, she scored it lightly with her teeth.

His arm came around her like a steel band, pulling her higher, closer. The kiss went from teasing to carnal so quickly she lost her breath. One of her hands clutched his hard bicep, the other anchored at his narrow waist.

His mouth ate hers with a single-minded intensity that torched her earlier intentions and had flames licking through her veins. She pushed his shirt over his shoulders, dragged it down his arms, all without relinquishing his lips. And then her hands stroked over the flesh she'd bared in a frenzy of exploration.

Her fingers skimmed over his hard back, traced the indentations of his spine, lowered to test the firm hardness of his butt. She'd never thought of a man's body as more than a means to an end. Never considered it as something to be hedonistically enjoyed. But his was different. *He* was different.

Abbie tore her mouth away to press her lips against his collarbone, against the wild beat of the pulse at the base of his throat. The evidence of his desire calmed something in her, had her wanting to stoke it higher before she became lost in her own.

And he was still overdressed.

She pulled his shirt off, took a few moments to skate her hands up and down the corded muscles of his arms, then unfastened his pants. Their fingers tangled as he struggled to help her free of hers. Eventually they had to pull away to divest themselves of garments in an impatient frenzy before walking into each other's arms again.

Pressing her lips to one dusky male nipple, Abbie flicked it with her tongue while her fingers went in search of his hard, straining length. Her breath quickened. She knew how to touch him now, what made him shudder, and what could fracture his control completely. The knowledge was heady, almost as exhilarating as the feel of him, hot and pulsing in her hand.

His belly quivered beneath her fingers as she worked the waistband of his boxer briefs down his lean hips. She went to her knees to bathe the tip of his sex with her tongue. There was a drop of pearly liquid on the head of his shaft and she scooped it up, then took him fully in her mouth.

She barely heard his oath, could hardly feel the grip of his hands in her hair as she tortured him with the wet suction. She reveled in the taste of him, and the slightly musky smell of desire. But it was his response that had her pulse careening madly. The bunched muscles of his thighs and stomach, his harsh groan, the unrestrained surge of his hips against her mouth.

His reaction stoked her own hunger. She couldn't get enough of it, of him. Every time they were together, it was a sensual battle to drive each other crazy. There was a hot spear of satisfaction at the knowledge that he was lost in the pleasure she brought him.

But that all changed in the next moment, when he stepped away from her and swung her up into his arms. The abrupt shift in positions was dizzying. She draped an arm around his neck to steady herself and dragged her heavy lids open to look at him.

His mouth was full, hard. The skin was drawn tightly over his cheekbones and his eyes . . . there was a flare in the pit of her belly when she caught his gaze. Narrowed and intent, the sexual intensity she saw there was an unmistakable promise.

Her veins went molten. She reached up to trace the seam of his lips with the tip of her tongue, but the kiss quickly grew desperate, with teeth and tongues clashing. There was a hammering in her blood, a wild tattoo beat that sharpened desire to urgency. Next time they'd go slow, tormenting each other with languid strokes and teasing touches. Right now she needed the release they found together, secure in the knowledge that he was as ready as she.

When he set her on her feet, she blinked, expecting to see the bedroom. But he stood in back of her before the vanity mirror in the bathroom.

"I want you to see yourself the way I see you," he murmured in her ear, before scraping his teeth down the side of her throat. Abbie gave a quick shiver, her focus on the sight of his taller broader form behind her.

"Soft." He cupped her breasts in both hands, rolling her nipples between thumbs and forefingers. "Yet firm." He dragged his lips over the sensitive area beneath her ear and she felt her knees turn to water. "Delicate." One hand lowered to splay over her rib cage, fingers tracing the place where flesh met bone. "But strong."

Her eyelids grew heavy with desire. There was as much enjoyment to be had watching him as in the exquisite feel of his hands on her bare skin. His voice was low, raspy with hunger. His touch was restrained, as if he had a tight leash on his control that could snap at any moment.

She smiled, slow and wicked, deliberately pressing her hips back against his. His reaction was immediate, unchecked as his hardness surged against the cleft of her buttocks. "And sexy," he rasped, his hands lowering to clench tightly on her hips.

Her head lolled against one of his muscled shoulders, and he took immediate advantage of the expanse of throat she bared. Hot stinging kisses were pressed in a precise line from shoulder to jaw, and her vision hazed.

But she wanted to see. Wanted to watch their reflections, his skin a shade darker against hers, his muscles hard and defined. Their position made it impossible to touch him as she craved, so she slid her hands over his arms, delighting in the sensation of hair-roughened skin beneath her palms.

Thoughts of the future had receded to a dim distant part of her mind. It was the present that mattered, the keen-edged appetite that could only be sated by this man, when he was buried deep inside her. She reached behind her, gliding her palms over his taut flanks, determined to shatter the ragged restraint he still clung to.

And instead she found herself going boneless, when Ryne skimmed his hand across her thigh to her sex, parting her with his fingers. "Sleek," he muttered, rubbing her rhythmically. "Like wet silk."

Their reflections blurred as need streaked through her. And when he stroked a finger inside her, explored her deeply, her breath broke into a sob as she climaxed, leaving her shaking and weak, unable to stand without his support.

"Greedy." He gave a purely male smile of satisfaction. "I like that, too." Turning her, he boosted her hips up to the counter and stepped between her open thighs. After their last shower together, he'd thought to stock the bathroom with condoms, too, but Abbie was past feeling grateful for his foresight. The head of his shaft was nudging her sex, and a desperation was building again that could only be satisfied in one way.

She took the latex from him and rolled it over the length of him with a deliberate slowness that had sweat gleaming on his brow, had his entire body quivering. When she'd sheathed him, she reached below his manhood to cup his heavy sac in her hand, stroking delicately until the harness on his restraint abruptly snapped.

He lifted her legs to his hips and pulled her hips toward him, entering her with one long deep stroke that drove the breath from her lungs. Distantly she was aware of his labored breathing, his clenched jaw, the glint of savage hunger in his gaze. Until he thrust again and her senses pinwheeled into a kaleidoscope of sensation.

She hooked her ankles behind his back, clutched his bulging biceps with her fingers and met every surge of his hips, straining to bring him closer. Deeper. Harder. Until he was imprinted on her body the same as he was on her mind. On her memory. A part of her that could never be completely separated.

His control shredded, he showed no mercy as he pounded into her. She wanted none. Dragging her eyelids open, she struggled to focus, wanting this sight, this memory to cling to.

Their sweat-dampened bodies slapped together, flesh against flesh, the sound calling to something primal from deep inside her. The pleasure careened and collided through her system. The world receded. Each individual sensation magnified. His slick muscles beneath her fingers, clenching and releasing with each movement. Their harsh mingled breathing, the tight grip he had on her hips, and the incredibly fullness of his possession.

Need fisted tightly in her belly, and she cried out brokenly, her release coming in a sudden brutal wave.

It seemed to trigger something savage in him. His hips jackhammered against hers until he stiffened, a low harsh sound of pleasure escaping him, as his body quaked violently against hers.

And while she was lost in the aftershocks of pleasure, it was even more satisfying to hear him groan gutturally, "Abbie."

———

Laura Bradford sat up in bed, the sheet low enough to reveal her perfect breasts. "Are you sure you can't stay?"

Listen to her. Trying to sound sweet and inviting but the petulance was there, right beneath the surface. Just like every other cunt, she thought fucking a man gave her rights. Women like her just never learned.

"I have an early meeting." The bathroom light provided a backdrop for the man, Warren Denton, before he exited it to reenter the bedroom, fully clothed. He stopped by the bed to drop a careless kiss on the woman's lips before he scooped up some personal effects from the bedside table and slipped them in his pocket.

"Do you have court tomorrow? If you do, maybe we could—"

"Not tomorrow. I'll be busy preparing for the Frederickson murder case for the next couple weeks. But I'll call you. The first chance I get."

A soundless laugh escaped as the scene played out. Pathetic bitch, trying to keep a smile plastered on her face even while she was getting the brush-off. Looked like ol' Warren was a fuck 'em and leave 'em kind of guy.

Would it make Bradford feel any better when she discovered that the police would soon be asking Denton some very embarrassing questions? Maybe even hauling him in to enjoy some jailhouse hospitality? The lawyer's appearance here tonight had been unexpected, but flexibility was always key.

And watching the fuck fest between the two of them had almost been worth the delay in plans.

"I'll see you soon then." Bradford's voice was heard, but

Denton was already walking away. A minute later the front door could be heard opening, and then closing again.

"Bastard." A pillow was heaved toward the doorway. After a moment, Bradford got out of bed and left the room.

One gloved hand pushed the bedroom closet door open wider. Sweat slicked under every inch of the leather mask and dark clothes. Damn closet had been hot. Time to adjust the air-conditioning before getting to work.

A smile of anticipation started, grew. No more vanilla sex for Laura Bradford. She was about to experience her destiny. The closet door eased open. The satchel was picked up and set within easy reach of the bed. A running faucet sounded, giving away the woman's location. And the feeling of anticipation surged, spreading through veins and arteries and sizzling across synapses in a rapid-fire frenzy.

Long stealthy strides. A peek around the corner and there was Bradford, standing naked in her kitchen setting an empty glass down forcefully on the counter.

Watching her brought a rush of emotion, something surprisingly close to affection. *Ah, Laura. I have such plans for you.*

Time slowed to fractions of seconds as the inner power built to an all-encompassing roar. Then stepping away from the wall into her line of vision. Relishing the instant she'd see the stranger in her home.

"Warren?" The one word was thin. Uncertain. A step closer. Two. No hurry. Let her see her future. Watch the fear take her.

"Who are you? What do you want? Is it money? Here." She stumbled to her purse on the edge of the counter.

Was she going to bargain for her life? That was always amusing. How much did the bitch think she was worth? And how satisfying to watch her realize there'd be no escaping her fate.

But it wasn't money she withdrew from her purse.

Shock bloomed. A gun? When had the cunt gotten a gun?

The muzzle flash was blinding, followed by a searing pain.

"I know who you are, you son of a bitch. It's in all the news."

Another shot, this one nearly as close as the first. The disbelief was gone, mingled rage and pain taking its place.

Drop to the floor. Crawl rapidly, clumsily backward, away from the gun and the crazy whore wielding it. Who did she think she was? How did she dare?

"Run, you bastard, you coward." Bradford's voice was shrill, hysterical. "That's what you are. I saw the news. You're a pathetic coward who preys on women because you're nothing but a fucking loser!" The last words rose to a shriek and a bullet buried itself in the wall just inches away.

The pain was jagged agony now, joyfully gnawing through flesh and muscle. There were no choices left. Clutch the injured arm, rise, run for the front door, leave the demented whore behind.

For now.

Breath turning into a sob, stumbling away faster. Jesus, how far was the car? Two blocks? Three?

Every step brought a fresh flood of pain. Fury. Humiliation. By God, Bradford would be sorry. She wouldn't be spared for a fate chosen especially for her. She'd die, in as hideous a death as could be fashioned. She'd merely delayed her destiny.

But first there was someone else to deal with. The bitch responsible for those news stories. She'd pay for ruining everything.

She'd pay with her miserable life.

Chapter 19

Ryne stepped gingerly, staying well clear of the UV light sources, and the plastic evidence markers that dotted the floor, and made his way to the spare bedroom, where Abbie had been interviewing Laura Bradford for the last hour.

The uniform at the door moved aside to allow his entry. Abbie was seated across from the woman on a chair dragged over from the computer desk tucked in the corner. Bradford sat huddled on the edge of the bed, wrapped in a robe, arguing with Abbie.

"He never got near me, I swear. I don't understand why I have to go to the hospital."

"We'd like an exam done to be sure you don't carry any forensic evidence on your person," Abbie explained. "We don't know where he was, or what he might have touched. You could have minute splatters of his blood on your skin. It just helps us collect more evidence against him."

The woman made a grimace of distaste, and apparently gave up the battle. "A few of us were just discussing it today at lunch." She had the robe's belt in her hands and was wringing it convulsively. "We got to talking about him, the

Nightmare Rapist. How it was like *Fear Factor*, that show, you know? Having to confront your worst nightmares. One gal told everyone how she was petrified of snakes. I admitted I was terrified of heights. We were joking about it. God." She swallowed convulsively. "How macabre is that?"

"Can you give me the names of everyone you were talking to, Laura? And anyone else in the vicinity?" Bradford rattled off several names, which Abbie wrote down.

"But it's not like it's news to anyone who knows me," Bradford added, winding the robe's tie around one finger. "It's a running joke at the courthouse. I get teased if I so much as wear high heels. People will ask if they're giving me acrophobia."

Abbie exchanged a look with Ryne, who'd taken up a stance next to her chair. "So your fear was common knowledge."

"I'm pretty open about it." Her face crumpled, and she shoved one fist to still her trembling lips. "I had no idea that anyone was even here. We locked the door after we came in, and I'm sure Warren locked it behind him. He's always very security conscious. That pervert had to have been hiding the whole time. *Watching* us."

"You've been through a terrifying experience. But the fact that you weren't alone tonight might have ended up saving your life."

At Abbie's words, Bradford managed a shaky smile. "That and my revolver. I'm sure I hit him. I saw him grab his arm. And then when I fired again . . ." She stopped, sending a guilty look toward Ryne. "Am I going to get charged for that? For shooting him, I mean? The gun . . . I don't have a permit for it."

"I can't make any promises," Ryne said, a glint in his eye, "but under the circumstances, I don't think you need to worry about it. Don't expect to get the gun back, though."

Twenty minutes later after the EMTs escorted Laura to the hospital, Abbie faced Ryne, finally able to ask the question that had been burning in her. "What has CSU come up with so far?"

"She's a lucky lucky lady. She probably did hit him," Ryne confirmed, a hard satisfied smile on his face. "We got a good-sized sample, and several smaller ones from the carpet. Another from the handle of the front door."

Abbie pumped one fist in the air. "That's a huge break." She was already calculating how long it would take the labs to run the blood analysis. And then there was the process of submitting the resulting data to CODIS, to see if it matched any DNA evidence left at any other violent crime scene in the nation. She was willing to bet it would. This UNSUB had been evolving, so he'd had to start somewhere. He couldn't always have been as fortunate as he'd been so far with this latest string of rapes.

But tonight it looked like his luck was running out.

She said as much to Ryne, adding, "He's had a couple of instances now when things haven't gone as planned." When Ryne raised his brows, she explained, "First he had to rush the Larsen job, when she didn't come home as expected. And tonight Bradford arrived home with company."

"The bastard's adaptable."

Although neither of them had gotten any sleep before Ryne had received the call, he looked as wide awake as Abbie felt. Her earlier exhaustion had dissipated, at least for the moment. She was still on an adrenaline high. "He would have been watching Bradford for a while, so he'd know Denton sometimes came home with her, but never spent the night." And Abbie hadn't missed the tinge of bitterness in the woman's tone when she'd divulged that fact.

"I'm not an advocate for citizens carrying concealed weapons—especially illegally—but she saved herself a horrible experience. The women of Savannah will probably give her a medal." He hesitated, and something about the pause alerted her. "And now for the bad news. Dixon wants another press conference."

She brought a hand up to rub the ache that had suddenly appeared between her eyes. "Why am I not surprised?"

"He's going proactive on this latest development. And he specifically asked for you to be there with me. He wants an updated profile, complete with your best prediction of what the UNSUB is likely to do next. Bring your crystal ball."

"I can make an educated guess. Highly intelligent offenders think they're smarter than anyone else. The cops and their targets. Being outmaneuvered by Bradford was probably a shock. But it's going to enrage him, even more so if it's made an issue in the media. It'll be a slap at his ego and may be the one thing that could motivate such an organized offender to act impulsively."

"Bradford's still in danger."

It was more statement than question, but she nodded anyway. "He won't let this go. And I don't even want to consider what he'd do to her if he catches her again."

"I can get a female officer to stay with her around the clock. Another one posted outside her house. At least for a while."

"If he's unable to get at her right away, he'll strike out in another fashion," she mused. "Possibly speeding up the selection and targeting the next victim weeks earlier than originally planned."

Ryne's face went grim. "So he's an immediate threat."

Lifting a shoulder helplessly, Abbie said, "That depends on a lot of variables. How badly he's hurt, for one."

"Hard to say." Ryne leaned a shoulder against the wall. "But it was most likely a surface wound, from the amount of blood left. He was able to walk out of here. We've got the streets blocked off, and as soon as dawn breaks, we'll canvass the area and see if we can pick up his trail."

"He'd have a vehicle stashed nearby."

"Unless he lives in the vicinity."

Recalling the map Ryne kept tacked above his desk at headquarters, Abbie mentally added Bradford's house to the locations of the other attacks. "He doesn't stick to a specific area," she murmured. That had been one more challenge to predicting his actions. "He'd have planned to transport her. Either with her vehicle or his own. Hang her over a cliff. Dangle her off the side of a building. God knows what he had in store for her." But it would have been specially designed with Laura's phobia in mind. Of that they could be sure.

"He left his bundle of toys."

That had her straightening. "Are they bagged yet? I'd like a look at them."

"Give the tech another ten minutes or so." He indicated the form in her lap. "Is that the completed interview form?"

Handing it to him, she said, "I asked if she'd done any volunteer work lately. I was disappointed when she said no."

Flipping through the interview pages, he made a non-committal sound, which she took for interest. "I didn't have a chance to tell you yesterday. Hornby's sister told me Ashley had been doing a lot of volunteering since coming to Savannah. She wasn't sure on specifics, but thought a couple schools, the free clinic. Maybe a homeless shelter. That started me thinking, because Amanda Richards had made all those public appearances before women's groups, schools, and a battered woman's shelter. I thought I might find some victim intersections using that angle, but haven't yet."

"It's probably like you said. He's using more than one method to find them. Any connections at all at this point could be useful."

The adrenaline high was fading. Abbie feared she was going to hit the wall of exhaustion soon, and she still needed to prepare for the meeting with Dixon. And the press conference.

She looked up, surprised at the expression of concern on Ryne's face.

"You look like you're ready to fall over."

Standing, she began gathering up her things. "Very flattering. Thanks."

"You know what I mean." He was silent for a moment, still regarding her with that enigmatic stare. "Bet you never slept at all last night either, did you?"

"I've gone without sleep before. I'll manage."

"I can have a uniform take you home. You could get a few hours in before the task force meeting this morning."

"I want to get a look at the scene first. And his tools." Standing, she worked her shoulders to free them of the kinks in her muscles. "Any idea how he got in yet?"

"Came in the bedroom window. Sliced the screen then cut out a piece of glass above the lock, reached in, and unfastened it. Must have seemed like a piece of cake."

Lack of sleep was making her punchy. "Well, there's nothing like a bullet to persuade him otherwise." They grinned at each other. "They should process her car. If he'd planned to use her vehicle to transport her, he may have used the time he was waiting to get it ready."

"We've got it covered."

She wasn't surprised. Of course, he'd have already thought of that. Ryne was a good cop. The best she'd worked alongside. His instincts would impress even Raiker, a difficult feat.

"If it's distance you're wondering about, I've got some facts for you. I've been doing some checking." Something in his tone alerted her. They'd gone abruptly from professional footing to personal. "It's about five hundred seventy miles from Savannah to Manassas. Less than two hours by nonstop flight." He took in her arrested expression with a lift of his brow. "Think about it, Abbie."

He left the room, but it was long moments before she'd be able to follow him. Unconsciously, she reached out a hand to the back of the chair to steady herself. She knew how long a flight it was between her home base and Savannah. She'd flown it, hadn't she?

But Ryne hadn't. He'd checked. And the implication of that held Abbie immobile.

She certainly would think about his words. She'd be helpless to do otherwise.

The task force morning briefing had been delayed by several hours, until the team had finished at Bradford's. "Contents of the satchel the UNSUB left behind are on this list." Ryne passed a sheaf of papers to Cantrell, who took one and passed the rest on. "The bag itself is leather, brand name *Volux*, which is sold primarily to scuba enthusiasts. Wayne, see what else you can discover about it. There's bound to be scuba shops in the vicinity. Maybe we'll get lucky. We'll also get started on the listed contents. Phil, you take the top half of the list and Isaac can work the bottom half."

Cantrell let out a low whistle. "I don't even know what half this stuff is, but this is one very sick fuck."

"Just like we figured—a handheld forensic vac." Holmes scowled. "No wonder we never got squat off the bedding. But what's the packaging tape for?"

Abbie consulted her own list. "My guess is he planned to use it to tape Bradford's eyelids open once he transported her to the arranged site. With her phobia, it was likely he was going to suspend her from a considerable height. After all his trouble, he'd want to force her to see every minute of it."

"He's going to want to replace what he's lost, so alert every merchant you chat with about our interest in these specific items." Ryne shifted his attention to the officer who'd been on surveillance detail last night. "Greenway, make my life easier."

The heavily muscled officer shook his head regretfully. "Sorry, Detective. I stuck to Juarez all night. He went to work, home, and then to Shorty's. Five a.m. he went home again."

"Shit," someone muttered.

Ryne tamped down a surge of frustration. "Did you get a visual during the time he was at Shorty's?"

"No, but he went there at one a.m. He can't be the guy at Bradford's place."

A murmur swept through the room, and Ryne flicked a glance at where Abbie was sitting silently in the front row. She couldn't have gotten more than a couple hours' sleep before making it back to headquarters. "Okay. We keep the surveillance on Juarez because at some point in time, he did come in contact with the rapist. Or at least came to his attention. It'd be nice to know how."

"My guess is at one of those dives he goes to a few times a week," volunteered Cantrell. "Where are we on those photos that have been taken at his hangouts?"

"We've identified several known scumbags, and a couple parole violators. A few people have been seen talking to Juarez when he's at one of the places, but all have been known acquaintances."

"You might want to compare the photos to the film taken outside all the crime scenes to those of any crowds that gathered to watch the police work," Abbie said.

Ryne nodded. "Phillips believes this UNSUB may seek to insert himself into the investigation in some way. And he wouldn't be the first one to hang around to watch the police work." He consulted his notes. "Vincent, Garcia, Lee, and Brooks, you can start on that comparison today. The rest of the officers will be needed to help canvass Bradford's neighborhood." When they'd left the scene that morning, the crime scene techs were searching Bradford's yard and the surrounding sidewalks, streets, and neighboring yards. He had uniforms there to control the perimeter, but he was anxious to hear what, if anything, CSU discovered.

"Any latents on the contents in the bag?"

"They've been wiped clean," Ryne responded to Malloy's question. "But further tests might bring something." It was harder than most people thought to get rid of bloodstains. If any of the devices in the satchel had been used on other victims, they could yet find proof of it. "We do have one valuable lead—a partial hair—blond—found in the seam at the bottom of the bag. No root, but still appropriate for mitochondrial DNA testing. We can compare results to the DNA blood sample, or see if it matches one of the victims." Richards, Larsen, and Bradford were all blond.

He gave a brief update on the Ketrum lead he'd be following, closing with, "Hopefully I'll hear from Sheriff Jepperson today. I want a verbal report on your progress before end of shift." The press conference was scheduled outside headquarters at three. Surely it would be over in time.

Memory of the press conference, and the prior meeting with Dixon, darkened Ryne's mood. As the detectives and officers filed out, he walked over to Abbie. "Get any sleep?"

Her gaze flickered over the men still within earshot and said noncommittally, "Enough. I've put something together for Dixon for this afternoon."

"Before we're expected over there, I'd like you to connect with Bradford again. You told her she can't go back to her place until CSU is done with it." He waited for Abbie's nod before going on. "If there's someone she could stay with, that'd be best. Or a motel. Either way I need an address, and I'll arrange her protection." Captain Brown had already okayed the expense.

"All right. I'll meet you at Dixon's office prior to the press conference." Her tone was almost studiedly impersonal. Which didn't account for the faint flare of color that washed her cheeks before she rose and hurried after the last of the men.

Ryne watched her departure, a faint smile on his lips. He knew intuitively that she was still grappling with the comment he'd made back at the scene. And it pleased him, more than it should have, that he'd taken her by surprise. She didn't know how to handle it. Any more than she knew how to handle them. And damned if he wasn't entitled to feel just a little smug about that.

He made his way to his computer and checked his e-mail. He was pleasantly surprised to find a message from Jepperson, and opened it first. It read, "Savannah, I think I got what you need. See below. Hope you have some results for me soon on that data I sent yesterday." Below the man's initials was a list of ten names.

Ryne pressed a command to have the e-mail printed and made a mental note to call the toxicologist tomorrow and give him a push. The scientist had cautioned him that a mere comparison of tox reports would show only similarities in what was present and absent in the victims' blood, nothing conclusive. But trace amounts of Ecstasy had shown up in all the Savannah victims' blood. If the same amount showed up on the tox screen of the Montana victim, that'd be enough for Ryne to suspect a link.

His cell rang. Glancing at the caller ID, he saw it was Mel

Thomas, the lead crime scene tech from this morning, and his gut tightened in anticipation.

"We've got a few more fresh bloodstains along a two-block path heading southwest from Bradford's," Thomas said without any preliminaries. "We're taking samples for matches. But we went another couple blocks in all directions and came up with nothing."

"So he stopped the bleeding or got in his vehicle and took off," Ryne surmised. "What do you have in the circumference of that area?"

"Streets are mostly residential. Lots of cul-de-sacs." Ryne could hear the faint sounds of traffic in the background. "Other than that, there's a convenience store, a twenty-four-hour fitness center, and a Subway, before we hit highway to the south."

"I'm on my way," Ryne said, taking a quick glance at his watch. "I've already dispatched a dozen officers to help with the canvass." He disconnected the call and grabbed his suit jacket off the back of his chair as he rose, instincts humming.

He'd relied on those instincts, in one way or another, since he'd first become a cop. And everything inside him right now said they were very close to nailing the Nightmare Rapist.

The bandage needed changing. An oath escaped as it was pulled off, the injury examined. The wound was ugly, red and angry, but despite the pain, largely superficial.

Swing the arm gingerly back and forth. It fucking hurt! But there didn't seem to be muscle damage. The bullet had passed cleanly through.

The interruption to the TV program was ignored. The cunt had just gotten lucky. Her other shots had gone wild. But who could have known she'd have a gun? There had been nothing in her files, nothing in her house to indicate it.

That couldn't have been foreseen. It wasn't a mistake. Not really.

Except for the bag of equipment left behind.

Carelessness. The old man's voice sounded as clearly as if he hadn't been dead for well over a decade. *You know what the punishment for carelessness is, don't you?*

The punishment had always been the same, regardless of the mistake. The old man hadn't been one to deviate from a proven method. Especially one that had given him so much pleasure.

Apply the antibacterial cream, tape on another gauze pad. Good as new. But four pain relievers this time, instead of two.

A familiar scene played on the TV screen. It had played many times already, and each time anger surged anew.

But wait. This wasn't a repeat of last week's press conference. This was a new one.

Grab the remote. Turn up the volume. And then let the rage flow as that bitch took the microphone.

Impulsive. Escalation. Did she actually think she could predict a mind so far above hers? What had she ever accomplished in her sniveling cowardly life? She couldn't possibly understand bold courageous moves and a vision staggering in its genius.

The remote hurtled through the air, smashed into the screen, and bounced off, leaving a crack right over her face. A portend of things to come.

Even Einstein had been misunderstood in his day. Being underestimated could be turned to an advantage.

Smiling now. Dressing carefully. One little setback couldn't be allowed to derail such masterful vision. There wouldn't be any staying low, healing in lonely misery.

There was hunting to be done.

———

"You didn't have to do this. Takeout would have been fine with me." Abbie felt slightly guilty sipping wine as she watched Ryne cook dinner for her. But that emotion was layered with pleasure.

He moved capably, the long sleeves of his white shirt rolled up to the elbow, as he stabbed at the spaghetti in the pot with a long wooden fork. The fabric of the shirt stretched across his back, hinted at the muscles beneath. She'd explored those muscles intimately more than once. She was looking forward to doing so again soon.

"I wanted to. Besides, you get to see the sum total of my culinary skills tonight."

"I figured," she said, amused. She took another drink. "When you told me my choices were pasta or pasta."

"I have endless variations, but it all comes down to the same thing. Thank God for the Italians."

Smiling, she let her gaze wander around his kitchen. He'd shown her the rest of the house, and it had struck her that despite his having lived there over a year, it didn't look much more personal than her rental.

He did have some books, movies, and CDs jammed into a bookcase in the living room. And a TV that rivaled the screen at the drive-in she'd once attended in high school. What was it with men and large-screen TVs? She'd always heard that it was cars that were supposed to be extensions of their manhood.

But there was nothing on the walls, nothing personal other than the comfortable utilitarian furniture that would stamp this as a man's place. Any man's.

There was a lone picture on the coffee table, of Ryne with his arm around an older woman she assumed was his mother. And that was it. While she spent most of her free time painstakingly leaving her own mark on her home and its contents, he seemed content to live in near anonymity. She wondered what that said about him. Or about her, for that matter.

"I got phone calls from Sommers, Larsen, and Billings after the press conference aired today," she told him as he picked up a spoon to stir the sauce he had simmering. "They all wanted to know if we were close to making an arrest."

"And you referred them to Commander Dixon, since the whole media blitz was his idea?"

She shook her head, although he couldn't see it. "I just said we had new leads we were vigorously pursuing and that we'd be in touch when we had something solid."

"Bureaucratic BS, but in this case, right on." Apparently satisfied with the contents of both pots, he picked up his beer and turned to face her. "This thing is closing in. I can feel it. We got a couple different clients at that twenty-four-hour fitness place near Bradford's who described the same vehicle in the parking lot when they came and left, even though they were the only ones in the facility at the time. Black Crown Vic, four-door."

"No one got a license plate number, I suppose?"

He shook his head, bringing the bottle of water to his lips. "But it gives us a place to start. Isn't there something about these guys wanting to buy cars like the police? They've got some hard-on about failing to join the force, or military or something?"

"I've worked cases where that was true." She almost hated to go on. "But I don't think that's this UNSUB's profile. I'm guessing you'll discover the car was stolen."

He gave her a wry grin. "Guess I should leave the profiling to you."

His smile deepened the attractive creases beside his mouth, making her realize just how rarely she'd seen him this at ease. The sight brought a pleasant flip in her stomach. The man was simply devastating to the senses. And she wasn't nearly as determined as she'd once been in maintaining an emotional distance.

Or a physical one. She hadn't forgotten his parting words to her at Bradford's about the ease of travel between her city and his. She suspected that had been his intent. But it had occurred to her throughout the day that she didn't think a thing of hopping a plane at a moment's notice and flying across country for a new case after a terse phone call from Raiker. That was the job. Why was it unthinkable to fly occasionally to see Ryne?

Because long-distance relationships were fraught with complications. Everyone knew that. At least, that's what she'd always heard. She'd never actually engaged in one. Hadn't ever been tempted to try.

But she was tempted now. As he bent to check the French

bread, she swallowed some more wine. The warmth suffusing her veins wasn't totally due to the alcohol. This could work between them. Why not? If they both wanted a relationship to succeed, how big a coward would she be to not even try?

Although she was afraid she knew the answer to that question, her decision had already been made. She wasn't ready to see the last of Ryne Robel. The thought of not having to walk away from him after this case had relief and joy mingling inside her.

Knowing he didn't want it to end was an even greater pleasure. For once in her life, Abbie was going to forget the lessons she'd lived her life by and reach out for what she wanted, without worrying about the possible consequences.

Her face must have given away something of her thoughts, because when he turned toward her again, he gave her a careful look. "You're looking awfully pleased with yourself."

"Well, I am sitting here drinking wine watching you cook me dinner," she pointed out. With a sly smile, she added, "The view isn't half bad."

His expression went pained. "Half bad? That's the best you can do?"

"How about a spectacularly stunning package of manhood?"

He winked at her, reached for his water again. "That's better. It's nice to know you've been admiring my package." When that rendered her speechless, he smirked. "Unfortunately, my Adonis-like physique and unflagging good nature don't come without a price, so you can set the table. Dishes are in the cupboard next to the stove."

It felt amazingly natural to sit across from him, watching him consume three times the spaghetti she did, while their discussion ranged beyond the case to politics.

"You're a bleeding heart liberal," he accused after she'd vehemently argued a position. He tipped more wine into her glass. "Who would have thought?"

"And you're a typical die-hard tough-on-crime conservative who believes the death penalty is the solution for most of society's ills," she retorted, leaning back in her chair, pleasantly full.

"Not all ills," he said lazily. "Just about half the incarcerated population."

"You act tough." She sipped slowly. "But you don't see things nearly as black and white as you pretend."

"Really." His tone was challenging. "And you know that how?"

"I'll bet you never reported the run-in with McElroy last night." It was a guess, but she knew immediately from his expression that it was an accurate one. "You never told Dixon. Or Captain Brown."

His gaze slid away. "There was no point. He isn't dumb enough to bother you again. He's a fuckup, sure. But just because he made his coffin, doesn't mean I want to be the one who nails down the lid."

She smiled, satisfied that she'd read him correctly. "I agree. He's dug himself a deep enough hole. And Dixon doesn't strike me as the type to be too tolerant of mistakes."

"Only his own." Ryne mopped up the remaining sauce on his plate with the last of his bread.

"How'd he ever happen to leave Boston?"

"I don't really know. There was talk that he screwed up big-time in the mayor's office, but then a few weeks after he'd left, I heard he'd landed this job down here, so it was probably just gossip."

"I understand his wife is the chief's niece." At his raised brows she said, "You're not the only one who hears talk."

"That's true, but he's done well enough for himself here." Pushing away from the table, Ryne crossed to the refrigerator and took out another water. Twisting off the cap, he asked, "Have you heard from Callie today?"

The question had a sliver of worry piercing Abbie's sense of well-being. "She isn't answering her cell or her room phone. She's staying at the A-1 Suites on Oglethorpe. I'll swing by and see her tomorrow." And make sure she was still taking the medication that had been prescribed. She'd feel better once Callie kept her appointment with the new psychiatrist. She also planned to go with her. Her sister couldn't always be trusted to be forthcoming with a new therapist. Abbie didn't really think Callie had any meaningful insights into her own behavior.

"You said she was bipolar. There's medication for that, right?"

A feeling of unease filtered through her. She'd never discussed her sister's problems with anyone other than Callie's therapists. It always felt disloyal somehow. "She's had a lot of diagnoses over the years, and accompanying treatments. Bipolar is probably the one that's most accurate. She's also been diagnosed with antisocial personality disorder." And truth be known, that was probably accurate as well. The identification of Callie's problems was really only of value in terms of treatment, and in understanding the choices she made.

He drank, then lowered the bottle to regard her steadily. "Prone to bouts of aggression and violence? Uncaring of the consequences her actions have on others? History of sexual promiscuity?"

Her earlier lighthearted mood evaporated, to be replaced with a sense of foreboding. Setting her glass down carefully on the table, she said, "What's all this about, Ryne?"

His expression grew dogged, a sure sign that she wasn't going to like what he had to say. "I've done a little research. Enough to know that you could probably get her put away for observation for a while. Just long enough to be sure she's getting the help she needs."

Her smile was tight. He was lecturing *her* on how to handle her sister? That was rich. Abbie was well versed in several different states' laws for involuntary committal. But legality never took into consideration the emotional price of taking such measures. A price she paid, along with her sister. "I know how to take care of Callie."

He looked away, his mouth drawn into a flat line she was beginning to recognize. "Sometimes we can be too close. Can't see what needs to be done because we're blinded by emotion."

"She hurt you, Abbie. You told me once that she never would, but she hurt you bad enough to send you to the emergency room. Even if she's not a danger to anyone else, she's sure as hell a danger to you. You have to recognize that. Hell, the profile you developed of the UNSUB should convince you of the kind of damage that can be inflicted by people with abuse in their backgrounds."

A steel band was constricting her chest. Abbie struggled to draw in a breath. That he would take what she'd confided to him about the childhood she'd shared with her sister and use it to bolster his argument was more than hurtful. His betrayal sliced through her like a blade. "You're comparing my sister—*my sister*—to this sick bastard we're hunting? Where the hell do you get off?"

"She's shown up in the photos. Lots of them that were taken at Juarez's hangouts. You have to admit there are parallels there . . ."

"There's a significant percentage of violent offenders with abuse in their backgrounds," she said, her voice shaking. Her hands balled in fists, her nails biting into her palms. "But those offenders represent only an infinitesimal percentage of all abuse victims. What happened the other night . . ." She hesitated as a sneaky splinter of doubt stabbed her. "It was a one-time thing," she said with a certainty she wished she felt. Ryne was responsible for this doubt. Questioning and advising in an area he knew nothing about, all to strong-arm her into making a decision she suspected would cost both her and Callie for years to come.

His expression was bleak, his voice low. "I don't want this to come between us. But it's clear to me that she's a ticking time bomb, and when she goes off, you're the one most likely to get hurt. Think about it. You of all people should know the value of listening to all sides of an issue."

The lump in her throat grew boulder sized. And in a quick flash of clarity, she understood exactly why she'd never allowed a man this close before.

Without another word, she stood, grabbed her purse, and headed for the door.

His chair scraped behind her. "Abbie, stop. I wouldn't say anything if I didn't care."

She stopped at the door, gave him one last glance over her shoulder. The sight of him, face resolute, fists clenched, carved a jagged furrow through her chest.

"Maybe you do. But if this is your definition of 'caring,' it comes at too steep a price."

Chapter 20

"I'll need to take some personal time tomorrow afternoon."

Given that they were the first words Abbie had directed toward him since last night, Ryne supposed he should have been grateful. He looked up from the ViCAP binder he was studying to where she stood beside her desk. She'd been gone most of the day, making a return visit to Amanda Richards to update her on the investigation, and then coordinating the removal of some personal things from Bradford's for Laura's stay in a motel across town.

There was no sign of the temper she'd faced him with last night. And, thank God, no sign of the shocked hurt he'd seen in her eyes before she'd left his place, the one that had lanced him with seven kinds of remorse. She wore the same composed mask he recalled from when they first started working together. Its reappearance made him irritable.

Although his mood could just as easily be blamed on lack of sleep. Or the self-reproach that had plagued him all night, lying awake in his bed, knowing he'd been the cause of her misery.

"But you're planning to be here tomorrow morning?" Hell, he could do the self-possessed thing as well as she could. Better. In the last year and a half, he'd become a master at ensuring his personal life never splashed over to his professional.

"I'll be at the briefing. Then I have an appointment to talk to Karen Larsen again." She unlocked the bottom drawer of her desk and withdrew her purse. "I want to get some more background from her, especially about the fire that killed her parents. See if I can find any parallels to the one that destroyed her house a few weeks ago." She straightened, clutching the strap of the bag tightly, and he thought for a moment she meant to say more.

There were smudges beneath her eyes that suggested she'd slept as badly as he had. He'd shoulder the responsibility for that, too, and add it to his growing list of regrets. He'd handled last night's conversation poorly. But identifying Callie in those pictures, cozied up against lowlives in places most women would steer clear of, had only hammered home his concern for Abbie's dealings with her sister.

That fresh slice in her arm, the stitches, and her refusal to talk about how she'd gotten them told a story that was all too easy to guess. And he wouldn't take back what he'd said last night, even if he could. Callie was an explosive waiting to detonate. And Abbie was the closest in her path.

When she failed to say anything else, Ryne forced his gaze back to the binder on his desk. "All right. See you then."

He felt, rather than saw, her hesitation and tensed in anticipation. Then a moment later he heard her footsteps as she walked swiftly away.

Jaw set, he turned to his computer screen and began submitting the names of the Ketrum employees into the databases.

He printed out each individual's report in turn, willing his focus away from Abbie and on to the case. As the last set of results were printing out, Detectives Marlowe and Cantrell veered toward him on their way toward the door, each of them shrugging into their suit jackets. "We just got a call," Marlowe informed him. "We might have found the Crown Vic the perp used for the Bradford assault."

Ryne's head snapped up. "Where?"

"Private parking garage over on York and Montgomery. Elderly owner called to complain that the vehicle's front end had been damaged, although she hadn't used the car for well over a week. We're on our way over to take a look."

"Private garage should have decent security. If there's any chance of this being the vehicle, let's get the tapes. I'll send CSU over if you find anything."

Mallory nodded and the two men fell into a low-pitched conversation as they headed toward the exit.

Ryne watched them go, a sense of excitement filling him. The walls were closing in on the perp. It was only a matter of time now.

Marcy Bennett swung by his desk. "I showed a visitor for you into the conference room, Ryne."

"Who?"

But the woman was already hurrying back to take her position behind the receptionist desk, where the phone lines were ringing in raucous chorus.

He collected the papers that had printed out, and shoved them in a desk drawer before making his way back to the conference room. But once he'd pushed open the door and seen the room's lone occupant, he wanted nothing more than to turn around and walk out again.

"Hear me out, Robel." Nick McElroy stood, a manila envelope clenched in one large hand. "I know things the other night got fucked up, but this is different."

"What are you doing here?" Ryne let the door shut behind him and leaned against it, fighting the burn of impatience. He didn't have time for this shit. Not now. McElroy had a gift for digging the hole he was in deeper and deeper, and there was nothing he could say that Ryne wanted to hear.

"I just wanted to give you these." McElroy opened the envelope and shook out some five-by-seven photos. "I told you

I could still contribute to the case. I've been hanging out at the places we had targeted. The ones Juarez frequents sometimes, and I saw something you should be interested in." He shrugged one beefy shoulder. "Hell, I got nothing else to do, right?"

Reaching for his flagging patience, Ryne said, "Nick, I told you before. More than once. Stay away from the investigation. You can't help us. Your involvement could screw things up."

"Just look at these." McElroy walked over and jammed the photos in his hand. "And if you think this doesn't have anything to do with the case, you're a damn fool."

Ryne glanced through the pictures, recognizing some of the places depicted. He already had officers staking the places out, which McElroy knew. Already had a stack of photos, similar to these, so there was no point in him . . . His interest sharpened as he stared harder at one picture, the woman in the tight long-sleeved sequined top instantly recognizable.

Callie Phillips.

"When was this taken?"

Pleased with Ryne's interest, Nick said, "Last night. Around midnight. You know who that is? Phillips's sister. She's quite a party girl. Everyone in these places seem to know her, and I mean *know* her." He reached for the pile and took out another to place on top. "She's not shy about spreading it around."

Although Callie was alone in some of the photos, most had her cuddled up against one man or another. Others showed her engaged in even friendlier poses. Once again Ryne was struck by how little Abbie and her sister were alike. There were a few familiar faces in the photos. He'd probably run across some of them in the pictures taken by the officers he'd placed inside these places.

"We've got similar pictures already," he said finally, looking up at the man. "You knew we had this angle covered, Nick. There's no point in you following up on this yourself."

"This is the one I wanted you to see." McElroy flipped through the stack and shoved another for Ryne to look at. "Interesting choice of companions, don't you think?"

Ryne froze, staring at the image of Callie laughing into a familiar face, one hand placed suggestively on the man's crotch.

Hidalgo Juarez.

Wadding up the wrapper from the deli sandwich he'd had delivered an hour ago, Ryne tossed it into the nearby waste-basket. The office was quieter after shift change. Made it easier to think. And after the events of the afternoon had raced to a mind-numbing blur, he needed time to collect his thoughts. Plan his next course of action.

They'd scored a possible link on the Crown Vic when CSU had discovered a dime-sized blood sample in it. It'd take a while to determine if any of the latents or fibers retrieved from the car matched anyone other than the owner. In the meantime, he was planning something bound to be very unpopular with at least one member of his team.

First thing tomorrow morning he was having Callie Phillips brought in for questioning.

Regret surfaced, but he shoved it aside. Morning would be best. If she was spending most of her nights boozing it up, she wouldn't be as mentally sharp after only a few hours of sleep. He already knew that the woman lied as easily as some people breathed.

And he wanted the truth when he questioned her about her relationship with Hidalgo Juarez.

How well did she know the man? Had she ever seen any-one else conversing with him, and if so, could she identify them? The employees and occupants at the dives Juarez fre-quented tended not to "see" anything. They admitted know-ing even less. Getting positive IDs on all the individuals pictured had been slow going, mostly done through matches with the electronic mug books.

He pulled out the envelope of photos McElroy had taken

and set them on top of his notes for the next briefing. Tomorrow he'd have the uniforms go through them and cross-check individuals already known, start identifying the new ones. He'd follow the same line of action he'd pursue for every occupant they identified, regardless of who they were.

Or whom they were related to.

Resolutely, he forced aside thoughts of how Abbie would react to his interviewing her sister. Would she be able to separate their argument of the other night from the facts emerging in the case?

He honestly didn't know. And that uncertainty kept him from calling her right now and alerting her of his plans. She was a complete professional. He recognized that. But she'd also been taking care of her sister for years. If there was even the slightest chance that she would warn Callie of the upcoming meeting, he couldn't afford to risk it. She'd find out tomorrow morning when she came in and discovered who he had in the interview room.

His chest burned thinking of Abbie's reaction, but he couldn't let that matter. Disconnecting logic from emotion was always a bitch. He was an expert on that.

But he was less familiar with the guilt weighing on him for doing what he knew had to be done.

He returned to the reports on the Ketrum employees identified as working on the TTX trials. Jepperson's list had included both scientists and techs, three women and seven men. But the background checks had turned up nothing on eight of the ten, other than one who didn't like to pay his speeding tickets.

The other two were worth investigating further. Dwayne Carsons had two recent domestic assault complaints lodged against him. It was entirely possible the guy had violent incidents in his past that had gone unreported.

He turned his attention to Trevor Holden's data and let out a low whistle. A sealed juvie record. Now that was interesting. No way to access that information at this point. The record had to be at least three years old. It took that long beyond serving the delinquency sentence to even request a seal.

Ryne was sufficiently intrigued to submit Holden's name to a few more databases, just to see what else he could dig up on the man. When that didn't pan out, he typed Holden's name into a search engine.

Not much came up. An old newspaper article listing graduation from a two-year technical school in Indiana with an associate of applied science degree. Ryne checked the dates. Could be the right guy. Then he spent an hour looking through telephone books from the town the college was located in, and even made a few calls to the Holdens listed. None claimed knowledge of Trevor Holden.

He took a break from the search to send Jepperson an e-mail requesting copies of Dwayne Carsons's domestic assault reports. Then he reluctantly turned back to the computer. He was gaining new respect for the computer techs or anyone who had to spend most of their day gleaning information from the Web. It was mind-crushingly boring, for one thing. And it was tough on the muscles. He had a nagging pain in the middle of his back from being hunched over the computer too long that day. And he was increasingly pressed for new and original search requests to type in that may yield information about Holden.

He did, however, discover that there was a whole lot of worthless shit on the Internet. And more people than he'd ever guessed who considered it their personal responsibility to post their every thought and opinion in cyberspace for the rest of the world to read.

His faith in people's intelligence, never at a high, sank a notch.

An hour later, his chin propped on his fist, he was skimming some broad's online journal. Or whatever they called it. Blog. Simpleminded musings. And there he found it. The reference to a Trevor Holden.

He straightened to read more carefully. It was an archived post dated two years earlier, complete with every excruciating detail of planning a ten-year class reunion. At the bottom of the post was a listing of six classmates the author still hadn't found, and a plea for readers' help if they knew the whereabouts of any of the individuals. Holden was fourth on the list.

Ryne did a search on the town that housed the named high school. Two hundred and fifty miles northwest of Madison, Wisconsin, its biggest employers were the school and the residential juvenile detention located there. The detention centers were a boon to shrinking school districts, as most of the institution's residents were educated at local public schools.

Anticipation tightened in his gut. A Trevor Holden working on the TTX experiments had a juvie file, and another Trevor Holden graduated from a high school located in a town with a juvenile detention center. He'd never been a huge fan of coincidence.

· He found no telephone listing for any Holdens in town, but places like that were limited, and could draw juveniles even from out of state.

The author of the blog post, a Cyn Paulus, was listed in the online phone directory and Ryne gave her a call. When there was no answer, he left a short message on the answering machine, sure she'd get back to him. He just hoped their conversation didn't end up on her damn blog.

———

"You can't smoke in here."

Callie looked up from the cigarette she was on the verge of lighting, her heavy-lidded eyes widening in amusement. "You gonna lock me up for smoking?"

Ryne gave a slight nod to the silent officer leaning against the wall, and the man left the interview room. "No." He strode over to the table and took the cigarette and lighter from her hands, shoving them back inside her purse. "I won't have to because you aren't lighting up."

A hint of a smile curving her lips, she leaned back in her chair and languidly crossed her legs. She looked like she'd been dragged from bed after a long night of debauchery, although the officers who'd fetched her from her motel room had assured Ryne she'd been alone. Her makeup was smudged, her long blond hair tousled, and her short shorts and tight long-sleeved shirt looked slept in.

"Long night?" Setting the folder and notebook he carried on the table, he pulled out a chair across from her.

She yawned, one long-nailed hand tapping her mouth. "Short one, actually. Didn't know I'd be rousted by your men so early. That's the term, right? Rousted." She purred it, as though savoring the taste. "One of the officers you sent . . . the big one? Roughed me up a little in the squad car." She slid an eye closed in a sultry wink. "I enjoyed it."

"We have video cameras in the squad cars," he said calmly. "I'll check out your claim."

"Well, damn." Her smile seemed genuine, not at all flustered to be caught in a lie. He imagined it happened frequently enough to register little reaction. "What am I suspected of, Detective? Last I heard, breaking the hearts of low-rent rednecks wasn't a crime."

"Is that what you were doing last night? Must have steered clear of Mr. G's. Had a vice sweep there."

She lifted a shoulder. "I've been there. Not last night, though."

He gave her a slow smile. "And you're no stranger to vice anyway, right?" He flipped open the folder, withdrew a piece of paper. "Petty theft. Possession of a controlled substance. Resisting arrest. Assaulting an officer. Solicitation." The criminal check he'd run on her had yielded no real surprises. But they did originate from varied locales. The lady got around.

For the first time she looked vaguely annoyed. "I hope you're not going to tell me that you had me brought down here to discuss my checkered past. I haven't been arrested for anything for years." She corrected herself almost immediately. "At least, not in the States."

"Good to know your crime spree is over."

She laughed, seeming genuinely amused. "You know, I like you, Detective. Ryne." Her foot, shod in toeless fuck-me heels, touched his leg under the table, not quite accidentally. "Don't ask me why. Normally cops are too humorless for my taste. God knows my sister is."

He was suddenly supremely aware of the one-way mirror on the wall to his left. He didn't think Abbie had come in yet, but if she had, she'd be behind it, watching. Fuming. "Your sister isn't a cop."

"Close enough." As if reading his thoughts, she slid a glance toward the one-way mirror. "Where is she anyway? Does she know I'm here?"

Ryne studied the woman carefully. She wasn't an easy read. "What do you think?"

"I think you didn't tell her. I think you're in for a real ass chewing when she finds out you talked to me."

The assessment was dead on. Eerily so. Skirting it, he reached into the folder again. "I had some questions I wanted to ask you about an ongoing investigation."

"I'll save you a little time. I don't know anything about the Nightmare Rapist."

His hand stilled for an instant in the act of withdrawing the photos. "I didn't say which investigation."

Callie lifted a shoulder, left bare by the gravity-defying strapless shirt she wore. "You didn't have to. The Nightmare Rapist is your case. Probably the only one you're working on. Least that's the take I got from those TV clips you and Abbie were in."

Not for the first time, he damned the press conferences Dixon had insisted on calling. They'd been more hindrance than assistance. He splayed the photos of her in the bars on the table before her. Some of the shots were McElroy's, others taken by the officers he'd placed there. She gave them a cursory glance. "You seem to be a popular lady."

She began drumming her fingers on the table, a rapid little tattoo. Nerves? Or boredom? "Maybe you'd like to see why I'm so popular." She leaned forward suddenly, propping her arms on the table and giving him an eye-popping view of her cleavage. "Cops like it wild. That's what I always heard. And crazy broads are the wildest in bed." She winked again, but there was no humor in her expression. "And we both know you think I'm crazy."

She'd managed to catch him off guard. Had Abbie told

her that? In the next moment, however, he recovered, noting her speculative expression. She was playing him, the same way he'd planned on playing her. And he had to admit she was good at it.

He nudged the photos closer to her. "I'd like you to take a look at these and identify the men in the pictures with you."

She picked up the photos, fanning them out in her hands like a poker hand. "Who took them?"

"How well do you know the men you're pictured with?"

Callie eyed him as she let the photos drop back on the table. "Well enough to fuck 'em. Is that what you want to hear?"

Ryne felt a flicker of sympathy for Abbie. Conversation with her sister was mind-numbing. But he still wondered how much of that could be attributed to her illness, and how much to sheer cunning. "Then you can tell me their names."

She laughed, genuine amusement lighting her face. "You aren't that naïve. Abbie, maybe. But not you."

Pitching his voice to a lower, more intimate tone, he cajoled, "You saying you don't want to help me? Help Abbie?"

Heaving a sigh, she slouched lower in her chair. "I'm saying I don't bother learning their names. Or remembering them. What's the point?" She singled out a picture, tapped the man in it. "But if I had to name them, he'd be EverReady. Doesn't take much imagination to figure why." She slid another photo out of the pile, smirked. "We'll name him Jackhammer." Another photo. "And him . . ." She pursed her lips. "I think we'll call him Handful of Disappointment."

Deliberately, Ryne slid the photo of her and Juarez across the table. "How about this one? How well do you know him?"

Something flickered in her expression, there and gone too quickly to identify. "I didn't fuck him if that's what you mean. He's not my type. He's too pathetic."

He surveyed the picture again, of Callie's hand placed familiarly on the man's crotch. "How's he different from the others?"

Cocking her head, Callie reached up one hand to trace the

rise of her top, where it stretched low across her chest.
"You're a cop, you know the type." She gave another shrug,
obviously losing patience. "He's the kind of guy bent over
from life continually kicking him in the ass. A permanent
victim."

———————

"Detective Robel? Can I speak to you?"

Abbie could tell her dispassionate tone didn't fool Ryne.
From the sidelong glances of some of the men departing the
conference room after the briefing, it didn't fool them either.

"Of course."

He remained behind the table, shoveling notes back into
the accordion binder. She followed the last uniform to the
door and swung it shut behind him.

Hauling in a deep breath, she struggled to rein in the temper that bubbled and frothed inside her before turning to face
him again.

"Why?"

The question split the room like a rifle shot. She didn't
mind the accusation that sounded in it. He deserved that, and
more. She just hoped he didn't hear the note of betrayal layered beneath the word.

"That was an exercise in futility. I only caught the tail end
of the interview, but it was enough to see you'd wasted your
time." Driven to move, she rounded the table then stopped
again, bracing her arms on its top. "She gave you nothing.
Because she knows nothing. Which I could have told you had
you seen fit to share what you were planning."

He didn't dissemble. She could appreciate that, even if it
likely meant he didn't care enough to bother. Instead he silently held out a folder, something suspiciously like pity on
his face. And that had the pent-up anger go molten again.

"Go ahead. Take a look."

She eyed the folder like she would a live serpent. Something else sliced through her ire. Trepidation.

It took effort to reach for the folder, flip it open. She'd
half expected something like the photos in it. Something in

her chest eased a fraction. She lifted a brow. "So? Callie frequents high-risk places. Indulges in high-risk behavior. This isn't news."

"Look at the last one."

Something in his eyes, in his voice, warned her. Steeling herself, she flipped to the bottom of the pile. But she still wasn't prepared for the punch of disbelief, the sick little sink to her stomach when she saw the photo in question.

Callie and Juarez.

"This doesn't mean anything," she said with remarkable calm. Remarkable, because her nerves were rattling like china dishes in an earthquake. Her mind whirled, possible explanations chasing doubt in fast-forward speed. She shook her head, attempting to clear it. "It goes to figure she'd run across him, given the places they both hang out." When Ryne said nothing, merely continued to look at her, she snapped, "Juarez is alibied for the night of Bradford's attempted rape. He doesn't fit the profile. You can't still believe . . ."

Ryne walked over to the coffeemaker in the corner, poured a cup, and returned, shoving it into her hands.

"Drink it," he ordered brusquely.

Her fingers wrapped around the Styrofoam, welcoming the heat that transferred. Her blood seemed to have gone to ice.

"Think. You're the expert on victimology. We're looking for intersections, you said. Juarez was a victim, you said. Well, this is a hell of a coincidental intersection, don't you think?"

Abbie took a gulp of the coffee, almost spewed it out again. Black as pitch and almost as thick, it was a vile brew. But it steadied her, had her thinking clearly again. "Juarez came across the UNSUB at some point, yes. But we have no reason to believe that Callie did, so the intersection angle doesn't hold."

"At the least she could help us with some of the guys in the photos we haven't ID'd."

Suddenly weary, she set the cup on the table separating them. "Maybe. If she felt like it. But it's just as probable that it's like she told you. She doesn't bother to learn their names. My sister is a lot of things, Ryne, most of them sad. But she doesn't have anything to do with this investigation."

"I can understand why you wanted to talk to her," she said stiffly when he remained silent. "But you still should have let me know first. If you didn't want me in on the interview, I still could have given you some suggestions on how to best handle her."

"I wanted to." His voice was low, his gaze direct. "Believe that, Abbie. But you're too close. You know that, even if you can't admit it. Right from the first you said we had to consider every option."

Her fingers gripped the edge of the table as she struggled for a calm to match his. "And what option haven't I considered?"

"That hospital Callie stayed at in Connecticut. Was she free to come and go or was she on a locked ward?"

The seeming non sequitur took her aback. "What does that . . ." Then comprehension filtered through and her temper ignited all over again, a lit match to a gasoline-soaked fuse. "You can't possibly be trying to link her to those sexual homicides in New Jersey three years ago!"

There was a muscle jumping in one tightly clenched jaw. But his voice was even. "Just tying up some loose threads. She was in the general vicinity at the time."

Her fingers let go of the table to ball into tight fists. Hauling in a deep breath, then another, she struggled for composure, but the effort seemed beyond her. "So were you, remember? For that matter, so was Dixon."

"I'm saying her presence here bothers me. Her background bothers me. Her connection to Juarez and the places he hangs out *really* bothers me. And then there's the fact she refused to give me jackshit in the interview this morning. Remember how you dismissed Juarez right away as a suspect?"

"You pushed me for an opinion that I told you wasn't based on any evidence, only—"

"Only your gut." He gave her a grim nod of satisfaction.

"Now my gut is telling me Callie could be linked to this case somehow. Maybe something she heard. Someone's she's met. I'd like your help getting her to cooperate."

She gave him a mirthless smile. "Little late to be asking me in on that, isn't it?"

"Abbie." He took a step toward her then stopped, as if reining himself back. But the misery in his voice was reflected in his expression. "Do you think this is easy for me? Any of it? But we follow every lead, no matter how slim. To do it, we have to separate the personal from the professional. We have to do the job."

Giving a jerky nod, she headed for the door. "Should be easy enough. As far as I'm concerned, there no longer is anything personal between us."

Chapter 21

Because she was driving like an automaton, it took Abbie twice as long as it should have to get to Larsen's place. Twice, she found herself having to backtrack because she'd missed a turn. Once she nearly sideswiped a car because she wasn't watching the light closely enough.

The near miss shook off the curious numbness that had encompassed her since leaving headquarters. She almost mourned the loss. A tangle of emotion weighted her chest. Ironically, she seized on the one thing Ryne had said with which she could agree without reservation.

They had to do the job.

Pulling to a stop in front of Larsen's, she turned off the car's ignition. It took an embarrassing amount of effort to pull back and achieve the distance necessary to objectively evaluate the bombshells of this morning. The hits had come so quick and furious that she'd been left inwardly reeling. But now she forced herself to evaluate the events on their own merits. And reached a conclusion that was inevitable.

Of course they needed to talk to Callie. The same way they needed to speak to Juarez's ex-girlfriend, his family, and known acquaintances. She'd crossed the man's path, and at some point Juarez had come to the UNSUB's attention.

Gleaning anything valuable from her sister, however, would be an uphill battle, even if she had anything worthwhile to share. Abbie strode rapidly up to Larsen's front door, rang the bell. The most telling part of Ryne's interview with Callie had been her remark about Juarez being a victim. Given her past, she'd empathize with the man, even while she derided him. And misguided sympathy would be enough to elicit Callie's obstinance, assuming she knew anything important.

When Karen Larsen swung the door open, and wordlessly stepped aside for her to enter, Abbie had the thought that the last few days had been rough ones for the woman. The careful makeup couldn't hide the circles under her eyes. And Abbie observed the way Larsen looked furtively past her before pulling the door shut. The careful way she secured what looked like a new deadbolt.

"How are you, Karen?"

"Fine." The tone, the smile, was almost normal. But the arms folded tightly across her chest, the jerky movements as she crossed to the couch, told a different story.

"So, I guess you haven't found him." The woman lifted a shoulder. "Or you would have told me already, right?"

"We're getting closer." Abbie sat down on the couch beside the woman, turned to face her. "I hope it will all be over soon."

"What about that last woman he attacked? People are saying she might still be in danger." Karen swallowed hard, but her gaze was direct. "Do you believe that? That he might come after his victims again?"

Abbie reached over to grip the woman's hand. "I can't discuss details of the last attempted assault. But I don't think you're in danger." Seeing that her words did little to alleviate the worry from the woman's expression, she added, "For your peace of mind, though, maybe you'd feel more comfortable staying with a friend for a while." She searched her memory. "What about your brother? Maybe he would come."

The woman shook her head. "He's in Louisiana. He's asked me to come down there and stay, but I can't afford to not work. I'll be fine." As if the words calmed her, Larsen forced another smile. "You said yesterday you had some other questions for me."

Pulling her notebook from her purse, Abbie flipped it open. "I'd like to ask you about the fire at your home when you were a teenager."

Larsen turned away, drew a deep breath. "Haven't we already covered that?"

"I'm sorry." Abbie's sympathy was sincere. "I know this is difficult. But I need to find out if there are any similarities between the origins of two fires."

"I don't see how." Larsen's voice was shaky. "The fire at my home in Minnesota started because of frayed wiring in the attic. At least that's what the police said after the fire department had investigated."

"Do you happen to recall the name of the chief of police there?" When Larsen shook her head, Abbie smiled. "Doesn't matter. I can track him down. I'd like you to tell me what happened that night." When the woman closed her eyes, Abbie felt a tug of guilt. That first fire had cost the woman her parents.

And the cost of the fire a few weeks ago had been equally devastating.

Slowly, laboriously, Abbie elicited the details from Larsen. How she'd awakened to find the hallway filled with smoke. Flames visible beneath her parents' door. The staircase engulfed in fire. How only the quick thinking of a neighbor had saved Karen, with a ladder the man had propped up to her window.

It occurred to Abbie then that Larsen had been fortunate twice in her escape. But her escape from the second fire was most likely not due to luck, but to design. The UNSUB had meant for her to get away, although perhaps not as quickly as she had. He would have wanted her terrorized as the flames got closer. Perhaps reaching the woman on the bed before she freed herself.

After more than an hour of questioning, Larsen looked wrung out. "I have to get to work soon." Consulting the slim purple and gold watch on her wrist, she grimaced. "The clinic is clear across town, and I'm not even dressed yet."

Abbie rose. "I realize this has been hard. But I appreciate your help. Have you remembered anything else about the night of your attack?"

Larsen hesitated, before shaking her head firmly, getting up to lead Abbie to the door. "No. Sorry."

But that slight pause had Abbie's instincts sharpening. She stopped inside the door, facing the woman. "It might seem insignificant to you. Maybe even not worth mentioning. But I'm interested in any detail you remembered, Karen. Regardless of how small."

"It's just . . ." Larsen crossed her arms over her chest. "I'm sure it's meaningless." At Abbie's encouraging smile, she plowed on. "But you asked before whether I'd told anyone about the fire that killed my parents. And I've only told one person here, so I didn't give it much thought. But your question got me thinking . . ." She halted, shook her head. "Like I say, it's really nothing. But I did check back with Paula, my friend. She said she hadn't told anyone what I said about the fire except for her boyfriend."

"Her boyfriend?"

"I don't even know the guy's name. Paula's always real coy about it. I think he's married or something. I just found it sort of odd she'd mention it to him." She gave a strained smile. "But then I'm no expert about conversational topics between lovers."

———————

Ryne checked the cell before answering it, feeling a quick clutch in his stomach when he saw the incoming number. "Abbie."

"I finished with Larsen and wanted to update you before taking personal time." She gave him a quick succinct rundown of her conversation. "Did Dixon tell you that he knew about the fire in Larsen's background?"

"I don't think so. But it goes to figure. He'd have gotten as much information as possible from his girlfriend before ever bringing Larsen to my attention."

"If I have time yet this afternoon, I'm going to follow up with some phone calls to Stratton, Minnesota." He could hear the sounds of traffic in the distance. Abbie was on the road. "I'd like to talk to the officer who responded to the scene of the first Larsen fire."

"I have a few questions to run by you." Conscious of the occupants at desks around him, Ryne kept his tone impassive as he reported Dwayne Carsons's dings on domestic assault and Holden's sealed juvie record. "Given the unlikelihood that we have an UNSUB traveling fifteen hundred miles to commit these rapes, what are we looking for here?"

"The relationship between the TTX supplier and the perp," she said immediately.

His muscles untensed a notch as the familiar back-and-forth exchange began. Whatever their differences, he could rely on Abbie to concentrate on the investigation.

"I started thinking about that at the debriefing this morning. About the origin of that relationship. Even if the perp doesn't let the supplier know what he's doing, the supplier recognizes the capabilities of the drug and can make certain presumptions. It takes a degree of trust, don't you think? So I'm guessing there is a long-standing connection between the two. This UNSUB is enacting the torture and rapes because of serious abuse in his background. That kind of abuse doesn't lend itself to the establishment of casual friendships."

"Why couldn't it be someone he happened across who could be of use to him, like Juarez?"

"If I had to speculate, I'd guess it isn't. This guy is careful not to be identified. I think he'd have gotten the biggest supply he could get his hands on and then made sure the supplier disappeared for good. He knows too much. Juarez was just a patsy."

Ryne scrubbed one hand over his face. Holden and Carsons were a start, but if a Ketrum employee were the supplier, none of the ten on the team was above suspicion. They'd be in a position to get their hands on the drug, as well as falsifying any records necessary to cover up the loss.

"Okay. I'll follow up on these two. If I strike out, we'll have to check the other eight members of the Ketrum TTX team."

"I look forward to your update tomorrow morning."

From her impersonal tone, she could have been talking to Cantrell or Holmes. There was no hint of the fury she'd faced him with that morning. Nor any remnant of the intimacy that had developed between them. An intimacy she'd declared dead earlier.

An unfamiliar clutch of nerves tightened in his gut. "Listen, Abbie . . ."

"You were right this morning."

Her words silenced him. "You had to talk to Callie. I'd have made the same decision."

It was the last thing he expected her to say. The last thing he wanted to hear. His throat went tight, as recognition of his mistake slammed home. "I should have let you know I was bringing her in."

"Yes, you should have."

He took a breath, looked around, not really seeing his surroundings. Dammit, he'd played it safe. By the book. How could that be a screwup?

Because it meant he'd underestimated Abbie. Badly. And she'd made it pretty clear what that was going to cost him.

His palms went damp. "Listen . . ."

"I'm stopping to pick Callie up now. I'll talk to you later."

The call disconnected. It took several long moments before Ryne put his cell away, mentally calling himself seven kinds of a fool. Damn, how could a decision that had seemed so right only hours ago make him feel like such a shit now? This was exactly why he'd always steered clear of relationships. They were full of minefields. The least misstep and they blew up in your face.

"Robel, call for you on line three," Marcy called.

But it took another moment for Ryne to reach for the phone. And more effort than it should have to shift his focus to the caller.

"Detective Robel?" The woman's voice was breathy, excited. "This is Cyn Paulus. I called back just as soon as I heard your message. I didn't get it until today because I was away from home a few days on a buying trip. I have this little shop, you see, and I sell all sorts of—"

Ruthlessly, Ryne cut through the woman's rambling. "Thanks for calling back. I have a question about a name I ran across on your blog. A former classmate of yours. Trevor Holden."

"Why, what's he done?"

Ignoring her question, he asked one of his own. "What can you tell me about him?"

"Weeell . . ." There was a pout in the drawn-out word. "I didn't know him that well. We didn't exactly run in the same circles. But I wanted to invite all the classmates, and he did graduate with us, even if he was only around a couple years or so."

Patience thinning, Ryne asked, "Why is that?"

"He was one of those delinquents from the State Training School." Ryne felt a flare of excitement at her words. "None of them showed up for the reunion, of course, which was just as well. But I told my girlfriend, I have to at least invite them, just to be fair. . . ."

He shifted to a more comfortable position. Something told him that this conversation was going to take a while. "Can you tell me what you remember about Holden in particular?"

"He was sort of creepy, I remember that. Had a way of looking at girls like he was stripping us naked in his mind, you know what I mean?"

Something in Ryne went still. "Schools are rumor mills, right? Did you ever hear what he was sent to State for?"

"If I did, I don't recall. We just sort of steered clear of the staties. Sorry, that's what we called the State School residents. And it's not like any of them wanted to be friends with us. They all sort of hung together."

"So you'd have no idea where Holden is now. What he's doing."

"Oh, I heard some talk at the reunion." The woman gave

an audible sniff. "Have a hard time believing any of it. One guy, Danny Sorenson, says Holden attended the same junior college as his cousin. Said they were in a lot of the same classes. He even tried telling us his cousin claims Holden is working for some sort of drug company."

Satisfaction surged. "Any idea where? Or for what company?"

"No, like I said, no one believes it. Danny said it's somewhere out West. Most of us figure the most likely place to find him out there is Yuma Prison."

Ryne probed further, until he was convinced he'd learned all the woman knew. About to end the conversation, he had a second thought. "You wouldn't happen to have a picture of Holden, would you? Something in a high school yearbook maybe?"

"Sure, he's probably in there. Most of the staties didn't get senior pictures, of course, but our principal had the high school yearbook staff take pictures to be sure they were included in the annuals."

"Could you find that picture and fax it to me?" Ryne gave her his fax number.

"Maybe," she responded coyly. "If you tell me what this is all about. Is Holden in some sort of trouble? I'll bet he is. Are you going to arrest him?"

Ryne rubbed one temple, to alleviate the throb that had suddenly appeared there. He reached for diplomacy, found it harder than usual to summon. "I'm just following a lead. I'm not at liberty to divulge any information, Ms. Paulus. But I can tell you your help could be vital to an ongoing investigation here."

Her voice perked up. "Vital?"

"Absolutely, ma'am," he said soberly, leaning back in his chair to stare at the ceiling. Some clown had thrown several pencils up to remain stuck in the soft tiles. Probably while having a conversation much like this one.

"Well, you can be sure I'll do anything I can to help. I'll get on it right away."

Given the enthusiasm lacing her tone, he had no doubt

she'd do just that. Recalling his earlier conversation with Abbie, he added, "Could you also send a photo of any of Holden's buddies?"

"I'm not sure I remember who he hung out with. Like I said, we didn't—"

"Run in the same circles. Right. But maybe one of your friends will help jog your memory."

"Maybe." She sounded dubious. "I'll see what I can do."

"Thank you. I appreciate your assistance." Looking up, Ryne noted Captain Brown heading toward his desk. "If you can send them as soon as possible, that will be a big help."

He disconnected the call as Brown halted next to him, looked up inquiringly.

"I just got off the phone with Commander Dixon," the man said without preamble. "He's going to be in my office in ten minutes and wants a recap on the case."

Jesus. Ryne just barely restrained an audible groan. Could this day get any worse? "All right. I'll run off my latest investigation report."

Brown's broad freckled face looked grim. "Better come prepared with more than that. He's on a tear, Ryne. He's talking about replacing you as lead detective on this case."

––––––––––

It was times like these that Ryne missed drinking.

He sat slouched in his desk chair, head tilted back, gaze trained on those pencils protruding from the ceiling tiles. There had been a time when Jim Beam had been a damn good friend after a long bitch of a day. God knew, this day had been the mother of all bitches.

But it wasn't alcohol he craved right now. It wasn't one of the nameless faceless women who'd matched him shot for shot, then invited him home for diversion of another sort.

It was one woman. The one woman who'd walked away from him today, making it very clear she considered them over.

He eyed the ceiling balefully. And that was far worse than the last few hours, although they'd been hell by anyone's standards.

McElroy was still fucking up this investigation. The idiot had gone to Dixon about getting reinstated, and the result had been predictable. In his eagerness to color himself indispensable, he made it sound like he was still actively involved in this case, citing the photos that he'd handed over to Ryne. That had shifted the focus of Dixon's ire from McElroy to Ryne. Believing that Ryne had ignored McElroy's suspension, the commander had delivered a world-class paint-peeling ass chewing that had to have traveled through the squad room and beyond.

It had taken some careful tap dancing around the facts to convince Dixon that McElroy wasn't being utilized in any way, while not broaching the subject of the pictures the man had taken. But Ryne couldn't help thinking Dixon's loss of control had been over the top. He must be taking some heavy-duty pressure on this investigation from the higher-ups.

Or maybe he just had woman problems. Maybe his wife had finally wised up and kicked his lying adulterous ass out on the street.

Serve the bastard right.

Ryne scrubbed both hands over his face. He knew from all too recent experience just how fucked up a man could get over a woman. He sure as hell wasn't going to sit here and brood about how he'd give anything right now to be sitting next to Abbie. Just looking at her. Bouncing ideas off her. Or burying himself inside her.

Because that would make him pathetic, as well as pissed off.

Straightening, he checked the time, mentally shrugged. It was close to dark, but there nothing to go home for. No one to go home to.

Wearily, he scraped back his chair and stood, crossing the office to retrieve the faxes Paulus had sent him. On his way he met Mallory, coming back into the squad room.

"Dale. What are you doing back here?"

The man gave a sheepish grin. "Couldn't shake the case off tonight. My wife finally got tired of repeating everything she said and told me to go on back to work. It's where my mind was anyhow."

Ryne grunted and reached for the faxes. "Understanding wife."

"More annoyed than understanding, but here I am. You may as well put me to work."

Only half listening, Ryne looked at the first sheet of photos. The black-and-white pictures were even grainier on a fax, but Paulus had circled Holden's picture and underlined his name. He was inclined to agree with her assessment. The guy was spooky.

Mallory peered over his shoulder. "That the same Holden working the Ketrum trials?"

"I'll scan the photo and e-mail it to Montana. See if the sheriff there can ID him for me." As he spoke, he looked at the second page. Stilled. This one also had a photo circled. A name underlined. Big loopy cursive letters formed a caption that read: *Holden's only buddy that we can recall.*

Ryne stared hard at the picture. Not trusting his eyes, he cocked again and looked again from a different angle.

"What is it?"

Ryne held out the second page. "Try to concentrate just on the face. Who does this look like?"

The detective frowned. Squinted. Bent to peer closer.

Then he let out a long low whistle and lifted his gaze to Ryne's. "Holy shit."

"Yeah," Ryne said grimly. "Holy shit."

"I thought Dr. Solem seemed nice. Competent."

Callie lifted a shoulder in response to Abbie's statement, hooking a finger in the front shades to look out at the street. "She's a shrink. They're all the same."

And so was her sister's response to therapists.

Abbie set her purse on the back of the couch. Callie had been candid with the doctor, she reminded herself, trying to lift her flagging spirits, although the session had been more of an initial information-gathering meeting than anything else. Callie had signed an authorization for an exchange of information between Faulkner and Solem at the hospital the other night, so the new psychiatrist had a copy of her case file.

And she seemed calmer. More settled. From experience, Abbie believed she really was taking the medication again. The challenge would be to get her to continue.

Watching her sister roam the small room restlessly, Abbie reflected that she'd learned to celebrate the small accomplishments, because the setbacks could be so disappointing.

It was Ryne's fault she wasn't more enthused about these steps Callie was taking. He was the reason for the doubt that even now circled, looking for hidden nuances in every word Callie uttered. Worrying every time her always secretive sister was less than forthcoming.

"You're jumpy." Abbie stood in the doorway separating the kitchen from the living room and surveyed her sister. As a matter of fact, Callie had seemed increasingly edgy through dinner, for once insisting on coming straight back here.

"Not jumpy. Eager. I have something I want to tell you. To show you."

Instincts and experience had her distrusting her sister's smile. But she made sure to keep the emotion from showing when she responded, "What's that?"

"I think the appropriate question would be 'Who's that?'" A figure stepped out of Abbie's darkened bedroom. With only the kitchen light behind her and the lamp in the living room, it was impossible to make out a face.

The voice was eerily familiar.

Callie threw the newcomer a sly smile. "You're so impatient, baby. I was getting to you." She went to the figure and slipped her arm around his waist.

Trepidation circling, Abbie stepped farther into the room, peering at the man her sister was hugging so intimately. And then she stopped abruptly, as recognition slammed into her.

She could be forgiven for not recognizing him at first. She was used to seeing the long blond hair curled. Full makeup. Nails neatly polished.

She was used to seeing him as Karen Larsen.

Callie's laugh gurgled out. "You should see your face."

She turned to Larsen and said confidingly, "I think you startled her, Sean."

"Is that your real name?" Abbie asked conversationally, her mind racing. She'd checked out Larsen herself. Had even spoken to one of the woman's former nursing instructors. Karen Larsen existed. The identification he'd shown was valid.

It just belonged to someone else.

"Don't be such a cop." Callie's voice was peeved as Larsen—or Sean—stared across the room at Abbie. "Of course it's his real name. Sean Grant. I wanted you to meet him because he and I have become . . ." She gave a wicked laugh and leaned in to nip at his neck. "Close."

Without releasing Abbie's gaze, the man slid his arm around her shoulders. Seeing the syringe in his hand, Abbie lunged forward. "No!"

But Callie merely seemed puzzled, looking from the needle in her arm to Grant. "What's that? This really isn't the time, baby. My little sister doesn't approve." The last word slurred and she gave a surprised laugh. "Was that smack? 'Cuz I don't do smack anymore. Had a bad . . . trip." She stumbled, clung to Grant for support, and when he shoved her away, she fell to the floor, giggling helplessly.

"Your bitch sister knows what it is." The man took a step forward. "At least she knows what it does." His smile was ugly as he addressed Abbie. "According to the news, you pretty much know everything. And apparently you're an expert on me. So why don't you tell her who I am. Better yet, tell us both just what I have planned for you two tonight."

Oh, God. Her lungs were strangled. Ice filled her veins. Abbie flicked a glance in Callie's direction, but her sister was lethargically trying to raise one arm, and frowning at the exertion it took.

"She isn't involved in this," Abbie said steadily. "It's me you want, isn't it? Let her go."

"On the contrary." Grant crossed his arms, surveying her with something like amusement on his face. "I want you both. And I'm still waiting for you to read my mind. Tell me what I'm going to do. You should know because *you're the fucking expert!*" With one quick movement, he picked up a framed picture from the mantle and sent it hurtling in her direction.

She ducked, never taking her eyes off him. It bounced harmlessly against the couch and clattered to the floor. Experience had her replying smoothly, without thinking. "I'm not an expert on you. You're far too smart for me to predict." Play to his ego, obviously outraged that she'd dared to evaluate him. His motives. His next move.

"Now that's the first true thing I've heard you say. Too bad the media isn't broadcasting this." He squatted to where Callie was trying to pull herself up on a chair and slammed a fist into her face.

Abbie used the split second to bend, grabbing for her weapon, but by the time her gun cleared its holster, he'd pulled a large knife that must have been secreted in the back of his waistband. The large blade glinted as he placed the tip against a motionless Callie's throat. "I don't think you want to do that, do you, Abbie?"

Her cell phone rang, the sound an incongruous thread of normalcy in an otherwise deadly situation. She swallowed, watching the blood well as the knife tip pricked the skin. *Never surrender your weapon.* Raiker's mantra had been drummed into his staff. *Once you've been disarmed, your chances for survival diminish drastically.*

"Put down the gun and slide it over to me. And then your purse."

After several rings the cell went abruptly silent. "I don't think so." Abbie edged to the side to get a better angle for the shot. He was too close to Callie. And the blood was flowing more freely from the increasing pressure on the blade.

"This is her carotid artery. She won't survive a blade through it." He shrugged. "No loss, if you ask me. She's just another worthless cunt. But I'm surprised you'd chance it." He increased the pressure on the blade and the blood oozed faster. "After all she sacrificed for you."

Sick fear congealed in her stomach. "All right." Abbie

lowered her weapon slowly but sidled inches closer. If she could get him to relax his guard, just for an instant, she may be able to take him by surprise. But she wouldn't risk her sister.

"Stop right there!" The venom in his voice had her halting in her tracks. "You still think you can outsmart me? Put down the gun *now* or I will kill her."

"I am." She bent and set the weapon on the floor. "You're in control here. I know that."

"You *should* know it, but you're still lying. Slide it over here." When Abbie obeyed, Grant smiled. "You'll understand before the night is over, though. I'll see to that." Because Callie had started to stir, he reached over to grip her hair and slammed her head against the floor. Then rising, he reached for Abbie's gun and slipped it into his waistband.

Abbie sent a quick glance to her sister, but she lay motionless, her eyes closed.

"Now the purse." His face twisted. "I've learned not to underestimate what a whore carries inside it. Toss it over here."

Her purse. Mentally she did a frantic catalog of its contents. There wasn't anything in it she could use to defend herself.

But her cell phone was inside it.

Mind racing, she reversed course and walked backward to the couch again. Reached for her purse. Opened it. "Nothing in here to be afraid of." She reached inside it, flipped her phone open. Retrieving her keys, she pulled them out, held them up. "These can't hurt you." She tossed them lightly in his direction. They landed near his feet.

His mouth twisted. "Do you think I'm playing games with you, bitch?"

Her breath was stopped up in her lungs. It took effort to haul in oxygen. Her hand dipped in her purse again, fingers fumbling with the phone. Hoping she pushed the right buttons. The ones that would redial the last number she'd called.

"Not much in this." She gripped her wallet, withdrew her hand to hold it up for him. "But robbery was never your thing, was it? Not enough pain involved." She threw it in the same direction the keys had landed.

"You're going to find out about pain. Even sooner if you don't *give me that damn purse*!"

Reluctant to push him further, Abbie set the bag on the floor, praying the call she'd made had gone through. With a slight kick, it skittered across the floor, coming to rest several feet from him.

She saw the fury fade from his expression. He was feeling in control again. "You made it almost too easy, you and Robel, you know that? All it took was setting the fire, injecting myself, and making sure the blood work got to Dixon's girlfriend. You practically fed me your progress on the case every time you talked to me." He shook his head in mock disappointment. "Not too intelligent, were you? Are you smart enough to guess what I have in store for you tonight?"

Abbie took the opportunity to glance at Callie. She appeared to be unconscious. How badly was she injured?

"All out of ideas?" Grant's voice was conversational. "Then I'll tell you. We're going to your bedroom and wait for your sister to wake up." His eyes narrowed and he smiled nastily. "She really needs to be awake to appreciate this. You both do. After I tie you both up, we'll play 'Father Knows Best.'" He laughed silently. "From what your sister told me, your dad had a lot in common with my stepfather."

"Is he the reason you always use electrical cord?" Abbie asked conversationally, gauging the distance between them. Now that he'd moved away from Callie, she had nothing to lose by springing at him. With the element of surprise, she might be able to disarm him.

The odds were dismal, but her options were limited.

"He was an electrician. Always had a spool of wire in the basement when he dragged me down there. But he paid for that. Just like your dad did."

She eyed him carefully. "My father died from a fall."

"Callie never told you she pushed the drunk bastard down the stairs?" He shrugged. "He got what was coming to him, same as mine. Just sorry I didn't get to watch the bastard burn. But yours . . . I think he'd appreciate tonight's events. You're going to get to listen to your sister getting fucked again tonight. Better yet, you get to watch. Be like old times, won't it, Abbie?"

Sick horror rose, nearly gagged her. What had possessed Callie to confide in him? And how much had she told him?

"I'll only tie one of your hands to the doorknob. Your other one has to be free to handle the razor blade, doesn't it?" His expression was alight with an unholy glee. "I'm guessing I'll be a lot more imaginative than Daddy was. Every one of those scars I've heard about will be reopened. And then once I finish with Callie, I'll start on you." He cocked his head. "Did you predict that, bitch, when you were pretending to the world that you know how I think?"

She abruptly switched tactics. Pandering to his ego had had no effect. Slowly, derisively, she applauded. "Very creative. You and my father *do* have a lot in common. You're both sick and twisted. But that doesn't make you special. Just the opposite."

Grant's face flushed. "You'll pay for that, cunt."

"That's what your whole life's been about, hasn't it?" She circled toward her sister, and he had to move farther from Callie to keep Abbie in his sights. "Making other people pay for what was done to you? That only makes you pathetic, not smart. It makes you weak."

"Maybe we'll start the cutting early." He brandished the knife and stalked toward her. "There's nothing like the first slice to bring clarity. Remember that first slice, Abbie? It almost feels like pleasure, doesn't it? Just at first?"

She wanted to check on Callie again, but couldn't afford to take her eyes off him. Although she trembled from the effort, she waited for him to get closer. Her muscles bunched. Her weight shifted to the balls of her feet.

"We'll have the lights out for the production. You like the dark, don't you?"

The shudder that worked through her was real. He saw it, and smiled. A step closer. Then another. The blade rose.

Abbie kicked out at the hand wielding the knife. He shifted

away and slashed downward, cutting her across the top of her foot above her shoe. He laughed at her sharply indrawn breath, perfect teeth gleaming. "You'll be begging me to end it before we're done. And this time I'll have to." He lunged to slice at her arm, but she dodged away. "Pity. You two just might be my most brilliant vision yet. I want Robel to find you. I'm good at research. Found out he fucked up a case in Boston. And now he'll discover he's fucked up a—"

She pivoted to lash out violently at his injured arm, surprising a howl of pain from him. While he was distracted, she followed up by kicking the wrist holding the knife. It clattered to the ground and she dove for it.

"Think that will do you any good, you miserable cunt?" He stumbled back, drew her weapon from his waistband, and aimed it at her. "You fucking worthless whore. It was your fault that bitch Bradford had a gun. You ruined that. You aren't ruining this. Drop the fucking knife!"

"Or what?" Her voice was deadly calm. An eerie sense of composure had glossed over her earlier panic. If he pointed the gun at Callie, should she relinquish the knife? Knowing what he had planned for them? Or was Raiker right? Was she giving up all chances of survival by disarming?

"You're not ruining this. Tonight is going to be perfect." Grant's face was mottled, and she caught a glimpse of the emotion she'd seen when she'd interviewed him the second time. He was a master of pretense, but he wasn't pretending now. He was losing control. And she could imagine too well the image he'd planted in her brain.

Reliving their past. Using it against them. Making their last breathing moments an unimaginable hell.

She'd have only one opportunity to make a bid for her and Callie's lives. She'd aim for the heart. At this range, it was doubtful he'd miss his shot, but there was a chance. There was always a chance.

"Really? Is this perfect? Did you plan this?" She waggled the knife at him, watched his face carefully for the right time to strike. "Face it, you're the one who fucked up. You're a fuckup and a loser who can't do anything right."

"You cocksucking whore!" His face twisted. His finger tightened on the trigger. Abbie lunged.

"*No-o-o-o!*"

Time freeze-framed. Each fraction of an instant slowed.

Callie. On her knees. Swaying. Hands flailing. Grabbing Grant's leg. Pulling him off balance.

The man stumbling, going to one knee. Abbie frantically changing position. Callie doing the same.

The sound of the shot punctuating the struggle.

The knife plunging into his chest. Blood spurting.

A scream. His. Or was it Callie's?

In the next moment the scene fast-forwarded, everything happening in a blur of motion. A tremendous crash as the front door smashed open. Bodies pouring into the room, weapons drawn. Shouted commands. Grant dropping slowly to the floor, hands on the knife handle protruding from his chest.

But Abbie's attention was focused on her sister. "Callie!" Blood poured from the hole in her back, and a sick panic welled up inside her. Abbie ignored the pandemonium around her. Ripping at her shirt, she wadded it up to stanch the flow of blood, praying to a God who'd always seemed absent when it came to her sister.

"Hang on. Just hang on," she pleaded. "C'mon, Cal." Abbie lay on the floor, one hand maintaining pressure on her sister's wound, so she could look into her face. "Look at me. Open your eyes. It's Abbie."

Callie's eyelids fluttered, but remained closed. Her lips moved, but no words emerged. But when Abbie squeezed her hand, she thought her sister's fingers moved. Squeezed back.

"We're okay," Abbie whispered. "We're fine." They were eight and twelve again, clutched together in the darkness, rocking to comfort each other long after their father slept. "Everything's all right now."

But the words seemed as empty now as they had then.

"Come on, Abbie. They've got her. Come on." She fought the hands that drew her inexorably from her sister's side, watched helplessly as uniformed officers knelt to take her place.

"Are you hurt?" She recognized Ryne's rough voice, felt his hands moving over her searchingly.

She responded to the emotion, rather than the words. "No. I'm okay."

He muttered an oath. "You're *bleeding*."

Dazed, her gaze left her sister, and she looked down at herself. There was blood on her wrist. On her foot. "Cuts. I'm all right." Her attention bounced back to her sister. "Is she okay?" she asked the officer nearest to her. "Is she . . ." *Alive. Breathing.* Her chest constricted. She couldn't manage the words.

"She's hanging in there," the officer assured her.

Hearing a siren in the distance, she sank against Ryne, grateful for the support. "I want to go with her. When the ambulance comes. I have to be with her."

His arms wrapped around her so tightly that her words were muffled against his chest. "I have to go with her," she said more insistently.

Ryne ducked his head, his voice husky in her ear. "They won't let you in the ambulance." Her chin snapped up, but he forestalled the argument she would have made. "I'll take you myself. We'll be right behind them."

A breath shuddered out of her as she craned her head to keep her sister's form in sight. "He was going to shoot me. She threw herself in front of the gun. She's been taking bullets for me all my life, in one way or another. How do you thank someone for that? How do you repay that kind of sacrifice?" Her voice broke, weighted by twenty years of tears.

He rocked with her a little, his arms feeling strong. Blessedly secure. "I guess you just live." His lips brushed her forehead. "No one can ask for more than that."

Epilogue

"Callie seemed good." Ryne shrugged at Abbie's sidelong glance. "She's still Callie. But a little less so, you know?"

She gave him a wry smile. "Yeah, I think I know what you mean. And she is making progress."

Fall leaves crunched underfoot as they strolled back to the parking lot, but the weather was still relatively mild, requiring only long sleeves. Indian summer was always a gift to be appreciated.

Abbie had a much longer list of things to be thankful for.

Her sister had come out of surgery like a trooper, and worked harder at rehabilitation for her injury than anyone could have expected. She'd been less willing, however, to focus on her emotional health.

With a grimace, Abbie recalled the unpleasant scenes they'd had a few weeks ago, before she'd finally convinced her sister to seek long-term intensive care for her mental health issues.

Callie could walk out of Hillside anytime she wanted. That was a reality Abbie faced every day. But as long as her sister stayed, she was receiving help. Over years of dealing with her sister's illness, she'd learned to take the positives where she could.

"So you got the serial kidnapping case in Phoenix tied up in record time," Ryne commented.

The case had occupied the better part of the last three weeks, which at times had seemed interminable to Abbie. She still marveled—and worried—at how quickly Ryne had become such an integral part of her life. She'd gotten used to seeing him a couple weekends a month, along with daily phone calls. Thoughts of him had often interrupted her usual single-minded focus on the kidnapping investigation. Something else she'd have to get used to.

She bumped shoulders with him companionably. "Perp turned out to be a local youth baseball coach. And the lead detective on the case was about as welcoming as you were when I joined the task force."

That seemed to amuse him. "Give you a hard time, did he?"

The Phoenix detective had been a bit of a jerk, but had thawed over the course of the case. "He came around. My charm and charisma eventually overwhelmed him."

"Yeah, that's what got to me, too," Ryne said musingly. "Your charm and charisma. Not to mention your killer ass."

Her tone was pure innocence. "That's exactly what he said."

Ryne stopped and tugged her into his arms with satisfying swiftness. "You know, it's not exactly safe to bait a frustrated man. We can be unpredictable."

Linking her arms around his neck, she inquired, "Pretty frustrated, are you?"

"What do you think?" he growled, lowering his face to nip at her neck, then soothe the sensitive spot with his tongue.

Her muscles took on the consistency of warm wax. "I think it was a long three weeks." His kiss had just enough demand to it to have Abbie mentally calculating the minutes by car to get back to her place.

"Young lovers engaged in public displays of affection on a brilliant fall day. Could there be anything more revolting?"

The familiar voice had Abbie jerking away. But Ryne kept

her close with one arm around her waist. "Adam. What are you doing here?" Having her boss catch her in a clinch with Ryne ranked right up there with getting caught in class passing notes.

Adam Raiker set both hands on top of his cane in front of him, and leaned his weight against it. His expression was cynically amused. "You mean other than being forced into the unwilling role of voyeur? I came to talk to you. Are your lips free?"

"Not for long," Ryne put in, not a bit embarrassed. "So talk fast."

Raiker fixed him with a gimlet stare from his lone eye. "Robel. Reconsidered my job offer yet?"

"Nope."

"You will." That absolute certainty of his put a lot of people off, Abbie knew. But Ryne just gave him an enigmatic smile and said nothing.

"Walk with me. I've got a meeting in a couple hours at Quantico and traffic is always a bitch." They fell into step alongside the man. "Got a call on my way there, as a matter of fact. Headquarters said you were here, Abbie, so thought I'd swing by and pass on the news."

"A new development on Grant?" She exchanged a look with Ryne. Karen Larsen, aka Sean Grant, had been in custody for months. But he'd lawyered up immediately and had refused to answer any questions. The last she'd heard, his attorney was trying to line up expert witnesses to bolster a diminished capacity plea.

"Indirectly. Ryne's contact, that sheriff in Montana, finally moved on Trevor Holden."

"They've had Holden under surveillance for weeks," Ryne put in. "Ever since testing on that tox screen he sent me matched those of our victims. Jepperson finally tracked down that runaway who had been assaulted and she tentatively ID'd Holden as the guy."

"No doubt now that he was responsible," Raiker said grimly. "They caught sight of him burying something in back of his barn. Got a warrant and swarmed the place."

"A body?" Abbie guessed.

Raiker nodded. "And they discovered four more before they were finished. All had been tortured. He had the barn equipped with a sort of home lab, where he was manufacturing the drug. Had a big enough supply to keep him and Larsen in business for a long time. The place was also outfitted with small cells and equipped with some pretty heavy-duty torture devices."

"He must have been stealing samples of TTX all along and running his own experiments until he had a perfect product for his perversions," Abbie surmised. "But I thought he was just a tech at Ketrum. How would he have the expertise?"

"It was your idea to look for a relationship between him and the rapist," Ryne said in an aside to Abbie. For Raiker's benefit, he added, "A high school classmate of his claimed he was some kind of chemistry brain. I got a yearbook photo of Holden and another of someone he'd befriended at the juvie center." He shook his head, as if the shock of recognition were still fresh. "I wouldn't have recognized the name. Larsen was the name of his sister and stepfather. But once I saw his face, things started coming together pretty quickly." His focus shifted back to Abbie. "Then I got your call. Heard enough to figure out you were in danger and headed over."

The phone call on her cell after she'd been surprised by Grant. The memory of the scene could still bring a prickle to her skin, despite the warm temperature. "Grant claimed the fire that killed his parents was deliberate."

Raiker scowled, the expression, coupled with his eye patch and the scar bisecting his throat, making him look like a ferocious modern-day pirate. "Three guesses who set it."

"Holden," Abbie breathed. Of course. It would have seemed the perfect crime. If the police had been suspicious, the first one they would have looked at was Sean Grant, who would have still been safely locked away.

"Not surprisingly, Holden's feeling pretty talkative faced with five homicide charges. He's spilling everything he knows on Grant in hopes of a reduced plea. He admits he was released three weeks prior to Grant, and set the fire at his request. Apparently he's been calling in favors, first for that and then for sharing the drug. He claims his last three victims were delivered to him by Grant."

"Busy little fuck," muttered Ryne.

Raiker's answering smile was chilly. "There's more. Holden also maintains that Grant killed Karen more than six years ago and disposed of her body."

"I was afraid of that," Abbie said softly. She'd done a thorough background check on Karen Larsen. The woman had existed. Long enough to establish an identity her brother could later don at will. He'd even followed his half sister into nursing school, although he'd only gotten a two-year degree.

"You said it all along," Ryne told her. "That women will confide personal stuff to someone they trust. That's got to be how he got to some of the victims. Maybe they came into whichever medical place he was working at as Karen Larsen. Or he ran across them at the volunteer sites. Whatever. They'd open up to a woman in a way they never would to a man."

Abbie's smile was sad. "I also said the perp might try to insert himself into the case, to try to keep tabs on our progress. But I sure never saw what was right in front of me."

His arm grew tighter around her. "Neither of us did. He made a believable woman. He's not a large guy. Might even have had electrolysis treatments on his face to help with the disguise."

Expression hard, he looked at Raiker again. "I sure as hell hope they aren't going to give Holden a plea bargain. We have more than enough to get life for Grant without his testimony. The bloodstains in Bradford's apartment and in the Crown Vic tie him to her assault. And his DNA matched the CODIS files for two other sexual homicides in the last few years, one in New Jersey and another in Tampa."

"Not to mention Amanda Richards's hair in the bag you recovered." Abbie shuddered, reminded again of just how easily Callie could have fallen victim to him. Had he trolled those bars for unwitting dupes, like Juarez? Or had he been looking for high-risk women to rough up, while he was in between attacks? With Callie's pattern of self-destructive behavior, she must have seemed perfect.

And then there had been her unwise openness about her relationship with Abbie, the profiler on his case. And about their childhood. Arming Grant with that knowledge then unlocking Abbie's bedroom window for him had almost sealed their fate.

Giving a hard smile, Raiker said, "I know the director in charge of Montana's FBI office. I've let him know exactly how strong the case is against Grant already. Tracing that key you found in his place to the apartment he was using as a safe house was the final nail in his coffin. The DVDs documenting the rapes will be the most damning evidence against him." He checked his watch. "And I'm going to be late." With his usual disregard for formalities, he abruptly left them, angling toward his car.

Watching him, Ryne noted, "Well, he can't be boring to work for."

"No." Abbie's tone was rueful. "That's an adjective that never comes to mind in relation to Adam Raiker." But she'd spent as much time as she was willing to discussing her boss. The case. Or anything that didn't directly relate to her and the man beside her. Their time together was always brief, and she could already feel the precious minutes ticking away. "Drive us back to my place. And then I'll let you cook me some of your famous pasta."

Dropping an arm around her shoulders, he steered her toward his car. "On the way here I started tallying how much time we spend on the road. Or in the air."

Panic slicked down her spine. Was he already tired of the schedule they were keeping? Granted, it was chaotic with the demands of their jobs, coupled with the distance between them. But the time she got to spend with him made every sacrifice worthwhile.

"Maybe it's time to rethink this whole thing." Reaching

the car, Ryne leaned against the driver's door, surveying her soberly. "We could be making it too complicated."

It took a moment for the meaning of his words to filter through her dismay. When it did, hope bloomed. "I could commute," she suggested cautiously. "When I'm not on a job, we're expected at headquarters three days a week for training. But maybe I could arrange those days all in a row, at the beginning of the week, or something."

"I was thinking, too, there's nothing tying me to Savannah. With my background, I could find something around DC."

"You'd hate the politics." But her mind was spinning, racing with possibilities. "Raiker's serious about the job offer, too."

He reached out and tugged on her hand, pulled her against him. "We don't have to decide anything right away. But we have options, so let's just start looking into them. Time spent traveling is less time we have together." One corner of his mouth kicked up. "A good cop knows how to manage his time efficiently."

Heart bursting, she linked her arms around his neck and smiled radiantly up at him. "Yep, that's what I love about you. Your head for efficiency."

Eyes glinting, he lowered his mouth to hers. Against her lips he whispered, "Know what I love about you? Damn near everything."

Turn the page for a preview of
the second book in Kylie Brant's
exciting Mindhunters series

WAKING EVIL

Available October 2009
from Berkley Sensation!

The helicopter landed in the clearing with a slight bounce before settling on the ground again for good. Ramsey Clark shouted her thanks to the pilot, shoved open the door, and jumped lightly to the ground, her lone bag slung over one shoulder. She ran in a crouch to avoid the rotors, heard the *whop-whop-whop* behind her indicating the pilot taking off.

She scanned the cluster of four people waiting nearby as she jogged toward them. The three men wearing suits each held a hand over his tie to prevent it from dancing in the breeze generated by the chopper's rotors.

"Director Jeffries." The hand she offered was engulfed in the older man's pawlike grip and squeezed until she had to hide a wince. The chief of the Tennessee Bureau of Investigation hadn't changed much in the years since she'd left its ranks. His craggy face might be a little ruddier. His mop of white hair a bit shorter. But his six-foot frame was still military straight and as lean as ever.

"Good to see you again, Clark. I hear you've been makin' quite a name for yourself with Raiker Forensics."

Since the director wasn't prone to flattery, and since he could have heard it only from Adam Raiker himself, Ramsey allowed herself to feel a small glow of satisfaction. "Thank you, sir. I think I've learned a lot."

Jeffries turned to the two men flanking him. "TBI agents Glenn Matthews and Warden Powell. You'll be assigned to their team. If you need more manpower, give me a holler and I'll talk to the boss."

Ramsey nodded her appreciation. Jeffries had no superior at TBI, so they were being given carte blanche. Raiker had told her to expect as much.

The director turned to the man in the sheriff's uniform on her right. "I believe you know Sheriff Rollins."

Frowning, she was about to deny it. Ramsey knew no one in Buffalo Springs, Tennessee. But the sheriff was taking off his hat, and recognition struck her. "Mark Rollins?" She shook her former colleague's hand with a sense of déjà vu. "I didn't even know you'd left TBI."

"Couple years ago now. Didn't even realize I was interested in movin' back home until the position of sheriff was open." Rollins's pleasantly homely face was somber. "Have to say, tonight's the first time I've regretted it."

"I assume you've looked at the case file."

Ramsey's attention shifted back to Jeffries at his comment. At her nod, he went on.

"Rollins has his hands full here calmin' the local hysteria, and after a week, we aren't progressin' fast enough to suit the governor's office. The area is attractin' every national media team in the country, and the coverage is playin' hell with his tourism industry expansion plans." The director's voice was heavy with irony.

"I understand." And she did. Being brought in as a special consultant to the TBI pacified a politically motivated governor and diminished some of the scrutiny that would follow the department throughout the investigation. If the case drew to a quick close, the TBI reaped the positive press. If it didn't . . . The alternative didn't bother her. Ramsey had served as shit deflector many times in the past in her capacity as forensic consultant. If the investigation grew lengthy or remained unsolved, she would be served as sacrificial lamb to the clamoring public. Or to the state attorney's office, if someone there decided to lay the blame on Jeffries.

"Raiker promised a mobile lab."

"It'll be here tomorrow," she promised the director. "But for certain types of evidence, we may need access to the TBI facility on an expedited basis."

"We'll try to speed any tests through the Knoxville Regional Lab." Jeffries beetled his brows. "Just help solve this thing, Clark. It's causin' a crapstorm, and I don't want a full-fledged shit tornado on my hands."

Ramsey smiled. She'd always appreciated Jeffries' plain-spokenness. "I'll do my best, sir."

"Can't recall a time that wasn't good enough for me." Clearly finished, he turned to his agents. "I'll expect daily updates. And keep me abreast of any major developments." Without waiting for the men's nods, he turned and strode briskly toward a road about a quarter mile in the distance. Ramsey could make out two vehicles parked alongside it.

"I'm guessin' you'd like to get on into town, drop your stuff off in the room we lined up for you," Mark was saying.

Ramsey shook her head. "I want to see the crime scene first." Since diplomacy was often an afterthought for her, she added belatedly, "If that's okay."

The sheriff raised a shoulder. "It's all right with me. What about you fellas? Want to come along?"

The two agents looked at each other, and Powell shook his head. "We'll head back into town." He shifted his gaze to Ramsey. "We're set up in the local motel on the outskirts of town. One room serves as our office. We got you a room there, too, when Jeffries told us you were comin'."

And by not so much as a flicker of expression did he reveal his opinion on her being brought in on the case, Ramsey noted shrewdly. She'd have to tread carefully there, with both agents, until she was certain how her presence here affected them.

"I'll check in with you when I get to town, and you can bring me up to date on your notes so far."

When the agents headed in the same direction Jeffries had gone, she turned to Rollins.

"Let me get that for you." He reached for her bag, but she deflected the gesture.

"I've got it, thanks." She fell into step beside him as they walked toward the tan jeep emblazoned with SPRING COUNTY SHERIFF in black lettering on a green background. "Tell me about the case."

"Same ol' Ramsey." A corner of Rollins's mouth pulled up. "Always with the small talk. Chatter, chatter, chatter." His voice hitched up a notch as he launched into a mock conversation. "Well, I'm just fine, Ms. Clark. And how have you been? How's that new job of yours? The wife? Oh, she's fine, too. Still adjustin' to small-town life, but the two little ones keep her pretty busy. What? You'd like to see pictures? Well, it just so happens I have a couple in my wallet. Got them taken at the local Wal-Mart just last month . . ."

"I can play the game if I need to," she replied, only half truthfully. "Didn't figure I needed to with you."

He stopped at the vehicle, his hand on the handle of the driver's door, his face serious again. "No, you don't gotta with me. Figure we go far 'nough back that we can just pick up. But you'll find you'll get further with some folks in these parts if you put forth the effort. I know you never had much patience for mindless chitchat, but the pace is slower 'round here."

She was more familiar than he knew with the unwritten customs and tradition demanded by polite society in the rural south. Had, in fact, spent her adult life scrubbing away most of those memories with the same ruthless determination with which she'd eliminated her telltale drawl.

Rather than tell him that, she gave him a nod across the roof of the car. "I'll keep it in mind." She opened the back door and tossed her bag on the seat behind the wire mesh used to separate prisoners from the law enforcement personnel. Then she slid into the front passenger seat.

He folded his tall lanky form inside and started up the Jeep while she was buckling in. Several minutes later, he abruptly pulled off the road and began driving across a field. After the first couple of jolts, Ramsey braced herself with one hand on the dash and the other on the roof of the car.

"Sorry." Rollins seemed to move seamlessly with each jar and bump. "It'd take half an hour for us to get there by road. The kids that found the body hiked across through the woods on the other side, but going in from this direction will be an easier walk, though I'm told it takes longer. Brought the body out this way."

"Has the victim been ID'd yet?"

"Nope. White female, between the age of eighteen and twenty-five. Found nude, so no help with the clothing." A muscle jumped in Mark's jaw. "Not from these parts, is all I know. No hits from any of the national missin' persons data-bases. The medical examiner took a DNA sample, and we submitted the results to the FBI's system, but no luck."

So a Jane Doe, at least for now. Ramsey felt a stab of sympathy for the unknown woman. Maybe she hadn't even been reported missing. She'd died alone and away from home. Was that worse than being murdered in familiar sur-roundings? Somehow it seemed so.

"How valuable have the wits been?"

"What, the kids?" Mark shot her a look. "Told us what they knew, which didn't turn out to be much. Both scared silly, of course. Spouting nonsense about red mist and screamin' and dancin' lights . . . Tell you what I think." The Jeep hit a rut with a bone-jarring bounce that rattled Ramsey's teeth. "I think half is fueled by that blasted legend folks 'round here insist on feedin' regularly."

"Legend?" The case file contained only facts of the case. But when facts were in short supply, other details took on more importance.

Rollins looked pained. "Guess you'll be hearin' it from 'bout every person you talk to in town. I know I can count of you, out of anyone, not to be distracted by nonsense." Still, it seemed to take him a few moments to choose his words. Or maybe he was saving his strength for wrestling the Jeep. Beneath the spread of grass, the terrain was wicked.

"We've got something of a local phenomena called the red mist. Someone else could explain it better, but it's caused by some sort of reaction from certain plants in the area comin' in contact with iron oxide in stagnant water, coupled with contaminants in the air. Once every blue moon, the fog in low-lying areas takes on a red tinge for a day or two. Nothing magical 'bout it of course, 'cept the way it makes folks 'round here take leave of their senses."

"So the kids that found the body saw this red mist?"

"That's what they're sayin'. And I do have others in these parts that claim they saw the same thing, so might've been true. But local legend has it that whenever the red mist appears, death follows."

The Jeep hit a rut then that had Ramsey rapping her head smartly on the ceiling of the vehicle. With a grim smile, she repositioned herself more securely in her seat and waited for her internal organs to settle back into place. Then she shot the man beside her a look. "Well, all nonsense aside, Sheriff, so far it appears, your local legend is more grounded in facts than you want to admit."

Rollins brought the Jeep to a halt a few hundred yards shy of the first copse of trees. "Don't even joke about that. My office is spendin' too much of our time dealing with hysterical locals who set too much store by superstitious hogwash. The truth is, this is a quiet place. The crime we do have tends to be drunk and disorderlies after payday at the lumber mill, or the occasional domestic dispute. Once in a while we have a fire or a bad accident to respond to. But violent crime is a stranger here. And when it appears, people don't understand it. They get scared, and when folks get scared, they search for meanin'. This legend is just their way of gettin' a handle on how bad things can happen near their town."

Ramsey got out of the car and stretched, avoiding, as long as possible, having to look at that expanse of woods ahead of them. "That's downright philosophical, Mark. Didn't learn that in the psych courses at TBI."

He reached back into the car for the shotgun mounted above the dash, and then straightened to shut the door, a ghost of a smile playing across his mouth. "You're right there. I understand these people. Lived here most of my life. I know how they think. How they react. Don't always agree with 'em. But I can usually figure where they're comin' from."

They headed for the woods, and Ramsey could feel her palms start to dampen. Her heart began to thud. The physical reaction annoyed her. It was just trees, for Godsakes. Each nothing but a mass of carbon dioxide. And she'd mastered this ridiculous fear—*she had*—years ago.

Deliberately, she quickened her step. "You hoping to go hunting while we're here?" She cocked her head at the shotgun he carried.

"Not much of a hunter. But we do have some wildlife in these parts. Those kids were downright stupid to come in here at night. There's feral pigs in these woods. An occasional bobcat. Seen enough copperheads 'round in my time to keep me wary."

When her legs wanted to falter at his words, she kept them moving steadily forward. Felt the first cool shadows from the trees overhead slick over her skin like a demon's kiss.

"Wish I could tell you there was much of a crime scene," Mark was saying as he walked alongside her. "But apparently a bunch of kids dared each other to come into the woods and bring back proof they'd been here. First ones back to town got braggin' rights, I 'spect. So they paired off and trooped out in this direction. Shortly after the two found the victim, a few others arrived. And then the whole thing became one big mess with tracks and prints all over the damn place."

Ramsey felt a familiar surge of impatience. No one liked to have the scene contaminated, but one of the few downsides to her job with Raiker Forensics was that she was rarely called to a fresh crime scene. By the time their services were requested, the crime could be days or weeks old. She had to satisfy herself with case files, pictures of the scene, and notes taken by the local law enforcement.

"The way Jeffries talked, you've gotten more than your share of unwanted media attention." They stepped deeper into the woods now and the trees seemed to close in, sucking them into the shadowy interior. She resisted the urge to wipe her moist palms on her pant legs. "Seems odd for national news to be interested in a homicide in rural Tennessee."

"I suspect some local nut job tipped them off. It's the legend again." Mark's face was shiny with perspiration, but Ramsey was chilled. She would be until they stepped back out into the daylight again. "Every two or three decades there's this red mist phenomena, and a couple times in the past there's been a death 'round the same time. The two circumstances get linked, and all of a sudden we have people jabberin' 'bout secret spells and century-old curses and what have you."

She made a noncommittal sound. Part of her attention was keeping a wary eye out for those copperheads he'd mentioned so matter-of-factly. But despite her impatience with idle chitchat, she was interested in all the details that would be missing from the case file. Evidence was in short supply. It was people who would solve this case. People who'd seen something. Knew something. The tiniest bit of information could end up being key to solving the homicide. And with no murder weapon and no suspects and little trace evidence, she'd take all the information she could get.

"Have you eliminated each of the kids as the possible killer?"

"Shoot, Ramsey they're no more than sixteen, seventeen years old!"

When she merely looked at him, brows raised, he had the grace to look abashed. "Yeah, I know what you've seen in your career. I've seen the same. But 'round here we don't have kids with the conscience of wild dogs. They all alibi each other for up to thirty minutes before the body's discovery. Witnesses place the lot of them at Sody's parking lot for the same time. Pretty unlikely a couple hightailed it into the woods, committed murder, and dumped the body knowin' more kids would be traipsin' in any minute."

Unlikely, yes. Impossible, no. But Ramsey kept her thoughts to herself. She was anxious to hear what Agents Powell and Matthews had to say on the subject.

There was a rustle in the underbrush to her right, but it didn't get her blood racing. No, that feat was accomplished by the trees themselves, looming like sinister sentinels above her. Hemming her in with their close proximity. She rubbed at her arms, where gooseflesh prickled, and shoved at the mental door of her mind to lock those memories away.

Some would have found the scene charming, with the sun dappling the forest floor and brilliant slants of light spearing through the shadow. They wouldn't look at the scene and see danger behind every tree trunk. Wouldn't feel terror lurking behind. Horror ahead.

The trail narrowed, forcing her to follow Rollins single file. "Whose property are we on?"

"Most of it belongs to the county. We've got little parcels that butt up against the land of property owners, but we're standin' on county ground right now." They walked in silence another fifteen minutes, and Ramsey wondered anew at any kids foolish enough to make this trek at night.

Sixteen or seventeen, Mark had said they were. She knew firsthand just how naïve kids that age could be. How easily fooled. And how quickly things could go very wrong.

One moment they were deep in the forest. The next they walked out into a clearing with a large pond. It was ringed with towering pines and massive oaks, their branches dripping with Spanish moss and curling vines. The land looked rocky on three sides, but it was boggy at the water's edge closest to them, with clumps of rushes and wild grasses interspersed between the trees.

Ramsey's gaze was drawn immediately to the crime scene tape still fluttering from the wooden stakes hammered into the ground. A plastic evidence marker poked partway out of the trampled weeds near the pond, overlooked by the investigators when they'd packed up.

And in the center of that tape, crouched in front of the pond, a man repeatedly dunked something into the water and then held it up to examine it before repeating the action yet again. A few yards away, a jumble of equipment was piled on the ground.

She eyed Rollins. "One of yours?"

Looking uncomfortable, the sheriff shook his head. "Now, Ramsey," he started, as she turned toward the stranger. "Better let me handle this."

But she was already striding away. "Hey. Hey!"

The man raised a hand in a lazy salute, but it was clear he was much more interested in the reading on the instrument he held than he was in her. Ramsey waited while he lowered the tool to jot a notation down in the notebook open on his lap then looked up and shot her a lazy grin. "Afternoon, ma'am."

"Interesting thing about that yellow tape all around you," she said with mock politeness. "It's actually meant to keep people out of a crime scene, not invite them inside it."

The sun at her back had the stranger squinting a bit at her, but the smile never left his face. And it was, for a man, an extraordinarily attractive face. His jaw was long and lean, his eyes a bright laser blue. The golden shade of his hair was usually found only on the very young or the very determined. Someone had broken his nose for him, and the slight bump in it was the only imperfection in a demeanor that was otherwise almost too flawless. Ramsey disliked him on sight just on principal.

"Well, fact is, ma'am, this isn't an active crime scene anymore. Hey, Mark." He called a friendly greeting to the man behind her. "Kendra May know you're out walking pretty girls 'round the woods?"

"Dev. Thought you'd be finished up here by now."

Ramsey caught the sheepish note in Rollins's voice and arched a brow at him. The sheriff intercepted it and followed up with an introduction. "Ramsey Clark, this is my cousin, Devlin Stryker. He's uh . . . just running some tests."

"Your cousin," she repeated carefully. "And does your cousin work for the department? If so, in what capacity?"

Rollins's face reddened a little. "No. He's a . . . well, he's sort of a scientist, you could say."

Stryker rose in one lithe motion and made his way carefully back to the rest of his belongings, which included,

Ramsey noted, a large duffel bag with unfamiliar-looking instruments strewn around it, along with a couple cameras, a night vision light source, and—she blinked once—a neatly rolled up sleeping bag.

"Odd place to go camping."

"Can't say I used the sleepin' bag much last night." He unzipped the duffel and began placing his things inside it. "Too worried about snakes. I thought I'd stick around a while to compare last night's readings with some from today."

With quick neat movements, he placed everything but the sleeping bag in the duffle and zipped it, standing up to sling its strap over his shoulder. "I'm done here for now, though."

"Done with what, exactly?"

Devlin sent her an easy smile that carried just enough charm to have her defenses slamming firmly into place. "Well, let's see. I used a thermal scanner to measure temperature changes. An EMF meter to gauge electromagnetic fields. An ion detector to calculate the presence of negative ions. Then there's the gaussometer, which . . ."

Comprehension warring with disbelief, Ramsey swung back to face Rollins, her voice incredulous. "A *ghost hunter*? Are you kidding me? You let some paranormal quack compromise the crime scene?"

COMING OCTOBER 2009

WAKING EVIL

BY Kylie Brant

A Killer, a Prophecy—and Three Deaths Foretold

Buffalo Springs, Tennessee, is a neighborly kind of place where folks leave their doors unlocked and crime is unheard of. But once every generation, a strange red mist settles over the town, and with it come omens of death...

PRAISE FOR KYLIE BRANT

"Kylie Brant is destined to become a star!"
—*New York Times* bestselling author Cindy Gerard